THE DEVIL THAT BROKE US

The Devil that Broke Us

Copyright © 2020 Shelly Wilson
Published by Backabity
Peru IN

Cover art by Michael Christopher
Cover design and formatting by Serendipity Formats

ISBN: 978-1-7323601-5-0 (eBook)

ISBN: 978-1-7323601-4-3 (paperback)

CHAPTER ONE

1914

A cold wind blew atop Mount Perish. Although the sun had been up for hours, it did little to tame the bite of the frigid air as it howled through the ancient trees. Nestled among the snow-covered pines, hidden and long forgotten, sat the ruins of what was once a cozy, log house. With no one to care for it, portions of the old roof had collapsed; sections of it now rested on the puncheon logs below. The weather-beaten floor planks were worn and battered, as warped and twisted as the hands that had hewn them so long ago. Tufts of dead grass and wildflowers were wedged tightly within cracks and holes, having fought each other valiantly for prominence as nature slowly reclaimed what had been left behind.

The sleeping loft, where a young girl once found solace, was now resting on the broken bed frame beneath. Bits and pieces of a table and chairs—broken fragments of the past— lay scattered about, protruding from small drifts of snow. In a corner, shielded from the brutal winter winds, a family of raccoons had taken up residence. Though they were just some of many vermin who had laid claim to the decay amidst the dilapidated structure, their tracks were the only obvious signs of life.

A tall, stone fireplace, standing sentry as it had since the very beginning, was still mostly intact and recognizable. Once as strong and sturdy as concrete, the crumbling mortar of the hearthstone structure released yet another rock, sending a startled mouse scurrying across the floor. The mantel, fashioned carefully with loving hands, had long since split and cracked, its beautifully engraved images now lost to time. Always the heart of the home, this, too, had met its demise.

The landscape on the mountain had changed considerably over the years. No longer unconquerable, the Devil's Fork River had been breached at last. Two large bridges spanned the mighty waterway, negating the need for bent trees and moonlit crossings. The first bridge was erected forty-one years prior, near the town of Granite Falls, followed by another in Ely shortly thereafter. With the bridges, came the people. They spilled across the once impassable river to lay claim to parcels of land now housing the sixty-eight homes dotting the mountainside. At night, light from fires flickered through what had previously been an imposing curtain of black against the starry sky.

The once sleepy town of Ely had seen many changes as well. Situated at the base of Mount Perish, it had become a bustling city, now sprawling far beyond the foothills of the mammoth mountain. As a major hub for the railway, Ely offered any service imaginable for the hundreds of travelers passing through each day. Its three grand hotels were no longer able to accommodate the onslaught of people. Construction of a fourth hotel would soon be underway.

On the busy main street in Ely, Burton Nicholas stopped

in front of a small building that looked out of place wedged between the multi-story businesses flanking it. He hooked his cane over his arm and caught his balance on the handrail to the stairs. Looking up, he squinted against the bright sun, studying the familiar façade as he paused to catch his breath.

Out of his peripheral vision, movement caught his eye. A construction foreman hurried toward him from down the street. They spoke briefly and Burton gave the man a few last-minute instructions. After a nod of understanding and a tip of his hat, the foreman hustled up the steps and disappeared inside.

The unseasonably warm sun bore down mercilessly from a cloudless, December sky. Burton took his handkerchief from the pocket of his sack-suit coat, removed his bowler, and dabbed his forehead. He shoved the damp hanky back into his pocket and placed his hat onto his head. With his cane in hand, he steadied himself as he scaled the three steps.

Pausing at the doorway, he ran his fingers over the wood sign hanging next to him: *Burton Nicholas, Attorney at Law*. His parents had been so proud when he graduated law school. They'd helped him remodel the building, turning it into his office. A wistful smile played on his lips as he recalled the day he had hung the shingle. The excitement he had felt that day had only been exceeded by his mother's pride.

A loud shout interrupted the memory. He looked over his shoulder and returned a wave to Gill Mackenship, who was puttering slowly down the street in an old Model T Ford. Gill had purchased the automobile from him three days prior. He was relieved to have found a buyer for the vehicle, since he had recently purchased a new Wescott Coupe, which was waiting for him in an outbuilding at his new home on the coast.

Burton glanced down at the steps. He felt off-kilter as a childhood memory came rushing back. He instinctively leaned against the doorway for support. In his mind's eye, he saw himself as a young boy. He was running and leapt from the top step all the way to the road in a hurry to get over to his father's trading post for a piece of candy. His lips, usually set into a serious line, were stretched into a smile. Burton could almost taste the memory of sugar on his tongue. He squeezed his eyes shut tightly, forcing the images to fade.

Turning back to the building, he thought of his mother again. A strong and capable woman, she had started the first hotel in the town all on her own. He hoped he had made the right decision by selling the place. It was time for him to move on and start the final chapter in his life. His doctor had told him that retirement was the best thing for his rheumatism. It had been suggested that the salty, coastal air would do wonders for the condition. He had sold everything and bought a little place near the ocean. Still, it was hard for the forty-nine year old man to walk away from this life—his life.

You're just feeling nostalgic. You know it's for the best.

A train whistle pushed him from his thoughts. He reached into his vest, followed the path of a golden chain, and pulled out his watch. "Twelve o'clock. Right on time," he mumbled aloud. He took one last mournful look at the building, which had held so many fond memories.

Grabbing the handrail, he swayed down the steps and merged into the mass of people. He walked as fast as his gait would allow, making his way toward the building that used to belong to his father. He had already sold the place, earning the extra money he needed to buy the costly beach house. Though he was ready to move on with his life, he still couldn't help but stop and watch as a man scraped lettering from the front window. All that remained were the letters LIX'S, a fragment of his father's name.

A man hurrying along the crowded street bumped into him, pulling Burton's stare from the large, plate glass window. The commuter offered a rushed apology before continuing on his way. Burton fell into the mix of people walking along the side of the street. His cane, along with his steps, sounded like an out-of-rhythm heartbeat on the wooden sidewalk. The dirt streets of his childhood could not have anticipated the sound.

As he made his way past the Ely Grand Hotel, his thoughts returned once again to his mother. So many changes had come to the town, and he couldn't help but wonder what she would have thought about them. How would she feel about demolishing her old home to make room for the seven-story hotel that would take its place?

At the train depot, Burton waited in line with the others. He was grateful for the chance to catch his breath, but still eager to take his seat. Thankfully, the line moved quickly. He pulled his ticket from an inside breast pocket, more than ready to get off of his feet.

He handed the ticket over to the conductor. With stub in fist, he climbed the steep stairway, impatiently waving off the hand offered by the usher standing at the top. *I'm not an invalid yet.* Making his way along the aisle, he took the first empty seat next to the window. He wasn't in the mood for conversation, so he hoped no one would take the seat next to him. However, looking out of the train window at the long line of people still waiting to board, he sighed heavily, realizing it was unlikely he would be that lucky.

As he stared out the window, he watched as a wagon

pulled up beside the platform. The driver jumped down and spoke briefly to someone outside Burton's view. What they discussed was of no concern to him. All that mattered was that the wagon had made it on time. It held a precious family heirloom—the desk from his law office. It had been in the building for as long as he could remember. Originally, it had been the reception desk back when his mother used to rent rooms. The hefty antique had seen better days, but he did not have the heart to abandon it. This piece of the old place would go with him to the new one, a reminder of his professional career. In truth, his attachment probably had more to do with the fact it was one of the last things belonging to his mother that he still had in his possession.

An older woman took a seat next to him, and they greeted each other warmly. He was relieved when she pulled out a ball of yarn and two large needles from her carpetbag and started to knit.

She'll keep to herself. Shouldn't want to talk much. He smiled inwardly at the thought.

The whistle blew and the train rolled out of the station with black smoke billowing from its stack. Burton relaxed back in his seat, watching as the landscape outside began to ease past.

"Excuse me, sir," a porter said, taking Burton's attention from the window. "I'm sorry for the interruption. The man who delivered your desk wanted me to give this to you." He leaned over the woman and handed him an envelope. "He said when they pulled out one of the drawers to load it, this fell out."

Burton eyed the yellowed, crinkled paper as he took it. "Thank you."

The porter nodded and made his way down the aisle, swaying with the motion of the train as it began to barrel down the tracks.

The paper felt brittle in Burton's hand and was so thin he could see the faint lettering within. A smeared ink stain, faded but still recognizable, brought everything rushing back. He recalled the day he had accidentally knocked over the inkwell on his mother's desk. The panic he had felt in his eight-year-old mind as he hurried to hide the evidence, rushing to stuff the letter back behind the bottom drawer, had been all but forgotten.

The woman seated next to him took her eyes off her knitting and looked at the aged envelope. "I don't mean to pry, but aren't you going to open it?"

Burton met her gaze. "It's not addressed to me." He traced the faded ink with a finger, then jerked his hand back, worried he might rub the ancient writing from the envelope. "It's from my late mother," he said, carefully placing the letter into the breast pocket of his suit.

She nodded and returned to her knitting, leaving him to his thoughts and the scenery rolling by the window. The letter had made him more emotional than he already was—much more than he expected to be. Tears welled in his eyes, unbidden. He turned sharply toward the window in an attempt to obscure his sadness.

To see his mother's stylish and prim writing after all this time took him by surprise. He recalled how she used to admonish him about his poor penmanship, insisting he take his time to do it right. At the time, he had found learning penmanship interminable, but it struck him hard now to know there was nothing he wouldn't give for one more handwriting lesson with his mother. She was the one who pushed him for all those years and dreamed of him getting the finest education. He felt a lump growing in his throat, but he swallowed it and inconspicuously wiped away a tear with his finger.

"I'm sorry to keep disturbing you," she said, placing her hand on his arm, "but I just have to ask. Are you going to mail that letter? I think you should. It must've been important or your mother wouldn't have written it."

"I suppose so. It's so old...I don't even know if the person it's addressed to is still living after all this time."

She removed her hand. "It's hard to say. But if I were you, I'd send it."

Burton smiled and nodded before looking away. He leaned his head back and closed his eyes. The gentle rocking of the car, a slight annoyance minutes before, became a welcome distraction. He let it carry him to sleep.

A loud whistle startled Burton from his slumber. He leaned up and looked at the woman seated next to him. "Granite Falls, already?" he asked.

"Yes."

As the train jolted to a stop, Burton stood up. He grabbed the seat in front of him to avoid toppling over in his haste. "Excuse me," he said, trying to step past her and into the aisle. He glanced down at her and cracked a grin. "I have a letter to mail."

She returned the smile with warm eyes.

He made his way down the aisle, managed the stairs, and

then stepped out into the blazing sunlight. Squinting, he walked along the main street and considered stopping at the Rowdy Rabbit for a brandy. There wasn't time, though, so he hurried on, making his way to the post office. Spurred by the brevity of his purpose and knowing the train had a schedule to keep, urgency carried him faster than normal. He waited impatiently for three cars to pass before he could cross the street.

As he pushed the door open, an overhead bell jingled, once again carrying his mind into the past. He had heard that familiar ring his entire life, every time he had opened the door at his father's store. He could almost smell the pomade his father had used to slick back his hair and to curl his mustache. A similar scent hung in the air—different, but familiar enough to make him yearn even more for the real thing.

Burton shook off the memory and approached the counter. He hung his cane on his arm and pulled the letter from his breast pocket. "I need to post this," he said, huffing to catch his breath. He placed the envelope on the counter.

The man eyed it and met his gaze. "You sure? Looks like you've been holding onto it for a while."

Burton nodded. "I'm sure."

"Well, you'll need a new envelope. I don't think this one will hold up during delivery." He bent down behind the counter and retrieved a new one.

Burton copied the address and gingerly placed the old envelope into the new one and then slid it across the counter.

The man sealed the envelope. "It'll go out today."

Burton paid for the services, took up his cane from his arm, and tipped his bowler. He thanked the clerk, hurried on his way, and made it back seconds before the train pulled out of the station. Out of breath and red faced, he plopped down in his seat.

The woman looked up from her knitting. "Are you all right?"

"I will be. Just need a minute to catch my breath."

As the train began to roll out of the station, she turned to him. "Feeling better?"

"Much, thank you."

Truth was, he really felt much better. All day long, he had carried around a heavy feeling, like a stone tied around his neck. He attributed it to the emotions he had been tamping down as he went about the business of selling off the family properties. Now, he felt lighter and free.

Somehow, mailing that letter had taken away the ghost of a burden he hadn't known he'd been dragging around. As he turned back toward the window, he could have sworn he saw his parents waving outside of the train—their kind gesture was the reassurance he needed that he had made all of the right decisions.

CHAPTER TWO

NEVA, CALIFORNIA 1914

A motorcycle tri-car roared down the road, crackling gravel under its three tires as it sped along, leaving great plumes of dust in its wake. The rumble of the engine echoing off the trees disrupted the tranquil countryside. The obtrusive sound startled the horses nibbling alfalfa next to the barbed-wire fence, causing them to stampede past the territorial mare that remained rooted in place.

The driver downshifted when he approached the end of a long driveway. A herd of grazing cattle stopped chewing, looking up as their attention turned toward the garish sound of the vehicle that rolled to a stop. The driver eyed several hawks circling high above before he waved a hand in front of his face, trying to clear away the cloud of dust that had caught up to him. He repositioned his goggles to his forehead, swung his leg over the seat, and spat out a wad of tobacco.

Orderly rows of dormant grapevines flanked the driveway and stretched as far as the eye could see. The pattern was broken by the large house that stood sentinel on the property. White, with two stories, it was situated in the center of the vast three hundred acre estate. The four-pillar house was a mansion compared to the two smaller ones sharing the property. Behind the sprawling home were three large barns. Split-rail corrals abutting one of them housed a variety of livestock.

He opened the rear compartment on the back of the motorcycle to retrieve a small bundle of letters. After placing the mail in the metal box, he remounted the motorcycle. With hardly a glance back, he lowered his goggles and revved the engine, tearing off in a rush to finish his route.

On the front porch of the home, a woman sat in a rocking chair, a sleeping dog stretched out at her feet. Although her hair was still as black as a raven's feather, fine lines at the corners of her eyes gave away the fact she was middle-aged. Her skin tone was that of her native ancestors. She noticed the faint cloud of dust rising in the distance. "Looks like the mail's here. C'mon, Toopy," she said, leaning forward. She patted the black and white spotted dog on the head.

Toopy jumped up, tail wagging, and together they navigated their way down the porch steps. They were careful to avoid stepping on either of the two cats lounging in the morning sun. As she made her way down the long lane, the dog bounding in circles around her, she couldn't help but think of spring. She longed for the scent of flower blossoms and the sounds of the workers among the rows. She stopped, picked up a stick, and threw it far ahead of her. Toopy bounded after it, beginning their ritual game of fetch.

When she returned, she was mindful not to let the screen door slam behind her when she went inside. She crossed the porcelain-tiled foyer and slid open the pocket doors to the parlor, but there was no sign of her mother. Noticing the dying embers in the fireplace, she added another log. She grabbed the poker and stoked the fire, inhaling the wonderful aroma of burning hickory.

The mountain scene carved into the mantel drew her attention as she set down the poker. Wildlife surrounded a cabin next to a stream. Although she couldn't remember ever being there, the stories of it shared by her parents had filled her head her entire life. She couldn't help but smile at one particular pine tree, etched into the wood beside the cabin. Though unattractive, the memory that sprang to life when she looked at it was so beautiful that the detrimental effect on the entire scene could be forgiven. The day her father let her carve it into the mantel was one she would never forget. Anyone who saw it knew it was unsightly. Still, her father had proclaimed it the prettiest tree he had ever seen.

Smiling, she pulled herself from the past and turned to fluff the colorful embroidered sofa pillows before continuing with her search. She made her way up the stairway, trailing her hand along the smooth mahogany banister as she went. At the top, she paused outside one of the four bedroom doors, her fingers tracing the ornate carvings in the wood. She had always admired its beauty. An image of her father, hunched over amid a pile of wood chips, with tools in hand, came to mind. She knocked on the door. "Are you awake?" she asked, turning the knob.

The nearly extinguished embers in the fireplace provided no light, and the furnishings within were lost in shadows. No matter. She'd grown up in the house and could navigate it blindfolded if necessary.

She made her way through the hushed darkness and pulled back the heavy fabric draperies, flooding the room with morning sunlight. Small particles of dust danced in the beams of light that pierced the gloom, revealing a room fit for royalty. However, no queen lay in the unmade bed. The blankets were tossed carelessly to the side.

Plush rugs covered most of the room's polished, wood floors. On each bedside table sat ornate lamps with hand-painted, glass shades. On the wall opposite the bed was a beautiful vanity. Its top was lined with neat rows of bottles filled with makeups, perfumes, and lotions, which had come from distant and exotic places the world over. Beside the vanity were two matching, tallboy dressers with their mahogany, inlay banding shining in the bright sunlight.

She placed the mail on one of the bedside tables and made her way back out into the hall, closing the door softly behind her. Downstairs, she stuck her head into the den. In the center of the room sat the familiar old piano, the one she, her brother, and sister had all learned to play as children. Hundreds of books packed the shelves of the surrounding walls. The smell of their old pages had always reminded her faintly of vanilla.

Tears prickled at the corners of her eyes. This room now sat quiet almost year round. Sorrow had robbed her mother of her singing long ago. Only on Christmas day would she allow herself the pleasure of song for the entertainment of her family.

She left the den and made her way to the kitchen. Her footsteps on the patterned, tile floor echoed through the spacious room. It was clean and tidy, with all the cooking implements in their designated places. Pots and pans hung over the butcher block in the center of the room.

At the sink, she peered over the herbs sunbathing on the sill, which overlooked the backyard. Chickens wandered the yard, pecking and scratching at the ground. The sounds of chirping birds could be heard through the window, their colorful shapes warped by imperfections in the glass.

On the outskirts of the lawn, past the small orchard and underneath the tall oak where the old swing used to hang, she saw her mother. The careworn woman was cleaning off the debris that had fallen on the three tombstones during the night. The dappled light coming through the thick branches overhead gave her housecoat a mottled look, making it appear as if she were part of the landscape. She seemed to blend with the stone slabs in front of her.

I should've known.

The distance from the window was too far for her to distinguish the words. No matter. She knew the McGinnis gravestones intimately. In her mind, she could clearly see the names etched on each granite marker.

She walked outside and over to where her mother knelt beside one of the headstones. "It's chilly out here," she said, placing her hand lightly on the frail shoulder. "Please, come inside."

"I will, dear." The elderly woman stuck a finger in the air. "In just a minute."

She tenderly rubbed her hand across her mother's back. "I miss him, too."

"I know you do," she said, looking up at her daughter. "He's been gone for so long, yet I expect to see him every morning when I wake up. Sometimes, I can feel him next to me. Do you think that's possible?"

She saw the redness in her mother's eyes, heard the sadness in her tone. "I do. I'm sure he's always watching over us. Protecting us."

"I hope so. It comforts me knowing he's close by."

Not wanting to upset her mother further, she changed the subject. "They'll be back soon."

"I didn't mean to sleep in so long. I didn't hear a sound this morning."

"I cooked everyone breakfast at my house," she said. "Oh, and I put the mail on the table next to your bed."

"Thank you. No wonder the house was so quiet. Usually when they're in the kitchen, it sounds like the circus is in town." She smiled as she took her daughter's hand and stood. "We'd best get started. Those grandkids will be disappointed if we're not ready."

The elderly woman returned to her bedroom to dress for the day. Glancing at the mail on the table, she slipped on her spectacles and took a seat on the edge of the bed.

She shuffled casually through the usual stack of correspondence, stopping abruptly when her gaze landed on one from Burton Nicholas. Slowly, she reached for the letter opener. Pulling the aged envelope from within, she gasped when the name of the original sender revealed itself. It had been a long time since she'd thought about Edith. Her fingers trembled slightly as she traced the faded writing. She held the yellowed rectangle of paper with the pale ink splotch, unsure how to proceed. If she tore it or gripped the aging parchment too hard, she'd lose this precious thing—this piece of her old friend.

She cautiously sliced the fragile paper and pulled out the delicate letter within. The folded paper was stuck together, and she had to tease it apart ever so gently in order not to tear it. After managing to get it opened, she could still make out most of the writing despite the few words that had been rendered illegible by the ink stain.

As she read, her heart thumped harder and her breath caught in her throat. She had to pause now and then to keep her emotions from getting the best of her. Some part of her almost wished the letter had stayed lost as it rekindled such painful memories.

After she finished, she held the paper to her chest, a heavy feeling in her stomach. She sank back onto the plush bed, clinging to the letter as if it were a lifeline tethering her to her past. Her chin trembled, and her stomach rolled. A tear spilled and made its way along the raised three-inch scar on her left cheek. Unlike the faint script on the page, the old wound was indelible. It was only after the nausea had passed that anger finally bubbled to the surface. She closed her eyes and allowed herself to fall back into time, back to that horrific day.

CHAPTER THREE

1873

Icy fingers of dread crept up Abby's spine when Jesse swung up in the saddle. She knew Jesse's past all too well. Even though she had somehow managed to survive a home invasion, a rattlesnake bite, a gunshot wound, and a catastrophic fall down a mountain crevasse, she was not reassured Jesse would beat the odds again. The gut-wrenching feeling returned—the same one she had felt the day she left Jesse alone in the woods with the Roberts brothers. It was just like when she watched Jesse walk away from the cabin after the twins were born. It all came rushing back to her, settling over her like a well-worn blanket, and she shivered in spite of the dry heat of the day.

"I love you," Abby said, doing her best to keep the quiver from creeping into her voice. She placed a loving hand on Jesse's leg. "Please be safe. I—we need you to come home to us."

Jesse took hold of her hand. "I love you, too," she said, clasping Abby's fingers, "and I will."

Toby handed her the reins. "Take care of yourself out there, and d-don't do anything foolish."

"I won't." Jesse took one last long look at her family, as if trying to burn their features into her memory. "I'll see you all soon." She turned Buck and, with a click of her tongue, had him quickly galloping down the grapevine-flanked lane.

Abby's resolve to remain strong in front of her children felt as fleeting as the dust left behind by Jesse's departure. Worry made her twist the ring on her finger. She thought of the promise it represented, the promise Jesse had always kept. Dark and unwelcome outcomes grabbed at her, attempting to drag her into a black and oppressive pit of despair.

Gwen's muffled sobs pulled Abby back to the surface before she could be dragged into the shadows. She knelt, embracing her children in a tight and powerful hug. "Everything is going to be fine," she said, drawing strength from the small arms wrapped around her. "Pippa will be back before we know it."

It was unusual for Gwen to cry, but it was more unusual for anyone to witness it. An angry, embarrassed flush covered her cheeks as she swiped the tears from her face. The scene in the barn earlier had upset her more than anything she had ever experienced in her young life. Seeing the one person she thought of as fearless and capable of anything break down and cry had profoundly affected her.

Jim was shaken but managed to present a brave face. He was only eight years old, but he wasn't too young to comprehend that something significant was happening. He found the courage to be strong for both his mother and sister. After all, for the time being, he was the man of the house. At least, he felt like it.

"Your ma's right," Toby said, affectionately tousling the twins' hair in turn. "No need to be frettin' any."

"How about," Abby said, withdrawing from the tight squeeze the children still had on her, "we all go inside and I'll fix us something to eat?"

"I'll get Aponi, and we'll be right over," Toby said. "Oh, remember. Pippa went into San Francisco to see about a job." He waited for the twins to nod their heads in acknowledgement and then turned away and started walking toward his home.

The moment Abby entered the kitchen, it took every ounce of strength she had to keep from breaking down. On the counter sat the lopsided ham—the one she had cut a hunk from to pack in Jesse's saddlebag. An image of Jesse, seated on a bedroll spread beside a fire, eating cold food all alone, came to her mind.

"How 'bout ham sandwiches?" Jim asked, not wanting to add to his mother's distress.

"Sounds good to me," she said, swallowing back the sob that had been building in her chest. "Why don't you two run out and pick us a couple of tomatoes?"

"Last one to the garden is a rotten egg!" Jim called out, trying to lighten his sister's mood.

"Well…" Gwen said, moving slowly past the table. "Well, it won't be me!" She bolted out the back door and took off running across the yard, Jim hot on her heels in pursuit. They raced eagerly to the garden, their sadness forgotten for the moment.

Abby crossed the room and closed the door behind them. She returned to the counter, reached for a knife from one of the drawers, and grabbed a loaf of fresh sourdough bread.

Although she tried her best to stop it, her mind kept returning to the frightening and unsettling landscape it insisted upon crafting. As she pulled the knife across the bread, she noticed Jesse's favorite coffee mug on the counter next to her—it was the one the twins had given her for Christmas. Jesse had used it that morning and there was still a cold sip left in the bottom. On a hook by the back door hung one of Jesse's hats. She fought the temptation to walk over and get it, resisted the urge to breathe in the heady scent of wood and leather she had come to associate with her. Next to her right foot, she saw the broken tile where Jesse had accidentally dropped a cast iron skillet. No matter where she looked, somehow Jesse lingered behind, reminders of her presence lurking everywhere.

Toby mounted the steps to his covered porch. "Get! Shoo!" He hollered, stomping his feet and waving his arms. He went inside to find Aponi at the sink, one hand vigorously working the pump. "Damn chickens are shittin' on th-the porch again." He shifted his weight to one foot and observed her for a moment. "Now, I was gonna do that."

She paused, throwing a skeptical look over her shoulder at him, before continuing with her work.

"What?" He knew all too well the meaning of the look she gave him. "I was going to do it."

Aponi knew her husband had a tendency to procrastinate. Usually he put things off as long as possible or until she couldn't take it anymore—whichever came first. She cocked her head at him amiably and continued rinsing the vegetables. "I don't mind."

"Now, dammit," he said as his long legs crossed the room. "I said I'd do it."

The words might have sounded harsh out of context, but they were delivered with kid gloves that she knew all too well. He kissed her on the cheek as he plucked the turnip from her hands.

She smiled at him. "I thought you were going fishing."

"No. Jes had to run into the city and see about a job." Using his thumb, he scrubbed the dirt off the root vegetable, laid it on the counter, and reached for another. "Couldn't you get comfortable last night? I don't th-think you slept a wink."

Aponi dried her hands, tottered over to the table, and struggled to lower herself onto one of the chairs. "Someone doesn't want me to rest." She placed a hand on her distended stomach. "I wish it would come."

Toby dried his hands and knelt at her feet. His palm, which was calloused and strong, seemed small and almost delicate when placed against her swollen abdomen. Movement beneath his touch caused an eager smile to spread across his face. "Probably be any day now. Maybe there's two—or even three, in there."

She put her hand on his, smiling at the thought.

"Are you hungry?" he asked, standing.

She braced a hand on the table as she moved to stand. "I can make—"

"No. Abby wants us to come over and eat." He took her by the arm and helped guide her to her feet. "I th-think she could use some cheering up. You know how she gets when Jes is gone."

~

Abby was deep in thought, lost in a world of what ifs and maybes, when Toby and Aponi entered the kitchen.

"Is everything all right?" Aponi asked, softly.

Toby pulled out a chair and helped his wife maneuver herself onto the seat. "She's just concentrating so she don't take off a finger," he said, and then raised his voice. "Ain't th-that right?"

"Oh, I'm sorry," Abby said, looking up from the cutting board. "Did you say something?"

Aponi studied her face. "Are you all right?" She wriggled in her seat, trying to find a position that didn't exacerbate the pain in her hips and back.

"Of course," Abby said. "I just hate when Jes goes to the city, that's all. We're making ham sandwiches. Can you slice it for me?" She passed Toby the knife, and he started cutting slabs of meat from the bone.

Aponi had known Abby for a long time. Over the years, they had become as close as sisters, so she was able to recognize immediately that something about Abby's behavior was off. She only caught a glimpse of it before the twins came rushing through the back door with their arms heaped with several ripe tomatoes. Letting them roll from their hands onto the counter, the twins took seats across from Aponi and resumed what seemed to be an ongoing argument.

Gwen wrinkled her nose. "Do you smell something?" she asked her aunt and uncle.

Both Toby and Aponi sniffed the air.

"No. I don't smell anything," Aponi said.

"Me neither," Toby said, continuing to carve.

Gwen took a long, audible breath. "I sure do. It smells

like…" She inhaled again, pinched her nose closed, and pretended to retch. "…a rotten egg to me."

"Ha, ha. Very funny," Jim said, trying to catch his breath. He knew he could have beaten her to the garden if he had tried, but today he had let her have the win.

"Gwen," Abby said, reaching for the glass pitcher, "be nice."

"Auntie, I still think it'll be a boy," Jim said.

Gwen pushed her brother on the shoulder. "Nuh-uh," she said with a simpering smirk. "It's a g—"

The sudden sound of shattering glass brought silence over the room. It settled among them like an unwelcome guest.

Abby held up her hand. "Don't come over here," she said, staring down at the shards strewn all around her. The last thing she wanted was to have to dig pieces of glass out of her children's bare feet.

"I'll take care of it," Toby said, setting down the knife. "You've g-got sweet tea all over you. Why don't you go on and clean up?"

She patted his arm. "Thank you."

Abby climbed the stairs and walked the long hall toward the room she shared with Jesse. Her insides churned like someone facing a firing squad, rather than one who just entered the sanctity of their own master bedroom. After shutting the door behind her, she crossed the room and pulled open the double doors of her oversized wardrobe. It was packed full of clothing, with fancier dresses for church and special events on the right. The more modest dresses and skirts for daily use were on the left. She stood staring at all the different choices—choices she had because Jesse worked so hard to give them to her. Without any more thought, she reached toward the left side and pulled a dress at random from one of the hangers.

Abby tossed the clothing on the bed and looked down at her dress as she unfastened the buttons. The wet fabric clung to her body in a way she recognized. It triggered a horrible memory, the one of Jesse in Kaga's arms as he carried her into the cabin, a blood-soaked shirt clinging to her lifeless body. The image had been seared into her mind that day, and it was one she always dreaded the return of the most. She peeled out of the wet clothing, discarded it to the side, and dressed quickly.

All sorts of disastrous endings continued to torment her, poisoning the already dying landscape her thoughts had become. Clutching her stomach, she sat at her vanity and stared into the mirror. The image peering back appeared hopeless and miserable, and she found she couldn't stand to look at herself. Her eyes drifted around the room, which had always known so much love. There had to be something, anything, she could find to help ease the ominous feeling looming over her like a storm cloud.

Finally, her gaze lit upon the marble tile surrounding the fireplace. Her despair was as black as the ash residue lining the hearth. *Why didn't I just burn the damn paper? If something happens to her, it'll be all my fault.*

The pitifully weak grip she had on her sanity threatened to slip, so she grabbed ahold of the vanity for support. The wood was strong and sturdy, but even that seemed powerless to keep her from falling over the thin edge she was already teetering on. She felt as though all it would take was a slight touch to make her shatter, but she didn't want her children to find her in broken pieces on the floor. She knew from experience some slivers could never be removed.

Abby glanced back toward the mirror, forcing herself to face the strange, pallid reflection staring back at her. She swallowed a strangled cry, and her breath hitched as she pinched her cheeks for color. *Pull it together. Just pull it together.*

Reluctantly she stood, smoothing the wrinkles from her dress, and walked toward the door. As she reached for the knob, another wave of emotion flooded her, incapacitating and threatening to drown her. She leaned with her back to the door, melting down against the wood until she was a crumpled mess on the floor. The skirt pooled into a floral puddle that surrounded her. *What have I done?* She bent her head to muffle the cries in the palms of her hands but was startled by a pounding on the door.

"It's Auntie!" Gwen shouted. "Something's wrong! She peed on the floor!"

Abby's breath hissed in alarm, and she sprang to her feet. She quickly wiped the tears from her cheeks with a shaking hand, took a deep breath, and opened the door. "I think her baby is coming," she said to a wide-eyed Gwen.

Abby rushed to follow her daughter downstairs and discovered Toby, his arm supporting Aponi, carefully directing her across the foyer toward the front door.

"Where're you going?" Abby asked.

"I need to walk."

Aponi's calm demeanor surprised Abby. "Are you having any pain?"

"No. Nothing yet."

"I'll go get Celia and we'll be right over," Abby said.

Gwen took hold of her mother's hand. "I'll go with you."

"Me too," Jim said.

Aponi smiled at them. "No need to hurry," she said with a wink at the twins. "I think it will be awhile before your cousin makes an appearance."

CHAPTER FOUR

The following evening, Jesse reined Buck to a stop on the east bank of the Devil's Fork. The rushing river thundered in her ears as she pulled a foot from the stirrup. Tired and sore, she swung her leg over the saddle and dropped to the ground. She barely managed to keep herself from falling as her leg gave out beneath her. With a steady hand clutching at the saddle, she shook the offending limb in an attempt to get the blood flowing again.

Every joint of her thirty-year-old body screamed in protest. Sleeping on the hard ground wasn't something she was accustomed to and, when coupled with the fact her mind wouldn't shut off, she hadn't gotten much sleep the night before. She massaged her balled-up fist into the small of her back, trying to relieve a burning ache that had been throbbing for hours.

Once her leg felt strong enough to bear weight, she took off her hat and hooked it onto the saddle horn. Combing back the hair from her face with one hand, she took in the scenery before her. There was a hazy mist coming off the river that looked mystical. On the air floated the earthy aroma of moss, lichen, and pine. Although she had been gone for eight years, the past seemed to vanish the instant she inhaled the familiar scent. Being home was a strange sensation, but even stranger was crossing the river in broad daylight. With a bridge in Granite Falls, however, there was no longer a need to keep her promise to Frieda.

The leaden clouds overhead matched her mood. Ever since she had opened her eyes that morning, the notion that she would never see her family again had been pursuing her like an irritating gnat. It had only been one day since she'd seen them, but already it felt like a lifetime.

"They're better off," she mumbled under her breath, slipping off her boots. Some part of her was still trying to be convinced that there was truth in the statement.

Her gaze was drawn to the river, where the current coursed rapidly over granite outcroppings. The water flowed effortlessly, as though being poured down a steep flight of stairs. Another river came to mind as she watched. "What do you think, boy?" she asked Buck, reaching down to pull off a sock. "You want to go see if it's as mighty as Abby says?"

Thinking about the Mississippi sparked a memory, and as an image came to mind, her face lit up in a smile. She remembered Abby nestled next to the twins on the sofa as she shared stories about the river she grew up on back in Missouri. Despite Jim's best efforts, every time he tried to say the word, it always came out as "Mippissippi". Her lips curved up in nostalgia, regardless of the fact that the memory pierced her heart deeper than any knife ever could. Her resolve to walk away from her family toppled like a fragile house of cards. There was no way she could leave them, and she'd been foolish to consider it. The only thing that mattered was finishing what she came to do so that she could get back home to them. The sooner, the better.

Once her boots and socks were packed securely in the saddlebag, she curled her fingers around Buck's reins and carefully led him down the reed-covered embankment. The cold and oozing mud between her toes did little to abate the fire which had been ignited in the barn, back when she had first read the newspaper article. With a deep breath, she drew on the anger twisting in her gut. Allowing it to focus her mind on the task at hand, she stepped gingerly into the water.

Two exhausting days later, Jesse finally reached the end of the marked path. She rode to the edge of the lake and dismounted. Shielding her eyes from the light reflecting off of the mirrored surface, she stood there serenely, absorbing the view. Of all of the beautiful places she'd seen since leaving the mountain, none of them could ever compare to this breathtaking display.

"C'mon," she said, running her hand affectionately down the horse's neck. "Let's get you taken care of."

By the time she had tended to Buck and started a fire, there was nothing more she could do than collapse onto her bedroll. Although her bed at home was preferable, it still felt good to be stretched out rather than to be cramped up in the saddle. The sound of lapping water in the background had a tranquil and lulling effect.

Her thoughts drifted back to the last time she had bedded down there. Abby was with her, the twins only a flutter of hope beneath her fingertips. She remembered the conversation they'd had on that very spot. Abby had said that even though Frieda had not given birth to her, she was as much a mother to her as her own. And how, Jesse recalled, any child would be blessed to have two loving and devoted parents, regardless of if they were the same gender.

At the time, it made perfect sense. Things had gone much differently than they had expected, however, and now it was more complicated than that. If only they had stayed on the mountain, they would have had no reason to hide who they were. On the mountain, there were no rules. No one was there to say two women couldn't love each other. On Mount Perish, they could just be.

Unfortunately, the only way to give Jim and Gwen the life she wanted them to have was to live a lie. She knew she couldn't earn an income to support a family in a man's world any other way. Constantly, she worried the twins would find out the truth. Hopefully, when the day finally came for her to explain her reasons for doing what she did, they would somehow find it in their hearts to understand. After all, she did it for them, though she didn't know what she would do if they were to reject her. In the restless light of the fire, she fell asleep, wishing more than ever she was back home with her family.

Bars of early light stabbed at her face, trying to penetrate her closed lids. Sighing in exasperation, she groaned and rolled over on the hard ground. It took several moments for her mind to fully come awake. Her eyes blinked rapidly against the morning sun. She sat up and reached for her boots. Nearby, untethered, Buck grazed on the dew-soaked grass. She stood and stretched her arms above her head, trying to shake off the last remnants of sleep and alleviate the stiffness that had settled into her joints. Crouching down by the water's edge, she drank from her cupped palms and then splashed a handful onto her face. Cold drops of water dripped down her shirt, sending shivers down her spine. She stood up, staring out over the lake, and contemplated her next move.

Just around the bend, the landscape was going to change drastically. She knew she would be forced to continue on foot, so it was probably as good a time as any to part ways with Buck. With so many predators in the area, she knew she couldn't tie him up to wait for her to return. To do that would paint a big red target on his back and, after everything they'd been through together, she felt she owed him a fighting chance.

She hadn't yet seen another living soul, but she knew there was no guarantee it would stay that way. Erring on the side of caution, before setting out for the Ponak village, she decided to stash the horse tack in some low, dense brush for safe-keeping.

To her surprise, Buck followed like a faithful pet, keeping up the pace behind her. She felt a deep level of gratitude and didn't discourage the pursuit. Soon, however, they came to the area where the terrain was much too difficult for him to maneuver. When she stopped, he nudged her back with his head and nickered gently. She turned to face him and stuck out her hand. He lipped her fingers affectionately while she stroked the other palm against his muzzle.

"This is as far as you go, my friend." She bit back her tears to keep from crying. Draping an arm around his neck, she buried her cheek against his soft hair, breathing in his scent. "I hope you're here when I get back." She never thought it would be so hard to walk away from an animal. This was her constant companion, though, a friend who had faithfully been by her side. She forced herself to turn away and began climbing over the large boulders. When she heard him whinny in confusion and despair, she refused to let herself look back.

Even before she neared the top of the bluff, she could sense something was wrong. The breeze blowing against her face was heavily polluted and fetid. The odor that rose up from the very earth was putrid, with a thick and disgusting flavor that coated her tongue and filled her nostrils. Her gorge rose immediately, and she tasted bile in the back of her throat. She swallowed back the urge to vomit and as soon as she reached the peak, she pulled a handkerchief from her pocket. Cinching the cloth across her nose and mouth, the smell was reduced enough so that she could breathe without gagging. With her finger on the trigger of her rifle, she took a cautious step.

Rounding a small bend, she stopped mid-stride, spying a large carcass lying up ahead. It was within the shadow of a large oak, and she almost missed it. Heart pounding, she forced herself to move in closer for a better look. The smell got stronger, and she pressed the cloth closer to her face. Scavengers had gotten to the body. The rib cage was frayed, punctuating the hollowed cavity beneath it. The soft meat had been picked off, but it didn't matter. Size alone told her exactly who it was. Ahanu had been the largest brave in the tribe. Now his empty sockets stared, unseeing, at the clear, blue sky.

Jesse stepped away and continued on shaky legs, stomach acid burning in her throat. She was terrified with what she was about to discover, but at least now she knew what to expect.

Once she had reached the outskirts of the village, she ducked safely behind a large elm. From the camouflage of the forest, she carefully watched for movement. Nothing crackled or shifted. There was only stillness and silence. After several minutes, she was convinced she was alone. Her legs trembling, she left the security of her hiding place and willed her feet to move forward.

She discovered what must have been the community garden and thought back to the day she had given seeds to Black Turtle. Anything that had been growing had been picked clean; all of the plants had been trampled or pulled up by the roots. Boot prints were still visible in the dirt. It was the malicious imprint of those who had no respect for life of any kind.

The last time she had been there she was helping her brother claim a bride. All along the mountain, there had been the blossoming signs of life. Phlox and clover, accentuated by the vivid purple, white, and yellow violets called johnny-jump-ups, grew abundantly in lush fields. Nuthatches and chickadees flitted jovially from tree to tree.

Now, there was only death. Bodies were left behind with white skulls gleaming. Clumps of flesh and clotted blood were all that remained of the scalps that had been ripped from their heads. She saw that their backs were peppered with bullet holes. What had happened was so obvious that if she had a brush, she could have painted the entire macabre scene. It *had* been an ambush, just as she had suspected.

Through eyes stinging with tears, she watched as a shadow passed over the ground in front of her. One of the vultures that had been circling overhead had chosen to land on the corpse nearest her.

"Go!" she yelled, waving her arms. "Get outta here!"

Suddenly, the carnage all around her became too much.

She barely managed to pull the neckerchief out of the way before she was overcome with a violent explosion of vomit. Doubled over with her shaking hands on her knees, she heaved until there was nothing left for her stomach to purge.

She wiped her mouth on the sleeve of her shirt, fighting against the dizziness that threatened to drop her. Once she felt fairly certain she wasn't going to pass out, she stood up straight and stared out across the field of bodies.

Though it had been nearly a week and a half since the attack, the cool mountain temperatures had slowed the decomposition process significantly. Most of the bodies were ruined, with their mottled flesh the color of an old bruise. However, as Jesse walked among the dead, she was still able to recognize most members of the tribe.

As she made her way through the village, she kept her lips clamped together tightly in an effort to keep from crying. When she discovered the lifeless body of Honovi, though, there was nothing she could do to stop the tears from flowing. Like all of the others, there were bullet holes in her back. Beneath her lay Onawa, the cornea of her one remaining eye a milky shade of gray. Honovi had died trying to shield the woman she loved. It was the most devastatingly beautiful thing Jesse had ever seen. She felt a wave of emotion crash over her and choked back a sob. The image of the two of them together was embedded in her mind. She knew the memory would haunt her until the day she died.

There was one more place she had to check: the cavern where she had met with the tribal elders. She hoped and prayed some of them had managed to hide. If they were, the secret hollow in the mountain was where they would be. When she got there, though, there was no one to be found.

There were only more of those dried, muddy boot prints. All around the fire pit, where her initiation had taken place, were the scattered pieces of the ceremonial pipe. Now, it too was broken, as shattered as the tribe it represented.

Jesse screamed out in anguish, her voice bouncing off of the cave walls. There was no way she could ever wrap her mind around this. It made no sense. They weren't interfering with the ways of white men. Why would white men kill these people for no apparent reason and leave them out to rot? Why couldn't this peaceful tribe live on top of the mountain when there was more than enough land for everyone?

Jesse placed her hand on the wall for support, her palm coming to rest on one of the pictographs. She glanced down the length of the wall. Her chin trembled as she realized the simple native drawings were all that was left of the Ponak now. Her eyes widened as she spotted a particular scene—one depicting a ceremony with a white man and a native woman. Her pulse quickened in recognition. Yes, there was a survivor —Aponi. Only then did it occur to her that her sister-in-law had probably given birth. Everything wasn't lost. But now, more than ever, she couldn't wait to get home.

Jesse exited the cavern and set out across the meadow again. She tripped, stumbling over a body concealed by the tall grass. Her breath hitched when she saw it was Lewonta, her arms still clinging tightly to the two small children she had tried to save. Jesse tore her eyes away from the interlaced hands. They couldn't have been much older than her own. There was no way she could walk away, leaving them there in the grass, lost forever.

"I'm so sorry," she said, kneeling down and placing her hands beneath Lewonta's arms. The decomposing flesh shifted underneath her palms and threatened to come loose. She secured her grip and as carefully as she could, dragged the once beautiful chieftain's wife into the cavern. Gently, she placed the body along the far wall. Tight-lipped and tense, she returned for the children.

After placing their bodies next to Lewonta's, Jesse realized that if she were going to be able to continue with the rest of the village, she'd have to devise a better system of transporting the bodies. Thinking back to her youth, she remembered how Frieda had taught her the method of making a native drag sled for transporting large game back to the cabin. She maneuvered two lodge poles away from one of the teepees. Using a tomahawk she had found, she hacked them down to size, crisscrossed them at one end, and tied them tightly with lengths of rawhide she found in one of the ransacked shelters. Finally, she laid sturdy branches across the splayed ends, lashing them together to make a platform.

With a functioning travois, she began moving the bodies one by one into the cavern. She continued the process with decorum, containing the urge to gag to the best of her ability. Putrefaction penetrated her nostrils and she knew she would never forget the smell. As the last vestiges of daylight descended upon her, she placed the final two bodies side by side. Wiping the back of one shaking hand across her forehead, she looked down at Onawa and Honovi. She was deeply moved knowing they would be together forever.

Throughout the night, by the scant light of the waning moon, she hauled rocks and placed them over the entrance of the cavern, sealing up the twenty-eight-body tomb. By dawn, she was left with one last task. Her booted feet dragged the ground heavily, and her body was consumed with exhaustion.

She retraced her steps to the spot where she had come upon Ahanu. Her arms trembled with fatigue as she struggled to cover his body with rocks. Finally, when the last stone was in place, she found the strength to jam a stick into the ground to mark the makeshift grave. Pulling the neckerchief from around her face, she tied it securely to the end of the stick and knelt down to touch the ground. Wearily, she looked to the sky as the morning light parted through the clouds. With a deep sigh, she closed her eyes respectfully.

"Now the Great Spirit will know where to find you, my friend."

CHAPTER FIVE

The pale light of dusk had filled the sky by the time Jesse reached the lake. Her hopes of reuniting with Buck were dashed when the only thing greeting her on the banks was a croaking army of frogs. Though there had been no sign of him since they had parted ways two days ago, she couldn't help but wonder if he was merely roaming the mountain or if something horrible had happened to him. A fleeting thought, the latter was something she refused to consider. Regardless, the outcome for her was going to be the same. She was in for a long trip down the mountain on foot. Completely exhausted, she let her belongings fall from her work-numbed fingers onto the same place where she had bedded down the night before last. The serenity she normally felt near the shoreline was gone, replaced by an overwhelming sadness that crashed over her like a tsunami.

The scent of decay clung to her and seemed to have permeated her very being. As there had been no other signs of human life since having set foot on the mountain, she hurried to strip off her tainted clothes. Using ash from her old campfire and an oval sandstone, she scoured her body and hair vigorously. Even as her skin throbbed as though a thousand wasps had stung her, she continued to scrape the sandstone against her flesh. It felt as though the stench would never come off. No matter how hard she scrubbed, she could still feel the heaviness of death.

She waded into the lake, splashing water against herself, and began sluicing away the gray residue. Once she was deep enough, she dunked down in an effort to get the ash out of her hair. When she broke the surface, her fiery hair caught the last of the day's light. Treading water, she glanced back at the vacant stretch of shoreline. She would give anything to see Abby standing there, waiting for her with a blanket in hand and a smile on her face. The homesickness and longing were so heavy that the weight threatened to pull her under while she swam toward the shore.

As she slipped into a clean pair of long underwear, the idea of collapsing into her own bed and sleeping for days had never seemed more appealing. Unfortunately, hers had never been so far away. She'd have to make the best of sleeping on the hard ground yet again, on what would be another long and lonely night.

The simple act of gathering wood for a fire was almost more than she could bear. Her feet stung and throbbed with each step. The heft of the kindling was strenuous and exhausting. She could only recall once before struggling to collect wood, and that was right after she'd been shot.

Soon bright orange flames pushed back against the impenetrable darkness. The crackling of the fire, along with the clatter of crickets, mixed in with a deep-throated croak of the occasional bullfrog, was a welcome respite against the isolation. Off in the distance there was a loud wail. She rubbed a hand on the nape of her neck anxiously as the idea of Buck, alone in the wild, ran through her mind again. The image of him lying lifeless while a bear feasted on him flashed through her mind. *Don't go there. He's fine.*

Shoving the gruesome thought away, her nose crinkled as she looked down at her dirty clothing balled up at her feet. Knowing the smell of death would never come out of the fabric, she booted them into the fire without a second thought.

Jesse spread out her bedroll and finally sat down for what seemed like the first time in days. Despite the unpleasant odor coming off the fire, her stomach growled. She reached for her saddlebag, rummaged through it, and pulled out a half loaf of stale bread. Dry and hard, she ripped off a piece and shoved it into her mouth. She chewed aggressively, struggling to swallow it. What she wouldn't give for a hot cup of coffee to wash it down with. Resigned, she made do with water from her canteen, finishing off the meal with a slice of ham and a hunk of cheese.

Once her hunger pangs had eased, she allowed herself to collapse back on the bedroll. Under a star-filled sky, with her pistol clutched in her hand, she was gradually lulled to sleep by the crackle of the campfire.

In the early-morning hours, before the sun had risen, Jesse was jolted awake by the sounds of rustling in the nearby woods. Someone, or something, was in the shadows just beyond the light of her fire. Eyelids pressed tightly together, she feigned sleep. It was better that whatever was out there come into her circle of light, rather than her venturing out into the darkness. Another sudden noise made her heart leap, and a tense vein throbbed wildly on the side of her neck. She placed her finger on the trigger of her pistol.

The harmless chatter of raccoons brought quick relief. She exhaled the breath she had been holding and released her grip on the gun. Wide-awake now, she gently eased herself into a sitting position. Her body groaned from the aches and pains in her joints. The muscles she hadn't used in years were screaming in protest. Coupled with sleeping on the hard ground, all of the bending and squatting had finally caught up with her. The simple act of adding another log to the fire was agony. She massaged the backs of her legs in an effort to alleviate some of the soreness and minimize cramps. As she rubbed, she contemplated the situation.

With the breaking dawn, she decided upon dousing the fire and set about packing up her supplies. After several calls and whistles, there was still no sign of Buck. Reluctantly, she accepted she had no other option but to leave his tack behind.

She flung her saddlebags over her shoulder and picked up her rifle. Turning to leave, it occurred to her to at least take something of his as a memento. When she placed his bridle in her bag, an encouraging thought flashed in her mind. Buck knew the area as well as she did.

Maybe he went to the cabin?

In truth, it wasn't her only reason for wanting to go. She knew it would be her last chance to go to the old homestead. After everything she'd seen, all of the bloodshed, the mountain was ruined for her now. She had no intentions of ever stepping foot on it again.

Knowing there was still a chance someone could be in the area, she hid her saddlebags in the brush to be safe. Rifle in hand, she set out for the old place, choosing to stick to the deer path next to the stream. Although it wasn't as conspicuous as it used to be, walking along it was as familiar to her as Frieda's old hat.

As she neared the cabin, the scent of burning wood warned her she wasn't alone. Her heart hammering in her chest, she raised the rifle, trigger finger ready, and cautiously continued forward. Once she had crested a small hill, she spotted something up ahead that stopped her dead in her tracks. She immediately crouched low to the ground, giving her mind time to puzzle out what she was seeing. When the pieces finally fell together, she took off in a sprint.

Lying face down, her head in the stream, the leather-clad body of a woman was sprawled on the bank. Long, black strands of her hair were splayed out and floating along the current. A large, brownish-red stain on her tunic had spread across her back, covering her shoulder blades like a morbid set of wings.

Jesse dropped her rifle, thrust her hands under the body, and rolled it over. Brown, vacant eyes stared back at her. Even in death, the woman was recognizable. Her features were a deep bronze, still as rich and beautiful as the day they had met. It was Tala—the young girl offered as a bride for Toby.

Jesse knew by the condition of the body it couldn't have been there long. She ran her fingers down over the lifeless lids, whispering an inadequate apology, as she closed them for the final time.

Grabbing her rifle, she clutched it tightly as she left the trail, moving silently and using the trees of the forest for cover. When a small portion of the old cabin came into view, she hunkered down behind a large hickory. Furtively, she chanced a quick look. Two unfamiliar horses were penned in the paddock. A bearded man was seated nearby on one of Frieda's old stump chairs. She leaned back against the rough bark and took a series of calming breaths.

Since seeing the carnage at the village, a slow rage had been building up and simmering inside her. This man wasn't wearing a military uniform, though, so she had to assume he wasn't involved in the attack. It was the only thing keeping her from charging at him, gun firing.

Curiosity pulled her closer and she moved as quietly as she could, careful not to step on twigs or disturb anything that could give away her presence. Once she reached the large pine next to the cabin, she crouched down low behind its boughs. Peering out from between the branches, she studied the bearded man. His skin looked like dried, cracked leather. Her heart was pounding so hard she thought for sure he would hear it. She eased the branches closed, set down her rifle, and waited for her pulse to slow.

Jesse's eyes skimmed the familiar landscape. Her fingernails dug crescents into her palms when she caught sight of the stump midway between the cabin and the stream. It hadn't been just any tree. It was the one she and Abby had planted. The one that represented their relationship. Like everything else she had seen, it had been chopped down in its prime. She had a lot of faith in the ritual, so she couldn't help but wonder if what had happened to the tree was a sign of things to come for them.

"Why don't you go get us somethin' to eat," said the man on the porch.

For one irrational second, she thought he was speaking to her, until she saw someone step through the cabin doorway.

He took a seat on the vacant stump chair without saying a word.

"Don't tell me you're still sulkin' over that squaw." The man with the beard leaned to the side and spat tobacco juice onto the wood planks.

"You didn't have to shoot her."

"Not my fault," he said with a scowl. The rumble of his bowels gurgled as he continued. "She shouldn't have tried to run. Ya know once 'em injuns get in the woods they scatter like cockroaches." He used the back of his hand to wipe the brown spittle from his lips. "Why don't you make yourself useful and go shoot us some grub?"

The younger man stood and retrieved his rifle that was leaning up against the cabin.

"And not another damn 'possum." His bowel gurgled louder. "That last one is shootin' through me something fierce. Try for a squirrel or rabbit."

"You ain't comin?"

"No!" He sprang to his feet. "I've gotta see a man about a dog," he said, hurrying down the porch steps.

Jesse assumed she must have misheard him, because his statement didn't make any sense. She watched as the men went their separate ways. The younger of the two headed off into the woods opposite from her, while the other one ran to the outhouse and closed the door. Good sense told her it was time to leave. Her inquisitive side pulled her toward the cabin for one last look inside her old home. Now was her only chance.

Leaving her rifle on the ground, she pulled her pistol from the holster and stepped from the security of the evergreen. She ran stooped over, moving covertly onto the porch until she was huddled beneath the window. Cautiously, she slowly craned her neck and peeked inside. After seeing no one else moving around, she entered through the open door, remembering to step over the spot that always squeaked just inside the threshold. She took in the entire scene in an instant.

The place was nothing like she had left it. The top of Frieda's trunk had been broken off and thrown to the side, its contents tossed about like confetti. Jars and tins that used to line the shelves lay open and scattered about. The table and four chairs were still intact, but the two rockers had been broken up for firewood. A wave of nausea hit her hard when her gaze finally landed on the mantle—the one she'd spent so much time carving to get the details right. Nails had been pounded into the cherished slab of wood with a string of scalps hanging from each one, drying from the heat of a large fire.

Wisdom, logic, intelligence; everything told her to run out the door and never look back. However, her respect for the Ponak, for all they had done for her since she was a young girl, pulled her toward the fireplace. At her feet was a small pile of the wooden carvings she had left behind—now just more kindling for their fire. She holstered her pistol, pulled the gruesome trophies from the nails, and frantically tossed them into the flames. She'd be damned if those men were going to profit from her friends' deaths.

Jesse's knees nearly buckled when she heard the familiar squeak of the floorboard behind her. In one swift move, she had her pistol out of the holster and cocked before she turned to face the young man standing at the threshold.

"Don't shoot." He raised his hands and rifle above his head. "I mean no harm."

Jesse could see the pistol shaking in her hand as she leveled the weapon at his chest. She steadied the gun with her other hand.

"I didn't know any of this was gonna happen. It was supposed to be a trapping expedition." Keeping one hand held out in front of him, he used his other to slowly lower his rifle to the floor. Then, he stood with his palms facing her. "Please! I never hurt anyone in my life."

Her green eyes flashed with rage. Gun hand steady now, she asked, "What about those?" She tilted her head toward the fireplace, finger ready on the pistol should he so much as twitch an eyebrow.

"We figured it couldn't do 'em any more harm since they was already dead."

"And what about Tala?"

"Tala?"

She pointed with her pistol in the direction of the stream. "The woman out there." She directed the gun at him again and watched the color drain from his face.

"When we came across their village, we found her hidin' in a cave. I told my partner we should leave her, but he said we'd probably get reward money or make good money by selling her. Much more than we'd make sellin' pelts." He wiped his nose on the sleeve of his shirt. "It was all his idea."

She heard a noise coming from inside Frieda's old trunk. Keeping her eyes trained on him the entire time, she took a few side steps, and risked a peek inside.

"She was holdin' it when we found her."

"Tala had a baby?"

"Said it wasn't hers." He shook his head. "Sure couldn't tell it by the way she protected it. She tried to sneak out of here with it this morning, but when it started crying, my partner woke up." His chin trembled. "She would've gotten away if she'd left it behind."

Jesse wasn't surprised by Tala's actions. She knew all too well the love one can have for a child—even if it doesn't come from your womb. She also knew the Ponak women were motherly to any child born into the tribe, bestowing all of the knowledge and love they could to the next generation.

She holstered her pistol and picked up the baby. It looked to be around three months old. "Hey, little guy," she said. "It's all right." She held the whimpering baby against her chest. "Shhh, it's all right. Shhh."

"Hurry," he said, stepping aside. "Take it and get out of here."

With the baby in her arms, she stepped out onto the porch.

He followed behind her. "I'll get you a head start. It's the least I can do. Now go," he whispered.

She stopped to retrieve her rifle and noticed him lifting the loop of rope on the paddock gate. He silently shooed the two horses out of the corral. She knew if his partner planned on tracking her and the baby, the delay in catching their horses would buy them a decent head start.

By the time Jesse returned to the lake, with the baby held in one arm and her other hand clutching her rifle, she felt as though her muscles were on fire. She leaned her gun against a tree and gently placed the baby on the ground. Quickly, she pulled her coat from the saddlebag, tied the sleeves together to create a makeshift sling, and slipped it around her neck. Carefully, she picked up the baby and placed it inside. With the saddlebags draped over a shoulder, she hurried toward the overgrown path that would lead her down the mountain.

She moved as fast as the terrain permitted, trying to put a good distance between her and the men at the cabin. After an hour, she finally felt safe enough to stop and tend to the baby. Next to a stream, she tried her best to comfort the crying infant. It was obvious it was hungry and needed a diaper change.

"What should I call you?" she asked in an attempt to get the baby to focus on the sound of her voice rather than its hunger pangs. "How 'bout Joseph? You like that?"

The baby only cried harder.

"Come on. It's not that bad." She carefully took the baby from the makeshift sling. "You're right. Not Joseph. How about Thomas?" She studied the infant's face for any sort of reaction as she placed it on the ground next to the babbling brook. "All right. We'll keep working on it." In desperate need of a diaper, she pulled her last shirt from her saddlebag and cut the fabric with her knife. "I know," she said, staring back into the large, teary, brown eyes watching her. "But it'll do." She wetted a rag in the water and removed the dirty hide and moss diaper. "Oh! No wonder you didn't like those names." A wide grin spread across her face. "Looks like we have a lot in common, little one."

After the baby girl was changed, Jesse reached into her saddlebag and pulled out what was left of her provisions. Unfortunately, none of it was suitable for an infant. She studied what she had as the baby wailed loudly: five hard-boiled eggs, two apples, a tiny chunk of cheese, a small hunk of ham, and a crust of stale bread.

As if on cue, a bird landed on a bush close by. Jesse knew then what to do. She hurried to peel a hard-boiled egg. As soon as it was shelled, she took a small bite along with some apple and chewed. Once it was ground to a pulp, she spat it onto her palm, placing small bits of the pureed mixture into the baby's mouth. The girl's lips pursed as she swallowed down the sweet concoction, and she whined for more.

"Oh, you like that, huh?" She repeated the process until the baby seemed content, and then placed her against her shoulder to burp.

It would have been much easier to descend the mountain with a cradleboard, but Jesse did the best she could with what she had to work with. When the baby was awake, she sang softly to her, calling on memories of the songs Abby sang to their children.

During the times when the baby slept, when the world was quiet all around, she was grateful to feel the tiny beating heart against her.

Jesse was furious, heartbroken. She had witnessed more horror in her lifetime than any one person should ever have to see. Her body and spirit had never known such weakness. She knew she had to persevere, though, like she had always done. She pushed the garish thoughts from her mind and kept focused on who was waiting for her at home.

Two days later, Jesse's heart leapt when she caught sight of Buck standing by the bent tree marking the river crossing. She flew to him and wrapped an arm around his neck, unashamed of the happy tears streaming down her cheeks. He nickered and nudged her with his head. "Hey, boy. You ready to go home, too?"

She placed the baby on the ground at the base of a willow

and carried her rifle to the water's edge. With her saddle and sheath atop the mountain, there was no way she could carry the baby safely and her rifle across the river at the same time. The gun was special; it was the one Toby had given her for Christmas years earlier, but she knew her priority was the safety of the baby. She took one last look at the gun and then pitched it into the Devil's Fork.

She removed the bridle from her saddlebag and slipped the bit in the horse's mouth. Once bridled, she reached down for the baby. "So, how 'bout Rose?" Russet eyes watched her as she secured the baby within the makeshift sling. As if in response to her question, the baby wrinkled its nose. Jesse winked down at her. "Don't like that either, do ya?" she said, draping her saddlebag across Buck's back. She noted the large tree. "I got it. How 'bout Willow? Do you like that?"

This time her question was answered with a smile and a coo. "Okay, Willow it is," she said, taking hold of Buck's reins. "Let's go home."

CHAPTER SIX

Both energy and provisions were exhausted. Willow let out a series of small, pitiful cries, sucking at her fist. Jesse urged Buck down the dirt road, knowing it would lead them straight to Big Oak. Thankfully, the smooth gait of the horse soon had a calming effect on the baby.

The road before them seemed twice as long as it had only days before, stretching on for miles with no apparent end on the horizon. Although Ely would have been much closer and more convenient, Jesse couldn't bring herself to go there. The rage she felt toward those who had slaughtered the Ponak was matched only by the newfound and poisonous animosity she had for both Edith and Felix. She didn't want to risk running into them. Realistically, she knew there was probably nothing she could have done to prevent what happened on the mountain. By not writing to her, though, they had taken away her chance to try. Underneath all of her hostility was something more difficult to manage. Their broken promise had been a stab to her heart, a wound that would probably never heal.

Her heavy eyelids widened as she recognized the shining

gaslights of the city off in the distance. She felt her energy surge and gave Buck a nudge. He nickered and picked up the pace.

With the baby sleeping in the sling hanging from around her neck, Jesse guided the horse toward the rear of The Drake and pulled him to a stop. Standing near the back door, passing a cigarette between them, were two women deep in conversation. By their attire alone, she could tell they worked at the saloon.

"Excuse me, ladies. Is Charlotte here?" Jesse asked.

The older of the two turned a steady, penetrating gaze upon her. "Never heard of her." She studied Jesse for a moment, scrutinizing her clothes and the horse, before finally turning back to the conversation with her friend.

"How 'bout Jules? Is she around?" She hoped to make contact with someone from Abby's past but knew it might be difficult. These women looked after their own and didn't give away secrets to strangers.

The woman dropped the butt of the cigarette and crushed it with the toe of her shoe. She turned to face Jesse. "Don't know no Jules. But looky here," she said, pushing away from the wall. "I'm Daisy, and I know I can scratch whatever itch you got." She moved to take a step toward Jesse, but her friend took hold of her arm.

"This one is mine," the younger woman said. "He's one of my old Johnny's."

Daisy gave a nod of understanding and disappeared through the door of the saloon.

Jesse sat astride Buck, watching as the young woman approached. She studied her carefully. She was wearing a dress which conformed to her svelte body and perfectly accentuated her small, pert breasts.

"I remember you," the woman said, trailing her fingers down Buck's velvety muzzle.

Even though she was standing right beside her and she could see each delicate feature in detail, Jesse still had no memory of the redhead. She removed her hat. "Ma'am, I think you might have me confused with someone else."

"Oh, I never forget a face," she said, looking up through her long lashes. "It's me. Scarlet Rose. Nice to see you're still the perfect gentleman."

Try as she might, Jesse could not put a name to the face. "I'm sorry, but I'm sure we've never met."

"Oh, we have. But, you'll have to forgive me. It's been years. I don't remember your name."

"Jesse McGinnis. I think you have me confused with someone else. I really don't recall ever making your acquaintance."

"Sarah," she said, her voice tinged with enthusiasm. "I used to go by Sarah. Remember?"

The years since they had last seen each other had obviously been hard ones for her. Searching for anything that could remind her of the honey-blond girl she had met long ago, the only thing Jesse recognized was the name she had been given.

"I do remember you." Jesse put her hat back on.

"I've never forgotten your kind—" Sarah craned her neck. "Is that a baby?"

Jesse swung her leg over the horse's back and slid down. "I need some help with her," she said, revealing the baby girl tucked inside her coat.

Sarah brushed her finger lightly over Willow's cheek. "Where's her mother?" she asked softly, reaching for the baby.

Jesse gently picked Willow out of the improvised carrier and handed her over to Sarah. "Did you hear about what happened up on Mount Perish?"

"Of course," Sarah said, cradling the child in her arms. "Everyone heard about it. Those Indians attacked our soldiers. It's all anyone can talk about." She cast an inquisitive glance at Jesse. "Why do you ask?" The baby started to fuss and Sarah looked down at her. "It's okay, baby."

"Horseshit! It was the other way around. Those soldiers attacked an unarmed village." The heat of her rage stained her cheeks as she continued. "Killed 'em all—even women and children. I've been there! Seen the aftermath with my own eyes. The bullet wounds in their backs say those soldiers are lying." Her hand inadvertently went to the revolver hanging at her hip. "If I had the chance," she said, finger tapping anxiously against the gun, "I'd shoot every single man responsible. Only I would look them in the eyes while I did it."

"Is that where you found her? At the village?"

Jesse looked down at Willow. Her cheeks were puffed in frustration, with one tiny-balled fist punching into the air. She cupped the infant's head with her palm. Simply touching her had a calming effect, and Jesse felt her heart rate begin to slow. "Not exactly," she said, her fury relinquishing its grip on her. "I stumbled across an old cabin. Two men had taken her there. One of them told me they found a woman hiding in a cave with her after the attack. They took them captive. When Ta— the woman tried to escape, they shot her. As far as I know, this little one is the only survivor." Jesse snorted derisively. "Those men didn't have a clue on how to care for a baby, and I damn sure couldn't leave her there. So, I took her." She softened her tone and looked at Sarah with pleading eyes. "Will you help me? She hasn't had anything proper to eat in days."

Sarah nodded. "I know someone who can help. But, she'll want to get paid. You got money?"

Jesse turned, reached into her saddlebag and pulled out the money-filled sock Abby had packed. "How much?" she asked, peeling back some bills from the small roll.

Sarah plucked two dollars from her hand and tucked it into her bustline. "This should cover it. Go on in. I'll meet ya inside when I get back?"

Jesse placed a restraining hand on her arm. "Where're you taking her?"

"I know a wet nurse. And you're right," she said, looking down at Willow's gaunt cheeks. "She could use a good feeding."

"I'll go with you."

"No. Best if you stay here. Millie don't fancy strange men showing up on her doorstep, especially this time of night. Trust me. She'll be in good hands. You have my word."

Jesse had no reason to trust her, but without any other options, she knew she didn't have a choice. She released her grip on Sarah's arm. "Thank you."

"Welcome. I won't be long."

Jesse watched her disappear around the corner of the building and hoped she wouldn't regret her decision. Behind her, she heard Buck flapping his lips. She turned and ran her hand down his face. "Hey, old boy. You're probably hungry too, aren't ya?" Securing his reins, she led him out of the back-street and down the main road toward the livery.

After Buck was fed and settled into a stall for the night,

Jesse took her saddlebags and returned to the saloon. She stamped the dust of the road from her boots and fell in line behind the others who were entering. Just as she placed her hand on one of the batwing doors, the place erupted in cheers. Her first thought was that a show was about to begin, but as the line of people in front of her thinned, she realized her mistake. The crowd wasn't cheering for an entertainer; they were cheering for the two uniformed men who had entered in front of her. She felt her stomach lurch, revulsion burning her insides. The thought of anyone applauding such heartless killers made her blood boil.

The soldiers acknowledged the praise with crisp nods and barely-contained grins, shaking hands along the way as they moved through the crowded, smoke-filled room. They took seats across from two other officers who were waiting at a poker table near the back of the room.

Jesse went straight to the bar, watching the men as nonchalantly as she could while she waited for the bartender to take her order. Several minutes later, when the man beside her staggered toward the door, she claimed his vacant seat. She sat with a glass of bourbon in hand, studying the room.

Disgusted by the continued praises she saw bestowed upon them, Jesse tilted her glass and downed the bourbon in one large swallow. Fire burned from her throat to her stomach, aping the rage she felt for the men seated across the room. They were laughing and joking, slapping one another on the back. How could they look so carefree after what they had done?

She wanted to know what they were saying so she left the bar, snaking her way through the crowd until she was close enough to hear. Leaning against a support column, now worn smooth from years of use, she casually crossed her feet at the ankles and feigned ambivalence.

"All in, boys?" one of the soldiers asked. After getting affirmation from everyone seated at the table, he tossed down his cards and revealed three queens. Scoffing, the other players tossed their cards on the table. The winner put his cigar in his mouth, leaned forward, and scooped the pile of winnings toward himself.

The dealer shuffled the cards and laid out another hand. As the first player tossed his ante into the center of the table, a saloon patron came along and clapped him on the back.

"Well done, boys." He applauded the seated men. "Don't have to worry about those filthy bastards coming down and attacking our women and children." He set a bottle of whiskey on the table. "Drinks on me." He pulled over a chair and sat straddling it, his arms resting on the back. "So, did they give ya boys a good fight?"

The praise had an instant effect on the soldiers. Jesse watched as all four of them sat up a little taller in their seats. It was obvious they were proud of what they had done. Her eyes and cheeks burned, but she knew it was neither the haze of the smoke-filled room nor the strong bourbon that were to blame. She clenched her jaw, fighting to stay in control as she continued to listen in.

The one seated closest to her removed the cigar from his mouth. His hand was fisted, the cigar resting on his fat middle finger, his index finger and thumb wrapped around it protectively. He eyed the cards in his hand as he spoke. "I don't know what the powers that be were thinkin'. Our orders were to relocate any redskins we came across. For days we didn't see any sign of 'em." He selected two of the cards from his hand, discarded them, and tapped on the table. "Just when we were beginin' to think there weren't any, we came across one of the biggest Indians I've ever seen—and I've seen a lot." He rearranged the cards in his hand.

"He's not foolin'," another soldier continued, his bottom lip pocketing a large wad of tobacco. "He was one huge som' bitch." He leaned over and hawked into the spittoon at his feet. "Old Clyde here," he said, lightly punching the shoulder of the man seated next to him, "nearly shit his britches when that injun charged."

"Yeah, yeah," Clyde said, tossing a coin on the table to up the ante.

"You're lucky Sergeant Tillet shot him before he could get his hands on ya," he said, turning back to the civilian. "After runnin' into that big fella, we knew the kind of savages we were up against. Captain gave us the orders right then. Shoot any redskins we seen."

The civilian shook his head. "Don't know how them government fellas would think you could even begin to negotiate with heathens. If you ask me, those reservations are a damn waste of land. Better to run cattle or somethin' on 'em instead."

The third soldier finally spoke. "The government ain't stupid. They know exactly what they're doing."

"How so?" the civilian asked.

"They put feuding tribes together on the same reservation. The land they give 'em ain't good for shit. If they don't starve to death, they end up killing each other."

Jesse's face was disfigured with rage. She wanted to draw her pistol and fire on everyone seated there, even the man not in uniform. The only thing keeping her hand away from her gun was thoughts of her family. What kind of legacy would she leave behind if she attempted to kill five people in cold blood?

Toby's words played in her mind, and she knew she needed to get out of there before she did something she would regret. She pulled away from the column, intent on walking away, when Clyde said something that froze her in place.

"You should've heard 'em hoopin' and hollerin' when they saw us," he said. "They took off running, scatterin like a bunch of scared chickens." He reached beneath the table and pulled something from the side of his boot. "Look at this beauty. I got it off one of them really old injuns." In his hand was a bone-bladed knife with an antler grip. He handed it to the civilian. "Gonna give it to my boy when I get back home."

Jesse recognized the blade. It was the same one Black Turtle had used for her initiation into the tribe. The knife was the final straw. The resolve she had, already gossamer-thin like the delicate silk from a spider, finally snapped. She wrapped her fingers around the grip of her gun and prepared to draw. Suddenly, a warm body pressed up against her, hindering the process.

"Don't do it," Sarah whispered urgently into her ear, placing her hand over the one Jesse had on the pistol. "They aren't worth it." She pulled Jesse's palm away from the gun and placed it on the curve of her breast instead. "Sure you can kiss 'em," she announced loudly, slapping Jesse's hand away. "But you have to do it upstairs!"

Those around them broke out in raucous laughter.

Before Jesse could begin to process what was happening, Sarah took her by the hand and led her up the stairs. She felt the heat on her face rise, but still, she was grateful Sarah had gotten there when she did. If she had pulled her revolver, she would have kept firing until every chamber was empty. Probably, she would have been killed in the process.

"Looks like I got back just in time," Sarah said, closing the door behind her. She walked over to the bedside table and turned up the wick in the lantern. "What were you thinkin'? You got a death wish or somethin'?"

"Where's Willow?"

"Don't worry," Sarah said, sitting down at her vanity table. "She's in good hands. Millie's keepin' her for the night. The poor little thing is starving. She wants to give her a few good feedings. You can get her in the morning." Studying herself in front of the mirror, she pulled out her hairpins one-by-one, allowing the magnificent coif of red hair to tumble down her shoulders.

It was an innocent gesture, but watching her do it caused Jesse's heart to hitch. What she wouldn't give to be at home, sitting propped up in her bed, while she watched Abby brush her hair out.

Sarah stood and then closed the distance between them in one swift motion. "Did I embarrass you downstairs?" she asked, noticing the splotches of color on Jesse's cheeks.

"No."

Sarah smiled. "I think I did." She ran her hands down the lengths of Jesse's arms. "You're so sweet. Would you like to spend the night with me? I wouldn't mind your company." She unfastened the top button on Jesse's shirt.

Jesse took a hurried step back, bumped into a table, and fumbled to keep a glass from falling to the floor. "I can't... I'm...I'm married."

Sarah let out a short, cynical laugh. "That's usually not an issue with most of the men who come through my door. Their wives are the last things on their minds."

"Do you remember Abigail Flanagan? She used to sing here."

"I haven't heard that name in years. Sure, I remember her. Is *she* your wife?"

Jesse nodded.

"I didn't know. So how is she? You two live 'round here?"

"She's fine. Abby and I have a place outside of a little town called Neva. Ever heard of it?"

"No. Where is it?"

"Not too far from San Francisco. I'm taking Willow there." Jesse laid some money on the bed. "A little something for your troubles this evening." She headed for the door but stopped, her hand on the knob. "I think it's best if I get a room at the hotel down the street. Can you bring her by in the morning?"

"Sure thing. Say around eight?"

"See you then. And thanks again for all your help tonight."

Sarah winked at her. "You're welcome. Goodnight, Jesse."

"Goodnight."

CHAPTER SEVEN

J esse paused at the top of the stairs, gritting her teeth, fingernails digging into her palms. If those men could at least have some level of decency or compassion to shut up about the massacre, just let the dead rest, but they didn't. She could hear them clearly, loud voices that refused to stop bragging about the abominable acts. They were repeating the same stories, and the gruesome details became more macabre as they tried to one-up each other. How could anybody with a heart live with themselves after that? But there they were, celebrating deep into the night, and allowing patrons to spoil them heavily with drinks, food, and women.

She twitched in self-constraint, trying to convince herself the best thing she could do would be to head straight for the door and walk away without so much as a glance at them. Jaw firmly set and her teeth locked in determination, she moved her boot to take the first step. With great effort, she descended the staircase. Just as she reached the bottom, and feeling certain she was going to make it, she heard one of the puffed-up and insufferable comments coming from the poker table.

"Drink up, fellas. Plenty more where that came from. They love us," said the one with a cigar, gesturing at the room with a wide sweep of his arm. "And all we had to do was kill a few dirty injuns."

Jesse stopped dead and slowly turned to face the men. Her glare burned deeply into the soldiers, hard as steel and twice as cold, from underneath the brim of her hat. She palmed her gun belt, cradling the holster in her hand. "You're all a bunch of cowards!" Her voice was a poisonous hiss in her throat. "You shoot unarmed people in the back and call yourself heroes? You're not heroes!" Without lowering her gaze, she spit on the ground in disgust. "You're murderers!"

An icy silence fell over the table. All eyes in the room turned to look in their direction. Everyone stared, and few dared to breathe. The man closest to her pursed his lips and scooted his chair back from the table. Standing, he grew to his full height. He easily had a half a foot on her and was twice as wide, thick with muscle. He drew close enough she could smell the whiskey on his breath.

"They attacked us," he said. "We were damned lucky to get out of there with our lives."

"That's bullshit!"

"You wasn't there," he said, jabbing his finger into her chest like punctuation. "You better piss off now if you know what's good for ya."

"Go to hell." She held his eyes and her position, unfaltering.

His upper cut knocked her flat on her back, and her head slammed against the wood-planked floor. She rolled and tried to stand, but he moved too fast. He was on her in an instant, his weight crushing her chest. She tried to raise her arms, but he was too strong. He secured them at her side, pinning them with his knees. Defenseless, she became his punching bag. He rained blows against her face, snapping her nose and shattering her teeth. She watched in horror as his uniform was splattered with blood—her blood. When he was tired of punching, he gathered up large fistfuls of her hair and bashed her head against the floor.

Every time her head struck, she felt the bones of her skull crunching until, finally, the pain no longer registered. *Am I dead.* If the sense of hearing was the last to go, she couldn't understand why the banging sounds were growing louder.

"It's me," Sarah said, knocking persistently.

Jesse shot upright, inhaling a ragged breath. Her heart knocked as she flung her hands up to her face. Though she wasn't sure what she was expecting to find, she was relieved to encounter only normal contours. She continued to pat her skin in disbelief, trying to convince herself it had all been a very lucid and horrible nightmare.

Sarah knocked again. "Jesse, you in there?"

Blinking rapidly, she bolted out of bed, rushed to her pile of clothes, and tugged them on. "Be right there," she called out, hurrying to button her shirt.

Jesse opened the door, still a little breathless but feeling much calmer. She was taken back by Sarah's appearance. Wearing a modest dress that covered her from her neck to her ankles, her features were accentuated by a mere hint of makeup, a contrast to the full face she had been sporting the night before. She looked like an entirely different person.

"I swung by Millie's," she said, walking into the room. "If it's alright with you, she'd like to keep Willow until sometime tomorrow. She wants to make sure she gets her fill on breast milk before you leave." Sarah held up a slip of paper. "She also gave me a list of things you should get before you go."

Jesse closed the door and went over to the edge of the bed. "Is the emporium open?" she asked, sitting down and pulling on her boots.

"Yes, and I'd like to tag along if you don't mind. I can help you get what you need."

"Thanks. I'd appreciate it."

"Oh, and I also wanted to apologize for last night."

Jesse craned her neck to look at her. "For what?"

"For the scene I caused. I really didn't mean to embarrass you. But, you know, I had to do somethin'. You looked like a guy who was about ready to explode."

"You have nothing to be sorry for." She tugged her pant legs over her boots. "What you did...well, you probably saved my life." She stood and reached for her hat. "Shall we?"

As soon as they entered the emporium, Jesse spotted their selection of saddles near the front. "I need to get a new one," she said, pointing toward the tack.

Sarah nodded. "While you're doing that," she said, holding up the list, "I'll get started on this."

As Sarah milled about the store picking up items for the baby, she found herself feeling as respectable as the other women who were there shopping. She had gotten used to being regarded as disreputable. However, when she passed by strangers in the aisles, they met her gaze, and she discovered they looked at her indifferently; there was none of the familiar disgust or coldness she had become accustomed to in her field of work. It was a sensation she hadn't been expecting. As she continued searching the rows for supplies, she held her head up a bit higher.

After Jesse made arrangements with the salesman for the saddle to be delivered to the livery later that afternoon, she found Sarah near a rack of dresses. "See one you like?"

Sarah gently ran her fingers over the lace collar of one of them before pulling it from the rack. "What do you think of this one?" she asked, holding it up to herself.

"It would look really nice on you."

"It's dreadful," Sarah said with a sigh, shaking her head as she returned it to the rack. "It's so plain and boring. The drab things women call fashion these days." She turned to Jesse. "Here. I got you the silver one instead of porcelain. Figured it would hold up better on your trip."

Jesse turned it over in her hands.

"Know what it is?" Sarah asked.

"Where I come from they're called gravy boats."

"They do look similar, don't they? I've never used one before, but I imagine you pour the pap in here and feed her from the spout." She held up her arm to show the fabric draped over it. "I got your material, too."

"Thank you. I really appreciate everything you and Millie are doing for us."

"You're welcome," Sarah said with a smile. "It's been kinda fun playing housewife."

Back in her room, Jesse placed the items on the bed and got right to work. Having neither the desire nor the time to wash dirty diapers during the trip home, she spread the fabric out on the floor. Using her knife, she cut the material down to the necessary size. While she worked, she caught a whiff of something redolent. She took a cursory sniff at the fabric before her, but it carried only the faint musk of the store. Tilting her head toward her shoulder, she smelled her shirt. Her nose wrinkled when she realized it was her stink that was so offensive. Her clothing was dirty and creased with filth from days spent on the trail.

After making what she hoped would be enough diapers to last the duration of the trip, she returned to the emporium to purchase a change of clothing. While she roamed the isles, she remembered that any time she went away, she always returned home with gifts for her family. There was no way she could disappoint them by going back empty-handed.

She sampled several different perfumes, finally deciding on a soft, flowery fragrance with a hint of spice she knew Abby would love. Jim was always easy to shop for. She stopped in front of a shelf and scanned the row of books. One title in particular stood out, and she pulled it from the shelf. She ran her finger over the gilt lettering on the red spine of *Through the Looking Glass* and then tucked it under her arm. Gwen was more challenging. Jesse had built her a dollhouse for her fifth birthday. It had been the only girly toy she had ever played with. Until recently, she really seemed to enjoy getting miniature furniture for it. Lately, though, it seemed her daughter had been losing interest. She continued to browse the aisles, hoping something would catch her eye. Finally, she came upon what she hoped would be the perfect gift.

Jesse piled her items on the counter. "Can I get a dozen of your peppermint sticks?" she asked the clerk. Knowing the twins had never been keen on sharing, she added, "Oh, and can you divvy them up into two separate bags, please?"

While she waited, she noticed a box of fine chocolates next

to the register. Seeing the candy gave her an idea, and she asked the man for a pencil and piece of paper. She scribbled a quick note, then handed the paper and pencil back to him. "Could you get these delivered to Sarah at The Drake?"

An hour later, when there was a knock on Sarah's door, she opened it to find a young courier on the other side.

He held up the wrapped package. "Got a delivery for you, ma'am."

"You have the wrong room," she said, moving to shut the door.

The boy stuck his foot between the door and the jamb. "You Miss Sarah?"

She paused. "Yes."

"Then I got the right room," said the kid, handing the parcel to her.

Sarah closed the door and pulled the note from the attached string on the gift.

Sarah,

Thank you for all your help. I'd like to show my appreciation by taking you out for supper this evening. I'll be out in front of The Drake at 6:30 if you'd like to join me.

Jesse

After bathing and dressing in the new outfit, Jesse arrived early that evening. She stood outside the saloon waiting for Sarah. Of the scores of men she saw entering, the number of those who appeared repulsive equaled the same amount as those who looked reputable enough to be headed to church. She sat down on the steps and thought of Sarah. Briefly, she toyed with the notion of having to be intimate with any one of them as a means of making a living. It nauseated her, leaving a foul taste in her mouth, and she spat into the dirt.

A pair of tall-laced shoes stepped into view, and Jesse sprang to her feet. "Sorry about that," she said sheepishly. As before, she found herself surprised by Sarah's appearance. The redhead had chosen to wear her fiery locks down, the soft curls arranged to frame her face. Her dress was as beautiful as any Jesse had seen hanging in Abby's packed wardrobe, and of course it fit her perfectly. Her eyes had been made up to stand out and her red lips were slightly puckered into a bow. She was a vision.

"You look lovely," Jesse said, finding her voice. She offered Sarah her elbow.

"Thank you." A slight blush spread across her cheeks. She placed her gloved hand inside the crook of Jesse's arm.

Before they could take a step, Jesse was shoved forcefully from behind. It knocked her free from Sarah's clutching hand, and she fought to maintain her balance.

"Don't want any trouble, Jonas," Sarah said, her voice taking on a slight waver. "Why don't you just go on inside?"

"I came into town for you," he said, his greedy eyes traveling over her in appreciation. "Now why don't you run on upstairs? We got business to take care of."

Sarah met his gaze. "I'm not workin' tonight."

"The hell you ain't. And if you know what's good for ya, you'll git that sweet ass inside right now." When Sarah made no attempt to move, he grabbed her by the arm.

Sarah jerked free and took a step back. "I said I'm not workin'!"

Jesse reached into her pocket and pulled out the roll of money. She peeled five bills away and offered them to him. "Here," she said, waving them in front of his face. "Buy someone else's company and leave the lady alone!"

Jonas snatched the money out of her hand and grinned. "You know what they call a whore in a nice dress?" he asked, his eyes glinting.

Jesse didn't respond.

His lips tightened, and he moved closer to her. "A whore!" He tilted his head back, laughing uproariously, and then stomped up the steps, shoving the money into his pocket as he went.

"I'm so sorry about that," Sarah said quietly. "He can be such an ass."

"It's not your fault, so let's not let him ruin our evening. C'mon." Jesse extended her elbow again.

They walked down the main street in silence until Jesse stopped in front of a glass-fronted establishment. Unable to see beyond the closed curtains, she had only the sign above the place to go by: Thee Ole Butcher's Chop.

"How 'bout this place?" Jesse asked, taking hold of the brass door handle.

"Alright." Sarah ran her hands down the front of her dress.

While they waited in line for a seat behind two other couples, Jesse took a glance around the restaurant. It was a nice place by Big Oak standards, with white linen tablecloths and candle toppers. Beside every candle was a small glass vase, a single yellow rose balanced primly in each one. She wondered where they had managed to find so many roses of the same color in a town that size.

Jesse became aware of an awkward silence between her and Sarah that had been building ever since the confrontation with Jonas. She wanted to end it but didn't know how or why it was even there. Every time she opened her mouth to say something, she couldn't figure out how to put two words together. Stringing together an entire sentence felt like an impossible task, so she said nothing. When a man in a black suit approached to escort them to their table, she had never felt more grateful to see another person.

As they crossed the room lit only by candles, she was still able to see the unwanted looks Sarah attracted from some of the other diners. Many of the women didn't bother to conceal their feelings, curling their lips in disdain as Sarah passed by. The men seated across from those women ignored Sarah completely. Judging by their guilty expressions, Jesse ventured most of them had paid a visit to her room on more than one occasion.

After what seemed like a mile-long walk through a gauntlet, the maître d' stopped at one of the tables near the back. When he pulled Sarah's chair out for her, Jesse quickly stepped around and took the seat opposite. It wasn't until he had lit their candle and walked away that Sarah finally broke the silence.

"I could get used to this," she said with a smile.

"Well, you deserve to be treated like a lady," Jesse said, relieved to have conversation going again. "Are you hungry? I could eat half a cow."

The waiter appeared with a pitcher of water. He filled their glasses and asked, "Could I interest you in something stronger?"

Jesse held up two fingers. "Your best port."

"Very good, sir." He turned and left the table.

"What's good here?" Jesse asked, unfolding her napkin and draping it across her thigh.

"I don't know." Sarah shrugged. She picked up her own napkin. "Never been here before."

"Why not? Is the food bad or somethin'?"

Sarah chuckled. "It's not the kind of place a girl in my line of work gets invited to often. Besides," she said, spreading the cloth over her lap, "I heard it's expensive."

Jesse changed the subject, not wanting Sarah to feel uncomfortable. "Can I just say, your dress is quite lovely."

"Do you really think so?"

"I've seen my fair share of dresses over the years," Jesse said, taking a sip of water, "and it's easily one of the nicest I've ever seen. Did you get it from the emporium?"

"Lord no," she said with a laugh. "You've seen what they have to offer. No, I made this. My dream has always been to start my own boutique someday."

"You want to start your own business?"

Sarah leaned across the table. "You think," she whispered, "that a whore can't have dreams, too?"

"I didn't mean any disrespect. I didn't know. So, why don't ya?"

"It takes a lot of money to start a business." She sighed. "I started saving, but it's a far cry from what I need. Besides, you see the way the folks in this town look at me. They know what

I do. You really think most women around here would step foot in a store run by someone like me?"

Jesse pushed the china plate aside and propped her arms on the table. "Why don't you go somewhere where no one knows you? Start a whole new life."

Sarah scoffed and waved her hand. "Again, that would take money and—" She stopped speaking when the waiter approached.

He placed two glasses and a small basket of sliced pumpernickel bread on the table. "Will you both be having the house special this evening?" he asked, pouring the wine. "It's a ten-ounce sirloin and baked potato."

They both nodded.

"Make mine rare," Jesse said before he could walk away.

Sarah took a sip. "So, what do you do for a living?"

"I'm a carpenter."

Sarah licked the residual wine from her lips and set the glass down. "Does Abby still sing?"

"No," Jesse said, buttering a piece of the dark bread. "She gave it up when she became a mother." She handed Sarah the slice.

"Oh. I didn't know you two had a child."

"Actually," she said, shaking her head, "we have two. Jim and Gwen. Eight-year-old twins." She smeared butter on another slice. "It's hard to believe they're that old already. Time's flying by. I can't wait to get home." She took a big bite of the bread.

"Does Abby know about Willow?"

Jesse held up a finger and swallowed. "No, not yet."

Sarah toyed with her wine glass before taking another sip. "I'm sure she knows a wet nurse who can help."

A smile spread across Jesse's face. "Actually, I reckon by now my sister-in-law has had her baby. I'm sure she won't have an issue feeding—" She fell silent when the waiter returned with their food. She leaned back, allowing him the room needed to set down her plate.

"I hope you enjoy the meal. And please, get my attention if you need anything else."

"Thank you." Jesse looked down. "Boy, does this look good." The steak was charbroiled, and the juices from the meat flooded the plate. Her mouth watered from the aroma alone. Picking up her fork, she cut into the meat.

As the night wore on, Sarah was able to relax and enjoy herself. It was nice to spend an evening without expectations, with someone who wasn't interested in the one thing all the other men ever wanted from her. The minutes passed like seconds. She found herself having such a good time that before she knew it, two and a half hours had flown by. Jesse made it easy to want what another woman had, and she realized how much she craved a life similar to Abby's. She was sad it had to end.

Afterward, Jesse paid the bill and they stood out in front of the restaurant, admiring the night sky. It was cloudless and sprinkled with stars.

"I think that was about the best cherry pie I've ever had," Jesse said, patting her stomach.

"It was very good." Sarah smiled kindly. "Thank you for supper. Would you like to come to The Drake? Drinks are on me."

"I can't. I'm going to go check in on Buck and then I need to turn in early. Got a lot of miles to cover tomorrow."

"I know a shortcut to the livery. And it's a nice night for a walk. Would you like some company?" Sarah asked, wanting to prolong the evening.

"Sure, I'd like that." Jesse gestured briefly, indicating for Sarah to lead the way.

As the pair made their way down an alley toward the stables, Sarah said, "Abby sure did get lucky to find you."

The mention of Abby's name made Jesse grin. "Actually, I'm the lucky one. I wanted to thank you again for all your help. And for your company this—"

She was cut off by Sarah's scream. It severed through the stillness, shattering the night, but the warning didn't come quickly enough. The pistol butt to the back of Jesse's head came out of nowhere, and she collapsed at Sarah's feet. Unconscious, Jesse was defenseless against the shower of blows raining down on her.

Sarah lunged at the attacker, pounding her fists against his back, but she was no match for the masked man. Intent on his task, he ignored her completely. With his hat pulled low and a bandana covering nearly all of his face, there was no way to identify him. She ripped at the shirt he was wearing, trying to pull him away and realized she had seen it before just a few hours ago.

"Stop it Jonas!" She pleaded with him, grabbing desperately at his granite-like arms. "You're going to kill him!" She struck him in the head with her fist, knocking his hat from his head.

"You little bitch! You'll get yours!" He shoved her aside as effortlessly as a ragdoll. She slammed into the side of a brick building and slid down the wall. He picked his hat off the ground, shoved it onto his head, and began rummaging through Jesse's pockets. After finding the roll of bills he had seen earlier, he took off running down the dark alleyway and disappeared into the shadows.

Sarah threw herself at Jesse and cradled her bloody head protectively in her lap. "Jesse. Jesse, wake up." Warm tears streamed unhindered from her eyes. "Please..."

Jesse sputtered in response, fighting to breathe and instead gagging on the sheer volume of blood coursing from her nose and busted lip. Her efforts sprayed the front of Sarah's dress in a fine red mist.

Sarah found her voice and screamed. "Help! Help!"

It only took a few moments for two men to come running from the other end of the alley, but it felt like several lifetimes.

"Help me, please! He's hurt real bad!"

One man knelt down and rolled Jesse onto her side. "Go fetch the Doc," he said, looking up at his companion. "Now! Hurry!"

Sarah watched in horror as the scene played out before her. Never had she felt so helpless and weak. She looked up at the stars, closed her eyes, and prayed silently for Jesse's life.

CHAPTER EIGHT

Jesse woke slowly, taking her time to readjust and feeling disorientated to the world around her. There was an indistinct humming in her ears which gradually evolved into an incessant high-pitched squeal. A metallic taste in her mouth was stale and awful. She ran her tongue across her dry, cracked lips and discovered the split. Her left eye was swollen so badly she couldn't open it. Through her bleary right eye, she saw a shadowy figure moving toward her and she recoiled.

"I'm a doctor," he said, standing next to her bedside. "Doc Harris. You were robbed and took a nasty beating. You're going to be sore as hell for a while, but you're going to live."

Jesse's skull felt like it had been crushed. Her nose throbbed with every heartbeat. She reached up and felt the sore spot on the back of her head, wincing as soon as her fingers touched the lump.

"You got one hell of a goose egg." He pulled the cotton packing from her nostrils. "Looks like the bleeding has finally stopped."

"Is it broken?"

He shook his head. "No." He dropped the bloody cotton into the wastebasket. "I heard it was Jonas who did this to you."

It wasn't until he mentioned the name that a few details of the evening swam into focus.

"Where am I?" she asked, her voice nasally and raw. Her words sounded foreign to her.

"You're in my home. This is my office."

"Something's wrong." She tried to sit up. "I don't feel right."

He placed a hand on her shoulder. "When you started to come around you were combative. You even took a swing at me. I gave you some chloroform. Helped calm you down so I could examine you."

She tried to swallow but found there wasn't enough saliva. "Could I trouble you for a glass of water?"

"I'd rather you not drink yet. I don't want you getting sick. There's too much risk you'll aspirate." He walked over to the bureau and poured a glass of water from an ironstone pitcher. "I'll let you rinse out your mouth, though. I'd imagine you're as dry as a Georgia cotton field."

"Aspirate?"

The doctor picked up the glass and examined it thoughtfully. "Yes. Aspiration. It means if you vomit, you could accidentally inhale it into your lungs. You could get pneumonia and be in worse shape than you already are."

The legs of a chair scraped against the floor as he pulled it across the room. He sat down next to the bed and handed her the glass.

Jesse leaned up on an elbow and almost dropped the glass. Someone had undressed her and put her in a long nightshirt.

"The wife is laundering your clothes. They were covered with blood. Oh, and I had to remove your...you know," he said, gesturing at her with his hand. "Needed to see if any ribs were broken. There weren't any, but I went ahead and bandaged you up as if there were."

"Who else knows?" Her spine felt like ice. She tried to steady her hand, but it shook uncontrollably. The water spilled over the rim and splashed onto the covers.

The doctor reached out his hand to steady hers. "Only me. When Miss Winslow and I started to undress you, of course I saw the binding. Knew right away what it was for. I told her you must've been doctored for broken ribs recently and sent her away before she could see what you were really hiding."

"Miss Winslow?" Her voice and vision were fading again.

He lowered his hand. "Sarah." He thought for a moment. "Oh, you may know her as Scarlet Rose." He picked up a spittoon from off the floor and held it up. "Now go on, rinse out your mouth. No swallowing." While she swished the water, he continued. "I also gave you some morphine. Looks like it's starting to work." She spat out the water, and he sat the spittoon on the floor. "You get some rest," he said, taking the glass from her. "I'll be back to check on you first thing in the morning. See how that eye of yours is doing. Hopefully, the swelling will be down by then."

He turned down the knob on the kerosene lantern on the bedside table. The morphine overtook her before he reached the threshold.

Jesse woke the following morning to the sound of a creaking hinge.

"Ah, good. You're up," Doc Harris said, stepping in and closing the door behind him. Approaching her bedside, he asked, "So, how are you feeling this morning?" He reached above her head and pushed open the curtains.

She craned her neck to look at him and winced. "Like I got trampled in a stampede. I can't see out of my left eye at all." Speaking made the cut on her upper lip throb. "And the right one is still blurry."

"The vision in your right eye should improve soon," he said, leaning down. Gently, he pressed his thumb against her lashes to try and pry open her swollen eyelid. "This concerns me," he said, straightening his back. "If we don't get the swelling down, you could lose sight in your eye permanently."

He went over to a cabinet with glass doors and retrieved a brown bottle from one of the shelves, along with a clean cloth. Sitting down beside the bed, he uncorked the bottle. He poured some of the liquid onto the rag and proceeded to daub the area around her eye.

Jesse was relieved whatever medicine he was applying was painless.

When he was satisfied the iodine had disinfected the area, he unrolled a leather case and carefully surveyed the assortment of medical tools inside. He selected a scalpel and held it up for inspection.

Sunlight coming in through the window caught the sharp edge of its blade. She squirmed uncomfortably. "Um...what are you going to do with that?" she asked, her voice taut as a bowstring.

"I'm just going to make a small incision. Drain off some of the blood."

Jesse placed her hand defensively in front of her face. The scalpel had grown much too close for her comfort. She was nobody's hero, but she was no coward either. Usually, she took pride in the fact she was brave enough to face whatever came her way. However, she was terrified about letting him slice open her eyelid. This bothered her more than she cared to admit.

"Please," she said, grasping his arm. "Tell me there's another way."

Doc Harris lowered the knife. "There is. Although, I'm not sure you'll like the alternative any better."

She released her grip on his arm reluctantly. "What is it?"

"Leeches. I can put a few on your eyelid. Let nature take its course."

"Oh, shit! There's really no other way?"

"No," he said, holding up the knife again. "It's this or leeches. Up to you."

Grumbling under her breath, she stared up at the ceiling, considering her options. Trust someone she didn't know to slice the already sensitive skin around her eyeball or put a parasite on her face. She hated both remedies.

"All right. Go ahead. Cut it."

"Good choice," he said, raising the scalpel.

She kept rheumy focus on his hand, which was remarkably steady. As the sharp blade passed the line of vision of her good eye, however, she lost her nerve. Her hand darted out and grabbed his wrist. "Wait!"

He hesitated and looked down at her. "I promise. I'll be gentle."

"Yeah…well, I changed my mind."

Many times over the years Jesse had handled leeches. She had caught some of the biggest fish ever when using them for bait. Even though she still wasn't keen on the idea of having them attached to her face, the glint of steel made leeches seem like a preferable choice.

Doc Harris tucked the tool back into the leather case. He ran his fingers over the instruments and pulled a different one from its slot. A brisk knock came at the door. "Come in," he said over his shoulder.

A heavyset woman, who appeared to be about the same age as the doctor, entered the room. She was carrying a tray of food.

"You can set it over there," he said, tilting his head toward the table in the corner. "Jesse, this is my wife, Mrs. Harris."

Mrs. Harris acknowledged Jesse with a small nod of her head. She set the tray down on the table and left the room without saying a word to either of them. Once she was gone, Jesse redirected her attention back to the doctor. He had gone to retrieve something from the cupboard. When he returned to the bedside, there was a black jar in his hand. Jesse's heart fell when she realized it wasn't the jar that was black, but rather the contents making it appear that way.

He twisted off the lid and placed it on the bedside table. "You sure you want to do this? No guarantee it's going to work. I may still have to lance it."

Jesse nodded slowly, hoping she was making the right decision.

Using a pair of rounded forceps, he reached into the jar and pulled out a leech. He selected three of the smallest ones and placed them on her eyelid one by one. "There," he said, when he was finally satisfied. "All done." He set the forceps aside and put the lid back on the jar.

Jesse opened her right eye, curious. She was surprised to discover she couldn't feel them at all. Just knowing the worm-like bodies were on her lid, she had to fight the temptation to reach up and fling them off.

He took a seat in the chair next to her. "Just going to make sure they take hold."

"I want you to know I have a good reason for looking the way I do," Jesse said after a moment. She gestured at her torso to indicate her meaning.

"I suspect you do. You're not the first woman wearing a man's clothes I've treated."

His statement stunned her. "You mean…there are others out there like me?"

"Sure. I have to say, I can't blame women for what they're doing. It's a man's world and you don't have too many options." He paused, considering. "Unless you plan on working as a cook, cleaning lady, or in a brothel, there isn't much else you can do to survive. I wish it wasn't like that. Women are putting themselves in harm's way. Look at you. You're the perfect example."

"I was careless. Made a stupid mistake. I thought I could trust Sarah, but she led me into an ambush. Her and Jonas probably split the money he stole from me." The reality of her situation hit her. "I don't have any money. I have no way to pay you."

He chuckled lightly and patted her shoulder. "Don't worry. It's been taken care of."

"Wait. How—who?"

"Miss Winslow. I think you're mistaken about her." He reached across her face to reposition one of the leeches. "She told me what happened and already paid for my services. She even gave the missus a little something to cover your breakfast." He hooked his thumb toward the tray. "She's been to see the sheriff and told him all about how Jonas assaulted you." He plucked one of the leeches off of her eyelid and studied it. "This one is being finicky. I don't think he likes the taste of you. Two ought to do the trick for now I suppose."

Jesse watched as he opened the lid and let the leech slide from his finger into the jar. "How long will this take?" she asked, pointing to her eye.

"Anywhere from ten minutes to an hour." He secured the lid back on the jar and walked over to the cupboard. "They'll fall off when they're full." Quickly, he gathered his tools and moved them out of the way. He replaced the vacancy with the tray of food. "Why don't you try to eat something? Mrs. Harris whipped you up a fine breakfast."

Jesse groaned as she struggled to sit up.

"Go easy now," he said. "I don't want you to reopen the cut on your lip. I'll be back soon to check on you."

Immediately, Jesse chugged down the glass of water. She took her time with the food, chewing around small mouthfuls. Each time she took a bite, the split in her lip felt like it was being pierced by razor shards of glass. Still, she continued to take methodical bites and worked around her plate. She had already consumed a fried egg and two strips of bacon when one of the leeches plopped onto her plate. It landed in the runny, yellow yolk of the remaining egg and squirmed languidly. Jesse looked at it in disgust, her appetite lost. She placed the tray of food back on the bedside table and stretched out on the bed. Closing her eye, she hoped the process wouldn't take much longer. Thoughts of reuniting with her family played out in her mind. Regardless of the pain, she smiled.

CHAPTER NINE

The hands on the wall clock appeared to be in the same position as the last time Jesse had looked. She fought the temptation to throw the pillow at it. Though the day had barely begun, she already felt irritable. She shifted her body, cursing the bed that seemed made for someone who was more the twins' size, while doing her best to not dislodge the remaining leech. She wanted—no, *needed*, the treatment to work and prayed it would. The sooner it did, the sooner she could leave Big Oak and get back to her family.

The room was too warm, so she rolled up the sleeves of the nightshirt to get some relief, and her hand ran across the old scar on her forearm. She thought back to when she was twelve, remembering how terrified she'd been when Frieda used a knife to slice open the skin over the punctures left by the rattlesnake. That experience would be nothing compared to what the doctor had in store for her if the leeches didn't work.

Bright, morning sunlight illuminated a framed document hanging on the wall opposite the bed. She realized the letters on the diploma were no longer blurred, and the vision in her right eye could clearly make out the words: Miami Medical College; Cincinnati, Ohio. She breathed a sigh of relief, grateful her vision seemed to be improving. She hoped she'd have the same fortune with the left eye after the leech therapy.

There was a knock on the door. "Come in."

The doctor crossed the room and bent down. "Oh good. I see you're down to one." He glanced at the pillow, searching for the other slug.

Jesse pointed to her plate.

The doctor grinned. "Looks like that one is a herbivore." He turned his attention back to her eyelid, gently prodding the leech with his finger. "I think it had its fill. It's not even attached anymore." Picking up the black slug, he held it up for inspection. "It looks nearly double in size." After returning it to the jar, he got a clean rag and returned to the bedside. "The wound will probably seep a bit today," he said, dabbing away small traces of blood.

"Is that bad?"

"No. It's exactly what I want. It will take down—"

He was interrupted by a knock on the door.

"Yes, what is it?" he asked over his shoulder.

"Sorry to interrupt," Mrs. Harris said, peeking her head inside. "But Miss Winslow is in the parlor."

"You up for a visitor?" he asked.

"Sure." She pulled the quilt up to her chin.

"All right. I'll give you two some privacy."

A few moments later, Sarah was in the room. She moved briskly to the chair next to the bed and sank down into it. "Oh, Jesse. I'm so sorry." She stared at the swollen, purple area surrounding Jesse's left eye. It reminded her of a man who used to ask for her whenever he came through town. He had a huge port wine stain covering half of his face. "It's all my fault."

"Why? Are you the one who beat me up?" When she tried to smile, the cut on her lip was a painful reminder of how banged up she was.

"No, but I know I'm the reason Jonas did this to you."

"It was my fault. I was careless." She studied Sarah for a moment. "The doctor told me you went to the sheriff. Did they arrest him?"

"No," she said with a strained laugh. "He asked if I actually saw Jonas. I told him his face was covered, but that I recognized the shirt he had on. He just laughed. Said he can't go and arrest a man based on the clothes he's wearing. Told me as far as the law was concerned, his hands were tied. And unless you can identify him," she said with a shrug, "there's nothing he can do." She stiffened her posture and placed her hand on Jesse's arm. "Did you get a good look at him?"

"No, I didn't see anything."

She slumped back into the chair. "It wouldn't matter anyway. The sheriff and Jonas go way back. I can't imagine him getting arrested even if one of us swore on a stack of bibles." She grumbled under her breath. "I hate this town."

"I owe you an apology," Jesse said after a pause. "I thought you set me up. Thought you and Jonas were in on it together. I was wrong. I'm sorry."

"No need to apologize. You don't really know me. I could easily see why you'd think that. After all, it was my idea to go down the alley." She reached over, hesitated, and then gently touched Jesse's cheek. "Does it hurt?"

"Only when I breathe." She gasped, her head coming up

in alarm. "Willow?" she asked, slightly embarrassed. She should have thought to ask sooner.

"She's fine. Millie's takin' good care of her."

Jesse eased back against the pillow. "The doctor told me everything you did for me. How you paid for everything."

"It was the least I could do," Sarah said, dismissing the statement with a wave of her hand. "I might as well put some of the money I've saved to good use. Not like I'll be needin' it anytime soon."

"I don't have any more money with me. Jonas took everything I had. But I swear, I'll repay you every last penny. It just might take me a few days to make it happen." She reached behind and rubbed the knot on the back of her head, which had begun to throb. "Abby's probably worried sick. I should've been home by now."

"Would you like me to send a letter?"

"No. I'm leaving in the morning. I can be home before one could reach her."

"You really think you'll be up to ridin'? More broken ribs on top of the ones you already had. Not to mention everything else Jonas gave you. I can't imagine how painful that will be."

"Doc did a good job mending me up. I'll be fine."

"My wife managed to get out most of the blood," the doctor said, walking in the room. He placed Jesse's neatly folded clothes on the foot of the bed. "I think I've done all I can. You ready to get out of here?"

"Yes, sir."

"Miss Winslow, if you don't mind. Can you wait in the parlor while my patient gets dressed?"

Jesse glanced over at her. "No reason for you to wait on

me. I'm just going back to the hotel to get some rest. Got a lot of miles to make up tomorrow."

"Okay," she said, standing. "I'll bring Willow to the hotel in the morning."

"See you then. And thanks again. For everything."

After Sarah had left the room, he leaned over and applied light pressure around her eye.

Jesse winced.

"It's really hard to tell with all the swelling, but I don't think any orbital bones are fractured. Come back in the morning. Hopefully more of the swelling will be down. I can examine it better, just to be sure."

"I'm sure it'll be fine. Besides, I'm leaving first thing in the morning. I really need to get home. I'm sure my family is worried sick."

The doctor scrutinized her. "Are you married?"

Jesse nodded.

He frowned. "And he's fine with you running around looking the way you do? Putting yourself in harm's way?"

"It's not like that. He's a she. She knows and understands why I—"

"Are you saying what I think you're saying?" His brows snapped together.

She nodded again. "I thought you understood. You've treated other women like me."

"No. I said I understand why a woman would dress like a man. Doing it as a means of survival is one thing. A woman having relations with another woman...well, that's a different matter entirely." He snatched her clothing from the foot of the bed and shoved them at her. "I think it's best you dress and be on your way."

Jesse sat up. "I'm sorry if I've offended you."

His eyes, warm and compassionate moments earlier, were now as cold and black as the slugs in his jar. "You're not offending me. You're offending God. I don't want any part of that in my home." He turned his back on her. "I'll pray for you."

Jesse threw back the covers and stood, her anger giving strength to her unsteady legs. She slipped the nightshirt over her head and tossed it on the bed. "Pray for me? Pfft," she said, pulling on her long underwear. "I'm not the one you should be praying for, Doc. Try praying for yourself and every other close-minded hypocrite like you. Oh, I know all about God. How He allows evil things to happen to innocent people. I've seen it with my own eyes. He does nothing to protect the people who worship Him." She shook out her pants and slid them on as she continued. "I figure with all the horrors He's allowed to happen to the people I love, He owes me some happiness."

Without turning to face her, he said, "The scripture says—"

"Don't go quoting scripture at me. I've read the Bible. 1 John 4:20. I know what it says. Do you?" She fastened the buttons on her pants and stepped into her boots. "Look. Thank you for tending to me," she said, feeding her arms into her shirtsleeves. "We're going to have to agree to disagree." She clasped the buttons on her shirt as she made her way toward the door. Stopping at the threshold, she turned to face him. "I'd appreciate it if you wouldn't mention my situation to anyone."

Finally, he looked her square in the eye. "You don't have to worry," he said with a sneer. "I'm a Christian man before everything else. I wouldn't want word to spread I'm treating people with your kind of sickness. Hell, I'd be run out of town."

Jesse opened her mouth but clapped it shut when she realized there was nothing she could say that would change his mind. The sooner she left his home, the better off both of them would be.

For the rest of the day, Jesse fumed in her room at the hotel, replaying the morning's events. Instead of calming down, her anger only seemed to intensify. With her mind in overdrive, she came up with several suitable responses to his prejudice. She only wished she would've said them during the confrontation. Instead, she was isolated in the tiny room, caught in a battlefield of wild emotions. One minute she was angry, and the next she loathed herself. It left her feeling as bruised and battered on the inside as she was on the outside.

The words the doctor hurled at her were nothing new. She had sat through many sermons promising the wrath of God for a sinner like her. In her mind, she couldn't come to grips with the idea of Him being vengeful. She believed Him to be compassionate, a just and benevolent being.

With all the evil in the world, how could He possibly ever look at the loving relationship she had with Abby and see it as a bad thing? Why would God see a tender partnership between any two people as sinful? It made absolutely no sense and made her question which deity she should be worshipping. Maybe the Great Spirit Frieda and Aponi worshipped was the one she should pay homage to.

It wasn't until late in the evening, when she was repacking her saddlebag, that she came across the book she had purchased for Jim. She remembered how God had answered her prayers the night she had asked Him to spare her son. Regardless of what the doctor or anyone else said, she knew the God she believed in. In her darkest hour, when Jim's fever had been so high, God *had* answered her prayer. Surely He wouldn't have done it if He had felt she was unworthy. She decided in that moment no one would ever make her doubt His love for her again.

The next morning, Jesse paced from one side of the room to the other, nervously chewing on the ragged edge of her thumbnail. She was beginning to think they weren't going to show when there was a knock on the door. She flung it open and found Sarah standing there. Beside her was a very pregnant woman cradling Willow in her arms. Peeking from behind the hem of her threadbare dress were the dirty faces of two small children. Except for the baby weight the woman carried, Jesse noticed she was rail thin. All three of them were.

"Jesse, this is Millie," Sarah said.

Jesse doffed her hat. "It's nice to meet you, ma'am. Please, come in." She closed the door behind them.

"Got your stuff," Sarah said, placing a burlap bag on the bed. "Your eye's looking much better today. Most of the swelling's gone. Can you see out of it?"

Jesse nodded. "For the most part, yes, but still a little blurry."

"It still looks painful," Sarah said, noting the black and blue area covering most of the left side of her face.

"It doesn't really hurt." Jesse turned to Millie. "Looks like you took excellent care of her."

In the short amount of time spent with the wet nurse, Willow's cheeks had filled out noticeably and had regained much of their natural, rosy coloring.

Millie carefully transferred Willow to Jesse's arms. "She's such a good baby." She pointed to the burlap bag. "I fixed you up two containers of pap."

Jesse asked, "What is it exactly?"

"I used a mortar and pestle to grind down corn, millet, and sorghum, then added water to make it smooth like a pudding." She opened the burlap bag and pulled out two apothecary jars topped with cork stoppers. "Each jar should last you a day. That'll be enough, won't it?"

"Yes, ma'am. I should be home by tomorrow evening."

Millie reached inside her corset and pulled out the two bills Jesse had given her. "Sarah told me how you found her," she said, extending her hand. "Please, consider my service a gift."

Jesse gently curled the woman's fingers around the dollars. "You keep it."

"I heard Jonas took your money," Millie said. "You might need this to get home."

Jesse patted the woman's hand. "I'll be fine. I'm riding straight through. Please, I want you to have it." She winked at the small girl clinging to Millie's leg. Walking over to the bed, she flipped open the flap on her saddlebag. She darted a look between the two children. "You two like candy?"

Shyly, both children nodded.

Jesse pulled out one of the bags with the peppermint sticks and held it out to them.

Neither child moved until their mother placed a hand on

the back of each of their heads, giving them a soft nudge. "What do you say?"

"Thank you, Mister," the little boy said, reaching for the bag.

The little girl tried to copy her older brother. "Tank ya, Mista."

"You're both welcome."

With her children clinging to her again, Millie walked over and ran her finger down Willow's cheek. "I couldn't get her to eat the pap at first, but then I added some cinnamon and honey. That did the trick." She stepped back and placed her hand over her chest. "I made sure she had her fill this morning. She definitely prefers mother's milk. Hopefully you can find a wet nurse when you get home."

"I have help." She smiled at Millie and Sarah. "I'll never forget what both of you have done for her. And for me. Thank you."

Millie placed her hand on Jesse's arm. "I'm sorry for what Jonas did. Lord will get even with him someday." She cupped her hand on Willow's head. "Thank you for saving her. I can tell you're going to give her a good life. She deserves it after all she's lost." She turned to Sarah. "Okay. You ready to go? I got chores needin' done."

"Jesse," Sarah said, "you be careful out there. Be sure to tell Abby I said hello."

"I will." She watched them until they turned at the end of the hall and then closed the door. She looked down to find Willow's dark brown eyes watching her. "Okay, little girl. You ready to go home?"

CHAPTER TEN

It was late morning when the bright, sunny sky turned black. Impending clouds, dark and pregnant with rain, soon crowded the horizon. A stiff wind began battering the treetops, and Jesse felt a large raindrop land on her hand. With no other options for cover, she quickly left the dirt road and slid down from the horse. She sought shelter beneath a large evergreen, hunching with Willow tucked against her body, just as the sky let loose.

Fortunately, it was a fast moving storm that produced no thunder or lightning. The spruce tree protected them from the worst of it. Even so, by the time the downpour was over, her backside was soaked through. She crawled out from beneath the branches. Small showers fell from the leaves of the tree as they trembled in the cool breeze, dripping all around her. She rummaged through her saddlebag for one of the apothecary jars.

Sitting on the ground, with her back propped against the trunk of a redwood, she poured the pap into the feeder. As she fed Willow, she inhaled deeply, expecting the evocative petrichor she'd come to love after a good rainstorm. However, something inside her had changed. For the first time in her life, she found the earthy aromatic smell unpleasant. Her eyes scanned the landscape. Normally, rain had a way of making everything clean and refreshed, but now, even that was different. After everything she'd seen, she wondered if anything would ever be normal again.

Placing a hand on Willow's downy head, she pushed the unpleasant thoughts to the back of her mind and focused instead on who was waiting for her at home. The images of her family were so vivid she could practically reach out and touch them. The scene she longed for most was the one where Abby and the children came running across the yard to welcome her home. Toby and Aponi would be waiting on the wide porch behind them, holding their newborn. She couldn't wait to meet the new addition to the family.

Overcome with a desire to get home, she hurriedly packed up as soon as Willow was finished and got back on the road. Unfortunately, she hadn't traveled more than a mile when she came to an area that had taken the brunt of the storm. Pulling on Buck's reins, she slowed his gait to an insufferable walk. The muddy road sucked hungrily at the horse's hooves. With each step came a squishing noise, which soon grated on her nerves, as the slow and torturous pace served to prolong the reunion with her family.

Late the following evening, Jesse rounded a bend and brought Buck to a halt. Off in the distance, bathed in late, golden sunlight, she saw the town of Neva. Never had it looked more welcoming.

As eager as she was to get home, she wasn't prepared for the questions she knew were sure to come if she rode down the main street with Willow in her arms. With no ready answers, she steered Buck to the left, opting for privacy instead, via a route offered by the countryside.

As she drew closer to home, she looked out over the pastures flanking her property as though seeing them for the first time. Cattle grazed on a hill in one; golden wheat swayed in the slight breeze in the other. They had never looked more beautiful than they did there in the setting sun. When her house finally came into view, tears stung her eyes. She shook her head in disbelief as she recalled the crazy notion of never returning. She glanced down at Willow and whispered, "Nothing but a dying breath would ever keep me away from them."

With a tap to the flank, she urged Buck forward, closing the distance between her and her family. Her enthusiasm to see everyone was matched only by her apprehension about having to speak to Aponi. During the ride, she had contemplated how much she should divulge initially. The things she had seen were hard enough for her to stomach. She couldn't begin to imagine how the news would affect her sister-in-law.

As she rode up to the house, to her surprise, she was greeted only by the sounds of chirping crickets. It was very odd. Normally, there was always some sort of activity happening at the homestead, especially with active eight-year-old twins running around. The homecoming was nothing like the one she had envisioned. Unnerved by the eerie silence, she slid down from the horse. Leaving Buck in the yard, his reins draped over his neck, she hurried up the porch steps.

"Anyone here?" Jesse called when she went inside. She pulled Willow from the makeshift sling.

Not a moment later, she was nearly knocked down by the twins who had come running from the parlor. Both of them wrapped their arms tightly around her waist and began firing questions.

"What happened to your face, Pippa?" Gwen asked. "Does it hurt?"

"Whose baby is that?" Jim asked, standing on the tips of his toes for a better look.

"Here," she said, handing Willow to him. "Hold her."

Oddly, Gwen showed no interest in the baby. She took hold of Jesse's hand in an effort to get her to follow her to the Baptiste' home. "C'mon, Pippa," she said, pulling her by the hand. "Come and see."

Unmoving, Jesse asked, "Where's your—" She stopped when she caught sight of Abby coming down the stairs.

"I didn't think you were ever coming home," Abby said in a trembling voice as she rushed toward her.

"I'm here now." She let go of Gwen's hand so she could envelop Abby in her arms.

"Was it true?" Abby sensed she already knew the answer. "Are they gone?"

"Yes," Jesse said softly, stepping back. "I'll tell you all about it later." She looked longingly at the three of them. "I missed all of you so much."

Abby reached out and lightly touched Jesse's cheek. "What happened?"

"It's nothing, really," she said, noticing Abby's strained

expression. She sensed something far worse was bothering her other than concern over the black eye. "What is it? What's wrong?"

"Oh, Jes. It's Aponi," Abby said, her chin trembling. "She went into labor the night you left." She choked on the words but forced them out. "We did everything we could, but we lost her."

The news of Aponi's death came as physical blow, and Jesse staggered. The warmth of being reunited with her family was gone, replaced by a cold so deep it felt as if her bones were caked in ice. From the corner of her eye she saw the twins watching her and forced herself to remain stoic.

Jesse reached down and took Willow from Jim. "Where is he?" She handed the baby over to Abby.

"Out back. Whose baby is this?" Abby asked, cradling her on her arm.

"Her name is Willow. I'll explain everything later, I promise. Will you see if you can get her to eat something?" She started to walk away but stopped as she realized the twins were trailing behind her. She turned and faced them. "You two go take care of Buck," she said, gently placing a hand on each of their heads. "Then go see if you can help your ma."

Jesse passed through to the kitchen and looked out the window. In the shadows, barely visible in the quickly fading light, she saw the silhouette of her brother. He was sitting beneath the oak tree she and Abby had planted with the twins. Next to him was a dark mound of soil marked in a fashion she'd come to know all too well. She continued watching Toby for several minutes, wondering what she could possibly say to him.

She crossed the lawn, still having no thought of anything

that could lessen his heartache. Instead, she simply placed a loving hand on his shoulder. When he glanced up at her, she saw the unrestrained grief in his deep-set brown eyes. It was an ocean of pain she knew well. Being hit with wave after unbearable wave of an ache that never went away. A sea of anguish so deep she thought she would drown in it. An agony and longing so raw, at times she wished she would. She experienced it when she lost her family. It happened again, when she lost Frieda. Still, she knew none of it compared to what she would feel if she ever lost Abby or the twins.

She sat down beside him, silence filling the space between them.

"It's all m-my fault," he finally said. "We sh-should have never tried to have kids. God wa-warned us twice it wasn't meant to be."

Faint cries came from the house. Jesse wondered if Willow's presence would serve as a reminder of the unbearable loss of his third child. She reached out and took his hand. "It's not your fault."

"Yes, it is. She never should have m-married me."

The fretful cries of the baby grew louder. Jesse tried to ignore it, wanting to give her brother her full attention. "You can't blame yourself. Aponi wouldn't want you to. She'd want you to go on." She sat there in silence and then said, "I know it won't be easy. But I'm here for you. We all are, and we'll get through this together."

His words tumbled out in a rush. "Black Turtle? Is he alive? Are any of th-them alive?"

"No, they're gone."

"Right before Aponi passed," he said, "she told us sh-she could see her tribe in the room with her. Said Black Turtle was holding her hand and he was there to take her to the Great Spirit. I didn't believe it, but maybe th-they really were with her." He palmed away the tears rolling down his cheeks. "I thought she was delirious from the blood loss. God, Jes, there was so much blood."

Jesse leaned in and draped an arm around him. "I believe they were with her. I'm sure she's in a good place, surrounded by her people."

He crumpled into her embrace. "I hope so," he said, sniffling. "I'm not sure how to go on."

"One day at a time, Toby. One day at a time."

"I wish you'd been here. Abby and Celia wanted to give her an elaborate funeral, but sh-she wouldn't have wanted all the fuss. It wasn't the way of her people."

"I'm so sorry I wasn't here for you." A shrill cry punctuated her remark, and she glanced over her shoulder at the house. After having spent several days with Willow, she felt she had come to know well the sounds the infant made. She had never heard her cry like that. Something wasn't right.

Toby stared at the mound of dirt. "I picked this spot. She always loved your family's special tree. I th-thought it would be the perfect place to bury her."

"You did good. This is where I'd want to be buried." She stood up. "Why don't you come inside? I need to go see what's wrong with Willow."

"Willow?" He scratched his temple. "It's not a bad name. But I've been th-th-thinking I want to name her Jamie."

"Jamie?"

"Yes. After our sister."

"I know who Jamie is." She felt a wave of bewilderment crest over her. "What are you talking about?"

"My daughter. I wa-want to name her Jamie."

Jesse's legs nearly gave out. "Your daughter!"

"Yes. You didn't know?"

"No! Abby told me about Aponi, but she didn't mention you have a daughter. Now you *have* to come inside and introduce me to my niece."

"Celia and Abby have been c-caring for her. I haven't even held her yet," he said, hanging his head. Guilty tears spilled over his tired face. "I've been b-blaming her. I know I shouldn't." His shoulders sagged. "But it's hard not to."

"No one is to blame." She reached down and offered her hand. "Aponi left you with a precious gift—a part of her. Come on. Let's go inside. I want to meet her."

When he stood, he was able to see her face in its entirety. He reached out, placed his hand on her jaw, and turned her head. "Good God! What the hell happened to you?"

"I had a run-in with some asshole in Big Oak. I'm fine. It looks worse than it is. C'mon."

Inside the back door, Jesse shucked off her boots and placed her hat on a hook.

Over at the table, Toby took a seat across from Abby. "I thought Celia brought Jamie by," he said. "Thought I heard her c-cryin'."

"Jamie," Abby said with a smile. "That's a beautiful name." She had no idea what Jesse had said to him, but whatever it was, at least it had finally persuaded him to pick a name for his daughter. She fed Willow another spoonful of mashed vegetable soup. "They did stop by, but Jamie got to fussin'. Celia figured you'd want to catch up with Jes since she just got home. Said she'll bring her over in the morning after she feeds her."

Toby reached over and held Willow's hand. Just when he was going to ask Jesse about the baby, Gwen and Jim, slingshot and book in their hands respectively, came rushing into the kitchen. Each of them had a peppermint stick poking out of their mouths.

Jim took a seat at the table. "So," he said, removing the candy from his mouth, "whose baby is that?"

Gwen stood beside Jesse and reached up to grasp her hand. With the other, she pulled the sticky mint from her mouth. "Yeah," she said, licking the sweet taste from her lips. "Where'd she come from?"

Jesse walked to the table, sat down, and lifted Gwen onto her lap. She brushed aside a strip of the straw-colored hair that had fallen into her eyes. "I found her up on the mountain. She has no kin left to care for her. I thought maybe she could live here with us." She looked at each twin in turn. "What do you two think? Would you like a baby sister?"

"Ooh, I've always wanted one," Gwen said.

Jesse asked Jim, "How about you?"

He plucked the candy from his mouth again. "A brother would've been better, but I suppose a sister will do." He shoved the peppermint back between his lips and sucked at it happily.

Jesse turned to Abby. "And what do you think?"

"I think we'd be blessed to have her in our home," she said, wiping the remnants of broth from Willow's mouth with a damp towel.

Jesse reached over and ran a finger across Willow's soft cheek. "I know Celia has her hands full right now, but do you think she can be a wet nurse to her until we get her weaned?"

"I imagine she won't have to do it for too long." Abby

pointed to the nearly empty bowl on the table. "Seems like she's taking to solid food already."

Gwen lightly ran her fingers over the bruise surrounding Jesse's eye. "What happened?"

Jesse gave her daughter a sheepish grin. "Oh, I fell off of Buck. Landed right on my face."

Abby looked at her skeptically. "See," she said to the children. "Riding horses is dangerous. You have to be careful."

Toby pushed back from the table. "Think I'm g-going to turn in." His eyes were dark and carried the weight of exhaustion. "I want to have my w-w-wits about me tomorrow when I hold my daughter." He clapped Jesse on the back. "I'm glad you're home."

Jesse expected to see him exit through the back door and was surprised when he made his way down the hallway instead. Leaning over Gwen's head, she asked Abby, "Where's he going?"

Jim pointed toward the ceiling with his peppermint stick. "He's going up to my room."

Abby smiled at her son and then looked back at Jesse. "He's been staying with us. I didn't want him to be alone so he's been bunking with Jim. Well, sort of."

Gwen tilted her head back so that she could see Jesse better. "Have you ever heard him snore? He sounds like a rabid grizzly bear."

Jesse couldn't help but laugh. "He kinda does."

"I've been sleeping on the sofa in the parlor," Jim said, "and I can still hear him."

"Oh, you'll survive," Abby said. She placed the rag on her shoulder and repositioned Willow so she could burp her. "Jes, the soup's on the stove. Also, I've heated you some water for a bath."

"Thank you. I'm not hungry, but a bath sure sounds good. I think I'm gonna get cleaned up and turn in. I'm beat."

Wanting to get Jesse alone to find out details of the trip, Abby said, "Why don't you go on ahead, and I'll get the kids settled down for the night."

"Aw, Ma. Do we have to?" Gwen asked.

"Yes, ma'am," Abby said.

Jesse kissed Gwen on top of the head and scooted her off of her lap. "Good night, you two."

"Night, Pippa," they both said.

Jesse placed her hand in an oven mitt and carried the steaming pot of water upstairs.

With Jesse in the tub, and Jim settled on the sofa for the night, Abby took Willow and followed Gwen up the stairs.

"Can she sleep in my room?" Gwen asked. "Please!"

"I don't see why not," Abby said. "Why don't you rock her while I fix her a bed."

Using Jesse's old method, Abby pulled a drawer from Gwen's dresser. She removed the clothing and lined the bottom with a blanket. Before she had even finished, Gwen's rocking had lulled Willow to sleep.

Abby placed the makeshift crib on the floor next to Gwen's bed and gently took the baby from her. "You come get me right away if she wakes up," Abby whispered. She leaned down and kissed Gwen's forehead.

"I will," Gwen whispered back. "Night, Ma."

"Night, sweetheart."

In the water closet down the hall, in the privacy offered by a closed door, Jesse was finally able to release her pent-up emotions. The news of Aponi's death hit her hard and it had taken everything she had to keep it together in front of her family. Eyes scrunched tight against the pain of yet another tragic loss, she lay soaking until her tears fell on water gone cold.

Her skin was pruned when she finally stepped out of the tub and slipped on a pair of long underwear. She pulled her robe around her and returned to her bedroom. She discovered Abby seated at her vanity, pulling a brush through her long hair. Quietly, she closed the door behind her.

Abby set down the brush and turned to face her. "I was just getting ready to come check on you. I thought you might have fallen asleep in there."

Jesse yawned and turned the lock on the door. She took off her robe and tossed it on the cedar chest at the foot of the bed.

Abby got up and crossed the room. She stood on the tips of her toes and lightly kissed Jesse's bruised cheek. "Now, what really happened? I know you didn't fall off the horse."

"I got robbed in Big Oak," she said, cupping Abby's face in her hands. "I'm fine, so don't fret. I've got so much to tell you, and I have a hundred questions about Aponi, but can it wait 'til tomorrow?" She covered Abby's mouth with her own, ignoring the pain of her busted lip. The kiss intensified as she guided her tongue inside. How many miles had thoughts of a scene like this kept her going, she wondered. When she could finally pull herself away, she stared deeply into Abby's bright blue eyes. "God, I've missed you."

"I've missed you, too." She took Jesse by the hands and led her to the bed.

Jesse didn't want to think. Didn't want to feel. All she

wanted was to fall asleep with Abby in her arms. She pulled back the covers and crawled into bed.

"I'm so glad you're home," Abby said, burrowing closer. "You don't know how hard it's been here without you."

Jesse tightened her arms around her, breathing in deep the subtle lavender scent of Abby's hair. "You don't know how good it is to be home."

"Tomorrow, we need to bring one of the cribs down from the attic. And we need to go into town so I can get some things for the baby," Abby said. She kept a firm grip on the arm draped around her waist, as if at any minute she might wake to find the whole scene had been a dream.

"Sure. I was going into town anyway. I need to make arrangements at the bank to send Scarlet Rose money for her services." She bit her bottom lip and waited for the response she knew was sure to come.

Abby flipped over on the bed and glared at her. "And exactly what services did this Scarlet Rose provide for you?"

"You remember little Sarah from The Drake?"

"Yes."

"She goes by Scarlet Rose now. She helped me find a wet nurse for Willow. And, she paid for everything after my money was stolen. I'm going to send money to pay her back."

Abby lay back down and took hold of Jesse's arm again. "I was hoping she got out of that place by now."

"Actually, I wanted to talk to you about that. I told her I'd send her the money to reimburse her for what I owe, but I was thinking about giving her a little extra. Would you be upset if I did?"

Abby craned her neck and kissed Jesse on the cheek. "Oh, Jes, how could I be upset?" She spooned her body closer to

Jesse's. "So, what's The Drake like? Does it still look the same? Did you run into anyone else?" She stopped when she heard Jesse begin to snore. It was highly unusual, and Abby knew then that the trip had taken its toll on her. She listened to her breathing, comfortable in the moment, and whispered, "Goodnight, my love."

CHAPTER ELEVEN

For the next few weeks, a dark shroud draped itself over the McGinnis house. It was as dark and heavy as the storm clouds Jesse had encountered on her ride home. She knew nothing would ever be the same. Especially for her brother. However, she knew that for his sake they needed to push forward, regardless of their pain.

Since returning home, Jesse found the best thing for her to do was to fall right back into her old routines. Always the earliest riser, the first thing she did each morning was to go down the hall and peek inside the children's bedrooms. It set her mind at ease knowing they were as safe as she had left them the night before.

One Sunday morning, after checking on Jim, she entered the room Gwen and Willow shared. Hearing coos as soon as she entered, she walked over, plucked Willow from the crib, and smothered her cheek with kisses. "Good morning," she whispered, trying not to wake Gwen. She carried her downstairs, sat her in the highchair, and began making breakfast.

Half an hour later, Gwen entered the kitchen yawning and stretching. "Morning, Pippa."

"Morning. Here," Jesse said, handing her a wooden spoon. "Can you feed her while I finish?"

Jesse removed crispy strips of thick bacon from the skillet and placed them on a plate. She looked over at Gwen, watching as she scooped some of the oatmeal into a bowl before heading to sit next to Willow. She couldn't help but smile at her daughter, who seemed to have become something of a mother hen.

Jesse reached above the counter and raised the kitchen window. A warm breeze blew into the room, stirring the curtains. She placed the heaping plate of bacon on the table and took a seat next to her girls. "It's going to be a scorcher today."

"Sheesh, it's hot already." Gwen blew on a spoonful of oatmeal and fed it to Willow. "It's going to be hotter having to wear that stupid dress." She plunged the spoon back into the bowl. "Why do people have to wear their Sunday best to go to church? Why does He care what we're wearing, as long as we're there?"

Jesse didn't have a good answer. She felt the same way. "It's just the way it is." She watched her daughter blow on another spoonful. "You're a natural at that. You're gonna make a great mother someday."

Gwen scrunched her nose. "To be a mother I'd have to be a wife first. Boys are…" Her face twisted as she tried to think of a word fitting enough for how awful she thought they were. She shuddered.

Jesse laughed so hard that tears came to her eyes, and she pulled a handkerchief from her pocket.

"What's so funny?"

Jesse wiped at the corners of her eyes. "You. You're so much like me. I said the same thing to my mother when I was around your age."

"You did?"

"Mm-hmm. Well, not about boys, of course. I think all children must feel that way about the opposite sex. But trust me, your feelings will change."

Abruptly, her laughter stopped. It had been a long time since she had thought about that conversation with her mother. The memory still hurt after all these years.

"What's wrong, Pippa? You okay?"

She pushed the memory out of her mind. "Oh, yeah. I'm fine. Morning, Jim."

"Mornin', Pippa," he said, approaching the table. He snatched a piece of bacon from the plate. "It's hot in here."

Jesse wrapped an arm around him and pulled him close. "Hey, how 'bout we beat this heat today? When we get home from church, you two wanna go for a swim? What do ya think?"

Their mouths stretched into broad smiles, the first genuine ones she'd seen since her return.

"Okay, you two go on and eat. I'm gonna go get your ma up."

Jesse hurried upstairs, sat on the edge of the bed, and watched Abby sleep for a moment before gently shaking her shoulder. "Hey, time to get up."

"What time is it?" Abby grumbled under her breath.

Jesse eyed the clock on the mantle. "Going on seven."

"I overslept!" She threw off the covers. "Willow is probably starv—"

"Relax. She's been fed."

Abby collapsed back onto her pillow. "Are the kids up yet?"

Jesse nodded. "They're eating. It's gonna be a hot one today. I told them we'd go for a swim when we get home. Thought maybe we'd pack a picnic. Make a day of it."

Abby rubbed the sleep from her eyes and yawned. "I thought you had to finish the Blair job today?"

Although Jesse had fallen behind on her deadlines and was still trying to get caught up, she knew she needed to put her family first.

"It can wait. I think we could use some fun. It'll be good for all of us." She stood and walked toward the door. "I'm going over to see if Toby wants to go to church with us. Oh, and breakfast is on the table." She paused in the doorway. Knowing Abby had a tendency to fall back to sleep, she clapped her hands. "Hop to! You know how I feel about being late."

Abby placed her feet on the floor. "I'm up, I'm up," she said, waving her hand. "Go."

Jesse made her way over to Toby's house, stomping at the chickens as she approached the door. She went inside and found her brother sitting in a rocking chair, Jamie cradled in his arms.

"Chickens are poopin' on the porch again." She sat in a chair next to him.

"I know. They got all that space out th-there and still they have to do their business on my porch. They keep it up, we're gonna have one hell of a barbecue."

"How'd she do last night?"

"Real good. You just missed Celia. I don't kn-know what I'd do without her."

"So, you feel up to going to church with us this morning? We're going on a picnic when we get home. Thought we'd take the kids swimming. Wanna come?"

He looked down at the tiny bundle in his arms. "I can't."

"Why not?"

"What'll I do with her?"

"Bring her along, silly. It'll do you good to get out of the house." She reached out to take Jamie. "Here, give her to me. You go get ready."

Toby handled Jamie as if she were a delicate piece of china. Jesse smiled, recalling her own similar behavior when her kids were that size. She looked down at the baby cradled in her arms. "Hard to believe the twins were ever this little. Boy, they grow up fast."

"Yeah, they sure do," he said, walking toward the bedroom.

She looked into the earthy, brown eyes staring up at her. "Your mother would be so proud of you," she whispered. "You look just like her." Knowing her niece would never get the chance to meet her own mother, Jesse felt herself starting to break. She forced herself to swallow her sadness when Toby came back into the room. "I need to go hook up the wagon and get changed." She gently handed Jamie back to him. "Go on over to the house. Breakfast is on the table."

Jesse made quick work of hitching up the team, pulled the wagon around to the front of the house, and set the brake. She hurried inside, taking the stairs two at a time, and headed to the bedroom. While she dressed, she could hear a muffled argument coming from down the hall. As she was tucking in her shirt, Abby came in.

She crossed the room in a huff and plopped down in front of the mirror. "Getting that child in a dress is like trying to catch a greased pig."

Jesse thumbed up her suspenders, walked over behind her, and took the brush from her hand. "She asked me why she has to wear a dress. I didn't know what to say." She pulled Abby's hair into a pile on top of her head.

"Maybe we made a mistake by letting her wear pants in the first place," Abby said. "Every week, it's the same old argument."

Jesse took the pin Abby offered and secured it in place. When she was finished, she cupped Abby's shoulders and admired her reflection.

"I think from now on," Abby said, checking her appearance, "you should be the one to get her ready for church. She doesn't give you any lip like she does me."

Jesse leaned down and kissed her on the cheek. "Okay. I will. Come on. Let's get going."

Once everyone was seated in the wagon, Jesse snapped the reins and got the horses moving. If there was one thing she hated, it was being late, especially for church. Although it had only happened once, she could still recall the frowns of annoyance as they filed past the congregation, forced to sit separately, filling in the empty spaces on the pews.

Ten minutes later, Jesse steered the horses next to a small white building set back from the road. Out in front, men and women were huddled together in their respective groups. On the edge of the lawn a small gathering of children were playing together.

She parked next to the wagon belonging to Armand and his family. As soon as they stepped down, Abby said, "Toby, why don't you let me take her for you." She handed Willow over to Gwen.

"No," he said, looking down at Jamie. "I'm good."

Before her mother could assign her another task, Gwen handed Willow back to her and ran off to join the other children.

It was their first time attending church since Aponi's passing. It was also the first chance for the townspeople to see Willow and Jamie. Usually the men talked about such things as crops, equipment, or the weather. That day, though, they continued offering condolences to Toby, while at the same time showering him with praises about his daughter.

Jesse watched as Abby, with Willow on her hip, approached the group of women. She rolled her eyes when she saw Elmyra Tallent turn her appraising glance on the baby.

Harvel and Elmyra Tallent were the owners of the mercantile in town. Elmyra was born into a wealthy family. She ran not only the business with an iron fist, but her husband as well. Her wealth provided her with all of the comforts she could ever want. She even had hired help to do all of her housework for her. With plenty of free time, Elmyra made it her business to know everyone else's.

"And who is this little angel?" Elmyra asked.

"This is our daughter, Willow."

Elmyra raised an eyebrow. "*Your* daughter?"

Abby repositioned Willow to her other hip and held Elmyra's gaze. "She was orphaned. We were more than happy to take her into our home."

Elmyra's eyes narrowed and she snorted air. She didn't believe a word Abby was saying.

Celia could feel the tension between the two women. "I had a bunch of apples to use before they went bad," she said to Abby. "Why don't you bring your family by the house this evening for pie."

"We'd love to." Abby turned her back on Elmyra. "Why don't you and Armand bring Armande and meet us at the swimming hole this afternoon? We're going to have a picnic."

Celia fanned her face with her hand. "That sounds wonderful!" she said, rubbing her very pregnant belly. "I'll just bring the pies with us then."

Jesse had no idea what the women were saying, but she was relieved to see Abby and Celia engaged in a conversation.

"So, which one?" one of the men asked Jesse.

Toby nudged her with his elbow.

"What?" she asked, turning her attention back to the group of men.

"They want you to settle an argument." Toby pointed to Garland Montgomery, who was the sheriff, and Emery Shumaker, who was both the undertaker and cabinet maker in town.

"The sheriff wants me to use pine for his hutch because it will be cheaper," Emery said, "but I told him oak or cherry would be a better choice. What do you think?"

Jesse looked at the sheriff. "I'd trust what Emery says. Same way I'd trust you when it comes to the law. But, if you can swing it, I'd go with oak or cherry."

The church bell started ringing. Jesse turned to walk away but stopped when she saw Emery grab hold of Toby's arm.

"I need to speak to you," he said to Toby.

Toby looked at Jesse. "I'll be right in."

She nodded, hurried over to Abby, and fell in with the others who were filing in.

After an opening prayer and hymn, everyone took their seats on the wooden pews. Jesse glanced around the room. She couldn't help but notice several parishioners looking at her. Leaning over, she whispered to Abby, "Is it my imagination or are people staring at me?"

Not wanting to speak during the service, Abby gave a slight shake of her head.

Gwen shifted on the hard bench seat. "Is he almost done?" she whispered, tugging on Jesse's shirtsleeve.

Jesse winked down at her and mouthed, "Almost."

Back at home, everyone hurried to change out of their church attire and into swimming clothes. With babies and a basket of food in hand, they headed into the woods to their favorite spot along the river. Jesse and Abby barely had time to get a blanket spread under a shade tree before Toby handed Jamie over to them. He stripped off his shirt, raced after the twins, and leapt into the water with a whoop.

Jesse and Abby sat side by side on the blanket, a baby on each of their laps. They watched as Toby dipped below the surface and gave each kid a turn at standing on his shoulders. Once their feet were planted, he would spring up and shoot them through the air. The children squealed with delight, waiting anxiously for their next turn.

Jesse caught the look on Abby's face. "I'll watch 'em. Go on in. I know you want to."

Abby laid Willow down on the blanket. "I hate that you never get to swim with us."

"It's fine, really. It's more fun to watch."

"Come on in, Pippa!" Gwen shouted. "We won't let you drown!"

"No way!" She glanced down at Willow and Jamie. "Besides, I've got babies to watch."

Jesse would have loved to swim with her children but knew it wasn't possible. Jim and Toby wore nothing but old pairs of pants, which had been cut off at the knees. Her kids would expect her to dress the same way. Years ago, in an effort to avoid questions, she had told them she was terrified of water. She fabricated a story of a near drowning incident when she was very young, which seemed to pacify the twins. It hadn't been a total lie. The Devil's Fork had tried its best to take her.

It felt good to see her family having fun and to hear them laughing again. Even Toby seemed to be finding a reprieve from his pain. He had somehow managed to persuade Abby to climb onto his shoulders. When she screamed as he flung her through the air, everyone roared with laughter.

Abby waded to the bank, wringing the water from her hair. She crossed the small stretch of grass and stepped next to the blanket. "I'm going to take her in for a bit," she said, slipping Willow out of her clothes.

As Abby made her way back to the water's edge, Jim came running up and spread out on the blanket beside Jesse. Sprawled on his back, he held up his book and read.

"You can't be done swimming already?" she asked.

"No, but I'm at a good part."

Reading was the one love they shared. She could understand him wanting to finish.

"So, it's pretty good?" she asked, repositioning Jamie in her lap.

"It's my new favorite. You'll have to read it when I'm finished."

She watched him as his eyes flitted across the page. Dappled light created a mosaic on the pale skin of his stomach. He had always been a slender boy, but his slimness seemed more apparent to her now, with the bones of his ribs standing out noticeably. He seemed so fragile. She had an overwhelming desire to cover his body, shielding him from anything that could ever cause him harm.

Jim felt her eyes on him. "Is there somethin' on me?"

"No."

She had a role to play. Fathers didn't display such gushing behavior. Though Jesse knew her father loved her, not once did he voice it out loud.

She smiled at him. "I'm so proud of you."

"Uh-huh," he mumbled, never once taking his eyes off his book.

"Look at me."

He lowered it and turned to look at her.

"I love you. You know that, right?"

He smiled at her. "I know. I love you, too, Pippa."

The look he gave her caused her throat to constrict. She knew if she didn't drop the subject, she'd break down and cry. "Hey, I heard someone bought the Leebolt farm. I found out the new owners will be moving in next week. They have a boy about your age."

Jim picked up his book again.

"I was thinkin'," she said, "maybe your ma can whip us up a buttermilk pie, and we could call on them. What do you think?"

"Uh-huh," he said absently, turning the page.

Toby swam to the bank and sat in the shallow water next to Abby and Willow. He cupped water in his hand and let it trickle down Willow's back, causing her to giggle. "Abigail McGinnis, did you know you're the town saint?"

Abby darted him a look. "Why would you say that?"

"It's what other people are saying. Heard it with my own ears."

"And what did you hear, exactly?"

He glanced sideways to make sure Gwen was out of earshot. "Emery told me th-this mornin'. Word's going 'round Jes had an affair with some squaw. Got her with ch-child on one of those work trips. Apparently, she didn't want a half-breed. That's why Jes wasn't here for Aponi's funeral. She was off fetchin' Willow. Had the nerve to br-br-bring her home for you to raise."

"That has Elmyra Tallent's name written all over it. I can't think of a single other person who would spread such a thing. No wonder Jes thought people were staring at her this morning. Wait 'til I tell her this one."

"No. Please," he said, "let me. I can't wait to see the look on her face wh-when she finds out she fathered another child." He waved at the Baptiste family, who were coming down the path. "Lord knows I can use a good laugh."

CHAPTER TWELVE

Jesse sat in the rocker on the front porch, enjoying the predawn hush. She blew across the top of her cup and took a sip of coffee. It was a cold December morning, and the heat from the mug felt good against her skin. Still, it was nothing compared to the subfreezing temperatures like those she'd experienced atop Mount Perish.

She watched the last few twinkling stars fade as orange light splashed across the horizon. The serenity was cut only by the sound of the curved gliders grinding against the wooden porch planks.

She glanced down at the worn paint on the arms of the rocker. The chair was one of the first things she had made for Abby soon after they moved in. One of the first pieces of furniture she had ever built, it wasn't something she was especially proud of. Although the rocker, along with its mate, were scratched and scraped from years of wear, Abby forbade her from replacing them. She claimed there were too many memories in their contours and insisted they stay. It was, after all, the place where they had spent countless hours rocking both the children, not to mention the hours they'd spent watching sunrises and sunsets. Abby tried to convince her the children would cherish inheriting them someday, but Jesse wasn't so sure. She was certain once they found out the truth about her —the awful truth—they'd probably want to pitch them onto the burn pile.

She understood Abby's need to hold onto things. Neither of them had many keepsakes from their pasts. She hoped their children would never know the kind of heartaches and struggles she, Abby, and Toby had endured. Realistically, she knew it was unlikely to think a person could go through life without acquiring a few scars along the way. So far, though, she thought they had done a fairly good job of giving the twins a life that was both happy and carefree. Most importantly, the children knew unconditional love.

In the distance, she noticed smoke rising above the tree-tops from the Baptiste chimney. Having spent countless mornings in their home, she could picture the scene clearly. Celia, after breastfeeding baby Claire, would stoke the cook stove and then prepare breakfast for Armand and their five-year-old daughter, Armande.

She thought back to their chance meeting and what a stroke of luck it had been. Somehow, he'd managed to take sandy soil and turn it into not only a successful vineyard, but a highly profitable one as well.

It had been the perfect partnership until recently. Armand wanted to expand the operation by producing wine, whereas she didn't feel the need to take on the more expensive endeavor. They were already making a decent profit by selling their yields to other wine producers in the area. She didn't see the point of taking on all of the added headaches of starting a new business. Plus, she knew there was no guarantee anyone would buy their wine. Unfortunately for Armand, without her financial support, there was no way he would have the means to produce wine on his own.

Still, Jesse smiled. Her life had been blessed by the serendipitous encounter. If not for him, she often wondered if her family would still be living in the confines of San Francisco.

Footsteps on the gravel path leading from the side of the house gathered her wandering thoughts. "Morning," she said. "You feeling better?"

"Much," Toby said, sitting down in the rocker next to her. "Thanks for looking after Jamie last night. I th-think I just needed a good night's sleep. How'd she do?"

"Good." She set her empty cup on the small table between them. "She was out as soon as we put her to bed. I checked on her before I came down. Her and Willow are still sleepin'." Overhead a lark trilled and she peered up at the sky. "Couldn't ask for a better day. Isn't it funny? The older we get, the more we appreciate the simple things. Like the sun shining."

He nodded. "Well, you are g-getting' long in the tooth."

"What's that's supposed to mean?"

He chuckled. "It's how you tell the age of a horse. The longer their teeth, the older they are."

Just then, the door opened. Toby and Jesse watched as Jim came toward them, a blanket draped around his shoulders.

"Mornin', Uncle Toby," he said, rubbing the sleep from his eyes. "Mornin', Pippa."

Jesse stopped rocking. "I thought you were campin' out back with Jonathan and Gwen?"

Ever since the day they had gone over and welcomed their new neighbors, Jonathan Plunkett and Jim had been best friends. The boy seemed to spend more time at their house than he did his own.

"I was," Jim said, settling on her lap. "But it got too cold last night." He tucked his head into the crook of her neck and closed his eyes, allowing himself to be rocked.

It was rare for a boy of Jim's age to want to be rocked by a parent, and Jesse couldn't help but smile. She appreciated the risk he was taking, knowing if Gwen or Jonathan saw him being coddled, they would almost certainly tease him—especially his sister.

After a few precious minutes together with her son, Jesse reluctantly brought the chair to a halt, knowing it could be so easy to spend all day rocking him. As usual there was work to be done. "Why don't you go on in and get changed? I need you to milk Curly and collect the eggs."

Jim untangled himself and stood, his eyes nearly invisible under hooded lids. He made his way toward the door, the blanket trailing behind him on the wooden planks.

"I best get started on breakfast," Jesse said, standing. "Got a lot to do today. Oh, can you help in the attic this morning? Abby wants the decorations brought down."

"Sure," Toby said, following her inside.

While Jesse headed to the kitchen, Toby took the stairs up to Gwen's room. He pushed open the door, quietly stepped into the room, and peered into Willow's crib. Both babies were sleeping soundly.

Sometime during the night, Jamie had managed to free

her feet from beneath the blanket. A pained smile pulled at the corners of his mouth. Her mother had been the same way. Aponi couldn't stand to have anything covering her feet. In the subtle light coming in through the window, he saw the resemblance of his late wife in the four-month-old infant. Jamie's skin tone, long lashes, and coal black hair were all vivid reminders of the woman he loved. He found he couldn't resist the temptation to hold her. As gently as though he was plucking a petal from a flower, he picked his daughter up and held her against his chest. When her eyes opened, he started to hum. In slow, lumbering steps, he danced with her.

"Good morning," Abby whispered, trying not to wake Willow. She placed her hand on Toby's shoulder and peeked at Jamie.

"Mornin'. Thanks for lookin' after her la-last night."

"She was no trouble at all. I take it you're feeling better?"

He nodded.

Abby leaned over the crib and repositioned the blanket on Willow. "Where's Jes?"

"Gettin' breakfast ready."

Abby went back out into the hall and down the stairs. When she got to the kitchen, she was surprised to find it empty. There were no signs of Jesse anywhere. No pans or dishes were out, none of the usual evidence indicating break-fast was underway. She made her way across the tiled floor and peered out the window. From there, she could see Jesse creeping across the lawn. At first, she had no idea what she was up to until Jesse stepped next to the tent.

Jesse grabbed hold of the tarp, shook it, and roared like some wild beast. Within seconds, the tent flap flung open and

Jonathan and Gwen came bolting out. As they raced toward the house, Jonathan tripped over his feet and fell.

Jesse doubled over in laughter.

Gwen stopped and turned around. "Not funny, Pippa! Not funny at all!"

"Come on. It was *kind* of funny." She walked over and offered a hand to Jonathan. "Good thing I wasn't a grizzly. You'd've been breakfast."

"Good one, Mr. McGinnis." He couldn't help but giggle as he got to his feet.

Abby came out and stood on the cement landing outside the backdoor. "I'm sorry, Jonathan. Sometimes my husband acts like a child. Are you okay?"

"I'm fine." He brushed the dirt from his pants. "He sure got us."

"I wasn't scared," Gwen said. "I knew it was Pippa the whole time."

"Mm-hmm," said Abby. "Why don't you two go inside and wash up before breakfast?"

The two of them raced toward the house, pushing and shoving one another in an attempt to be the first one through the door. As they jostled their way inside, they were still arguing about who had been scared and who had known it was Jesse all along.

Abby rolled her eyes and gave Jesse a sheepish grin.

"What?" Jesse asked.

"You're so bad." She looked behind Jesse. "Where's Jim?"

"He got cold. He's inside getting dressed."

"After hearing you tell ghost stories last night, I'm surprised all of them didn't sleep inside."

"Oh, it's good for 'em." Jesse chuckled. "What kid doesn't like hearing scary stories?"

Abby shivered and pulled her robe tighter. "You won't think it's so funny when they start sleeping in our bed."

Jesse gave her a wink and swatted her on the behind. "C'mon, let's go inside. It's cold out here."

CHAPTER THIRTEEN

As soon as the children finished their breakfast, they raced outside to play in the barn. Jesse and Toby quickly stole into the attic. In the far corner of the dusty room, they found the collection of Christmas decorations, which had been accumulated over the years. Pinecones woven with brightly colored ribbon and awkward candles the family had dipped themselves were some of the more precious, eye-catching baubles. One by one, they carried the crates downstairs. Abby, who was sitting in the parlor with Willow and Jamie, directed them on where to place each box as they entered the room.

After two more trips, Jesse said, "This is the last one." She put the container on the floor next to Abby. "You ready?"

They had started a family tradition when they had first moved to Neva. Every year, a few weeks before Christmas, the entire family would bundle into the wagon and ride out into the woods to pick out the perfect fir tree together.

Abby searched through the newest box placed at her feet and pulled out the stockings she had knitted years ago. "I think I'll stay here with the little ones," she said, laying the socks on the arm of the sofa. She turned her attention to Jamie, who was stretched out on her back beside her. She placed her hand on the baby's stomach and gently tickled her belly, eliciting a giggle. "It's pretty chilly outside. I don't want them coming down with anything."

"No," Toby said, adding another log to the fire. "You go on. I'll stay."

"You sure?" Abby asked. Her eyes were lit up in excitement. "I don't mind." An element of relief flickered in her voice, obvious though she tried to hide it. She looked forward to this tradition all year, every year, and her family knew it.

"You g-go on," he said, gingerly stepping over Willow, who was attempting to crawl across the floor. He made his way over to the sofa and held his daughter, waving Abby on.

Without another word, Abby hurried to the foyer to fetch her coat and gloves.

When Jesse and Abby got to the barn, they discovered Jim, Gwen, and Jonathan taking turns swinging on the rope hanging from the hayloft. Jesse used their distraction to make quick work of hitching up the horses. Once the wagon was ready, she hollered at the kids, and then climbed up and took a seat next to Abby.

With a gentle snap of the reins, she drove across the pasture to the tree line at the edge of their property. Before the wheels had rolled to a stop, the kids leapt from the bed of the wagon and took off running, each of them eager to be the one who found the perfect tree.

Jesse set the brake and jumped down. She walked around and extended a hand to Abby. As she helped her step to the ground, they heard Gwen shouting exuberantly in the distance.

"How 'bout this one?" she yelled, pointing to a fir near the edge of the woods.

"Too small," Abby called back. "Think bigger!"

Jesse reached into the back of the wagon and picked up a handsaw. Well-versed from years of experience, she knew it would take Abby a long time to decide. "I'm going to get started on collecting some boughs while you look. Holler at me when you find one."

For the next hour, they roamed the woods. The children pointed out potential prospects, confident with each selection that they had chosen the perfect one. Each time Abby shook her head with a kind nod. "Little smaller," she said more than once. "The branches aren't full enough," she said about another. "Maybe a bit bigger," she said with a smile about a tree no taller than herself.

The kids ran off after each rejection, giddy in anticipation of discovery.

"What about this one, Ma?" Jim asked, his mittened hand pointing toward a majestic fir.

It could have been one they had already passed over or one they were seeing for the first time. The tree had an almost ethereal glow, highlighted by the transitioning sun overhead.

Abby pulled her coat around herself more tightly and approached the tree. The children watched, holding their breath as she gave it a meticulous inspection. She shook the branches, eyed the height, and gauged the aesthetics. "It's perfect."

Jim cheered. "We'll go get Pippa! Last one there's a rotten egg!"

Several minutes later, Jesse returned with the children. She set to work, cutting immediately into the base of the tree before Abby could change her mind.

"Timber!" Everyone shouted as the tree toppled over.

It was easily the largest tree they had ever harvested, and it took all of their combined strength to drag it back to the wagon.

Jesse stole several glances at Abby along the way. Her face was red from the effort and the cold. It reminded her of Abby's first trip up the mountain. She felt her stomach flop. *My God, she's more beautiful now than she was then.*

By working together, they managed to hoist the tree into the wagon. The large evergreen, along with the pine boughs Jesse had collected, filled almost the entire bed.

On the way home, Jesse intentionally kept the horses at a leisurely pace. She knew it wouldn't be long before Abby started to sing. It was one of her favorite parts of the tradition, and she knew it would be fleeting no matter how slow she kept the horses.

Abby started softly at first. As her voice rose, all three children joined in. It wasn't long before *Hark the Herald Angels Sing* could be heard resonating across the open pasture. Even Jesse, who was utterly tone deaf, found it impossible to resist and joined in on the chorus.

Though it was obvious Abby was the only one of them with any musical talent, Jesse knew she had never heard anything more beautiful than the off-key harmony of her family that December morning.

They spent the rest of the afternoon making multiple strands of pine garland, each one adorned with red ribbons and bows. With the help of Toby and the children, Jesse wrapped them around porch rails and columns, while Abby used the excess pine boughs to weave a wreath.

Once the outdoor accents were completed, the wreath hanging proudly on the front door, they turned their attention to the inside of the house. Each decoration was put into a designated place and meticulously arranged. Candles were placed strategically and drawings displayed. In one corner of the parlor, the large evergreen intentionally stood untouched. Tradition mandated the trimming of the tree was reserved for later that evening.

After supper, with mugs of hot chocolate in hand, everyone gathered in the parlor. Jesse handed out ornaments to the children while Abby guided them on placement. Once Jesse helped Willow place the twig star atop the tree, there was only one thing left for them to do.

Toby added a generous dollop of lard to the cast iron pot, poured in dried corn kernels, and swiveled the crane to put the kettle closer to the fire. While they waited, Abby seated herself on the sofa, coddling Jamie. Perched next to her was an eager Gwen, who wiggled impatiently in anticipation of stringing popcorn. Jim and Jonathan sat on the floor, concentrating on an intense game of chess. Nearby, Jesse was lying on her stomach, encouraging a hesitant Willow to crawl toward her.

Toby handed Gwen the first bowl of popcorn and she started measuring out the thread. "Pippa, come sit next to me."

"In a bit." She kept her focus on Willow. "Did you see that? I think she's about to do it!"

Gwen concentrated on pushing the needle through the popcorn, a petulant pout on her lips. She focused diligently on each kernel, working it onto the ever-growing strand. She tried to ignore Jesse and Willow, but no matter how hard she tried, they remained a distraction. Her exasperation was palpable, and her eyes continuously darted between them. The more she tried to pretend they weren't there, the more their interaction bothered her. After accidentally poking her finger with the needle yet again, she threw the garland in a huff and stood.

"Pippa, will you please come with me?" Gwen asked, standing over her. "I want to play you a new song I learned on the piano."

Jesse didn't look up. "In a minute. Look. I know she's about to crawl."

"Why does she have to live here?" Gwen crossed her arms in front of her chest. "You never should've brought that stupid Indian baby home."

Jesse came up off the floor and snatched her by the arm. "What did you say?" she said, raising her hand.

"Nothin'." Gwen saw the change on Jesse's face and instinctively moved her hands to shield her behind.

"Move 'em now!"

Still trying to protect her bottom, she tried backing away. "I'm sorry."

"Don't make me tell you again."

Gwen lowered her hands. "I'm sorry," she said in a tiny voice. "I didn't mean it."

Jesse was furious, with an unmarked rage she had never felt before. Somehow, she managed the force of her spankings, but it took conscious effort.

Before the next blow had landed, Gwen could no longer keep her emotions in check. She jerked away from Jesse's grip and glared up at her with seething, tear-filled eyes. "I hate you!"

Jesse's hand fell to her side when she realized what she had done. Physical punishment on her children was unprecedented and completely unexpected.

"Gwyneth McGinnis!" Abby said. "Go to your room this instant!"

Gwen stormed from the room, stomped up the stairs, and slammed her bedroom door shut as hard as she could. She flung herself on her bed, rare tears streaming down her flushed cheeks. She wasn't crying because of physical pain. She'd had falls before with worse wounds. Her tears came from the fact it was the first time her father had ever needed a reason to spank her. Her heart was broken. To make matters worse, Jonathan had witnessed the entire humiliating scene. She buried her face into her pillow, screaming in frustration and embarrassment.

Abby was always the one who meted out punishments. Even then, she rarely resorted to anything physical. It was usually nothing worse than a tugged ear lobe or the flick of a dishrag. She transferred Jamie to Toby. Before leaving the room, she ran a consoling hand down Jesse's arm and then headed toward the stairway.

With each heavy step, Abby wondered how such a beautiful day turned into something so ugly. She went into Gwen's room and took a seat on the edge of the bed. "Are you alright?"

"I d-d-didn't me-mean it." Her voice was muffled by the pillow. "I d-d-don't hate Pippa."

"Look at me." Abby put her hand on Gwen's back, but she didn't move. "I said, look at me."

Gwen pulled her face away from the pillow but couldn't meet her mother's eyes.

"I know you don't hate Pippa." She brushed aside Gwen's

long, blonde bangs. "You have to be mindful of what you say, especially when you're angry."

Her daughter looked up at her with tear filled eyes and listened.

"Remember, words can't be taken back."

Gwen's cheeks were mottled red, and her body shook uncontrollably. She rested her head in her mother's lap. "Do you th-th-think Pippa will ever forg-g-give me?"

Abby patted her back. "Of course. But I don't ever want to hear you say anything like that again. Do you understand?"

"Yes, ma'am. I'm sorry." Gwen sniffled. "I didn't mean wh-what I said about Willow. She's my sister. You know I love her." Timidly, she asked, "Will you please tell Pippa I'm sorry and I don't hate him?"

"I will." She gave Gwen a hug and stood. "It's been a long day. Go on and get ready for bed."

"Goo-good n-night, Ma."

"Good night."

When Abby returned to the parlor, Toby informed her that Jesse had gone outside. She stopped in the foyer and quickly slipped on her boots and coat. When she didn't find Jesse on the porch, she went to the barn. She found her hunched over the sawhorses, aggressively carving at a piece of wood. Red faced from exertion, Abby knew some of her coloring was from a flush of emotions, as well.

Walking up to her, Abby asked, "Are you okay?"

The chisel in Jesse's hand came to an abrupt stop. She stared down at the slab of wood intently. "I'm fine. I can't believe she would say something like that about Willow."

Abby rested her hand on Jesse's back. Her muscles were hard and knotted. "You know why she said it, don't you?"

Jesse lifted an eyebrow.

"Jealousy. It got the best of her."

"Jealousy? What does she have to be jealous of?"

"She's still getting used to sharing you with Willow." Abby's smile was slow. "She wanted you all to herself."

The chisel fell from Jesse's hand. Tears burned the back of her throat. "And I spanked her for it."

"She had it coming. She needs to learn that words have consequences. I was going to spank her myself. You just beat me to it. You didn't do anything wrong, Jes."

"Well…she hates me now. Do you think she'll ever forgive me?"

Abby chuckled. "She asked me the same thing about you. You know if your children say they hate you, then you're probably being a good parent." She rested her hand on top of Jesse's. "Why don't you go talk to her?"

"I don't think I can face her right now."

From the light cast off by the lantern, Abby could see tears shining in Jesse's lashes. She squeezed her hand. "If you don't, neither one of you will sleep tonight," she said, picking up the lantern.

As soon as they came through the door, Jesse kicked off her boots and hung her coat on the hall tree. At the stairway, however, she stood frozen.

Abby gave her a gentle nudge. "Go on."

Jesse had always considered herself to be brave. She knew she had faced greater challenges than this and conquered them all. Still, the last few steps on the long staircase were the hardest she had ever climbed. She thought back to her own childhood—to her mother and Frieda. She called on their strength as she trudged down the hall.

She stood outside Gwen's door for a moment, clutching her stomach as she tried to conjure her courage. Then, she knocked on the door and entered.

The moment Gwen saw her, she threw back the covers and leapt from the bed. She flew into Jesse, almost knocking her over in the process, and wrapped her arms tightly around her waist. "Pippa, I'm so s-sorry. I didn't mean wh-what I said about Willow! And I don't hate you. I could never hate you."

"I know. I know." She could feel Gwen's body trembling. "I think it's fair to say we both did something we regret." She tilted Gwen's chin. "You know I love you more than anything in this world, right?"

Gwen nodded.

"And I know you love me, too. Sometimes we mess up. The best thing we can do is learn from our mistakes, move on, and try not to make the same ones again." Jesse gave her a small grin and a wink. "How about you and me put this one bad moment in an otherwise perfect day behind us?"

Gwen's red face and puffy eyes filled Jesse with an overwhelming sense of remorse for the way she had acted. She never wanted to be responsible for causing that kind of pain in anyone again.

Jesse turned to leave, afraid she was about to break down and cry.

"Don't go." Gwen grabbed hold of her hand. "Will you stay until I fall asleep?"

It had been more than an hour since Jesse had gone up to check on Gwen, and Abby couldn't stand it any longer. Unable to control her curiosity, she padded up the stairs. The door to Gwen's room was slightly ajar. She pushed it open to find Jesse asleep on top of the covers, an open book resting on her chest.

Gwen was sleeping with her head snuggled in the crook of Jesse's shoulder.

Abby smiled. They were so much alike, stubborn and headstrong, yet softhearted to a fault. She gently pulled the book out from under Jesse's hand, marked the page, and put it on the bedside table. From the chest at the foot of the bed she pulled out an extra blanket and covered them. She put out the light and tiptoed quietly from the room. Pausing in the doorway, one hand on the knob, she looked back over her shoulder. "Good night, you two," she whispered. "I love you."

CHAPTER FOURTEEN

CHRISTMAS EVE

It was after ten o'clock when Jesse discovered Abby in the parlor, sleeping in a chair next to the warm and cozy fireplace. "Get up," she said, gently shaking her awake.

Abby stirred and her eyes flew open. "Oh! I must've fallen asleep after you left." She stretched and then grinned brightly. "Did you get them?" she asked, her voice an excited whisper.

Jesse nodded, her smile mirroring Abby's. "Yeah. Toby's getting 'em settled."

"I can't wait to see the looks on their faces in the morning." Abby's eyes sparkled in anticipation.

"Me, either. C'mon and have a look."

Jesse lit a lantern, took Abby by the hand, and led her across the yard.

Inside a stall toward the back of the barn, Toby was brushing down a black horse with a snowy, white face. Another lantern was hanging nearby, but it provided minimal light. Jesse held hers up higher for a better look.

Abby ran her hand down the horse's neck and noticed his deep, blue eyes. "Oh, he's beautiful. What's his name?"

"Phantom," Toby said. He tilted his head toward a sorrel and white-spotted gelding standing in the next stall. "That's Gypsy."

Abby studied the horses up and down, taking in their size. "Jes? Are you sure they're not too big? It would be an awfully long fall."

"They'll be fine." Jesse handed the lantern to her and pulled a piece of paper from her pocket. "It's not like they haven't ridden before." She smoothed out the wrinkles and nailed the note to the stall's wooden beam. "Don't worry," she said, noting the furrow on Abby's brow. "I'll make sure they're comfortable before I turn 'em loose."

Toby stood and patted the gelding. "She's r-right. These two are well broke. They're as tame as old house cats."

"I'm going to worry anyway," Abby said with a resigned sigh. "I hope we don't regret this."

Jesse draped an arm around her shoulders and pulled her close. "They'll be fine. I promise."

"I'm gonna hold you to that," she said, settling comfortably into Jesse's arm.

Jesse enjoyed the moment and then took hold of her hand again. "C'mon, we still have a lot to get done tonight."

The three of them began transferring the presents hidden at Toby's house to theirs. Abby arranged the room with an artist's eye, creating what she thought the perfect Christmas morning should look like. She wanted the day to be an indelible memory for her children that would bring back powerful feelings of family, tradition, and love.

Though more than once they had to pause, certain that one of the kids was waking up, they managed to pull it off without so much as a peep from any of them. When they were finished, the ambience of the parlor was warm and inviting, the essence of what Christmas should be. The base of the tree was crowded with presents, and the stockings hung from the mantel, heavy with fruit, homemade candy, coins, and small toys. Captivating as it was, they finally turned out the lights and climbed the stairs to their room, knowing it would be a very short night. As exhausted as they were, they tossed and turned, thoughts of the children's reactions keeping them awake long after they had gone to bed.

Only a few hours later, Jesse and Abby were awakened by the shouts coming from downstairs. Although they were tired, they hurried to put on their robes, giddy to see the joy on their children's faces.

Before heading to the parlor, they stopped down the hall to get Willow. Already awake from the sudden commotion, her brown eyes stared up at them, wide and curious. Jesse scooped her up and headed down the stairs behind Abby. Shouts of, "Santa was here!" and, "Pippa, Ma, come see!" guided their descent.

No sooner had they stepped into the parlor than the twins rushed at them, nearly bowling them over. The children had already pulled out the small toys and candy from their stockings. Toby was sitting on the sofa with Jamie nestled on his lap. Two wrapped packages sat at his feet.

Abby carefully stepped over the dominos and glass marbles scattered on the floor and took a seat next to Toby. "Merry Christmas," she said, patting him on the leg.

"Merry Christmas, Abby."

"Look, Pippa!" Jim said. "Look at all the presents!"

Jesse passed Willow over to Abby. "I bet they're all for me," she said over her shoulder. She could tell by their expressions that they were considering it.

After a moment, Gwen said, "Nuh-uh, I already read the tags."

"Well, then," Jesse said with a twinkle in her eye, "let's see what Santa brought." She sat cross-legged in front of the tree, picked up a gift, and read a tag aloud. One at a time, she handed out the presents.

Jim and Gwen wasted no time. The sounds of ripping paper, along with an occasional *ooh* or *ahh* filled the room. "I love this!" squealed Gwen, and, "Oh wow!" gasped Jim. Jesse and Abby frequently exchanged glances, their own merriment echoed in their eyes.

Of course, most gifts were practical in nature—socks, mittens, scarfs, and other clothing—something they needed. Each child, however, also received a present more to their own predilections. Jim's face lit up when he saw the cover of *At the Back of the North Wind*. Gwen couldn't wait to sharpen her charcoal pencils and begin drawing in her new sketchbook.

Toby handed each twin one of the large boxes near his feet. "A little something from me."

Eagerly, they ripped off the paper. Jim finished first and lifted the lid off of the box.

"So, whatcha th-think?"

Jim pulled out a black, Stetson hat and positioned it on his head. "Do I look like Pippa?"

Toby smiled. "I think so." He looked at Gwen, who seemed hesitant to open hers. "Well, you gonna open it?"

Gwen wasn't sure she wanted to. She was afraid it would be the kind of hat her mother wore, all fancy and adorned with silk ribbons and bows. If that was what was inside the box, she knew she wasn't going to like it. Still, she didn't want to hurt her uncle's feelings. She braced herself, preparing a stellar act for Toby's sake, and removed the lid. When she peered inside, her mouth stretched into a smile that travelled from ear to ear.

"Oh, thank you, Uncle Toby!" She placed a tan Stetson on top of her head. "I love it! I love it so much!" She ran down the hall to admire herself in front of the mirror hanging in the foyer.

Jesse took a seat between Abby and Toby. Stretching out her long legs, she crossed them comfortably at the ankles and leaned her head against the back of the sofa. "I think we did a pretty good job this year," she said. "Oh, I almost forgot." She reached into her robe pocket and pulled out a small box. "Merry Christmas, Abs."

Abby pried open the lid, revealing the delicate cameo necklace inside. "It's beautiful!" she said, holding it up. She smirked and looked at Jesse. "It sure beats an iron."

Jesse's smile faltered. She reached across to fasten it around her neck. "You're never going to let me forget that, are ya?"

"Not in your lifetime." Abby reached under the sofa and pulled out a wrapped package. "Merry Christmas, Jes."

Jesse ripped off the lavish paper, eager to dig into the box. She held the dark, green sweater under her chin. "I love it. Thank you so much!" She kissed Abby on the cheek and then looked over at her son. "Jim," she said with a wink.

Jim jumped up, ran down the hall, and disappeared into Jesse's office. He returned after a moment with Gwen, carrying something behind his back.

"Here, Uncle Toby," he said, offering him a small box. "This is from all of us."

Jesse and Abby leaned forward, excited to see his reaction. The room was quiet in anticipation.

"You didn't have to do th-this."

Jesse nudged him on the shoulder. "Just open it already."

Toby removed the wrapping paper, slowly lifted the lid, and looked inside. He was quiet for a long moment. "Oh, you r-r-really shouldn't have." His voice was nearly a whisper.

Abby asked, "Don't you like it?"

"I love it. It's just…you sp-spent way too much."

"Nah," Jesse said.

"Flip it over," Jim said.

He turned the gold pocket watch over on his palm.

"Read it out loud," Gwen said.

Toby swallowed the lump of emotion caught in the back of his throat. The calligraphy inscription was precise, as beautiful as the words themselves. "Until the end of time, we love you."

Surprised by the unexpected cache of tears cascading from her brother's eyes, Jesse quickly stood and raised her voice to redirect the twins' attention. "Well, I guess that's everything. Looks like Santa was good to everyone this year." Walking across the room, she said, "Guess it's time I get started on Christmas dinner."

Toby looked over at the twins and said, as though suddenly remembering, "Oh, I forgot to tell you! I'm p-pretty sure I saw Santa coming out of the b-b-barn last night. I wonder what he was doing out there?"

Jim and Gwen glanced at each other and simultaneously let out small gasps.

"Well," Jesse said, "maybe we should go out and see."

The kids were already halfway to the front door when Abby called out, "Slow down! Wait for us!"

Everyone hurried to slip into their coats and boots and then dashed outside. Jesse slid open the barn door and made a show of peeking inside.

"Well, I'll be," Jesse said, feigning surprise. "Would you look at that?"

"What is it?" Gwen asked.

Jim tried to sneak a look. "What's in there?"

The twins couldn't contain themselves and, bursting with excitement, pushed past her to see with their own eyes.

"Are those Santa's horses?" Jim asked, his voice a whisper of awe. He pushed up the brim of his hat to get a better look.

"Santa don't have horses, Jim!" Gwen said with a roll of her eyes. "He has deer!"

"Looks like he left a note," Abby said, interrupting the bickering. She shifted Willow to her other hip and tugged at the paper nailed to the wooden beam. "Interesting." She began reading aloud to the children:

"Dear James and Gwyneth,

I know you've both been very good and helping out as much as you can this year. Because of this, I thought you both deserved something extra special. For you James, is the black horse, Phantom. To Gwyneth, I'm giving the paint horse, Gypsy. Take good care of them, and remember, I'm always watching. I'll know if you've been naughty or nice.

Hope to see you next year,

Santa Claus."

Jim shot a smug look at his sister. "See? He does too have horses!"

Gwen's forehead wrinkled in consideration. She looked up at Jesse and asked, "How'd he get them in his bag?"

Jesse shrugged. "Must be magic." She unlatched the stall door and waved for the children to come closer. She hoisted Jim onto Phantom's back and sat Gwen on top of Gypsy. She stepped back, but although she was smiling, she began to understand Abby's apprehension. The twins truly did seem small and fragile sitting on top of the powerful geldings.

"Now, these aren't toys," Jesse said. "And I better not see either one of you messing around, being careless. The first time I catch either of you breaking the rules, I won't hesitate to sell 'em. Do I make myself clear?"

As the twins nodded from on top of the horses, Jesse rubbed at the sudden prickle of hairs on the back of her neck. Doubt nipped at her, and she wondered quietly if she had made a mistake in convincing Abby this was a good idea.

CHAPTER FIFTEEN

DECEMBER 13TH, 1880

Jesse pointed toward a break in the trees. Fourteen years of hunting in those woods, and the terrain was as familiar as her own reflection. Besides being the place where she could escape the demands life put on her, it was the one place that made her feel less homesick for the mountain she had once called home. She felt anchored there. Grounded. In many ways, it was almost like being back on Mount Perish. Even better, though, was the quality time she was able to spend there with her children, teaching them the life skills they needed to survive and live off of the land.

"Remember what I showed you," Jesse whispered to Willow.

The seven-year-old knelt quietly, her brown eyes keen and aware.

Several yards away, a ten-point buck stood grazing, its neck extended in an attempt to reach leaves from a higher branch. Suddenly alert, the deer turned and looked in their direction. They froze. For a long moment, the buck remained focused on their position, seeming to stare straight at them. Jesse and Willow didn't move until, with a final flick of the ears, the deer sensed there was no danger. It lowered its head and nibbled at the foliage at the base of the tree.

"Easy now," Jesse said in a soft voice. "Right behind the shoulder."

"I know." With the heavy barrel resting on a fallen tree, Willow positioned the rifle carefully and took aim. Confident she had the gun trained accurately, she pulled the trigger.

A loud bang rang out and the large stag danced away, its white tail a flash through the vegetation. Willow said, "Dammit!" In less time than it took her to say the word, her hand was already flying to cover her mouth, as though somehow she could shove it back in.

"Excuse me!" Jesse used the sternest tone she could manage, though she had to bite her lip to keep from laughing. "You know better."

"Sorry. It makes me so mad that I missed!"

"You know, I miss sometimes, too." She took the rifle away from her and set it on the ground. "And so does Gwen. I'm sure you'll get the next one." She rested her back against the downed tree. "You might as well get comfortable. Might be awhile before we see another one."

"You ain't gonna tell Ma I swore, are ya?" Willow's small face was pinched with concern. "She'll give me more chores to do."

Jesse couldn't help but chuckle. She remembered being that age. "I won't tell her." She extended her little finger. "Pinky promise."

With their fingers hooked together, it was impossible for Willow not to see the differences in their skin tones. For as far back as she could remember, it was the one thing truly setting her apart from the rest of the family.

Abby and Jesse had never hidden her adoption from her. What they deliberately kept from her, however, were the graphic details of how they had come to be her parents. All she knew was that her biological parents had passed on from illness. From the very beginning, she had never been treated any differently or loved any less than the twins.

"I wish I looked more like you," Willow said.

"Now why would you want that?"

"I look so different."

"Being different is a good thing. It's what makes you special."

"I wish we shared the same blood. Like you do with Jim and Gwen."

Jesse put an arm around her daughter. "We do." She opened up her hand to display the faint, but still visible scar on her palm. "Years ago, before you were born, I cut my hand. Chief Black Turtle cut his, too. When we shook hands, we mixed our blood together in brotherhood. So, you see, we do share blood."

Willow sat silently, trying to process this new information. Her brow furrowed. "You and me don't, though."

Jesse rubbed the scar on her forehead. "Give me your hand," she said finally, pulling her knife from the sheath.

Willow's dark brown eyes went wide when she saw the long blade. She tucked her hands into her armpits. "You ain't gonna cut my hand like yours, are ya?"

Jesse poked the tip of her own finger against the sharp point of the knife. "Now, let me see your hand."

Willow watched intently as a dot of bright, red blood

formed on the end of Jesse's finger. Squeezing her eyes shut tightly, she quickly stuck out her own hand, palm up.

Jesse smiled at Willow's bravery and then she balled up her tiny hand, leaving one finger exposed. As gently as she could, she quickly tapped the end of the blade against Willow's fingertip. "There," she said. "That wasn't so bad, was it?"

Willow peeked through the small slit of her right eye. Seeing a small drop of blood on the tip of her finger, she opened both of her eyes and studied it. "No." She sighed with relief. "Not bad at all."

Jesse held out her finger and Willow pressed hers against it.

While their fingers were pushed together, Jesse recited a few sentences in the Ponak language, wanting to give her the most authentic ceremonial experience she could.

Willow stared at their hands, her eyes wide with awe and respect.

"Now," Jesse said, after the speech was complete, "you and I share the same blood."

Although Willow seemed satisfied by the ritual, Jesse was riddled with sudden guilt. She wished she would have realized sooner how much it bothered Willow to look different from the rest of the family. Even though they had told her of her heritage, she should have anticipated it wouldn't be enough. She decided then she would teach Willow the language of her people. She might not be able to give back everything the little girl had lost that day, but not everything had to die on the mountain.

"How 'bout we go back to the house? I'm sure your ma has breakfast waiting on us. And I've got a lot of work to get done today."

"Thank you, Pippa." Willow leaned over for a hug. "I love you."

Jesse squeezed her tight in return. "Ee kee tah lahee."

Willow pulled back to look at her. "What'd you say?"

Jesse gave her a wink. "I said, I love you more."

When Jesse and Willow reached the trailhead, they saw Gwen approaching. She had come to see if they needed any help with field dressing a kill.

"Get anything, Squirt?" Gwen rested her hand on top of Willow's head.

"No." Willow hung her head. "I missed a big one."

"It's okay. I've missed several myself."

"Yeah, but you don't anymore." Willow looked up at her big sister. "Now you're really good."

"It took me a long time to get really good." Gwen smiled. "Keep trying. You'll get better."

Jesse didn't say anything. She grinned at her daughters' interaction as they continued to the house.

When they reached the edge of the woods, Gwen came to an abrupt stop. "Pippa, Jonathan is here. I can't let him see me like this." She glanced down at her rabbit pelt coat, buckskin pants, and old boots.

Jesse glanced toward the house and noticed Jim and Jonathan sitting on the front steps. She looked over at her fifteen-year-old daughter with a mixture of confusion and amusement. She found herself wondering when Gwen started caring about her appearance. Especially when it came to

Jonathan, who had always been like a big brother to her—or so she believed.

Jonathan had been away for the last three months visiting his grandparents. In the short amount of time he had been gone, something had noticeably changed in Gwen. Jesse wasn't exactly sure when it had happened, but it was obvious her daughter was growing up, right before her eyes it seemed. She wasn't sure if she wanted to laugh or cry.

"Wait here," Jesse said. "I'll go distract him for you. When we get inside the house, you make a run for it. I'll make sure he doesn't see you."

"I'll stay with ya," Willow said.

Jonathan was on his feet by the time Jesse reached the covered porch. "Good morning, Mr. McGinnis," he said. His hands fidgeted nervously at his sides before he finally shoved them into his pockets.

"Morning," Jesse said, shifting the rifle to her other hand. "When did you get back?"

"Last night." Jonathan pointed over his shoulder toward the house. "I like the Christmas decorations. And your tree is one of the nicest I've ever seen." He smiled awkwardly, trying to find words to use in the conversation. "I wish I would've been here this year for the search. Mrs. McGinnis sure picked out a nice one."

Seated behind him, Jim rolled his eyes and shook his head at Jonathan's noticeable apprehension.

Jesse admired the pine garland running the length of the porch banister and then moved her gaze to the large wreath hanging on the door. "Yeah, she really does have a knack for it. So, what are you boys up to today?"

Neither one said anything until Jim finally stood and gave Jonathan a nudge. They were best friends, after all, and it was painful to watch him struggle.

"Go on. Ask him already."

"I...I was wondering," Jonathan said, "if I could maybe speak with you—in private. You know, one man to another."

Jesse chuckled inwardly. Jonathan was still just a boy in her eyes. "Well, sounds serious. We better go to my office." She could sense Gwen watching as they climbed the stairs. She led the way into the house and entered the room first. "Have a seat," she said, pointing to the chair across from her desk. After closing the door, she walked over, placed the rifle on the desk, and sat down in her chair. "What's on your mind?"

Jonathan couldn't have sat still if his life had depended on it. He squirmed in his seat, his nervous eyes darting about the room in an effort to avoid eye contact with her. He moved his focus to a black hat, Frieda's old one, which Jesse prized more than almost anything, hanging on the wall. The front door slammed, causing him to jump.

Jesse glanced toward the ceiling, tickled by the sound of Gwen and Willow's running feet overhead, which sounded like a herd of cattle. Turning her attention back to Jonathan, she said, "My mother used to say if you have something to say, best to just spit it out."

Instead of making him feel more at ease her words only seemed to make him more nervous. He blanched visibly.

Jesse worried he might pass out. "You don't look so good." She pointed to the leather settee up against the wall. "Do you need to lay down?"

Jonathan licked his lips and swallowed against the walnut

sized lump that seemed to be wedged tightly in his throat. His mouth felt bone dry and when he tried to speak, his voice cracked. "Uh…no…uh…" He took a deep breath, and tried again. "Jim told me you're getting ready to leave for a job in San Francisco. He said since you'll be away, none of you are going to attend the Hawkins' Christmas party this year. So, uh. I…I was wondering…" He took another breath and said in a rush, "If it would be alright with you, could I escort Gwen Saturday night to the dance? And, um. I'd like your permission to begin courting your daughter, sir."

Jesse sat quietly. She knew this day would come eventually but hadn't expected it to be so soon. Gwen was still her baby girl, after all. Although she was quite fond of Jonathan Plunkett, she wasn't keen on the idea of him courting her daughter, or anyone else courting her for that matter. She took off her hat, tossed it on the desk, and pulled open one of the drawers.

Jonathan could tell by Jesse's strained expression he had crossed a line. Intuition told him to get out of the room while he was still capable. He slowly pushed his chair back, cringing openly at the noise the legs made against the polished wood. He stood, certain the next thing he was going to see would be a protective father reaching for his gun. "Ne-ne-never mind. I shouldn't have asked."

Jesse reached into the drawer and then pulled out a jar of cleaning oil and a rag. "Sit back down," she said, but not unkindly, and placed the items on the desktop. After pouring some of the liquid onto the rag, she began cleaning her rifle. "Ever heard of a town called Lagro?"

"No, sir," he said, taking a seat again.

Jesse thought back on the town. It was nothing more than

a single building used as a stop for the stagecoach. She knew there was nothing else there but dust for as far as the eye could see.

"Just the other day I read in the paper they have a female doctor there." She shook her head, all the while sliding the rag up and down the long barrel of the gun. "A woman doctor," she said with a smirk. "Can you imagine?"

Jonathan shrugged, unsure how he was supposed to respond to such a peculiar question.

Jesse set the rag and rifle off to one side, rested her elbows on the desk, and looked him straight in the eyes. "Don't you think a woman's place is in the home? In the kitchen? Taking care of their husbands and having babies?" She stared, unfaltering, into the boy's eyes. "If Gwen ever got a crazy notion in her head like that woman doctor out in Lagro, would you be man enough to put her in her place?"

Jonathan looked down at the scuffed toes of his shoes. When he raised his head, there was no hesitation in his answer. "No disrespect, sir, but I want Gwen to do whatever makes her happy. If she wants to be a doctor, I would encourage her to follow her dreams."

The leather in Jesse's chair squeaked as she leaned back and rested her steepled hands in her lap. Although his response wasn't the one she had been anticipating, it was exactly the one she wanted—needed to hear. Moreover, she knew by Gwen's reaction earlier, this was what her daughter wanted as well.

"If that's the way you feel." Jesse stood and came around to his side of the desk.

Jonathan watched in frozen fear.

"Yes, you certainly may have my blessing."

Jonathan released his held breath and relaxed in the chair.

It dawned on Jesse the Hawkins' dance was a fancy affair by Neva standards. She knew his parents struggled financially. However, since they had never attended the event in the past, she had always assumed they would have felt underdressed for the occasion. She considered offering Jonathan some money to purchase the appropriate attire but knew his pride would keep him from accepting it outright. There were plenty of chores she could have him do around the farm to earn the money, though.

"You do know the dance is kind of formal, right?"

"I know, sir." He sat up taller. "That's why I've been with my grandparents. I did some work for 'em. My grandmother took me to a shop and helped me pick out a nice suit."

What he had done spoke volumes about his character. It only then occurred to her that he had been planning this for months.

"I couldn't think of anyone better to take my daughter to her first dance." She placed a hand on his shoulder. "Now, how would you like to stay for breakfast?"

"Thank you, sir. I'd like that. And I promise, I'll be the perfect gentleman."

"I expect nothing less." She glanced down pointedly at her rifle.

While Jesse and Jonathan were in the office, Jim had been waiting in the kitchen with his mother. Sitting on a stool in the center of the room, beside the big butcher block, he filled her in on what was happening in the other room.

"Do you think Pippa will let her go?"

Abby handed him a knife. "Here, finish cutting these for me." She reached up and grabbed another skillet hanging from the rack above their heads. "I don't see why not, especially since you'll be going."

Jim's head shot up, and he narrowly missed chopping off his finger. "Me? Why do I have to go?"

"Because that's what brothers do," she said, placing the pan on the stove. "They always look out for their sisters." She added a small dollop of lard to the cast-iron skillet and watched as it started to melt.

"She'll be with Jonathan. She'll be fine."

"You can be sure of that." She looked at him over her shoulder. "I won't have to worry about anything happening to her because you'll be with her, too. Besides, it won't hurt you to get your nose out of a book once in a—" She turned to face him. "Are you crying?"

Jim's nose wrinkled as he sniffed. "No, Ma. It's the onion."

Abby walked over to him and kissed him on top of his head. "You know we've always had a good time at the Hawkins' party. Who knows, you might find a nice girl to dance with."

Jim's shoulders sagged. "I doubt that."

Abby scooped up the diced onions and dropped them into the sizzling skillet. Her mind shifted to Gwen and what she was going to wear to the dance, which was only five days away. She began imagining the possible choices hanging in her daughter's wardrobe.

"Ma. Can I ask you something?" When she didn't answer, Jim repeated himself louder.

"Of course," Abby said, snapping out of her train of thought. She stirred the onions in the skillet. "You know you can always ask me anything."

His fingers absently stroked the few sporadic whiskers on his chin as he spoke. "How come Pippa doesn't have to shave?"

Abby was totally unprepared for his question. The wooden spoon fell from her hand, hitting the side of the stove before landing on the floor. She had no idea how to respond, but thankfully, at that moment, Toby and Jamie walked in.

"Where's Willow?" Jamie asked.

"I think I heard her and Gwen go upstairs." Abby picked the spoon up off the floor, laid it in the sink, and retrieved a clean one from the drawer. Her mind was racing on how to answer her son.

Jamie ran from the room and hurried to join the other girls.

Toby had overheard Jim's question. During the time he spent with the Ponak, he witnessed how the men of the tribe groomed themselves, by plucking their hair rather than shaving. In actuality, he had no idea if their hair grew back in or not. He only hoped the explanation he was about to give would satisfy his nephew's curiosity.

"It's because Jes grew up on the mountain with th-the Ponaks. You w-w-won't see an Indian with facial hair like this." Toby combed his fingers through his thick beard for effect. "When Indian boys come of age, all of their hair is pl-plucked out. It's unlikely it'll ever grow back."

Abby, cracking eggs into the skillet with the sautéed onions, glanced over at Jim. She could tell by his expression that he was believing every word Toby said. All of the kids knew details about Jesse's life on the mountain and her strong kinship with the tribe. Jim had no reason to question the validity of his uncle's words.

"I noticed I'm starting to get facial hair," Jim said to Toby. "When do I have to start plucking?"

Toby couldn't help but laugh. "Well, we do things a l-little different 'round here. I have a razor at the house. Why don't you come with me and I'll show you wh-what to do."

Toby winked at Abby over his shoulder as he followed Jim from the room.

She mouthed a silent thank you to him.

"Where's Jim?" Jonathan asked when he and Jesse came into the room.

"He's over at his uncle's," Abby said. "He'll be back shortly."

Having spent so much time at the McGinnis home, Jonathan knew exactly what needed to be done without having to be asked. After washing his hands, he went into the dining room to set the table for breakfast.

"He's such a good kid," Abby said to Jesse. "You didn't scare him, did you?"

"Now, would I do that?" She snatched a small piece of fried ham from a nearby platter. "Yeah, he's a good kid and all, but I still don't like it. She's growing up way too fast."

"I know. And just think! In a few years, you and I are probably going to be grandparents."

Abby's declaration caught Jesse completely off guard. She started coughing from the tiny piece of ham she inhaled.

Just then, Gwen, Jamie, and Willow came parading into the kitchen. Gwen's long hair was tied back with a silk ribbon. Her face had been scrubbed clean and her cheeks were rosy.

"Ain't she pretty?" Willow asked, staring up proudly at her big sister, who was wearing one of her good dresses.

"Isn't," Abby said, transferring the scrambled eggs into a

porcelain, serving bowl. "Isn't she pretty." She took in Gwen's appearance, noting she looked more like a young lady rather than a child. It tugged heavily at her heartstrings, but she swallowed back the sudden ball of emotion. "And, yes, she is. Very." Quickly, she changed the subject, unwilling to dwell on the reality of the passing of time. "Let's eat breakfast now, before everything gets cold."

CHAPTER SIXTEEN

Later that night, Jesse was stretched out on her large four-poster bed, her back resting against the headboard. Burrowed close beside her were Willow and Jamie, listening intently as she read aloud to them.

Abby came into the room, her silk robe wrapped loosely around her. "Alright, you two, time for bed."

"Aw, Ma, it was just gettin' to the good part."

"Just a couple more minutes, Auntie?" Jamie's brown eyes pleaded along with her cousin's. "Please."

"She's right." Jesse sat up, marked the page, and closed the book. "It's past your bedtime. C'mon, hop to."

Taking a seat at her vanity, Abby peered at them in the reflection as she reached for the bottle of her favorite perfume. She dabbed a little of the sweet fragrance behind her ears, on her wrists, and in the hollow of her neck.

Both girls gave Jesse a hug and a peck on the cheek before rolling off the sides of the bed.

"Night-night, Pippa," Willow said.

"Goodnight, Nugget."

"Night, Uncle Jes," Jamie said.

"Goodnight, sweetie. You both sleep well."

After giving Abby a quick kiss, both girls raced from the room and down the hall.

Abby got up and padded across the room to lock the door. When she was seated at her vanity once more, she pulled the pin from her hair. Her loose braids rippled down her shoulders, releasing the delicate, rosemary scent of her homemade shampoo.

Jesse watched her, mesmerized by the mundane task.

"Are the new spectacles still giving you headaches?" Abby asked, glancing at Jesse's mirrored image as she pulled the brush through her hair.

Jesse placed the book on the bedside table and took off the wire-rimmed frames. "No, but when did I get so damn old?" She pinched the bridge of her nose.

"We're both getting up there, ya know. Hard to believe you'll be turning forty pretty soon, isn't it?"

"Pfft. That's three years away." Walking over to the fireplace, she added another log and picked up the metal poker. "Don't rush it."

"Did you get a chance to read Sarah's letter yet?" Abby gestured toward the envelope on the bedside table with a tilt of her head.

Sarah Winslow had originally moved to Chicago where she worked under a well-known seamstress. Finally, after three years, she had managed to save enough money to move to New York City, where she opened her own boutique. Her business had flourished ever since. She knew it would be considered inappropriate to correspond with another woman's husband but wanted to express her gratitude to Jesse in some way. Every December for the past four years, she mailed one of her latest, highly sought-after dresses to Abby. The dresses and letters were her way of saying thank you for all Jesse had done for her.

"No." She repositioned the log toward the center of the grate. "What'd she have to say?"

"She's going to France in the summer," Abby said. "The dress she sent me this year is the one she'll be showcasing at a fashion show in Paris."

Jesse's eyes shifted to Abby. "Put it on. I want to see you in it."

Abby studied her own reflection in the mirror, running the brush through her silken hair, before responding. "I was actually saving it for the Masquerade Ball at the Davenports' next month. I want you to be surprised when you see me in it."

Jesse leaned the poker against the tile surround. "Glad to hear Sarah's doing so well." She walked up behind Abby, watching her brushing her hair for a moment. "So, it really doesn't bother you that Jonathan is going to start courting Gwen?" When Abby looked at her, Jesse held her gaze in the mirror.

"No, I think it's sweet. Our little girl is growing up, isn't she?"

"Too fast, if you ask me." Jesse cupped Abby's shoulders in her hands.

"She probably won't sleep a wink tonight. She's already fretting over what to wear."

Jesse gently plucked the hairbrush from Abby's hand and began making long, even strokes. She smiled at her in the mirror. "Bath sure felt good this evening, didn't it?"

"Mm-hmm." Abby let out a delightful moan and leaned

against Jesse for support. "So, did you get the Davenport job finished?"

Two years ago, Jesse had done some custom carpentry work for the owner of the San Francisco Press. He had liked her work so much, he asked if he could send a reporter to interview her for an article in his paper. She agreed, knowing the exposure would be good for her business.

Soon after the story ran, Mr. Frank Davenport hired her to design and build his grand staircase. A railroad tycoon, his mansion would take up an entire city block and was proposed to be the largest estate in San Francisco. It was her most profitable job to date. Jesse knew the time she had available would need to be fully invested in the project, so she declined all other work to focus solely on his job. Finally, after months of reduced sleep and endless hours spent carving in her shop, not to mention traveling back and forth to the city to take measurements as the construction developed, she was finally finished.

The fact it was so close to Christmas wasn't to her liking, but it couldn't be helped. Now, the only thing left was to load up the intricate parts and transport them to San Francisco. Once there, she, Toby, and Armand could erect the staircase which she hoped would be as easy to assemble as the pieces of a puzzle.

"Yes," Jesse said, nodding. "I did."

"Oh, good. Does that mean you're free tomorrow?"

"I wish." Jesse sighed. "Armand is bringing his wagon over so we can start getting everything loaded up and ready to go." She thought for a moment, considering. "Just loading all those spindles and packing them in straw is going to take most of the day. There's over two hundred of them, and I don't want them to get damaged during transport. I want the wagons ready so we can be on the road by first light the day after tomorrow." Jesse paused. "Why? Did you need me to do something?"

"No. I was hoping maybe we could slip off to the city. I'm sure Gwen would like to pick out a new dress. Jim could use a new suit. Plus, I'd really like to do some last minute shopping."

"You should go." Jesse set the brush on the table. "I'm sure Toby wouldn't mind taking you around. Armand and I can manage." She lifted Abby's hair away from her neck, leaned down, and gently traced the soft skin with her lips. "Go out to lunch, make a day of it." Knowing the little ones could be a handful, she said, "I'll look after Willow and Jamie. You know, this will be the last chance you have before Christmas. If I could go, I would, but if I don't meet Mr. Davenport's deadline, we might get uninvited to his gala." She nibbled delicately at the base of Abby's neck. "And I really want to see you in that dress."

"I wish you didn't have to go away," Abby said, curling her arm around Jesse to pull her closer. "Especially this close to the holiday."

"I know." She kissed the top of her head. "Me, too. But with Toby and Armand's help, I should be home next week. Don't worry, I'll be back in time. You know I wouldn't miss it."

Abby tilted her head back for another kiss. "You better be." She ran her hand down Jesse's arm. "It's bad enough you won't be here to see Gwen and Jim all dressed up."

"I can't believe I'm going to miss their first social. When I get back, I want to know every detail."

"I'll tell you everything." Abby swiveled around in her seat.

She plucked at the sleeve of Jesse's long underwear, tugging her closer. "Aren't you hot in these?"

The one-piece garment was still the best option Jesse had for sleeping attire. "It is a bit warm," she said, noticing the twinkle in Abby's eye. "If you're so worried about my well-being, why don't you help me out of it?" Pulling Abby to her feet, she pressed her body firmly against her and slid her hands down Abby's familiar curves. She captured Abby's lips, teasing her mouth open with her tongue.

Abby broke the kiss and slipped out of her robe, leaving it in a heap on the floor. She took Jesse by the hand and led her to the bed.

Jesse reached for the buttons of Abby's nightgown. She slowly unfastened them, leaving lingering kisses over the smooth, soft skin of her shoulders. The garment slid off and Jesse's heart took off like a spooked stallion. She snaked her hands between Abby's legs, slowly ran her hand up her inner thigh, and teased her with a finger.

Abby gasped, moaning in pleasure, and then devoured Jesse with another kiss. Now, there was a sense of urgency as she peeled her out of her clothing and unwrapped her binding.

For a brief moment, they took in each other's naked form lit up by the firelight. A few seconds was all that either of them could stand. They fell onto the bed, grappling sala-ciously, with Jesse letting Abby come out the winner on top. She straddled Jesse, kissing her way down her chest, letting her long hair fall loose around them. Her tongue focused on Jesse's nipple and she felt it hardening with each tender lashing.

"My God, I want you," Jesse whispered, her voice over-flowing with need.

"I want you, too." She moved her hand down Jesse's ribs, over her navel, and down below to the wispy curls.

Jesse moaned and arched her back when she felt Abby slip inside. She gripped Abby's thighs, making no effort to hold back the moan that escaped when Abby went deeper.

Abby teasingly brushed her lips over Jesse's, staring deep into her eyes as she slid in and out of her. She matched her speed to the ever increasing intensity of Jesse's moans.

Jesse moved her hips in sync, writhing in pleasure, until the pace grew frenetic. She cried out in sudden release, her body throbbing in ecstasy.

"Your turn." Jesse barely paused, her voice husky, as she rolled Abby onto her back. She positioned herself between the open and inviting thighs and found her already slick with desire. She whispered kisses all the way down, taking her time, exploring Abby with her tongue. Even after she felt Abby climax, she didn't stop, drinking her up like she was dying of thirst.

"Jes. Please!" Her head tossed from side to side, her fingers scrabbling for purchase in Jesse's hair as she continued to beg. "Please. I can't take it anymore. You're making me crazy."

Jesse moved on top of her, battling Abby's tongue with her own, and then slipped inside of her. Right away, she could feel Abby's muscles clamp around her fingers. Panting loudly, Jesse increased her pace and energy.

Abby dug her fingernails into Jesse's sweat-soaked back, rocking her hips and grinding against every thrust. It didn't take long until her body shook with tremors.

"Oh, Jes." Her voice quivered as she held Jesse's hand firmly in place.

Jesse waited for the contractions to cease before removing

herself. She placed one last kiss on Abby's shoulder and rolled off to lay beside her.

"That was incredible," Abby said, her voice still wavering. "Why don't we do that more often?"

Jesse pulled her closer, breathing in deeply the scent of rosemary in her hair. "I don't know why we don't, but we definitely should." She sat up, rolled out of bed, and grabbed her clothes from off the floor.

"Where are you going?"

"Over to let Toby know about taking you into the city in the morning." Jesse studied her face, then leaned down to kiss her.

"Well, hurry back." Abby patted the sheets and grinned. "I'm not done with you yet."

Quirking an eyebrow, Jesse tossed her clothes on the floor. "I'll just tell him in the morning." She crawled back into bed and positioned herself on top of Abby once again.

CHAPTER SEVENTEEN

The morning light had barely begun to illuminate the early hours of the day, but both Abby and Jesse were already awake. They lay snuggled under the covers, enjoying the warmth of each others bodies atop their billowy-soft mattress. Still reeling from their encounter during the night, neither one was quite ready to get up and face the day.

Abby eyed the family portrait hanging proudly on the adjacent wall. Gwen had sketched the drawing and had given it to Jesse on her last birthday. The likeness of each person was true to life.

"Do you remember when Gwen was little, and you'd let her stand on top of your feet so you could dance with her?"

Jesse recalled the memory of Gwen holding onto her thumbs as she took small steps around the den while Abby played the piano. Scenes of dancing with her daughter throughout the years played out in her mind. Gradually, the little girl of the past morphed into the young woman she had become.

"Yes. I'll always remember that." She lightly trailed her

hand through Abby's hair. "I wonder if she'll be as nervous as I was the first time you and I danced together. I remember worrying I'd forget how to move my feet."

"I'm sure she will be." Abby nestled in closer to the heat of Jesse's body. "I think she'll do fine. She had a very good teacher, after all."

Jesse smiled and shifted her focus. "Well…as much as I'd love to spend the entire day in bed with you, I think we'd best get moving." She lightly brushed her hand over Abby's bare behind. "We both have a lot to do today."

Abby didn't budge. She gripped Jesse tighter. "I wish you weren't leaving tomorrow."

"Me too," Jesse said, but when Abby didn't move, she added, "but the sooner you leave, the sooner you'll get home. Then we can spend this evening together." She gently bit her bottom lip in anticipation. "You know I wouldn't mind a repeat of what we did last night."

"Mmm." Abby considered the proposition and then released a deep-weighted sigh. "I'm really going to miss you. You'll be home next Wednesday for sure, right?"

"I will. I figure a week will give me plenty of time to get the job finished." She lightly patted Abby on her behind. "I'm going to miss you more."

"That's not possible. And you better be because Christmas Eve is next Friday."

"I know." Jesse kissed her on the lips and then stared into her deep, blue eyes. "I've never missed one before." She brushed a strand of hair from Abby's face. "I'm not going to miss this one either. Trust me."

"Alright," Abby said in resignation, lightly trailing her hand down Jesse's cheek. The soft and smooth skin suddenly reminded her of the incident with Jim. "Oh, I forgot to tell you." She leaned up on an elbow. "Yesterday, while you were speaking with Jonathan, Jim asked me why you don't shave."

Jesse cocked an eyebrow. Queasiness began to build up in her stomach at the thought of those types of questions crossing his mind. "What'd you—"

Abby put a finger on Jesse's lips. "You don't have to worry. Toby handled it." When Jesse's brow furrowed in confusion, she continued. "He told him you grew up among the tribe. Explained how the young men pluck their hair out rather than shave, and that it doesn't grow back."

A heavy, awkward silence lingered before Jesse finally spoke again. "I think," she said quietly, "maybe it's time I tell the kids the truth about me. They're fifteen now. It's time they know." She traced her thumb delicately across Abby's bare shoulder. "What do you think?"

Abby paused for a moment, considering, then nodded. "Yeah. And it's we, Jes. You and I are in this together, always. You aren't the only one who's kept a secret from them. I'm the one who didn't want them to know about Sam." She rested her head on Jesse's bare chest and caressed the soft skin beneath her fingers. "We'll both explain it. It might be hard for them to understand, initially. I think in time, though, they'll come around. Don't worry. I know how much they love and adore you. They would never push you away."

"God, I hope you're right. The last thing I ever want to do is hurt them." Jesse placed an arm across her belly protectively. Just thinking about their rejection made her insides cringe.

Abby lifted her head abruptly. "But, can we wait until after Christmas?"

Jesse pulled her arm out from under Abby. "That's probably for the best." She slid out of bed, shivering in the sudden cold. Quickly, she collected her clothes that were strewn across the floor. "I'm going to run over and tell Toby to start getting ready."

Abby sat on the edge of the bed and wrapped the quilt around her shoulders. "You do know I'm quite capable of driving myself."

"I know you are, but I'll feel a whole lot better knowing he's going with you." She pulled clean clothes from her dresser drawer and placed them on the bed. "He won't mind going," she said, binding her chest. "Especially when I tell him you're taking him out to eat. He'd do about anything for a good steak."

After sharing a rushed breakfast, Abby returned to their bedroom and pulled Jesse's best suit from the wardrobe. She removed the black tailcoat with the silk lapels from the hanger. She took the blue, double-breasted, brocade vest from underneath it and placed it on top of her ball gown, which was still inside the dress box.

But, I don't need a new vest. I already have too many the way it is, and it would just be a waste of money. Abby could hear Jesse's protest in her mind as she secured the lid, knowing full well if Jesse saw what she was planning, there would be some sort of rebuttal. Matching her attire to Jesse's whenever they attended these lavish events was something she had always fancied and was worth any chastisement should she get caught.

The first thing she intended to do when she arrived in San

Francisco was to swing by the tailor's shop and hire him to make Jesse a new vest. He could take any measurements he needed from the old one. Hopefully, he would find a material that could pair closely to the fabric of the new gown she was planning on wearing to the Davenport Ball.

Abby returned the suit to the wardrobe so Jesse would be none the wiser and then carried the dress box downstairs. Placing it on the table in the foyer, she stared at her reflection in the large mirror. She pushed back a few loose hairs. Satisfied, she put on her hat and tied the ribbon. She had just pulled it taut when Jim and Gwen came down the stairs.

"They're bringing the carriage around," Abby said, reaching for her coat and gloves. "You both ready?"

Gwen was bouncing on the balls of her feet in anticipation. She couldn't wait to get to the city to find the perfect dress for her first official outing with Jonathan. Jim's mood was as obvious as the nose on his face. Wrinkled in disdain and almost comical, he looked like someone soured with the unfortunate task of picking out the coffin for his own funeral.

"You'll be fine." Abby chuckled inwardly at his expression. She reached for her parasol, and then indicating the dress box with a tip of her head, asked, "Could you carry that out for me, please?"

Jim picked it up, hung his head sullenly, and stayed silent as he followed them out the door.

Outside, two large draft horses stood in front of a waiting carriage. Toby waited patiently at the reins while Jamie and Willow sat astride the horses. Jesse was bent over, polishing away with her handkerchief at a smudge of dirt on the new black carriage. The salesman had sold her on the Landau model when he mentioned President Grant owned the exact same brand during his second term. She stood back to survey her handiwork, observing the paint critically, and then leaned in for another swipe at an almost-imperceptible smudge.

"You're going to rub the paint off that thing," Abby said as she came walking down the steps. She secured the parasol beneath her arm and began pulling on her gloves.

Jesse didn't turn around, dismissing the comment with a wave. She gave it one more wipe before stuffing the handkerchief back into her pants pocket.

"Pippa," Jim said, opening the carriage door so that he could put the dress box inside, "do I *have* to go?"

"Oh, I think you'll survive one day in the city." She plucked Jamie down from the mare.

"Why can't you go, too?" Jim asked.

Jesse circled around the front of the carriage, pausing a moment to run a hand down each horse's face. "I wish I could, but I've got to finish loading the wagons so they'll be ready to go in the morning." She lifted Willow down.

Jamie tugged on Gwen's coat sleeve. "What color dress you gonna get?"

"I'm not sure," Gwen said, a small smile playing at the corners of her mouth. "I guess I'll know what I like when I see it."

"I wish we could go," Jamie said mournfully, tilting her head toward Willow.

Abby leaned down, kissing Jamie and Willow in turn. "You two behave and I'll bring you back something special."

At the promise of a treat, the girls readily agreed to be on their best behavior. After a round of quick goodbyes, they raced off to the rope swing hanging in the barn.

Toby looked down at Jim from the driver's seat. "Now, why th-the long face?"

"I hate shopping. I can't think of anything worse."

"It's not m-my favorite thing to do either." Toby patted the cushion next to him. "How 'bout you do the dr-drivin'?" He held up the reins.

"Uh, wait," Abby said. "I don't think that's such a good idea."

"I'm sure he'll do fine," Jesse said. "Don't worry."

Abby shot her a look—the look. She knew exactly how meticulous Jesse was with the new carriage. "I'm not worried about him driving. It's fine with me." She looked pointedly at Jesse. "But if it comes home with a scratch on it, I don't want you getting upset. Alright, we best get moving. We've got a lot to do today."

Jim was smiling from ear to ear. He eagerly handed his mother a book he had brought along to read and climbed up into the driver's seat beside his uncle.

Jesse opened the carriage door. "Ladies," she said with a little bow, offering her hand to help Abby and Gwen manage the step. Watching as they moved to sit opposite one another on the leather seats, she noticed the dress box. "Why are you taking that? Does it need to be altered?"

"What? Oh, no," Abby said, nonchalant. "I was going to see if I can find a hat to match the fabric."

"Okay—oh, I almost forgot." Jesse reached into her back pocket, pulled out an envelope addressed to Mrs. Felix Nicholas and handed it to her. "Would you drop this off at the post for me, please?"

Jesse had harbored strong animosity toward Edith for years, blaming her for the genocide that had occurred on

Mount Perish. Ever since, a rage had simmered deep within her. The faces of the slain haunted her dreams, a nightmare that followed her around even when she was wide awake. She had held Edith accountable for each and every one of the senseless deaths, a vicious anger that boiled up whenever she allowed herself to think too long about it.

If only Edith had been true to her word and had written to warn her about the bridge being built in Granite Falls like she had promised she would, things might have turned out differently. Maybe she could have done something to prevent the massacre. Since Edith had never sent out the crucial information, there was no way of ever knowing. Edith had taken away her only opportunity to find out.

Throughout the passing years, Jesse had periodically received letters from Edith. She let them go unanswered until finally, the letters ceased completely.

Mercifully, the passage of time had a way of healing over even the worst of old wounds, and Jesse came to terms with the fact that her anger had been misguided. After all, the only information Edith had been given was to let her know if men ever found a way to cross the river. If only she had been honest with her, it might have changed the outcome, especially if Edith had known innocent lives were at stake. When Jesse came to realize it was her own self who was solely responsible, she immediately started composing a letter in her mind on what she would write to Edith.

After seven long years, Jesse had finally swallowed her pride and penned a letter. Though she was still mindful to be vague in what she divulged, she made sure to mention she had never received a letter about the bridge being erected over the Devil's Fork.

When Edith had replied back, Jesse eagerly tore open the envelope. As she read the familiar handwriting from one of her first and oldest friends, tears filled her eyes and spilled down her cheeks. Edith swore to her that she had sent word, insisting her letter must have gotten lost somewhere in route. Jesse was stunned to discover Edith had kept her word all along and for the past seven years, she had been holding a grudge for absolutely no reason at all. As soon as she finished reading, all the anger, hurt, and bitterness she had been holding on to vanished completely.

With the misunderstanding behind them, Jesse and Edith picked up correspondence where they had left off. It was as though nothing had ever happened, and the relationship was completely restored to its former confidence. They communicated frequently, catching each other up on everything which had taken place over the better part of a decade.

Jesse's hostility had been like a crushing boulder throughout the years. By writing one simple letter, all of it had floated away like dandelion fluff in the wind.

Abby noticed the changes straight away. Unable to deny the results, she decided it was time to write a letter of her own. Her hope was that if she wrote out her feelings on paper, she, too, would get closure on something which had eaten away at her since she was a child.

As a parent, Abby had discovered an underlying wisdom and found there was much more she understood now. She knew she couldn't really blame her father for turning to alcohol after the death of his wife and baby. Thoughts of losing Jesse or one of the twins was unfathomable to her. While she herself wouldn't have tried to muffle the pain from a bottle, her father's actions were understandable when she considered them from that perspective.

Though it had been well over a month since Abby had secretly sent the letter to her father, she still hadn't received a response from him. She knew she shouldn't be surprised. Her father had stopped being reliable the day her mother and sister died. Getting all of her emotions out and forgiving him, regardless of whether he read the words or not, had not completely healed all the festering wounds. It did, however, help scab over some of the very raw ones, and she was grateful for that.

Abby happily tucked Jesse's letter into her handbag.

"Bye, Pippa," Gwen said.

"Bye, sweetheart." Jesse grabbed the carriage door. "You girls be safe."

"We will," Abby said. "And don't forget, if Willow and Jamie get bored, you can always have them work on their lessons."

"I'm sure if I threaten them with that, they'll get unbored real quick," she said with a grin. "I'll see you later this evening." She closed the door. An image of the carriage returning home, scratched and scraped as though it had been buffed with barbed wire flashed in her mind. She walked over to Toby, pulled on his pant leg discreetly, and whispered up to him. "Take over when you get close to the city."

Toby gave a crisp nod as she stepped back and then he turned back toward his nephew. "You be c-careful now," he said, clapping him on the back, "and don't get us killed."

CHAPTER EIGHTEEN

It was Saturday and exactly one week before Christmas. Even though it was late December, the temperature was unusually mild. There wasn't a cloud in sight—perfect weather for the yearly, holiday gathering. Gwen couldn't believe the big day had finally arrived. From the moment she had gotten up, there had been a queasiness rolling around in the pit of her stomach. She was growing more nervous than a bride on her wedding day with each passing second. In her parents' bedroom, her mother was assisting her with getting ready, which helped to somewhat keep her mind off of her rising anxiety.

"I wish Pippa was here to see us all dressed up," Gwen said, holding onto the bedpost for support.

Abby tugged at the strings of the corset with an experienced hand. "Me too," she said, pulling the laces taut. "I know he's disappointed." She picked up the lilac dress and admired it again. The color was vivid, but not ostentatious, and quite flattering to her daughter's features. She was careful not to disturb Gwen's hair, which had been styled with complicated twists and rolls. The coif hung beautifully to her shoulders and complemented the style of the dress perfectly. She helped her carefully slip the garment over her head.

Gwen tugged on the white lace cuffs, pulling the sleeves down to her wrists. Her strong hands appeared almost dainty against the crochet. "Pippa really is the best father a girl could ever have."

Reminded briefly of her own father, Abby couldn't help but wish she had the same close relationship with him as Gwen did with Jesse. She knew all too well how fortunate her daughter was to have a loving, paternal relationship in her life.

Thoughts of her own blessings flashed through Abby's mind. She compared the volatile relationship with her late husband, Silas, to the one she had with Jesse. The two were at opposite ends of the spectrum. Silas had ruled over her with a heavy fist. She couldn't even remember a time when Jesse had raised her voice to her. Thinking of how lucky she was to have Jesse, how grateful she was to have her in her life, made a smile tickle at the corners of her mouth.

"I think so too," Abby said, standing behind her daughter. "We sure are blessed." She gazed at Gwen in the full-length mirror. She hitched in her breath and tears formed in the corners of her eyes. "Sweetheart, you look beautiful." She walked over to her vanity table. "Come over here, please. Sit down."

Gwen smoothed out her dress, turned, and sat on the chair. "What's this?" she asked, noticing a tiny pot on the table. She picked it up and inspected it.

"It's rouge." Abby placed a decorative comb in her daughter's hair. "It adds a hint of color to your cheeks and lips."

Gwen removed the lid from the container, revealing the reddish salve inside. "Can I use some?"

Abby smiled at her in the mirror. "You don't need any. You're beautiful just the way you are."

Willow and Jamie came rushing into the room.

"Jonathan is here!" Jamie squealed, clapping her hands.

"Whoa!" Willow lightly touched a sleeve of soft fabric on Gwen's dress. "You sure look pretty."

"Thank you," Gwen said, trying to smile confidently. She placed her hand across her stomach in an attempt to calm her rattled nerves.

Abby turned to the girls. "Go tell him she'll be down in a minute."

They ran out of the room as fast as they had entered.

"There. Perfect," Abby said, making a final adjustment to the hair comb. "Are you ready?"

Gwen twisted her hands in her lap. "As ready as I can be." She took in a series of deep breaths, trying to calm her pounding heart.

Abby looked at her sympathetically. "Why don't you take a minute to compose yourself? Come down when you're ready."

Gwen nodded and released a pent up breath. "Okay."

Abby kissed her on the cheek, went downstairs, and joined Jonathan and Jim, who were waiting in the foyer. Jim had done what was necessary to seem presentable in a suit, though it was obvious from his fidgeting he was uncomfortable. Jonathan, however, had obviously put great thought into his appearance. He radiated confidence, though she could see his hands trembling at his sides.

"You boys look so handsome," Abby said, her eyes welling up. She fussed over Jim's tie, straightening it.

Gwen arrived at the top of the staircase. She stood there quietly, trying to mask her anxiety by fussing with her gloves.

Jim was the first to notice her. He gasped when he saw his sister. He thought she looked beautiful.

Abby glanced over at Jonathan. She couldn't help but smile at his reaction.

Jonathan's jaw hung slack. His eyes were wide saucers, focused solely on Gwen, who seemed to be moving in slow motion as she descended the stairs. He extended his hand and helped her navigate the bottom two steps. He couldn't take his eyes off of her. "You-y-you look good. I mean, pretty. You look very pretty." His high collar suddenly felt too stiff and tight. He tugged at it with one finger, trying to breathe.

"Yeah, who knew there was a girl in there?" Jim said.

Abby nudged him.

Gwen threw her brother a quick sneer and then beamed up at Jonathan. She placed her gloved hand into the crook of his arm. They went out onto the front porch together. Abby followed close, closing the door behind them.

Immediately, Gwen noticed a horse galloping up their long lane. She squinted, tenting her hand over her eyes to identify the rider. "It's Pippa!"

Jesse, riding bareback on one of her large draft horses, noticed Jonathan's horses had been hitched up to her prized Landau carriage. His family's dilapidated wagon was parked out next to the barn. She came to an abrupt stop at the bottom of the porch steps and slid from the lathered horse's back. "Phew," she said. "I thought I was going to miss seeing you off."

Abby stood there for a moment, shocked, and then

hurried down the steps to greet her. "What are you doing here? Are you home for good?"

"No. I have to ride back tonight. But, there was no way I could miss…Gwen," Jesse said, choking back emotion, "you look like a princess." The similarities between her and Abby were truly striking. She reached into her coat pocket, pulled out an oblong velvet box, and removed the lid. "I have something for you."

"Oh, Pippa." Gwen's fingers touched her parted lips. "It's lovely."

Jesse took a thin, silver necklace from the box, slipped it around Gwen's neck, and kissed her cheek. She climbed the remaining two steps and stood beside Jim. For a moment, she felt certain her knees were going to give out. *When did he get so tall?* She glanced down to make sure they were standing on the same step. She almost didn't recognize the young man before her, in his new, double-breasted, black suit.

The changes to him seemed as drastic as the ones to his sister. However, she saw no resemblance to Abby with him as she did with Gwen. The black hair and dark brown eyes her son had were reminiscent of the handsome, good looks of his biological father—Sam Bowman. Jesse's jaw unconsciously clenched, knowing if the two should ever meet, it would be obvious to both of them they were father and son.

Jesse pushed aside the frightening thought and reached into her other pocket. "You're going to have the girls smitten this evening," she said, looking up at him. She dangled a pocket watch before him. "Thought it was time you had one of your own."

Jim ran his thumb over the large J and M initials, which were skillfully and elegantly engraved, on the front cover. He pressed a button and it flipped open. He noted the time, six thirty-three, and pinched it closed. "Thank you. I've always wanted one."

"You're welcome." She watched him struggle with the gold chain for a moment. "Here, let me." She passed the fob through the buttonhole on his red, silk vest and placed the watch securely in his pocket.

Of course, she knew exactly what Jim and Gwen looked like before she left. But, in just the few days she had been gone, coupled with them being all dressed up, both of them appeared older. They really weren't children anymore. They were practically adults.

Jesse finally turned her attention to Jonathan and nodded in appreciation. "I have to say, I couldn't have picked out a better suit myself." Glancing back at the twins and biting back a swell of emotion, she continued. "Well, you best get a move on. You don't want to be late." She put her arm around Abby's waist.

Jonathan helped Gwen maneuver the carriage step. Once she was safely seated, he fell in beside her and closed the door behind them.

Jim climbed up into the driver's seat, met Jesse's eyes, and said, "I still don't understand why I need to go."

Jesse shook her head with a wide grin. "You'll be fine."

Jesse and Abby waved as the carriage rolled away and watched until it turned on to the main road.

"Well," Abby said, "I guess you caught us, didn't you? Gwen felt like Cinderella, so when she asked me yesterday about using the carriage, I couldn't say no. I hope you're not mad."

"Mad? Not even a little. You did good, Ma," she said, clapping Abby on the behind. When Abby gave her the look, she couldn't help but laugh. She knew Abby hated it when she called her that. "So, where are the girls?"

"They're playing Old Maid in the kitchen." She took Jesse by the hand. "Come inside and let me fix you something to eat before you have to leave."

~

Fifteen minutes later, Jim steered the carriage alongside the others parked near the Hawkins' barn. Even from a distance, he could hear the music spilling out through the tall double doors, which were slid wide open since the weather was pleasant. Jim tightened the reins, set the break, and jumped down. He opened the door and held it for Gwen and Jonathan. As soon as their feet were on the ground, Jim stepped up inside, and grabbed the door handle.

Gwen looked over her shoulder. "Aren't you coming?"

Jim reached under his suit coat and pulled out the book he had hidden in the waistband of his pants. "Nope." He waved his copy of *The Adventures of Tom Sawyer* at them. "You two go on." He closed the carriage door, a huge grin on his face, and got comfortable on the leather bench seat.

Jonathan turned away from the carriage and smiled at Gwen, offering her his elbow. She took it gratefully and allowed him to lead the way into the barn. However, no sooner had they walked through the doors than Mr. Hawkins approached them.

"Where's your folks?" he asked Gwen.

"My father's finishing a job in the city."

"That's too bad. I wanted to speak with him." He studied

them for a moment, stroking his chin thoughtfully. "Well, when he gets back, tell him the Fullerton's vineyard is starting to show signs of the infestation."

Gwen knew all about the louse invasion. Phylloxera had been devastating vineyards throughout the area over the past few years. She'd overheard Jesse and Armand talking about how concerned they were that it would destroy everything they'd spent years cultivating. Only recently had they learned that the root-eating lice couldn't thrive in sandy soil. Their vineyard had gone unscathed, whereas others in prime soil had been completely destroyed.

"I'll let him know," she said. The fiddler ran his bow across the strings and took her attention.

"All right," Mr. Hawkins said. "Enough about that. You two go on in and enjoy the evening."

"Thank you, and you too," Gwen said. Jonathan squeezed her hand insistently, so she allowed him to pull her away.

He led her to the area of the barn where the wooden dance floor had been set up. In front of them was a small band, consisting of men playing a banjo, fiddle, accordion, and a guitar. One industrious fellow was blowing a hollow tune across the mouth of a jug, doing his best to keep up with the rhythm of the music. Around the perimeter of the dance floor, small groups of people had gathered. Lost in conversations, many talking loudly to compensate for the blaring music, the room was filled with the cacophony of merriment. Jonathan and Gwen didn't hesitate for a moment in joining other couples on the dance floor.

Jim stayed holed up in the carriage until the daylight had faded away. Once he could no longer make out the words on the page, he reluctantly closed the book and laid it on the seat beside him. Frustrated, he grumbled under his breath and headed toward the barn in search of something to drink.

Jim allowed his gaze to skim over the scene. He noticed Gwen and Jonathan mixed in with the other dancers, oblivious to everything except each other. He rolled his eyes, cringing in mild disgust. It bewildered him how his sister could ever enjoy something so silly. He shook his head and made his way over to a long table against the wall, which was covered with a variety of tantalizing foods.

Jim bypassed the smorgasbord and made a beeline straight for the punchbowl. The first was delicious and went down quickly, so he helped himself to another. Just as he was dipping the ladle, he heard a familiar female voice from behind him. He recognized it instantly—Maggie Hawkins, the feisty redhead he knew from church.

"I saw your sister come in earlier," Maggie said, smiling at him. "But I didn't see you. I figured you weren't coming this year."

Jim poured punch into a cup and offered it to her. "I didn't want to." He shrugged. "But my parents made me."

They were the same age, and Maggie couldn't remember a time when she hadn't had feelings for him. What had started out as mild infatuation had developed into something stronger over the years, at least for her. She took a dainty sip, stalling as she struggled for something clever to say and tried to appear more confident than she felt.

Maggie gazed over her shoulder at the dancing couples and was quick to notice Gwen and Jonathan. She pointed them out to him. "Looks like they're having a good time out there," she said, casting a suggestive glance in his direction.

Jim poured himself another glass and fumbled with the drink, his Adam's apple working nervously.

Before he had a chance to respond, Maggie's older sister, Judith, approached. She scrutinized Jim from head to toe, hungrily eyeballing him like a piece of meat, and then elbowed her way between them without so much as a glance at her sister. "Care to pour me a glass, too?" she asked him, staring into his eyes.

Judith was the gorgeous brunette all of the boys wanted. Maggie had auburn hair and maybe one too many freckles. It was no secret, either, that Judith liked the older boys. Jim was a full two years younger than her. Judith had never once paid him any attention at all until that moment.

Maggie seethed with irritation at her sister's interruption, lips curled into a scowl she was having difficulty hiding.

Jim poured another glass and passed it to Judith, trying not to spill it in the exchange.

Judith let her hand graze his fingers as she took it from him. "So, James McGinnis," she asked, her gaze unwavering. "Do you know how to dance?"

He ran his hand over the back of his head. "I...I never have. So, I really can't say." He paused, watching the other dancers for a moment, and shrugged. "Doesn't look hard."

"It's so easy," Judith said, batting her dark lashes at him. "Especially if you have a good partner. All you have to do is move your feet in time with the music." She took a step closer to him. "You should pick a partner. Give it a try."

Jim knew he was smart when it came to books and figuring things out in his head, but females had always been this awkward and confusing mystery to him. Even so, he found he understood exactly what this other girl was suggesting. At first, he was surprised and a little flattered. All of the boys in the county, himself included, thought Judith was about the prettiest thing they had ever seen. She knew it, too, and wore it like a badge of entitlement whenever a fresh face caught her fancy.

"So you're saying," he said, studying her for a moment, "I should pick someone I think would be my ideal partner?"

"Only the best for you." Judith smiled sweetly.

"I see." He held eye contact with her. "Would you like to dance…" he said, stepping back from Judith and gazing at her sister, "Maggie?" He extended his hand.

Maggie stared at him in disbelief, for a moment unable to understand what had just happened. When it finally dawned on her that he was speaking to her, and not her sister, her whole face brightened. She took his hand without hesitation, and they turned away from Judith without a second glance.

Maggie's heart pounded as though it were going to beat through her chest. How often she had imagined being in his arms, and now, he was going to hold her close during a dance.

"I have no idea how to do this," Jim whispered as they joined in with the others. He held up his palms helplessly.

Maggie whispered back. "Just hold my hands and move your body the way I do."

Either would have sworn that from the second their bodies began to sway, the only music loud enough to dance to was the rhythm of their own heartbeats.

Not thirty seconds later, the slow song ended. The band started another, but it had a much faster tempo. Jim wrinkled up his nose.

Maggie nodded in agreement and mouthed silently, "Want to get out of here?"

Jim nodded back emphatically.

She glanced around and made sure nobody was listening, before whispering into his ear. "Meet me at the back door in a couple of minutes." She pulled away from him and headed in the opposite direction. Making her way toward the back wall of the barn, she watched as he went the other way and became lost in the crowd.

A few minutes later, he appeared by her side. "So, what'd you have in mind?"

Maggie scanned the crowd, looking for her parents. Her mother was busy serving pie to one of their guests at the back tables, laughing at something being said. Her father was harder to find, surrounded by a group of men and heavily engrossed in conversation. Maggie watched them for a moment and then turned to Jim. "Follow me."

They slipped out the back door and disappeared into the dark. A quick glance back proved they were not followed and secure in their escape. They sighed in relief.

Maggie led him toward the back of the yard and stopped underneath the branches of a large tree. He observed her movement as she took hold of a weathered plank and began to climb. He stepped behind her to follow but became flustered when he looked up and caught a glimpse of frilly bloomers. Immediately, he stopped in place and looked down at the ground sheepishly.

Her head appeared through the trap door of a large tree house. "Well, what are you waiting for?"

He snickered, shook his head, and quickly ascended the ladder. Once inside, she secured the door, found a candle, and lit it. She settled herself comfortably on top of a large cushion. Jim crossed over a well-worn rug, which occupied most of the floor, and took a seat next to her underneath a window. Although they were a significant distance from the barn, they could still hear the music.

"So, what do you want to do?" Her eyes twinkled in the candlelight. "Do you want to play a game?"

He crossed his legs. "What sort of game?"

"Do you know how to play chess?"

Jim had loved the game from the moment he had picked up his first chiseled knight. Though he considered himself to be an excellent player, it was easy to downplay his level of skill. He had nothing to gain through bragging. "Yeah, I've played a couple times."

Maggie's hand trembled slightly as she arranged the figures on the board. For the last three years, her crush on him had grown stronger. Ever since he had selected her in a schoolyard pick one day after church, her feelings had only continued to increase. She was used to being overshadowed by her sister. There was no way he could have ever known that being chosen by him would mean so much to her. Now there he was, sitting right beside her, and there was no one around, including Judith, to bother them.

"Your move," she said.

He slid his pawn. They played in silence, contemplating each other's moves suspiciously. One after another, they darted around the board, capturing each other's pieces.

At last, she said, "Checkmate!"

Though he'd had the opportunity to declare the same thing several times, he had deliberately chosen not to. As a result, the game had been significantly prolonged.

He smiled and started gathering his pieces. "Well played. Want to play again?"

She shook her head. "No, not really. How 'bout we talk, instead?"

"Okay." He leaned his back against the wall and stretched out his legs in front of him. "So, what do you want to talk about?"

"Tell me about you." She pushed the game out of the way and lay on her side, resting her head on a pillow.

"Me?" His dark eyes flitted over her face, memorizing every inch of her. "There's nothing really to tell. I'm not very interesting."

"I'll be the judge of that," she said primly. "So, what do you want to do for a living? You gonna work on your family's vineyard? Or do you wanna do carpentry work like your father?"

"Neither." He didn't hesitate. "I'm going to Harvard."

"Harvard?" Her brow furrowed. "Where's that?"

"Cambridge, Massachusetts," he said, eyes gleaming.

She chewed on her bottom lip. "You're going to find work there?"

"No. Actually, it's a college. A big one."

"Oh, so what are you hoping to learn there that you can't learn here in California?"

"They have the best dental school there." He rolled onto his back beside her. "I really want to be a dentist." He pillowed his head on his arm and faced her.

"A dentist?" Maggie rolled the idea around in her mind. "Mouths and teeth?"

"Yep. So what are your plans?"

Maggie scoffed, shaking off the notion. "Besides being a wife and mother, I don't have many options. So, there's your answer."

Although he had never heard of one, he said confidently, "I'm sure there are plenty of schools girls can go to."

"Oh, so you think I could go to Harvard then?" she asked, an edge of sarcasm in her voice.

"Uh…no—but I'm sure there has to be one for females, right?"

She rolled flat onto her back and didn't answer. She stared at the knotty pine ceiling. "I know your folks. I can't believe they're going to let you travel across the country."

"They're going with me to get me settled in." He thought about Jesse and laughed. "I think my father's more excited than I am. He's always wanted to ride on a train."

Maggie faced him again. "How long will you be gone?" Her sadness was obvious in her tone.

"A few years. But I'll come back on holidays and for visits whenever I can."

"Will you visit me?"

Jim shrugged. "I guess it depends."

"Depends on what, exactly?"

"Depends if you're married, for one. I can't think your husband would take kindly to a man making regular visits with his wife. I know if I was lucky enough to be your husband, I wouldn't like it if some man thought he could come calling on you."

Maggie felt her heart skip. "James McGinnis," she said through numb lips. "Now you be honest. Do you have feelings for me?"

"Uh…that's not what I meant."

"Well…I like you." She placed her hand on his cheek. "I have for a long time."

Jim's heartbeat thrummed in his ears, deafening. Yes, he

liked her. Whether or not he could admit it out loud was another thing entirely. He had no idea what he was supposed to say or do.

Maggie lowered her hand. "Do you want to kiss me?"

His mouth was very dry and his tongue felt enormously heavy. He wished for another glass of punch. He gulped and nodded.

"You can," she said, looking up through her lashes, "if you want to."

Gathering his courage, Jim leaned over and gave her a quick peck on the cheek.

Maggie giggled. "I'm not your mother or sister. Like this." Puckering her lips, she pressed a brief smooch firmly against his mouth. She leaned back to observe him and giggled again, despite herself, at the dazed expression on his face.

With his lips still pursed, he slowly opened his eyes and allowed his mouth to transform into a wide grin. Nowhere in sight was the well-read, overachieving young man who longed only to go to college. Now, there was only a young boy in way over his head.

Maggie squared her shoulders. "Now," she said, craning her neck toward him. "You kiss me."

Jim released a long breath and took in another, deeper one. He closed his eyes, leaned forward, and hoped he wouldn't miss. As soon as she felt his lips brush against hers, her hands laced around the back of his neck and pulled him close. In one awkward move, he crashed down on top of her. Trying to slow his fall, and failing miserably, he winced as he felt their teeth clack together.

"Are you okay?" he asked. "I'm sorry!"

Maggie ran her tongue over her lips and teeth. Everything

seemed fine. She laughed. "If you're gonna be kissing girls like that," she said, "well, let's just say you'll probably make lots of money being a dentist." She reached out and took hold of his hand. "Let's try it again."

This time, when their lips met, Maggie snaked her arm up his back. She could feel his muscles tense at her touch. She accredited it to the fact he was nervous; well, so was she. Using her tongue, she teased open his lips. His entire body went rigid and he rolled off of her, gasping for air as he fought to catch his breath.

Seeing him struggling, she was overwhelmed with panic. "I'll go get help," she said, jumping to her feet.

He reached up, grabbed her arm, and held up a finger. Slowly she sat back down beside him, holding his head in her lap as he continued to gasp for air.

After a couple of minutes, his breathing gradually returned to normal.

"You scared me half to death!" Maggie smoothed back his hair. "What happened? Are you okay?"

"I didn't mean to scare you." He took in another deep breath. It was easier that time. "I'm okay. I had the fever when I was a kid. Sometimes I have trouble breathing." He felt humiliated. She had witnessed one of the few things that truly made him feel weak. Embarrassed, all he wanted was to get out of there. He knew how frail he must look to her, completely unworthy of her affection.

It was only then, in the heavy moment of silence, they became aware the music had stopped. "It sounds like the dance is over," he said, almost eagerly. "I should probably get going anyway."

"Let me go first," she said, blowing out the candle. "Make

sure no one is around." She opened up the door and descended the ladder. Glancing around furtively, she called up quietly, "C'mon down." She watched him climb the planks. "Hey," she said when he dropped to the ground beside her. "Don't think I do this sort of thing all the time. I've never actually kissed a boy before."

He stared, expressionless.

She finished, in a rush. "I just really like you, and I always have."

He contemplated how to respond to her confession. "I think you're nice," he said, cringing. It was the best he could do, but once again he was humiliated by his lackluster response. He couldn't remember having ever felt this foolish.

Taking their time, they meandered their way around to the front of the barn. Guests were in the process of piling into carriages and buggies. Jim looked over and saw Jonathan and Gwen waiting patiently by theirs. They were smiling and didn't seem at all in a rush to end the evening.

Jim stuffed his hands into his pockets and scooted his foot against the ground. "I guess I'll see you at church next Sunday," he whispered to Maggie.

"We're leaving in the morning. We're going to visit my grandparents in Sacramento for the holiday."

"How long will you be gone?"

"Two weeks."

"I guess I'll see you in two weeks."

She put her hand on his arm and smiled at him. "I'm already looking forward to it."

As soon as they approached the carriage, Gwen tried to make herself appear stern. "Well, it's about time. I thought you walked home, at first, but I knew you'd never leave your book behind." She noticed how Maggie ogled Jim. "And, just what were you two doing?"

"Nothing. Don't you worry about it." He glanced at Maggie. "See ya later." He did his best to wave inconspicuously as she walked away. Turning back to his sister, he said, "Get in so we can go."

"Um, sure," Gwen said with a snicker. "But you might want to get some of the rouge off first, before Ma sees you."

Jim pulled a handkerchief from his pocket, anxiously wiping at his lips. When she laughed uproariously at his attempts, it only made him increase his efforts. "What's so funny? Did I get it all off or not?"

"Oh, Jim," his sister said between peals of laughter. "She wasn't even wearing any!"

CHAPTER NINETEEN

It was Monday evening, five days before Christmas. Jesse was scheduled to return in two days, and Abby was taking full advantage of her absence by working around the clock to finish the wool sweater she planned on giving her. She set the knitting needles aside and gently kneaded her hands.

Jim was stretched out on the sofa beside her, his feet resting against her thigh. She reached back and pulled a woven blanket from behind the sofa. As she draped it across his legs, he glanced up from the book he was reading long enough to give her a grateful smile. When he shifted his focus back to the page, she took a moment to study him.

It was bewildering to her that he could concentrate on what he was reading with the continual stream of piano music drifting down the hall. Had she been more observant, perhaps she would have noticed her son hadn't turned the page in quite some time. However, her mind was heavily distracted with everything she needed to finish before the holiday.

Jim's eyes were staring at the words, but his mind was somewhere else entirely. It had only been a couple of days since the dance. Since then, Maggie had been the only thing he could think about. Something magical had happened to him up in that tree house. The moment their lips met, everything had changed. All of his well thought-out, meticulous plans for the future vanished, wiped away as easily as chalk from a blackboard. Lingering on that kiss was enough to turn his cheeks the same deep crimson as one of his mother's prized roses. One thing he knew for certain was that as soon as he finished at Harvard, he was going to ask Maggie to be his wife.

Abby relaxed against the back of the sofa and let the sound of the piano wash over her. Gwen had been playing all evening. Normally, she wouldn't have had so much uninterrupted time. Since her sister and cousin were having a sleepover with the Baptiste girls, she took full advantage of it and was running through her entire song catalogue.

It was amazing to Abby that she could play so well, especially after the resistance they'd gotten trying to get her to take lessons. It had been nearly impossible to keep her sitting on the bench long enough to teach her anything. She always wanted to be outside. Not surprisingly, it was Jesse who had convinced her to stick with it.

Jim sighed contentedly and Abby looked over at him. A stray section of his bangs had fallen across his forehead. They had done the exact thing ever since he was a baby. He wasn't so little anymore, Abby thought wistfully. Neither of them were. In his suit, Jim had looked every inch like the man he would become someday. When Gwen had come walking down those stairs, Abby had never seen a more beautiful young woman. It was frightening to her to see how fast they were growing up. She was so proud her heart was as warm as the glowing embers in the grate.

Her knitting forgotten for the moment, she glanced around the room, letting her gaze linger on some of the more precious gifts Jesse had given her over the years. She was an excellent provider and worked tirelessly to give them a comfortable life and a beautiful home. Most importantly, Abby and the children knew how much they were loved.

Light from the fire caught on something inside her periphery. Abby turned to gaze at the hand-painted, porcelain vase near the mantel, with the tiny, intricate flowers done in shades of purple. It was her favorite thing in the parlor. She fondly recalled the night Jesse had given it to her, describing in detail the large West Coast Emporium where she had gotten it. It wouldn't be the last gift she got from there. Over the years, it became Jesse's favorite place to shop, as they carried a variety of novel and beautiful items from all around the globe. With a deep sigh of longing, Abby picked up her needles, but something on the Christmas tree caught her eye.

The popcorn garland, which they had strung together as a family, was hanging at a strange angle. Abby set the knitting aside and walked over to the tree. She lifted the strand and placed it back on the branch where it belonged. Satisfied, she returned to the sofa and picked up her knitting just as the grandfather clock in the hall struck ten.

"Well," she said to Jim, stifling a yawn, "I don't know about you, but I'm ready to call it a day."

Snapping his book closed, he pushed the blanket off of his legs, gathered it into a ball, and passed it to his mother. "Goodnight, Ma." He placed a kiss on her cheek.

"Goodnight, son," Abby said with a smile. She gave his hand a small squeeze and watched as he walked from the room.

Abby gathered her knitting garb and carefully placed it into her sewing basket. She made her way down the hall to the den, her ears attuned to the music. She stood silently against the doorframe. Gwen was playing *God Rest Ye Merry Gentlemen*, one of Abby's favorites. When the song ended, she stepped closer and gently placed her hands on Gwen's shoulders.

"I only messed up once this time," she said, tilting her head back and smiling up at her mother.

"I didn't even notice. I'm sure by Christmas Eve it'll be perfect."

Normally, Abby would be the one playing while the rest of the family gathered around the piano. That year, however, Gwen would begin carrying on the tradition. She had been working extra hard to master all of the songs. Every spare moment was spent practicing.

"Do you think Pippa will make it home in time?"

"Of course. There's no way he'd miss it. He told me the other night he underestimated how long it was going to take to install the staircase. He said even if he wasn't finished, he's still coming home."

"I hope so," Gwen said, stretching. "Is it bedtime already?"

"Mm-hmm, it's after ten."

Gwen stood and kissed her mother on the cheek. "Goodnight, Ma."

"Goodnight, sweetheart."

Abby turned down the lights and checked the door locks. After peeking in on both of the kids, she finally made her way down the hallway to her bedroom. Closing the door behind her, she took a seat at her vanity. As she was about to pick up her hairbrush, she caught sight of the large bed in the mirror.

The thought of crawling into it all alone made her miss Jesse even more. It had been five days since they had last slept together.

She stared at her reflection. Her skin was pale and there were dark smudges under her eyes. If she crawled into bed right then, she knew it would only mean another long, miserable night spent tossing and turning. Setting the brush aside, she pushed back from the vanity and went downstairs.

In the kitchen, she busied herself putting away clean dishes, which had been left on the counter to dry. The only sound was rolling thunder growing increasingly louder. As she was putting the final glass up in the cupboard, she heard a noise coming from Jesse's office. A knowing smile came over her face. It wasn't the first time Jim had snuck out of his room in the middle of the night to read in there. She closed the cupboard door and stepped into the hallway. With her ear pressed to the door of the office, she strained to make out any other sounds.

It crossed her mind how Jesse always got a kick out of startling the children, jumping out with a shout, and then everyone would laugh. Now, with Jesse on her mind, she couldn't resist the temptation. Snickering to herself, she turned the knob and quickly pushed open the door.

"Ah-ha!" She yelled, leaping into the room. "And just what do you think—?"

Abby was halfway across the room before she realized it wasn't Jim. There was a total stranger sitting in Jesse's chair. His feet were propped up on the desk, most of his face lost in the shadow underneath the brim of his hat. His hand was a tight fist clenched around a glass of whiskey. Behind him, curtains fluttered from the gentle breeze.

"What are you doing in here?" She hoped her voice sounded outraged and not tremulous. With the children sleeping right above her, there was no way she would let the bastard see her fear. Adrenaline pumped through her as she started to devise a plan, trying to think of a way to protect her children.

The stranger threw back the whiskey and banged the empty glass onto the desktop. He swung his legs to the floor, slowly and methodically. Reaching across the desk, he turned the handle on the kerosene lamp. The room was flooded with light. Despite the brightness, though, most of his face was still obscured, save for his days-old beard.

"If you're looking for my husband—"

The man slammed his fists, causing some of Jesse's belongings to clatter. Hands still balled, he stood and walked around the desk. He stopped a foot in front of her. "You sure have done well for yourself," he said and then spat on the floor. He took hold of one of Abby's curls, letting a strand of her hair play loosely through his fingers.

She jerked her head to one side, flinging her hair behind her back and held her ground. "I don't know who you are, or what you want, but you need to leave—now!"

"In time, my dear. In time. These moments need to be...*savored*."

"Look," Abby said, taking a step backward as he moved closer. "I don't want any trouble." She glanced at the door, keeping her eyes on him as she edged her way toward it.

He was as fast as a rattlesnake. He struck, grabbing her by the upper arm as he pulled her back. His breath was redolent with whiskey and hot in her face.

"Now, where do ya think you're going?" he asked, his voice

taking a playful and sinister tone. "We have so much catchin' up to do." He pushed up the brim of his hat with his finger, allowing her to get a good look.

With stunned dismay, Abby realized she knew him. His hair had once been as black as midnight, but time had shadowed it with strands of gray. In his youth, he was longer, lean, and trim, but now his potbelly protruded generously over the holster cinched around his waist. It had been more than twenty years since she had last seen him. Though physically, his features had changed significantly, Abby still recognized him.

She looked into his tyrannical, hazel eyes in disbelief. "No," she said. "Silas?" Her legs grew soft and threatened to buckle underneath her.

"And here I thought you'd forgotten all about your husband," he said with a deviant smirk.

She jerked her arm back in an effort to escape the tight grip he had on her, but it only enraged him further. He redoubled his hold on her.

"What do you want?" she asked, trying to fight his grip.

Silas reached into his coat pocket. "Can you imagine my surprise when I got your letter?" He tossed an envelope on the desk.

She recognized it. "Did my father give that to you?"

"Naw," he said, studying her face. "Your old man died a long time ago. Luckily, I've got a friend who works for the post. He gave it to me." He watched her expression closely. "What, no tears for your old man? You really must've hated the son of a bitch."

Abby didn't know how to process the news. Her father was like a total stranger to her. She had mourned him so many years ago, it was nearly impossible to register the loss now. "Why are you here—how?"

Silas shoved her across the room and pushed her down onto the settee. "You mean, how am I alive?" He leaned heavily on the back of the sofa, his face mere inches from hers. "I spent two months in the hospital with no fuckin' idea who I was. Sure, I'd see flashes of you here and there, but I didn't know who you were. Then it all came back to me. Every last detail." His nose pressed against hers and the wood of the settee creaked. He was so close she could almost taste the alcohol on his lips. "I remember how you bashed me in the head—and pushed me in the river." He grabbed her face in his hand. "Do you remember?" He squeezed her cheeks. Her lips pursed and he brought his lips down to hers, giving her a cold smooch.

Abby wanted to scream out and warn the twins. She needed to tell them to run as far and fast as they could. The nagging voice of experience told her to remain silent. Many times similar scenarios had played out in the past, and she knew how volatile he could get. In an effort to keep him from becoming enraged and possibly hurting her children, she thought it best to patronize him. She relaxed her struggle and he stepped back.

"When I woke up," he continued, staring hard into her eyes, "the doctor told me a couple fishermen found my body caught up in some branches near the bank. When they saw I was bleedin', they ferried me down to St. Louis." He rubbed the back of his head and then scratched the hard, needle-like whiskers on his cheek with dirt-caked fingernails. "Once I got my wits back, I left that damn hospital." He spat again. "Course, I didn't have any means to get back to Saint Charles.

I saw a man get off his horse right in front of me and go inside a building, so I stole his horse."

His eyes glinted. "Didn't get a block before I got caught. They hang people for horse stealing. Did you know that?" Then oddly, he snickered in sudden merriment. "Come to find out, there was seventy-five dollars in the man's saddlebag. That money saved my life. Without it, it would have been a simple case of horse theft. I would've been swinging from the end of a rope. But, because of the cash, I was charged with robbery. I did three years of hard labor in the state penitentiary for theft. Do you have any idea what that was like?" He roared in sudden rage and drew back his fist to strike.

Abby flinched.

"Naw," he said, lowering his hand. "You've been livin' the good life. It's alright. Gave me plenty of time to plan what I was going to do to you when I got home." He smiled coldly at her. "Oh, that's right. Imagine my surprise when I finally got home and found some son of a bitch living in my house." His backhand flashed out and connected with her face. "My house!" he screamed, pointing to his chest. "My home!"

"Silas. Please don't—"

He slapped her again, knocking her face against the wood frame of the settee. "Not only that, my faithful wife went and vanished without a trace." He grinned. "Thought I'd never see you again until your letter came."

"Please. I'm begging. Don't—"

He leaned so close she could see the stray, black hairs coiling out of his nose. "The only thing I'm going to do now is take my wife home, with me, where she belongs."

Abby trembled uncontrollably. She clenched her teeth, determined to maintain control over her mounting fear. Her only priority was her children. The sooner she got him away from the house, the safer they would be. "Alright," she said through pressed lips, "let's go home."

"Oh, you bet we will, sweetie," he said, pulling her close. "But first things first. I got an awful itch that needs scratchin'." He kissed her cheek, his whiskers abrasive against her soft skin. "It's been a long time," he whispered in her ear, rubbing his pelvis against her leg.

Abby could feel his intentions poking insistently against her. She shuddered when she felt his grimy hand slide up the smooth skin on her calf. "Don't do this. Not here. Please."

He leaned back, looking deep into her eyes. "The way I see it, you can let this feel really good for you." He sneered. "Or don't. Up to you." He pressed his lips against hers.

His tongue forced its way inside her mouth, tasting like whiskey and old cigars. She wanted to retch. Thinking of her children, asleep in their beds, she fought back the temptation to bite his tongue.

He knelt, forced her legs apart, and pulled her hips toward him. His breath was ragged and excited when he lifted her dress. "Mmm, just the way I remember."

The lust in his eyes made her wish for something to bash him over the head with. Squeezing her eyes shut, she flinched when she felt him kiss her knee. She turned her head in shame as he bit and licked his way higher, his tongue lapping at her skin. Denying the tears straining at her lashes, she allowed him to explore her body with his mouth and fingers.

Suddenly, the full weight of his body fell on top of her. Her eyes flew open.

"Get off of my mother, you bastard!"

Jim had his arm wrapped around Silas in a fierce chokehold, holding tightly as Silas whipped his body in a fight for air. The tendons in Jim's neck stood out and the muscles of his forearm and bicep bulged with effort. Bookworm or not, years of working hard on the farm had made him quite strong.

Silas clawed at the sinewy arm around his throat, trying for the pistol on his hip. Jim felt the arm moving and went for it, catching a grip and sliding it behind the man's back.

Jim dug in his heels and pushed back with all his weight. They flew across the room, stumbling. Jim regained his footing first and threw himself on top of Silas, creating a brick with his fist and pounding it into Silas's face.

"Don't you ever touch my mother again!" Jim yelled, slicing punches as punctuation. "Don't you ever! Don't you *ever!*"

With pure rage, Silas threw everything he had into dislodging the boy. Jim stumbled backward, windmilling his arms to keep his balance. Instead, he hit the floor hard. Silas stood up and found his pistol. The report of the bullet leaving the chamber was deafening in the small room.

"Better luck next time, kid."

"Jim!" Abby screamed in raw anguish. She dropped down beside him, her ears ringing from the loud blast of the gunshot.

Jim stared up at her with wide, terrified eyes. A trail of blood trickled out of the corner of his mouth as he spoke. "I'm scared." His voice gurgled, thick and clotted. "Oh, God, it *hurts*, Ma. It really hurts!"

"You're going to be fine." Abby applied pressure to the wound in his abdomen. Warm crimson blood spilled up and cascaded between her fingers.

"Shut the fuck up!" Silas yelled, yanking her by the arm. "Move!"

Abby jerked her arm free and placed both hands over the wound in a desperate attempt to stop the bleeding. "Stay with me, Jim. You're going to be alright. I promise."

"Dammit!" Silas reached down, lacing his fingers through Abby's scalp. He yanked her up by the hair.

The pain she felt was nothing compared to the agony in her heart.

"I said *move!*" He shoved her out of the room, manhandling her all the way down the hall and dragged her by her hair when she showed signs of slowing.

They got to the front door. As he reached for the lock, Gwen plowed into him from behind, using all of her force to shove him against the wall. He turned, instinctively drawing back his balled-up fist but laughed when he saw it was only a young girl. He palmed her face, shoving her out of the way. "Get out of here and go play with your dollies." She pitched backward and fell, striking her head against the bottom tread of the stairway.

Abby screamed and moved to run to her, but Silas was much quicker. This time he used his fist, landing a blow on the side of Abby's face that sent her crashing to the floor. He picked up her limp body and tossed her casually over his shoulder, carrying her out of the house with no more effort than if she were a sack of potatoes.

Gwen's eyes fluttered open, and she sprang to her feet. Through the open door, she watched the intruder draping her mother over his saddle. She took a step toward the door.

"Ma," Jim said, struggling to speak.

Gwen hesitated, torn. She cast an uncertain glance back over her shoulder.

"Ma? Where are you?"

Gwen looked through the open door again. Her mother dangled lifelessly from the horse as the intruder was mounting without a backward glance at the house.

"Ma," Jim called out again in a weak voice barely above a whisper. "Ma?"

The rider took off. For one split second, Gwen considered charging out after her mother. Something about Jim's cries, though, let her know he needed her more. She raced down the hall to the office, skidded to a halt, and dropped down beside him. "Oh, Jim!" She cradled his head in her lap and placed her hands against the wound. No matter how hard she pressed, however, blood kept gurgling out of the hole.

"Gwen," he said, raising a shaking hand to wipe at his stained lips. "Is Ma alright?"

"She's fine, Jim," she said, the lie rolling unbidden off her tongue. "She went to fetch Doc Montgomery. She'll be back soon."

He placed his hand over hers. "You never were a—" He winced. "A good liar."

"I'm not lying." Her trembling chin betrayed her. "Swear it. Help's on the way. You have to hang on. Can you do that for me?"

"Sis," he said, reaching up to touch her cheek. A streak of blood blemished her skin where he caressed her face.

"Yeah?"

"I don't think I'm going to make it."

"Don't say that," she said with a hitching breath. "You're going to be okay."

"Terrible liar," he said with a small smile. Then it disappeared and his expression grew both pained and serious. "I need you to do me a favor. Will you tell Ma and Pippa I love them?" He was having difficulty finding words and his voice was growing so faint it was barely audible.

"No!" Gwen said firmly. She brushed a lock of hair out of his face. "You tell 'em yourself."

"I love you, Sis." Blood trickled from the corner of his mouth. His eyes widened into round circles of surprise. "Hey, it doesn't hurt anymore."

"Oh! That's good. You're going to be—"

Jim's hand fell to the floor.

"Jim?"

Silence.

"Jim? Jim!" She shook him by the shoulders, thumping his body against the floor with her efforts. "Wake up! Wake up this instant!"

His brown eyes stared past her. She bent down and placed her head on his chest. Her vision blurred through her tear-filled eyes. She watched her brother's torso diligently for the gentle rise and fall, listened for the heartbeat she had known since they shared their mother's womb. Twin trails of grief seeped from her eyes and coursed down her cheeks when she was finally able to lift her head. She wiped her face on the sleeve of her nightgown and rose unsteadily to her feet.

She ran down the hall and out onto the front porch. With a sinking heart, she stared at the empty lawn. There was no sign of her mother. She knew she needed to get help as soon as possible. Bunching up her nightdress around her knees, she took off on her bare feet, running to the barn as fast as her legs would carry her.

Yanking Gypsy's bridle from the hook by the stall, her bloodstained hands trembled as she rushed to slip the bit into his mouth. Wasting no time with a saddle, she tore out of the barn, spurring the horse along in the darkness.

In a matter of minutes, she was at the Baptiste home. She flung the horse's reins over the hitching post and leapt over the steps to get to their porch. "Celia! Celia! Help!" She beat her fists against the wood door. "Celia! Help, please, help!"

The door flung open within seconds. A wide-eyed Celia stood at the threshold. "Gwen? What is it? Wha—" A bolt of lightning flashed and gave her a clear view of the girl in front of her. "Oh my God, Gwen!" Her hand flew to her mouth at the sight of all the blood. She reached out immediately, grabbed hold of Gwen, and pulled her inside. After closing the door behind them and making sure it was securely latched, Celia guided her over to a chair at the kitchen table. She turned up the wick on the lantern and took both of Gwen's hands into her own. Her eyes swept over the girl, taking in her bloodstained gown and the streaks on her face. "Are you hurt? What happened? Talk to me."

Willow, Jamie, Armande, and Claire all stood nearby. The shock of what was going on made them too afraid to move, and so they huddled together in a cluster. Outside, there was a loud grumble of thunder. The younger girls jumped and squealed.

Gwen's words came out in a broken rush. "A m-m-man was in our h-h-house. He took Ma." She buried her face in her hands, fresh tears beginning to flow. The reality of the situation was dawning on her, and her body felt cold and numb. "Jim's dead!"

There was a stunned silence and then the room erupted in

wails. Willow and Jamie collapsed against each other, their grief haunting the room with sorrow.

"Did you hear where the man was taking your ma?" Celia asked.

"No." Her normally blue eyes were red-rimmed and like ice, the irises the color of impending storm clouds. Gwen's gaze was drawn to her blood-covered hands resting limply in her lap.

"Was he alone?"

"I th-think so," Gwen said with an uncertain shrug.

Celia placed her hands on Gwen's shoulders. "I'm going for help. I need you to stay here."

Gwen found Celia's gaze and nodded in agreement.

As Celia hurried into her bedroom to dress, Willow and Jamie rushed to Gwen's side. The three of them pressed together, sobbing tears of grief only they could understand, while their two young neighbors looked on helplessly.

At the door, Celia put on her boots and coat. She looked over at the group of terrified girls. The storm was getting stronger and she had to raise her voice to be heard over the sound of rain hitting the metal roof. "Lock this door behind me when I leave. Don't let anyone in. I mean it. No one."

With their horses in San Francisco with Armand, Celia had no choice but to take Gypsy. After freeing his reins from the post, she led him over to the porch and used the steps to mount. She was soaked instantly, and the cold was miserable. Still, she rode on with her head down, pushing on through the torrent of rain to reach the sheriff.

She found him at home, playing cards with his cousin, Doc Montgomery. Celia quickly explained the dire situation, and they followed her back to the McGinnis house.

As soon as they arrived, the sheriff started his investigation, searching the property for any sign of the intruder or clues he might have left behind.

Celia, meanwhile, followed the doctor up the porch steps. She nearly fainted when she reached the doorway of Jesse's office. Seeing Jim's lifeless body was more than she could bear. With her hand covering her mouth, she watched as Doc Montgomery knelt down beside Jim.

The large pool of blood told him everything he needed to know, but still, he placed his fingers on the side of Jim's neck and waited. "He's gone," he said after a long moment. "Nothing I can do."

Celia felt her knees buckle, and she reached out to the wall for support. The room swam before her eyes, and she blinked, clearing her vision.

He stood and made his way over to the window where a gust of wind caused the curtains to flap wildly. Avoiding the water on the floor, he reached up and closed it. Next, he went over to the wall clock and opened the glass cover. Stopping the hands at twelve twenty-two, he paused for a moment out of respect, and then turned back to Celia. Resting a consoling hand on her shoulder, he said, "I'm so sorry. I wish there was something I could've done."

The sheriff entered through the kitchen door, his muddy boot prints trailing him as he walked toward them. "Damn rain!" he said, shaking off the water.

"The man must've come through the window because it was open when we came in. Did you find anything outside?" Doc Montgomery asked.

"Nothin'. If there were any tracks, the rain's washed 'em away." He looked to Celia. "Did Miss Gwen know the man?"

"I don't think so."

"I'll need to speak with her to find out what happened," the sheriff said. "And we need to find Jesse, let him know what happened. Your husband's with him, right? Do you know where they are?"

"They're in San Francisco. Doing a job for a Mr. Davenport."

"I'll head to the city and see if I can find them." The sheriff glanced down and noticed a book lying on the floor. He walked over and picked it up. "Odd," he said, turning it over in his hand.

"I'm sure it was Jim's," Celia said. "Abby was always getting on him for getting up and having his nose in a book all night."

"I wonder," the sheriff said, worrying the brim of his hat, "if maybe he got up to read and accidently crossed paths with him." He set the book down on the corner of the desk and turned his attention back to Celia.

She gasped. "Abby! What about Abby?"

"I'll gather up some men. We'll search up and down every road if that's what it takes to find her."

The doctor turned to his cousin. "I'll go to the city and track down Jesse. That way you can start searching for her. Oh, and I'll stop by Emery's and get him out here before I head out." He looked sympathetically at Celia and said, "Listen, there's nothing more you can do here. Why don't you go on home? I'm sure Miss Gwen needs you now."

Celia swiped at her eyes. "Oh, that poor child," she said, sniffling.

Doc Montgomery picked up his black bag. "I can swing by and give her something to help her sleep tonight."

Celia sniffled again and nodded. Then, her eyes went wide

with a promising thought. "Gwen is a talented artist," she said. "I bet she could sketch the man for you."

"That would be helpful," the sheriff said, nodding at her suggestion.

"I'll go up and get her things," she said, turning toward the stairs.

Glancing around the room, Celia spotted a sketchbook and charcoal pencils atop Gwen's bureau next to a carved wooden box. She was certain Jesse had made it for her. It dawned on her. If she could feel her own anguish building like a dam ready to burst, she could only imagine how Jesse was going to react to the news.

CHAPTER TWENTY

A loud clap of thunder rolled overhead and shook the ground. Abby's eyelids fluttered open. As she slowly regained consciousness, the first thing she noticed was the canvas of the tent stretched out in front of her. It was being battered by the rain, which was now coming down in sheets. The ground beneath her was cold and hard. The rocks and clumps of earth bit painfully into her hip and shoulder. Panic clawed at her when she realized her hands were tied with a thick rope. Her feet felt heavy and when she tried to move them, she could hear a chain rattling. With ankles fettered in iron shackles, even if she could free her hands, there was no way she would be able to run.

No sooner had she strung all these facts together than she remembered her children. A stream of ghastly images raced through her mind as her memory fought to recall the horrible night—Jim bleeding and gasping for air—Gwen lying motionless on the floor. A wounded sound escaped her, guttural noises even the howling wind could not mask. Tears flowed unrelenting from the corners of her eyes. *Please, God, let them be alright*, she silently pleaded.

Silas pushed through the flap of the tent and let it fall shut behind him. Shaking off the rain, he removed his hat and coat and tossed them onto the horse tack laying in the corner. Reaching over, he turned up the wick on the lantern hanging from one of the tent posts. Silently, he stared at her. After a moment, he knelt down beside her. "You're still so beautiful," he said, tenderly brushing strands of hair away from her face. His fingertips lingered on her cheek.

"Don't touch me!" She jerked her head away from him. That's when she noticed the freshly cut tree in the center of the shelter.

The remaining stump was roughly a foot and a half in diameter. It was easily three feet tall and had a hole drilled through its center close to the base. All around her, there were remnants of wood chips and sawdust. He had deliberately chopped down a tree and set up his tent over it, that much was obvious, but for what she hadn't a clue.

Every inch of her body hurt. The process of opening her mouth and speaking was excruciating. Her jaw felt as though it had been dislocated. When Silas had landed his blow, she vaguely remembered feeling a dull pop. Filled with rage and seeing red, she knew no amount of pain would be enough to stop her from killing him if she got the chance. Should the opportunity present itself, she would take it and do the job right this time. She struggled against the bindings around her wrists. All she wanted was to free her hands, wrap them around his neck, and squeeze until she could feel the life drain from his body.

"I can see you're going to be a handful," he said with a chuckle.

Blinking away her tears, still trying to loosen the rope, she focused on her surroundings. There had to be some way out of this hell. In one corner, there was a surplus of canned goods. Some were unopened, while others had been cleaned out and tossed in a pile. In the opposite corner, his tack, saddlebags, and a hand drill had been discarded. The ground around them had been firmly tamped down and the space carried a certain lived-in odor. It was easy to conclude he had been holed up there for some time. Since she had been unconscious, there was no way to know how far away from her home they had traveled.

In the past, Abby had learned to kowtow to him. She was always too frightened to face his wrath, knowing all too well talking back would leave her black and blue or with a busted lip. She had changed since then. There were things she had learned which had taught her how to face her fear and to stay strong during a crisis. Now, she wasn't anything like the scared, naive girl she had been back when they were married.

She met his gaze with bloodlust, the fury of her stare rivaling the wrath of the storm outside. "I'm going to kill you."

"Yeah." Silas blew out a breath like flatus that rattled his lips and sprayed tiny drops of saliva. "Sure you are." He reached behind himself and pulled out the knife he had tucked beneath his belt. "You've tried that before," he said, pointing the tip of the blade at her. "Remember?" He pierced a can with the knife and continued cutting along the rim until he was able to pry back the lid.

Abby found her eyes drawn to the knife. She recognized it

instantly. It was the one she had given Jesse on her twenty-first birthday. It was usually kept in the top drawer of the desk.

"Hand to God," she said calmly. "I won't fail next time." The ground thrummed with thunder, but her gaze was unfaltering.

Silas scooped out some beans, ignoring her threat, and asked, "You hungry?" He held out the can, offering it in her direction.

She glared at him, refusing to answer.

He shrugged and noisily slurped the beans off the blade, and went back into the can for more. "Suit yourself." He licked juice from his hand and addressed her with a flick of his knife. "So, the way I see it, you owe me."

Her eyes narrowed. "Owe you for what?"

"When you up an' left, the house was considered abandoned and auctioned off. I sure as hell didn't get one red cent. So, how much money you got tucked away in that fancy house of yours?"

The first thing flashing through her mind was the gold hidden in her and Jesse's bedroom. Several years ago, Jesse had come to the conclusion that paying a monthly fee for safety deposit boxes was a waste of money. Just as Frieda had done, Jesse fashioned a place underneath the planks beneath their bed. The secret cubby blended in seamlessly with the other floorboards.

She scowled and her cobalt eyes flashed him with righteous anger. "I wouldn't give you a penny if my life depended on it."

He gave her a slow and sinister smile. "Well, I guess I can go over to the house and ask that girl of yours. What'd you call her…Gwen? She sure is sweet. I'm bettin' we could find plenty of things to talk about." His smile widened to expose his stained, yellow teeth. "One way or another, I'm not leaving here without my money."

His words set her pulse racing. Now he was threatening Gwen. Suddenly, it dawned on her what he had said. If he was thinking of going to the house and talking to Gwen, they couldn't have traveled far from her home. With an icy chill, she now understood her daughter was in danger. Silas was planning on going back to her house.

The children were vulnerable and it filled her heart with dread. She knew their lives depended on her. Silas would turn the house upside down, looking for anything of value and hurting anyone who stood in his way. She needed to escape, somehow. Keeping her family safe was her only priority.

As calmly as she could manage, she said, "We keep money in the desk in the office."

He took another sloppy bite, the juice already congealing in his beard, and pointed the knife at her. "Bullshit! Don't lie to me. I already looked there."

Even though she knew Jesse was supposed to return home soon, she chose to lie. "There will be when my husband gets home in a week."

She hoped she was a convincing liar. If her plan worked, it could buy her the time she needed to find a way to get loose and run home to warn them. Come hell or high water, she'd find a way to escape within the next day or two. Considering her options, she knew if it came down to it, she was willing to die in order to save her family.

"He always puts it in the top drawer of his desk when he gets home. Hides it near the back."

"Really," he said, his knife of beans momentarily forgotten. "How much?"

"A thousand." She thought for a second and then shrugged. "Maybe two."

"I'm listenin'."

She thought quickly. "While they're sleeping, you can sneak in and get it. After you get your money, you can leave. I won't tell anyone I know you."

"Leave. I'm not going anywhere without you, darlin'." He locked a steely gaze on her. "And don't call him your husband!" He pointed the knife at his chest. "Dammit, woman, I'm your fuckin' husband! Way I see it—and the law sees it, that marriage you think you have is nothin' but a sham." He reached into his vest pocket and pulled out a ring. He rolled it along his fingers and held it up to the light. "So, I guess you won't be needin' this anymore." He shoved it back into his pocket and took another bite.

Abby let out a small gasp as she recognized her ring. He must have taken it off of her when she was unconscious. It was the Fede wedding ring Jesse had given her. In all the turmoil, she hadn't noticed it wasn't on her finger anymore. She was more than a little upset she hadn't noticed it sooner. Her head shot up. "Jesse is more of a man than you could ever hope to be."

Silas backhanded her, the blow landing across her mouth. The sound was quite loud despite the rain. "I don't know why you always make me do it. You know better than to talk to me like that." His eyes flashed maliciously. "Seems like you've forgotten your manners."

Three years of marriage to him had taught her how to deal with his moods. Not much had changed. He was still as easy to read as shifting weather patterns. However, Abby knew she was in no position to fight back at the moment. It was probably best to bide her time until an opportunity presented itself. She eased herself down onto the ground and curled up on her side. The iron shackles clinked when she pulled her knees up to her chest. Behind her, she could hear him gulping down beans as if it were merely another day. The sounds of him eating were repulsive and disturbing.

As soon as he had scraped the last bean into his mouth, he lobbed the can over in the corner with the others. He stretched his arms up over his head and yawned deeply. "Oh, I'm gonna sleep good tonight. Full belly and a warm woman."

When she felt him curl up behind her, she feigned sleep. Her heart contracted and she had to fight against the strangled cry rising in her chest. Throughout the night, her mind replayed the recent events in a brutal back and forth battle. She fought between coming to terms with what had transpired at the house against trying to find the optimal solution of escape. As her mind fretted and raced, she unconsciously rubbed the bare spot where her wedding ring should be until sleep finally took her.

A short time later, Abby woke to find herself covered with a blanket. A heavy arm was draped familiarly across her waist. For one split second, she entertained the thought she was back at home, with Jesse beside her, and everything had been nothing more than a horrible nightmare. When she opened her eyes and saw the filthy canvas, her heart dropped. It was all real. Carefully, she lifted the weighted arm to try to slide out from underneath Silas.

No sooner had she started to move than he stirred and

rolled into her, pulling her body closer to him. He breathed in deep, inhaling her hair. "Damn you smell good." He grabbed her hips, grinded up against her backside, and pressed in tightly. "Miss that?"

"I have to do the necessary," she said, wrestling loose from his grasp. "Would you please untie me and take these things off so I can go?" Her breath clouded the early morning air, and she shivered.

"I'll undo your hands." He pointed to the iron restraints. "But not those. And don't think for a second I'm lettin' you out of my sight." Reaching down, he pulled her up by the rope and worked quickly to untie it.

Abby entertained the thought of lunging at him, but with her feet shackled there wasn't much she could do.

Silas grabbed her forcibly by the arm. "Don't try anything." He wrenched her arm and yanked her close. His face was only inches from hers and he enunciated every word. "I mean it. Don't try me."

"Alright!" she said, wincing from his tight grip. "I won't."

He stepped into his boots, picked up his pistol, and pushed her through the opening ahead of him.

The early morning sky was beginning to change from charcoal to smoky gray. She exited the tent, stretching out her aching muscles. Her body was already covered in gooseflesh. She shuffle-stepped as best as she could in the hobbling chains. The rough iron scraped at her ankles, clicking at the bone with every step. Mud squished up between her toes, cold and unpleasant, as he escorted her to the nearest tree.

She turned, lifted her dress, and squatted. Her eyes darted feverishly, scanning the landscape for anything familiar in the scant morning light. Several yards away, she spotted what appeared to be an ordinary old stump. To her, however, it was so much more; it was a bright shining beacon of hope. Several years earlier, that stump had been left behind from a fir they had harvested for Christmas. Memories from that day stood out in her mind as she stared at it. She could remember how Jesse and Toby had tried hard to convince her to pick one closer to home. Stubborn as always and unwilling to budge in her decision, she had never forgotten the torrent of good-natured harassment as they struggled to maneuver her large evergreen out of the woods. The sight of the decayed stump left no doubt in her mind. She was in her own backyard.

Abby glanced in the opposite direction. Silas's horse was tethered to a rope fashioned between two trees. The grass surrounding it had been well picked over, which solidified to her he had been camped out in their woods for several days. Propped against one of the trees next to his mare, she spotted an axe.

"You know where we are, don't ya?" He watched where her eyes moved and studied her expression.

"No. Why? Should I?"

"You probably think I'm daft," he said with a shrug, "but it's the ones searchin' for ya who really are. They ain't smart enough to look right under their own noses." He chortled. "Hell, I bet they're miles away lookin'." He held up his pistol. "If they do mosey this way, I'll be ready." He extended the gun out in front of him. With one eye closed in a wink, he aimed at an invisible target and pretended to fire.

Abby lowered her dress as she stood. She considered shoving him and making a run for the axe, but knew she wouldn't get far with the six-inch strides the irons allowed. He would catch her easily and be ready for it the next time. If she screamed, they were way too deep in the woods for anyone to hear her. Anything she tried right now might make the situation worse. The time to escape wasn't right. She needed to watch and wait.

Silas took her by the arm and steered her back inside the tent. "Sit your ass down." He guided her until her back rested against the stump. He reached for the rope and fed it through the hole he had drilled through the wood. Tying her hands down at each side, he checked to make sure they were secure and then covered her with a blanket.

"I'll be back soon."

"Where are you going?"

"Just want to make sure no one is following us." He pressed his lips to hers. Lightly, he stroked her bruised cheek with his thumb. "When I get back, we'll pick up where we left off. It'll be like when we first got married."

She lurched away from his touch and the blanket fell away from her shoulders.

"See what happens when you act like a spoiled brat?" He reached for the blanket again, tucking it securely around her bare legs and underneath her muddy feet. "Ya start pissin' 'round while I'm gone, I won't be here to cover ya back up." He draped the blanket over her shoulders. "Gonna get mighty cold in here," he said, cinching on his holster. "If you're smart, you won't move an inch." As he fastened his coat, he looked down on her in disapproval. "You never was very smart though, was ya?" With a shake of his head, he disappeared through the flap in the tent.

A few moments were all Abby could stand before she squirmed, feverishly working the short length of rope back and forth through the stump. After several minutes, it became quite clear to her it was useless to continue. She was a puppet on a string. Whenever she lifted her right hand, the rope slid through the hole, placing her left hand next to the base, and vice versa. There was no way to cut the rope loose. She did discover if she tilted her head down as far as she could, there was enough slack for her fingertips to touch her lips.

Abby felt defeated. She looked around, hoping to find some way to free her bindings. Her eyes landed on the pile of discarded cans in the corner and a plan started to form. If, somehow, she could reach one of the opened cans, she might be able to use the sharp edge of the lid to cut through the rope.

She slid down the stump until she was stretched out on the ground as far as possible and kicked the blanket off of her feet. Using her toes, she tried to grasp hold of one of the can lids. Repeatedly she tried, twisting, turning, and pulling as much as the rope allowed. No matter how hard, or how many ways she tried, the cans were always just out of her reach. At the end of her efforts, the only things she had achieved were bloody wrists from where the rope had dug into them and the loss of warmth from the blanket.

Gwen woke up in Armande and Claire's bedroom. Next to her, laid out on a pallet on the floor, were Jamie and Willow. All of them were still fast asleep. Gwen sat up and rubbed at her tired and dry eyes. Recalling the night before, at first she was convinced it was a figment of her imagination. Seeing where she was and how her body hurt, she realized last night really did happen. She had an overwhelming desire to go home. Quietly, she slipped from the room. Pausing outside of Celia's closed door, she debated on whether or not she should knock. After a moment, she decided it was likely Celia would only try to stop her, so she crept from the Baptiste home without anyone knowing.

The sun was just beginning to peak over the treetops. Only a few fluffy clouds scudded across the sky, but the air was deeply frigid. Gwen walked from one house to the other in her bare feet, the frost making every rock and twig a painful obstacle for her cold heels. Wearing only a thin, flannel nightgown Celia had given her, since hers had been saturated with Jim's blood, she wrapped her arms around herself in an attempt to hold onto what little body heat she had as she trudged forward.

Consumed with conflicting bouts of rage, shame, and remorse, the events of the previous night played over and over in her mind. A part of her died the moment the last breath faded from her brother.

It should have been me, she chanted repeatedly, each piercing step in the direction of her house less forgiving than the last. *It should have been me.*

There was no way for her to know Silas was watching her, well hidden within the tree line at the edge of the pasture. Right across from the house, as she made her way up the porch steps, his eyes narrowed as he studied her. She reminded him of Abby when he first met her.

When Gwen entered the house, she noticed the mirror in the foyer had been covered with a black cloth. There were noises coming from the parlor, so she peeked her head into the room. She was surprised to see Emery Shumaker's wife, Hannah, set to work taking down the Christmas tree.

"What are you doing here?" Gwen asked. "Why are you doing that?"

"Oh! You startled me," Hannah said, placing one of the ornaments from the tree into a crate. "I need to get this room cleared out." She approached Gwen and put a warm, comforting hand on the girl's shoulder. "I'm so sorry for your loss. If there's anything I can do for you, please ask."

Gwen walked over to the tree. "Why do you have to clear out the room?" She ran her fingers over an ornament Jim had made years ago.

"We have to get the space ready for when Emery comes back with Jim."

Celia wasn't at home, still sleeping, like Gwen had thought. Instead, she had arrived hours earlier to tidy up the house. After mopping away the sheriff's muddy boot prints, she finally went into the office. With a deep breath and a strong sense of duty, she dropped to her knees without a word to scrub away at the large bloodstain on the floor. By the time she heard chatter coming from the room down the hall, she had gone through four buckets of water.

Celia dropped the brush and stood, drying her hands on her apron as she walked. She went right over to Gwen and pulled her into an embrace. "How are you doing this morning?" she asked.

Gwen tilted her head toward Hannah. "She's taking down our tree."

"I know. But it has to be done. We're going to need this room for Jim's wake."

"Did they find Ma yet?"

"Not yet, but they're still searching." She squeezed Gwen's hand reassuringly. "They won't stop 'til they find her."

Gwen turned back to the tree. "I want to help." She removed one of the ornaments and placed it in the box.

Celia could see Gwen's body trembling, but it was difficult to tell whether it was from fear, shock, cold, or a combination of the three. She glanced down at Gwen's muddy, bare feet. "Let's get you warm and cleaned up first," she said, guiding Gwen toward the stairs. "I've got water heating on the stove. Why don't you go on and I'll bring it up to you. We can draw you a nice, hot bath."

After Gwen had washed up and put on clean clothes, she and Celia came downstairs to a commotion outside. Celia opened the front door to discover Mr. and Mrs. Tallent standing on the porch. In one hand, Elmyra held the McGinnis Christmas wreath she had just taken off the door. In the other, there was an unsightly black wreath with a single white ribbon dangling from it. Elmyra had made it herself and was fully intent on replacing the McGinnis wreath with her own.

Her husband stood off to one side, a large dish full of his wife's prized ham and potato casserole in his outstretched arms. His expression was both exasperated and apologetic. Behind them, two other wagons were coming down the lane. Word had traveled fast, as either a curse or perk of living in a small town, and the townsfolk were already riding out to offer their condolences. Celia put on her best smile and prepared for the onslaught of well-wishers.

CHAPTER TWENTY-ONE

It was close to ten o'clock in the morning when Doctor Montgomery steered his buggy in front of an ornate, three-story Victorian mansion. He hailed a workman, who was pulling boards from the back of a wagon. "Pardon me. Is this the Davenport residence?"

The man nodded and kept working.

"I'm looking for Mr. McGinnis? Is he around?"

"He was." He shouldered three milled planks of walnut and tilted his head toward the house. "Saw him leave a little while ago. His brother's inside. He could probably tell you when he'll be back."

"Thank you."

The doctor left his buggy and made his way up the walk. The heavy double doors, which were carved from one majestic and very impressive piece of mahogany, were wide open. He stepped inside.

Standing within the regal, high-ceilinged foyer, he scanned the room and spotted Toby hunched over, sanding an area on the handrail near the bottom of the staircase. Doctor Montgomery took in the extraordinary carvings as he approached. Unable to resist, he reached out and ran his hand over the wooden mane of one of the two four-foot-tall seated lions at the base of the stairs. "My God, your brother does exquisite work," he said in absolute astonishment. "I've never seen anything like this. It's incredible."

"Doc," Toby said, with a jerk of his head. "What br-brings you here?" He dropped the sandpaper on the stair tread and extended his palm.

"I'm trying to find your brother," he said, shaking his hand. "Do you know where he is?"

Toby pointed to a scuff on the handrail. "We had a little d-d-damage during transport. Jesse went to go p-pick up some varnish and then make a deposit at the bank. Should be back pretty soon." He arched an eyebrow. "Why? Is something wr-wrong?"

Doc glanced around at the other men. He gestured discreetly. "Is there a place where we can speak privately?"

Toby brushed the dust off his pants, his brow knitted with worry. "We can go in here." He pushed open a set of pocket doors next to the staircase.

The doctor followed behind him. He took in the lavish room as Toby closed the doors. The newly delivered furniture had been covered with white sheets but did not detract at all from the elegance of the room.

"W-what's this all about, Doc?"

"There's no easy way to say this, and I'm sorry to have to be the one to tell you." He cleared his throat and struggled for words. "Last night, Jesse's house was broken into. It got violent. Jim was shot."

"Is he alright?"

The silence was heavy and cold.

Doc couldn't bring himself to say the words. He tried to think of something to say that would dampen the blow, anything which might make the truth less painful to hear. His sorrowful eyes were filled with compassion when all he could do was slowly shake his head.

Toby went as pale as the sheets covering the furniture. His legs buckled, and he collapsed onto the nearest chair. His eyes went wet with tears, and he buried his face in his hands.

The doctor placed a consoling hand on his back. "I'm so sorry for your loss."

Toby's head snapped up. "The girls? Are they—"

"They're fine. Jamie and Willow were spending the night with the Baptiste girls. But, Miss Gwen was in the home." He cleared his throat. "She was with Jim when he passed. She's fine physically. It's her mental state I'm concerned about."

Toby pulled a handkerchief from his pocket. "What about Abby?"

"Here's the thing," Doc said with a deep sigh. "The man who broke in took Mrs. McGinnis. Garland and some of the other men are already out searching for her." He reached into his coat pocket, pulled out a piece of paper, and unfolded it. "Since Miss Gwen is the only one who saw the intruder, we had her do a couple sketches of him. Garland has one, and he's showing it around. Hopefully, someone will recognize him." He handed the paper to Toby. "Have you ever seen this man?"

Toby blew his nose and reached for the drawing. "No," he said after a moment. Never s-s-seen him before."

"I spoke with Emery earlier. He and Hannah were going over to the house to take care of Jim and do what needs done."

The paper in Toby's hand shook when he offered it back to him.

"No. You keep it."

Toby stood on unsteady legs. "I th-think it'd be best if you let me be the one to tell Jesse."

"I understand completely. If I can do anything to help, please don't hesitate to ask." He reached out to shake Toby's hand and cupped it warmly with the other. "Might I offer some advice?"

Toby nodded.

"Don't tell Jesse about Jim yet. Mrs. McGinnis needs her husband more than ever. She should be his only focus right now."

Toby nodded again.

"We had a storm come through last night. It washed away the intruder's tracks." Doc shook his head. "Listen, my cousin's a decent sheriff, but he's in way over his head on this one. So are the men helping him. You know they're only simple crop farmers."

"W-what do you suggest?" His eyes were red with contained emotion.

Doc thought for a moment. "Honestly, if it were me, I'd take the drawing and go hire me a private detective here in the city. I'd hate for Jesse to lose his wife, too. I pray there's still time to save her."

Toby considered what the doctor had said as he followed him down the walk. By the time Doc's buggy had turned at the end of the street, he had decided not to mention anything about Jim to Jesse yet. He turned back toward the house and went in search of Armand to fill him in on everything that had happened.

Not half an hour later, Jesse steered the team of Belgium horses up in front. She was annoyed to see Toby and Armand sitting out next to the street when she knew there was work to be done. Delays meant it would take that much longer for her to get home to her family. She forced her mouth into a hard line. "Did you get it sanded?" When they jumped to their feet, she cracked a smile. She was in too good a mood to let anything get her down.

Toby walked over to the wagon to retrieve the can of varnish. Having already checked out of the hotel earlier that morning, he expected to see their packed bags, but was surprised to find several new packages in the back, as well. He knew then she'd already been to the emporium to pick up gifts for her family. His heart sank at the sight of the book he was certain she had purchased specifically for Jim.

"I think this year, I'm really going to pull off Abby's present," she said. "As soon as we get finished up here, I want to go hire a photographer. I'm going to have him come out to the house and take a family portrait."

Jesse could already see the black and white tintype photograph in her mind. Abby would be sitting in the parlor wearing her favorite dress, with Willow beside her. Jim and Gwen would be standing on either side of their mother, wearing the same outfits they had worn to the dance. She envisioned herself standing behind the twins with her hands resting proudly on their shoulders. It would be, by far, the best gift she had ever gotten Abby.

"Then, I want a photograph with all of us in it." She looked at Toby. "You and Jamie." She turned to Armand. "You, Celia and your girls. What do you two think?"

Jesse noted how Armand hung his head and was unable to look at her.

"Yeah, Jes," Toby said, his voice cracking. "She'll love it." He handed the can of varnish to Armand. "He's g-g-gonna finish up here. I need you to come with me." He climbed up and scooted her over with his hip so that he could be in the driver's seat.

"Can't it wait? Mr. Davenport paid me this morning." She reached into her pocket and pulled out a pair of envelopes. She handed one to him and the other to Armand. Each contained five hundred dollars to pay them for their help. "I promised him I would have it finished by noon." Her eyes twinkled. "Abby isn't expecting me until tomorrow. I want to get home this afternoon and surprise her."

Armand stuffed the envelope in his pocket and managed to swallow his emotions. His face was blank. "You need not worry. I will have it completed before twelve o'clock. You have my word."

Jesse could sense something was amiss. She glanced over at her brother, searching his face for the answer. "Are you sick or somethin'? Your color doesn't look so good."

Toby reached into his pocket and pulled out Gwen's drawing. "You ever seen th-this man before?"

She glanced down at the sketch. "Nope. Why?"

"Doc Montgomery came b-by while you were gone." He swallowed deeply. "This man broke into your house last night. Gwen saw him and drew th-that." He pointed to the charcoal image. "That man took Abby."

For a split second Jesse's breathing stopped, and she reached out and grabbed hold of his arm. "My God, Abby—

what about the kids?" she asked, tightening her grip. "Are th—"

"They're f-fine, and Garland is out s-s-searching for her now." He looked at her thoughtfully and then flicked the reins. "Doc and I think you sh-should hire an experienced lawman. I asked some of th-the guys. Got the address of a fella named Obie McCreary. He used to be a d-detective for the Pinkerton Agency."

Jesse didn't speak as Toby steered the wagon through the winding streets. She already felt the guilt of not being home to protect her family starting to fester, like a raw and open wound.

He stopped in front of a two-story, red brick home. "This is the place."

Jesse jumped down from the seat and flew up the walk, her pulse racing. The staccato of her fist on the door matched the thumping of her heart.

"I'm comin'! I'm comin'!" said a gruff voice from inside the house. A tall, heavyset man with thick sideburns and a generous mustache opened the door. His chin was shaved so clean it nearly shined. "Where's the damn fire?" he asked, casting an annoyed eye at them.

"Are you Mr. McCreary?" Jesse asked in a rush.

"Who's askin'?"

"I'm Jesse McGinnis and this is my brother, Toby." She gestured over her shoulder. "I need your help." She held out Gwen's sketch. "This man took my wife. I want you to find her."

"Now, hold your horses." He studied them for a moment before taking the piece of paper. He looked it over. "Come on in. There's things we need to discuss."

Jesse and Toby followed behind him into a tidy room, which served as his office.

"Please, sit," McCreary said, motioning toward two chairs across from the desk. He took a seat himself and placed the sketch on the desktop. Leaning over it, he studied the drawing more closely. "So, what do you know about this fella?"

"Nothing. Other than he broke into my house last night and took my wife."

He looked up from the paper, leaned back in his chair, and laced his fingers behind his head. He scrutinized the pair of them but didn't speak.

"Do you th-think you can f-f-find them?" Toby asked.

"Well…anyone can be found if you know where to look." He stroked his chin thoughtfully. "Anyone see which direction they headed out of the city?"

"We don't live in San Francisco," Jesse said. "We live in Neva. We were here on a job when it happened. As far as I know, no one knows which way he went."

Toby said, "It also poured there last night."

"Well, that will make it a bit more difficult," McCreary said. "Are you offering a reward? Money can be a good motivator for someone to speak up if they've seen somethin'."

"I'll pay whatever it takes to find her. I need to get home now, so I can go out and look for her."

"No," McCreary said. He picked up his pipe. "You let me do the lookin'. I want you to stay home." He struck a stick match and puffed until the rich smelling tobacco caught. "This man may contact you somehow," he said, chuffing out smoke. "He might be holdin' your wife for ransom. I can arrange to have some wanted posters made up." Clamping down on the pipe, he held the paper loosely in his hands and leaned back in his chair again. "How much you willin' to pay for his capture?"

Jesse had seen numerous outlaw posters plastered throughout the town over the years. Depending on the crime, some of them were hardly worth the effort. There was often a watchful eye out, though, for the posters of extreme interest. "Five thousand," she said, without hesitation.

McCreary lost his balance and nearly toppled from his chair. Quickly, he leaned forward, all four legs of the chair coming down hard on the floor. "You should know," he said, "I require five hundred for my services. Two fifty up front, the rest when I bring him in."

"No problem," she said, standing.

"Wait." The detective held up a finger. "Here's my terms. I get paid the remaining two fifty regardless of whether I bring this man in, or someone beats me to it—even if your wife has perished. Just so there's no confusion, I expect to get the five thousand whether I bring this guy in dead or alive." He looked square at Jesse. "You good with that?"

From the moment she heard him say "wife" and "perished" in the same sentence, Jesse's world had begun spinning. Her legs finally gave out from the hard blow of his brashness, and she plopped back onto the chair. It wasn't a possibility she wanted to consider.

"Yes," Toby said, noting her condition. He locked eyes with the detective. "Just hurry up and f-f-find her. The longer we sit here flapping our lips, th-the farther away they're gettin'."

Obie slid a blank piece of paper across the desk. "Jot down your address."

Jesse took the pencil he offered, but her hand was trembling so badly it was a struggle to write legibly. After sliding the paper back, she reached into her coat pocket. She had already deposited five thousand dollars in the bank, out of the seven thousand Mr. Davenport had paid her. She counted out five hundred dollars from the remaining thousand she had left and slapped it down on his desk. "Bring her back alive and I'll give you a thousand more."

The silence was palpable, and the detective sprang to his feet. "I'll need to gather up my things. I'll be ready within the hour. I need to do some checking around on my way to your house." He reached across the desk and shook her hand. "I'll see you this evening. Who knows? Maybe by then, this fella will have reached out to you."

Jesse and Toby left his home in a hurry. They both remained silent as Toby raced them through the city. Each of them carried the weight of their own heavy thoughts as they obsessed with how to proceed. Jesse was consumed with worry over Abby, while Toby was frenzied with notions on how and when to tell Jesse the truth about Jim.

As soon as they reached the countryside, Toby hurried to steer the wagon to the side of the road. He brought the horses to a sudden stop and clutched his abdomen with one arm. "I'm going to be sick." He groaned and leapt from the wagon, a heave in his throat.

Jesse moved over in the seat and set the brake. She waited patiently, looking in the opposite direction to grant him some privacy. "I know how you feel," she said, jumping down. "I'm sick over it, too. I really feel she's fine, though. I think I would know if she were gone. I'd feel it in my soul."

Toby spat one last time and straightened his back. He wiped his mouth and stared at the ground for answers. He looked up and down the dirt road. There was no one coming in either direction. "Jes," he said. "I have to tell you something."

There was something about his tone that made her blood run cold.

"What is it?"

"I lied to you," he said, bile burning his throat.

"About what?"

"Jim…"

"What about Jim, Toby?" Her mouth felt numb and it was getting difficult to form words. She stared hard at him, her eyes round and terrified. Tears were already forming.

Toby choked on a sob, and tears dripped down his face. His eyes mirrored hers. He had to force the next words out of his mouth. They tasted rancid and offensive. "He was shot last night."

Her eyes were bright and unblinking. "Is he okay?" The lump in her throat made it difficult to swallow.

"Jes," he said softly. Everything around them was perfectly silent, waiting for what he was going to say next. "He died."

She flinched as if someone had doused her with ice water, and her body went limp.

When he saw her start to collapse, he caught her in his arms and guided her gently to the ground. Her wails clawed at his heart and gripped his spine, threatening to snap him in two. It was the most horrific scream he had ever heard, and he knew he would never forget it as long as he lived. He wrapped his arms around his sister and held her tightly until she fell silent.

Jesse looked at him. "Why didn't you tell me sooner?" she asked through gritted teeth. Her eyes flashed out at him.

"You know he was like a son to me. Th-there's nothing we can do to bring him back. But, there's still time to s-save Abby. That's wh-what we need to focus on now."

Jesse felt a new wave of anxiety crash into her. "Oh, God, Toby. If I couldn't feel it in my soul about Jim, what if I'm wrong about Abby?" She felt as though one of her draft horses had kicked her in the stomach.

"Don't think that w-way. There's still hope." He stood up and pulled her to her feet. "Listen. Maybe th-there are still tracks left behind."

"You think so?"

Toby was quick to nod his head. "And I kn-know you are Abby's best chance at finding them."

CHAPTER TWENTY-TWO

As soon as Toby pulled to a stop at the end of their long lane, Jesse jumped down and crouched next to the wagon. The ground all around her was covered in a cross-crossed pattern of well-defined wheel grooves. She traced her fingers over one of the hoof prints preserved in the dried mud. From the impressions peppering the area, it was unclear which, if any, belonged to the intruder.

"I wouldn't know which ones to track." She fought hard against the tears she felt welling up. A bitter sneer crawled across her face and transformed her normally cheerful expression into something dark and sinister. Quivering with rage, she swore revenge on the monster who had killed her son and abducted Abby. Already she was planning his excruciatingly slow and painful death, should they ever come face to face.

"C'mon," Toby said, distracting her thoughts. "Let's get up to th-the house."

Jesse climbed up beside him, the weight of so many unanswered questions crushing down on her shoulders painfully. How was she supposed to walk into their house and not break down? How could anyone expect her to stay there and wait, instead of going out and searching for Abby? Most importantly, what was she supposed to say to her girls?

"I'll see to the horses and be r-right in," Toby said.

Jesse made no effort to reply as she hurried up the steps. She paused briefly, noticing that the Christmas wreath Abby had made for the door was missing. In its place was a ghastly black one encircled with a white ribbon. She took a moment to glance up and down the length of the porch, noting someone had taken down all of the holiday decorations.

It was eerily quiet when she entered. As she hung her hat on the hall tree, she spotted the black crepe covering the mirror. She glanced around, noting the closed doors of the parlor. A question furrowed her brow. The parlor doors were always kept open. A pressure started to form in her chest.

She was visibly startled when she heard a clamor coming from the kitchen. She turned quickly in the direction of the sound.

"Oh, I didn't hear you come in," Celia said as Jesse entered the room.

Jesse stood in the doorway, staring blankly at the copious amount of food, which had been brought over by the members of the community. It was everywhere. There was so much of it that it covered every bit of counter space, as well as the large butcher block. One chair balanced two pies and a loaf of bread precariously.

Celia stood there looking at her, unsure of what to say. "I'm so sorry," was all she could manage.

"Where are the girls?"

"Gwen's up in her room. Willow and Jamie are at my house with Hannah," Celia said, approaching her. She reached out and placed a compassionate hand on Jesse's arm. "Did you go in the parlor?"

"No. Why?"

Celia lowered her voice. "Jim's in there."

Jesse looked up sharply.

"When Emery and Doc carried the coffin in, Gwen saw Jim and became hysterical. Doc had to give her something to calm her down." Celia fiddled with her apron. "Jonathan came by a little while ago. I told him Gwen was resting and it would probably be best if he came back tomorrow. And Emery and Hannah are coming over in the morning to go over all of the arrangements with you."

Jesse nodded.

Celia watched as Jesse slowly turned and made her way back down the hall. She started to follow, but decided to give Jesse some privacy.

Jesse placed her hands on the parlor doors, a scream building at the back of her throat. The muscles in her face tightened as she fought to keep her emotions in check. Taking in a deep breath, she pushed back the doors.

An entire lifetime of experiences couldn't have prepared her for what was on the other side. At first, Jesse couldn't believe it was the same room. Because of the closed shutters and drapes, sunlight was barred from the room. Only several strategically placed candles lit the space, although they did nothing to brighten the gloom. What little furniture still remained had been pushed out of the way to make room for the coffin. It sat atop ordinary sawhorses, which had been covered with a white, silk sheet.

With his arms crossed over his chest, Jim looked like he was tucked away and ready for bed. He was dressed in his finest suit, the one he had worn to the dance. She remembered seeing him in it, thinking fondly of the man he was becoming. Standing there looking at him, a quiver rippled her chin. All she could see now was the man he would never be.

Somehow, she gathered enough courage to make her legs move. Her boots felt as heavy as boulders, and it took conscious effort to walk toward the coffin. She felt herself swaying. Jim looked close enough to sleep that her mind was convinced he would wake up any moment with a smile on his face and an adventure in his heart.

Jesse placed her trembling hand on top of his. It was cold and waxy, but she paid it no mind. "Oh, Jim." She tried to gulp down the grief caught in her throat, but it was thick and felt permanent. She looked up at the ceiling. "Why couldn't it have been me?" She waited for any indication God was listening to her, but there was only silence. "Why would you take him when he was just starting out? How could you take my son?"

Toby came up behind her and wrapped his arm around her shoulders.

Jesse used her fingers to push away her tears. "It's my fault. If I'd have been here, maybe this wouldn't have happened. It should be me laying there—not him."

"Don't. That's not fair to you or Jim. You aren't to blame for this."

Jesse's hand trembled as she reached over and placed it on her son's forehead. She traced her thumb along his brow. Whenever Jim would get to the good part of a book, there was a heavy crease that would form above the bridge of his nose when he concentrated. She smiled in recollection, and then her own heavy crease formed when she realized Jim would never read another book again.

The wave of sadness finally crashed and flooded her emotions. She choked, drowning in her sorrow. "God!" she screamed to the ceiling. "Why?" Unable to stop the flow of hot, stinging tears, she leaned down and kissed Jim's forehead. Her whole body shook with tremors. "My son," she whispered. "My son. I'm so sorry." One of her tears left a trail on his ashen cheek, and she lightly thumbed it away.

Toby pulled up a chair and guided her onto it. He stood over her, rubbing her back in soothing circles while she buried her face into her palms and cried inconsolably.

When she regained some of her composure, he asked, "Where are the girls?"

"Little ones are over at Armand's," she said, voice breaking. "Gwen's upstairs."

"I th-think you should head up and check on her. She needs you now." He patted her back once more and left a comforting hand on her shoulder. "I'll go on over and b-b-bring the girls home."

Jesse took a long, ragged breath and rose to hug her brother. She took one last glance over her shoulder before leaving the room. Toby gave her a look that said he knew all too well the pain she was feeling.

As she climbed the stairs, it was nearly impossible for Jesse to fathom everything that was happening. She couldn't begin to imagine how hard it must be for her girls, especially Gwen, who had been holding her brother when he died.

She found Gwen's bedroom door ajar and gently pushed it open. "Gwen?" The bed was empty. With her mind racing frantically, she rushed down the hall. The door to Jim's room was open. She discovered Gwen, asleep in her brother's bed, clutching one of Jim's shirts tightly in her hand.

Gwen's eyes spasmed restlessly beneath her lids, her mind lost in a nightmare she could never wake up from.

There was a pain in Jesse's throat as she swallowed a strangled cry, and she clamped her lips together to keep from making a sound. She backed slowly from the room and closed the door. Quickly, she hurried to her own room. It felt like there was an ice pick jammed in her heart. The door had barely clicked behind her before she crumpled onto the floor, pulling Abby's robe off of the hook on her way down. It smelled so much like her: the perfume, the herbal hair tonic, and the warm scent of her soft skin.

For the next hour, the tears flowed unhindered. She used Abby's robe to mask the sound of her agonized sobbing. Brain on fire, Jesse was consumed with thoughts of what-ifs and if-onlys. Then, as quick as striking a flame to a match, her emotions shifted. She gritted her teeth and squeezed the robe tighter, wishing it were the throat of the man responsible.

Jesse didn't know who he was, but he had to have been strong to overpower Jim and ride off with Abby. Good sense told her that if she ever did get the chance to confront him, it was likely he would kill her. She didn't care. Death would be a compassionate end to the unbearable pain.

Gwen woke up to peculiar mewling sounds coming from down the hall. She swung her legs over the edge of the bed and sat up. Alarmed, she got up to investigate. Outside her parents' door, she placed her ear on the wood. The sounds she had heard were coming from inside the room, but she didn't recognize who it was.

Softly, Gwen knocked. "Are you alright in there?" she asked.

"Just a minute," Jesse answered, her voice thick with emotion and exhaustion. She leapt up from off the floor. Tossing the robe on the bed, she quickly went over to Abby's vanity to check her reflection in the mirror. Her appearance was disheveled and pallid. She didn't want to add to her daughter's distress. She hurried to dry her eyes, dragging her sleeve across her face, and then combed her fingers through her hair. Releasing a weighted breath, she opened the door.

"Pippa!" Gwen cried out, wrapping her arms around Jesse's waist.

"I'm here now, sweetheart," Jesse said, folding her arms around her. "I'm here."

"Did you find Ma?" Gwen asked right away.

"Not yet," Jesse said, unwrapping Gwen's arms. She took a hand in each of hers. "But everyone is out searching. You know your Ma. She's a fighter." Jesse squeezed Gwen's hands and smiled. "She'll find a way to get back to us."

Gwen's stomach rumbled loudly.

"Have you eaten today?" Jesse asked. Emotions were insignificant when compared to her daughter's well-being.

Her chin quivered obstinately. "I'm not hungry."

Food was the last thing on Jesse's mind as well. For Gwen's benefit, however, she knew she would need to lie. "Well, I sure am," she said. "Your Uncle Toby is bringing the girls home. How 'bout we go wait for them in the kitchen? I'm pretty sure I saw some of Miss Dottie's doughnuts in there."

The bright orange of the setting sun was visible for a moment when Silas pushed through the tent flap. He glanced over at Abby and chuckled spitefully. "I thought I told you not to move."

Her lips were purple, her skin was pale, and she shivered uncontrollably. "Will you please start a fire," she asked through chattering teeth.

"I may have been born at night," Silas said, picking up the blanket, "but it wasn't last night. You know the wind can carry smoke for miles." He shook out the leaves and debris, and then tossed the blanket back over her. "Nice try, though."

"Bastard." She spat at him.

"You best watch your tone, woman," he said. "So, I got some good news. Looks like my money's arrived."

Abby gasped.

"Your place was crawling with people today. Might be another day or two before things quiet down enough so I can get it." He gave her a wry smile. "I guess that gives us more time to catch up." The smile dropped. "For your sake, you best not be lyin'."

Abby had seen Jim's injury. There had been so much blood. She knew it was likely to be a mortal wound. Still, she held onto the smallest glimmer of hope that Jim was going to be fine. It was so dim she could barely see its glow. Leaning forward, her eyes wide, she asked, "Did you see my son? Is he alright?"

Silas thought she was batshit crazy for asking, but he didn't change his expression. Surely, he thought, she had to know there was no way her boy could have survived. The shot had been point blank. He had known from the moment the kid had hit the ground he wasn't ever getting back up again.

While spying on the homestead, Silas had seen the men carry a coffin inside the house, which validated his belief the boy was dead. Although he would have loved nothing more than to give Abby the news personally, and watch her happy world crumble with hopelessness, he did have his limits. The last thing he needed was to be stuck in a confined space with a grieving and hysterical woman.

"I didn't see him," he said, picking up a can. "You hungry?"

Abby turned her head away and pushed out her chin defiantly.

"Suit yourself." He shrugged.

After lighting the lantern, Silas set to work cutting open one of the cans. He scooped some beans onto the knife and held them out to her. When she turned her head again, he lipped the beans off the blade. "You wanna know somethin'?"

Abby showed no interest.

"I got married again," Silas continued, as though she had asked. "She was the sweetest little thing, too, in the beginning. Had just turned seventeen, tightest little body..." He scooped out another bite. "Just thinking about that...mmm." He slurped at the bean juice salaciously. "Anyhow, she bore me two daughters," he said, swallowing. "Can you imagine? Pfft, what's a man gonna do with daughters? They're worthless. Can't even carry on the family name."

Abby was only halfway listening. There had to be some way to escape. With Jesse coming home early, she knew she had to get away. Time wasn't a luxury she had anymore.

An idea came to her. She looked longingly at the beans. "You make those sound so good," she said. "I think I might be hungry after all. Could I have some, please?"

Silas set the can down in front of her. He eyed her suspiciously for a moment before reaching over to untie the rope. "Don't try anything stupid. I mean it."

Abby rubbed her wrists and stretched her arms, grateful to be out of the constrained position. She looked down at the half-eaten can of beans and arched him a questioning brow.

Silas snickered. "Like I'd give you a knife. Use your fingers." He reached for another can and pierced the lid. "Now, where was I?" he said, cutting along the rim. "Oh yeah. So, after we were married, she started to get a mouth on her." He narrowed his eyes at her. "Kind of like you. But, same as I used to do with you, I taught her how to be a proper wife." He pried back the lid and dug in with his knife. "She wasn't like you. She was a slow learner. Real slow."

Abby paused, the beans scooped on her fingers momentarily forgotten, as she thought about the poor girl and the hell she must have gone through. She remembered all too well what it was like being married to him and bit back a reaction. The next bite she swallowed felt like jagged stones, but she forced it down anyway. Her mind was focused on the task at hand.

"The oldest had just turned two." He scratched his cheek with the blade. "And the baby was only a few months old. One day, I came home from work to find my wife sitting under the kitchen table." He scooped up some beans and gulped them down. "She was sittin' there rocking back and forth, back and forth." He mimicked the motions. "I was scratchin' my head and said, 'Woman, what you doing under there,' but she wouldn't say a word." His body came to an abrupt stop. "I found the girls lying in our bed. They were dead."

Abby's heart lurched. She couldn't imagine what he had done to push his wife to her breaking point. She didn't want to imagine it.

"Would you believe the crazy bitch suffocated her own babies?" The knife clanked on the sides of the empty can as he rounded up the last morsels. "I buried 'em in the backyard." He tossed the can into the corner. "You know how much I've always wanted a son. So, we kept trying anyway."

Abby choked down the final bite of beans. Realizing her opportunity had arrived, she discreetly took aim and tossed the empty can. Her heart leapt like a frog when it landed. It was exactly where it needed to be when the time came. Now, all she had to do was wait. She turned her attention back to him. He was so caught up in his story he didn't register what she had done.

"She only got crazier." He put the blade near his head and moved it in circles. "I had to keep her tied up when I was gone so she wouldn't hurt herself." His brow darkened. "But that shit got old real quick." He stared thoughtfully at her. "I never did get my son."

Thank God, Abby thought.

"Anyway, I finally had enough—packed her ass up and took her home to her folks. Haven't seen the crazy bitch since." He leaned closer to Abby. "And I'm a happier man for it." He pointed a finger at her. "I always wondered why my seed never took root in you. Hell, you had me thinkin' it was me. But now I know the truth. You did somethin'."

"What are you talking about?"

"I know you crazy bitches have ways of gettin' rid of babies while they's inside ya. You can be sure of one thing." He cupped his crotch. "When I put my seed in you next time, I'm not letting you out of my sight. I'll keep you tied up the whole nine months if I have to, but you will give me a son!"

Abby's body stiffened. "I'm not giving you anything. I'd rather die than let you touch me."

"Oh, yeah?" He licked his fingers. "You think you're too good for me?" He tossed the can he was holding. It hit the one she had so carefully placed, knocking both of them well out of her reach.

Silas grabbed her hands forcibly and looped the rope around them. Once he had secured her binding, he glared down at her with hateful black eyes. "I'll get you off your high horse, woman," he said, yanking a handful of her hair and twisting it around his fist. "You ain't no better than me." He placed the knife dangerously close to her throat and then, in one quick motion, sliced off the lock of hair.

She stared at him with a look of shock, but he already had another handful.

With short, jerking motions, he used the knife to slice off large fistfuls of her hair, which gathered in a pile at his feet. When he finally stopped, he looked down at her with disgust and kicked the hair aside. "Now you look as ugly as that mouth of yours."

Casually, he stretched out beside her and curled up under the blanket. A quick puff of the lantern and everything went dark.

Jesse got Gwen, Willow, and Jamie tucked in for the night and went downstairs. Pausing outside the closed parlor doors for a moment, she could picture the scene in the room as plain as if she were inside. The window was cracked a couple of inches, along with a cold grate in the fireplace, all in an effort to keep the room temperature low. Toby was in there and she could hear his muffled cries. She purposefully avoided going in.

It was easy for her to understand why Toby had chosen not to go along with the strange custom of displaying the deceased after Aponi died. She knew it wasn't her son in there. It was his body, yes, but she believed wholeheartedly she knew exactly where Jim was now. Frieda had once given her a glimpse at what was on the other side of life. Jesse saw now what a gift it had been. Whether or not there was any truth to it, she didn't know, but it was what she chose to believe—had to believe.

She could see it so clearly in her mind, too. There was Jim, inside the cabin on top of Mount Perish. He was surrounded by her parents, Daniel, Jamie, Aponi, Frieda, Nathaniel, and Patrick. She could think of no better people for him to be embraced by, if she and Abby could no longer be the ones wrapping their arms around him. The belief that he was somewhere with family being loved was the only thing bringing her any shred of solace.

Jesse knocked on the door. When Toby came out into the hallway, she said, "I can't stay here and do nothing. I'm going to go join the search."

"Remember wh-what McCreary said? He wants you here in case the ma-man tries to contact you."

"Toby..."

"No, there are people out there searching for her. Besides, Abby would w-w-want you to be here to make sure Jim gets a proper burial. And what about the girls? They need you here."

Jesse was torn. She wanted to leave but knew her brother

was right. She chose instead to pace the hall, squeezing her eyes shut against each horrible scenario her mind conjured about the hell Abby was surely going through.

It was a quarter past ten and Jesse had all but given up hope the detective would show, when she finally heard a knock on the door. Anticipating news about Abby, she raced to answer it. She flung open the door and saw Obie McCreary. "Did you find her?"

"Not yet and my apologies for being so late," he said.

"Come in," Jesse said, shoulders sagging.

"Do you know how the man got in?"

Jesse nodded and led him down the hall to her office. "We believe," she said, pointing to the window, "that he came in through there."

"Was anything missing or out of sorts?" McCreary glanced around the room.

Jesse pointed to her desk. "I had a knife in the drawer. It's gone."

The detective wandered the space, casting a careful eye for anything that might have gone unnoticed.

"Oh, there was a bottle of whiskey and a glass left on the desk. He must have helped himself, because my wife doesn't drink."

McCreary nodded. "I'm sure he was probably going through your things. Any money missing, or anything else of value?"

"I don't think so. The money we do keep in the house is still here."

After thoroughly inspecting the windowsill, McCreary walked around the desk and took a seat in her chair. He reached inside his coat, pulled out a cigar, and lit it. He tossed the spent match in the ashtray. "Have a seat," he said, motioning.

Jesse eyed him wordlessly as she sat across the desk from him.

"I got a good lead on my way here." McCreary took a drag from his cigar. "I stopped in at the mercantile over in Holling's Gulch."

Jesse knew the town well. It was midway between Neva and San Francisco.

"I showed the sketch to the owner," he said, tapping his ash. "He recognized the fella right away. Told me he'd been in the store within the last week." He took another puff and exhaled. "He purchased some canned goods along with a hand drill, axe, lantern, and some kerosene."

Jesse leaned up on the edge of her seat anxiously. The words tumbled from her mouth. "Did the guy know him, or know where he was from, or where he was headed?"

"Nothing," he said, leaning his elbows onto the desk. "But he did mention he thought the fella was a miner." He shrugged slightly. "It's my professional opinion the man was probably passing through the area, and…well, after seeing your home, I think maybe he saw an opportunity." He shook his head and looked at Jesse. "Listen. I know several mines in the area. I'll check out each one. Show the picture around. Tell anyone who'll listen there's a five thousand dollar reward for his capture." He tapped the ashes again and sat back comfortably in the chair. "That should entice someone to speak up if they happen to see him or know him." He chewed on the end of his cigar.

"It's ten thousand now. The man who has my wife killed my boy." Her voice was calm but vicious, dripping with venom. "I want the son of a bitch hunted like the animal he is."

The detective nearly inhaled the butt when he heard the increase of bounty. McCreary stood up quickly and snuffed out his cigar. "I'll find him—and her. You have my word." He nearly tripped over his own feet eagerly walking toward the door. The ten thousand dollars was practically already in his pocket.

Jesse followed him back down the hall toward the front door. She nearly bumped into Toby when he stepped out into the hall.

The detective looked into the parlor. He saw Jim's body lying in repose and his expression softened. He glanced over at Jesse. "May I?" he asked, gesturing.

Jesse gave a simple nod. Her eyes were trained on the floor as she trailed slightly behind him.

"He was a fine-lookin' young man," McCreary said, placing his hat over his heart. "Very sorry for your loss. I can't imagine." They stood there together while the detective gave a moment of silence. "Rest assured," McCreary said with a new level of determination, "I will find the man who did this and bring him to justice. I won't stop 'til I do." He pressed his hat on as they left the room and then turned to Jesse. "I'll be in touch real soon."

At the foyer, Jesse reached for her coat. "I'm going to go out and look for her."

"No," McCreary said. "You need to stay here. He took your wife for a reason—money. There's a good chance he'll try to contact you soon." He adjusted the brim of his hat and opened the door. "Trust me. I'll find her and bring her home." He turned and walked out into the night.

Jesse stood in the doorway until he was gone and then glanced over at Toby. "It's been a really long day," she said, weariness edging into her voice. "You should go get some sleep."

"That g-goes for you, too," Toby said, hugging her tightly. "Goodnight. I'll be over first thing."

As soon as Jesse closed the door behind him, she realized she had never felt more alone. She was lost but too keyed up to sleep. Like a boat cut loose from its mooring, she wandered from room to room, allowing herself to be guided but avoiding the parlor at all cost. Leaning against the large butcher block in the kitchen, a thought struck her. Curiosity piqued, she hurried to the den and began pulling certain books from the shelves. She placed several under her arm and went to her office, plopping them down on the desk.

Sitting there, flipping through the pages, her agitation gradually increased as she realized she couldn't find the word she was looking for. She opened a cupboard and removed the books from the front, revealing the very expensive bottle of unopened scotch Sam Bowman had given them as a house-warming gift years ago. She pulled it out, poured two fingers of whiskey into a glass, and downed it in one swallow. Refilling the glass absently, she opened another book. Skimming the pages, she still hadn't found what she was looking for and pushed the book aside.

Jesse drained the glass again and eyed the bookshelf in the office. She pulled every book she could think of that might hold the answer and placed it in a pile on the floor. Taking the bottle with her, she sat down, crossed her legs, and continued flipping through pages.

A few hours later, Jesse's green eyes were watery and bloodshot. She twisted her hands through her hair and bit back a scream of frustration as she tossed the last book aside. She had to conclude what she was searching for didn't exist. There wasn't a single word in any of the books she owned to describe what she and Abby were now: parents who had lost a child.

She cursed the fact that she was put in the position to know. She reached for the half-empty bottle of Scotch and brought it to her lips. Taking another large swallow, she hoped, at the least, it might numb some of the pain for a little while.

CHAPTER TWENTY-THREE

Early the next morning, Toby walked the well-beaten path to his sister's home and entered through the back door. Normally, at that time of day, the kitchen would be abuzz with activity and conversation. Breakfast would be well underway, with everyone preparing for their day. Now, the room seemed as stony and silent as a mausoleum.

He turned up the knob on the gas lighting and then hung his coat on a peg next to the door. His boot heels were loud against the tile floor as he made his way through the kitchen and into the hall. He came to an abrupt stop when he reached Jesse's office.

The room was a complete mess. All of the cabinet doors were open. Things that were usually neatly arranged on the desk were now either on their sides or had been knocked carelessly to the floor. The books, normally lining the shelves in orderly rows, lay scattered about the room. Passed out in the center of the chaos, in the exact spot where Jim had taken his last breath, was Jesse. She was sleeping next to a small pool of vomit. In one hand she clutched an empty liquor bottle like a lifeline.

Toby weaved his way through the mess and knelt down beside her. "Jes," he said softly, lightly tapping her shoulder. "Wake up." He shook her a little harder.

Jesse groaned, released her grip on the bottle, and drew her knees up to her chest.

"Hey," Toby said a little louder. He took her by the arms and pulled her into a sitting position. "It's t-time to get up. Come on."

Jesse sat slumped with her eyes closed, her head hanging like a wilted plant. She pressed her palms against her temples. "Alright," she said finally, her voice gravelly. She licked her lips. They felt rough when her tongue slid over them, like a cheese grater. "I'm...I'm up." Slowly, she opened her swollen and bloodshot eyes. After blinking several times, her vision finally cleared.

Jesse focused on the mess surrounding her. Glancing down the front of her shirt, she realized she had gotten sick during the night. She wiped her mouth with the back of her hand and tried to swallow, but there was no saliva. A horrible taste lingered on her tongue. She grimaced, disgusted.

The room was still spinning and her head felt like it was too heavy to hold up. She pointed at the books scattered all around her and then looked up at him. "Ya know we...we're orphans," she said, slurring slightly, "'cause we lost our parents. You're a widower 'cause you lost Aponi." She shrugged help-lessly. "But wha...whaddya call us? Parents who have lost a child. There's not a word. I know, because I looked." She blinked at him and held up her hands incredulously. "Why's that, ya spose?"

Toby bent down and draped her arm across his shoulders. He helped her to get to her feet and stood there patiently while she gathered her balance. "I don't know th-the ans—"

"I do!" Jesse let her gaze fall on the book at her feet. "There's no word because..." She used her bare foot to kick the book across the room. "Because it's so God-awful no one has ever been able to come up with one that can even begin to describe how h-horrible it is! That's why!" She started to fall.

Toby struggled to keep her upright, using his hip to support the bulk of her weight.

After hearing all the commotion, Gwen had come downstairs, then stood watching silently from the doorway. Eyes lowered to the floor, she hugged herself tightly, one lone tear slipping down her cheek. Her arms were no protection against the raw emotion in her father's voice, and she felt it pierce her heart like an arrow.

Toby caught sight of Gwen standing there and cleared his throat.

Jesse raised her head and saw her daughter. "I'm sorry. Oh God, I'm so sorry. It's all my fault. It sh-should've been me."

"Pippa, don't say that!" Gwen rushed over and draped an arm around Jesse's waist. "It's not your fault. Nothing about this is your fault."

"We're going upstairs," Toby said to Gwen. "Would you please heat up some wa-water for a bath and put on some coffee." He stopped at the threshold. "Ma-ma-make it strong. Then straighten up in here the best you can." Toby hefted Jesse to better distribute her weight. "The Shumakers will b-be here in a few hours. I'll be back down to help ya as s-soon as I can."

Toby somehow managed to get Jesse up the stairs and down the hall to her bedroom without a single trip or fall. He sat her on the bed and helped her out of her soiled shirt, leaving her binding and pants in place. He waited until she had her robe on and was curled up into a ball on the bed. Then he hurried downstairs to fetch the warm water from the stove.

Once he had drawn her bath, he went back to the bedroom and led her down the hall to the water closet. "I'm going to step out so you can g-get cleaned up."

As he looked at Jesse sitting on the edge of the tub, memories of the night Aponi died came rushing back. He had felt so alone sitting at his kitchen table with the barrel of a pistol pressed against his head. He rubbed his temple and could still feel the cold, hard metal. It would have been so simple, too. One twitch of his finger and all of his pain would have been gone. As strong as he was, though, he found he simply didn't have the strength required to pull the trigger.

Toby was scared for his sister. He had never seen her like that before, and it worried him. He knew the kinds of dark thoughts she was undoubtedly having. Thoughts of self-blame and inadequacy. They were the kinds of thoughts that could sink her into a hole so deep he wouldn't be able to reach her. He knew he would have to keep a close eye on her.

"Will you b-b-be okay in here?"

Jesse kept her head lowered.

"You aren't going to do anything s-s-stupid, are ya?" He waited for an answer. When none came, he put his hand on the knob, closed the door, and crossed his arms over his chest.

Jesse finally looked at him. "I'll be fine. Go."

Toby let his arms fall. "You sure?"

"Yes. Now go."

"I'm gonna go help Gwen st-straighten up. Holler if you n-n-need me."

She had to acknowledge him with a nod before he would leave. Slowly, Jesse unwrapped her binding and stripped out of the rest of her clothing. By the time she stepped into the tub, she was sobbing. She sank down into the warm water, letting it embrace her, and allowed the tears to flow.

Every few minutes, concern for his sister pulled Toby up the stairs to the closed door of the water closet. "You okay in there?" he asked one time. "How's the temperature of the water?" he asked another. "Can I get you anything?" Each time he asked a random question, anything to ensure that her head was still above the water. He refused to leave until he got a response from her.

Jesse knew what her brother was doing. She also knew he needed to hear in her voice that she was okay. Though she did her best to reassure him each time he knocked, her tears continued to drip, rippling the surface of the water. Her heart felt like it had been shattered into tiny, razor-sharp pieces. It hurt to breathe.

Jesse stewed in the tub, only slightly aware of the fact that the water had gone cold. She glanced down at her overworked and calloused hands. They reminded her of Frieda. She recalled a conversation with her, when Frieda had explained why Patrick's death had not been in vain. It had led them to each other.

Jesse had thought about that particular conversation a lot. She had spent years questioning why God allowed so many bad things to happen. It took a long time, but eventually Jesse realized something positive had come from the loss of her family. Without that experience, she never would have found Abby.

Now, after losing a child herself, Jesse understood her old mentor better. What she needed to know was how Frieda managed to carry such a heavy loss for all of those years. Jesse laid her head on the edge of the tub and closed her eyes. She contemplated what possible reason God would have for taking her son away from her so soon. She could never see anything good coming from his death.

Jesse let her grief drag her under the water and held her breath until her lungs felt like they were going to explode. Just when she had opened her mouth to scream, she was plucked violently from the tub. She began coughing and retching up the bathwater as Toby pounded her on the back. Instinctively, she moved to cover her chest with one arm, while trying to push him away with the other. "Stop." She coughed and retched again.

Toby finally let go of her and averted his eyes. "I know wh-what you were trying to do. I'm not gonna let you do it." He set his jaw firmly. "Not on m-my watch."

"It's not what you're thinking." She was able to clear her throat but it burned like she had swallowed the sun. She belched out water and spit into the tub. "I'm fine."

"Swear it?"

"Yes! Now get out of here."

Only slightly reassured, Toby left the room.

Once she was dressed, Jesse made her way downstairs to the kitchen. A fresh pot of strong coffee was waiting on the stove. She poured a mug full, took a sip, and then joined Toby and Gwen in the office. Together, they finished straightening the room. Jesse had only managed to drink half a pot of coffee by the time the Shumakers arrived. Jonathan was right behind them.

Toby excused himself, taking Jamie and Willow with him over to his house. It was much easier to discuss details without interruptions or worrying about what the kids might hear. Jesse, Gwen, and Jonathan gathered with Emery and Hannah in the kitchen over another pot of coffee.

Jesse sat at the table listening but not fully understanding the proper protocols for a funeral. Her primary concern was making sure Jim would have the sort of funeral Abby would want for him. It was very important to her that Abby's wishes were prioritized.

In the back of her mind, she was still holding out hope that Abby would show up at any moment and take over the planning. Regardless, Jesse knew it was in her best interest to hire the Shumakers. She had to trust in them to make all of the necessary arrangements and use their best judgment.

Aware of the fact that in such matters, time was of the essence, it was quickly agreed upon that they would have his burial service the following morning. Several times throughout their meeting, Jesse had to excuse herself from the room. Fearing a complete breakdown in front of everyone, she fled to the privacy offered behind a closed door. There, she struggled to regain her composure.

By noon, all of the details had been put into place, except for one. For Jesse, it was the most important of all. She escorted the Shumakers out through the back door. Together, they walked over and stood underneath the oak tree next to Aponi's tombstone. Toby had purchased it not long after her death. Jesse glanced at the words carved in the stone.

Mrs. Aponi McGinnis
Beloved Wife, Mother, Ponak
Died August 1873

Jesse pointed to where she wanted Jim's final resting place to be. He would be close to his aunt, but there would still be enough space left on either side of him. When the time came, she wanted to make sure he would be between her and Abby.

Emery nodded his understanding. "Me and my boy will be back later this afternoon. We'll see it gets done."

"Thank you, both," Jesse said. "For everything."

Emery paused. "Would you like me to order the headstone?"

"No." Jesse didn't hesitate. "Abby will take care of it when she comes home."

Hannah knew Abby well. They were friends. She turned to Jesse and placed a hand on her arm. "I promise, nothing will be overlooked. Everything will be carried out exactly the way Abby would want it to be."

Jesse nodded and smiled gratefully. She, Gwen, and Jonathan walked with the Shumakers around to the front of the house. The three of them stood on the porch steps, watching as the wagon rolled down the lane and out of sight.

Jesse had no desire to go back inside the house. She put her hand on Gwen's shoulder and then looked at Jonathan. "You two want to get out of here for a little bit? Maybe go for a walk? Get some fresh air?"

Gwen and Jonathan agreed, and the three of them headed out across the pasture beside the house. As they headed toward the tree line beside the property, they were completely unaware of being watched.

Silas was concealed in a tree, right along the edge of the woods. Slowly, he pulled his pistol from the holster, leaned his weight across a hefty branch, and cocked the gun. Lining up the barrel, he aimed just above the brim of Jesse's hat. When she came within range, he placed his finger on the trigger. A second away from squeezing, he heard a loud whistle.

Jesse, Jonathan, and Gwen all turned around. Someone was riding up to the front of the house.

"It's the sheriff!" Jonathan said.

Silas swore under his breath and lowered his weapon as he watched them hurry back to the house.

Jesse looked up at Garland Montgomery with pleading eyes. "Did you find her?"

He threw a leg over the saddle. "Not yet," he said, sliding down. "But I have a good lead." He nodded a hello to Gwen and Jonathan and then turned back to Jesse. "I showed Gwen's sketch around at the train station, but nobody seemed to recognize him. So, I did a little searching around the tracks."

Jesse looked at him quizzically.

"You know, vagabonds are usually nearby, jumpin' trains. Anyway, I finally found a man who said he was pretty sure it was the same fella who came up to his fire last night. He was begging around, asking for food. Told some story about him and his wife trying to get down south."

"What about Abby?" Jesse asked. "Did he see her, too?"

"Well, no, he didn't actually see a woman," Garland said. "But that doesn't really mean anything. If the man did have Mrs. McGinnis, he could have easily left her tied up some-where close by." He frowned and shook his head. "I looked all over for 'em, but they were long gone. Honestly, I think they jumped the train." He pulled out a piece of paper from his vest and held it up. "I have the schedule here. I'm going to stop at every depot on the route. I'll ask around and see if he's been spotted." He tucked the paper back into his vest. "I wanted to swing by and let you know what was goin' on."

It occurred to Jesse that the sheriff was working alone. "I thought you had help?"

"I did, but they all rode home this morning. Don't worry. I don't need help now that I have a solid lead."

Jesse scoffed. "So no one is going with you?"

"No. It's just me. 'Sides, with Christmas only a few days away, I knew none of us would be back in time for the holidays."

"I'm coming with you," Jesse said.

He shook his head. "I just ran into Emery and Hannah down the road. They told me Jim's funeral is set for tomorrow." He put a hand on her shoulder. "If you come with me, there's no way you'll make it back in time."

"Sheriff Montgomery," Jonathan said. "I'll go with you."

"But, Jonathan," Gwen said. "If you go, you'll miss Jim's service."

"I know." Jonathan took her hands in his. "Jim was my best friend in the whole world." He looked desperately into her eyes. "But you know he'd want me to help find your Ma. Let me do this for him—for you."

After a moment, she nodded slightly.

He turned and faced the sheriff.

"I don't have time to dilly-dally," Garland said, putting his foot in the stirrup. "I need to get movin' now, while the lead is hot."

"My horse is already here," Jonathan said, pointing over his shoulder toward the barn. "All I have to do is saddle up."

Garland looked at Jesse and she gave him an approving nod.

"Alright," he said, swinging up into the saddle. "Get movin'. We don't have a minute to spare."

Both Jonathan and Gwen took off running toward the barn.

Jesse tilted her head to look up at him. "Give me a minute, will ya? Let me get some things put together for the boy. I'll be right back."

Jesse hurried into the house and got her saddlebags. She tossed in some food and a change of clothes for Jonathan. After filling up a canteen and fetching him a bedroll, she went back outside.

In the barn, as Gwen helped him with the horse, she told Jonathan, "Please bring her back." Her eyes were white with fear.

"I will," he said, leading his horse by the reins. "I'll do my best. You have my word." He pressed his lips against her forehead.

When they returned with the horse, Jesse secured the saddlebags and bedroll to his saddle. Once Jonathan mounted, Jesse said, "You two be careful out there."

"I promise you," Garland said. "We'll beat every bush 'til we find her." He tipped his hat at Gwen.

She offered a slight smile in return but kept her focus on Jonathan.

Jesse and Gwen watched the two of them gallop away until they were small specks on the horizon.

Jesse looked at Gwen. "I really don't want to take a walk anymore," she said, placing a hand on her upset stomach. "I'm not feeling so well. I think I'll go lay down for a while." She turned toward the house and then glanced back at her. "Why don't you go on over and help your uncle Toby with the girls."

That evening, Abby was exactly where Silas had left her, still tied securely to the stump. She was surrounded by wood chips and the long strands of her hair.

"I think tomorrow night," he said, "I'll be able to get inside your house. After I get my money, we'll get outta here. Get some miles in while it's still dark." He ran his hand through her short locks. "I've been thinkin'. Maybe we could start fresh. What do you think of Oregon?" He tilted her head back and pressed his lips against hers.

Abby allowed the kiss, barely managing to suppress the shudder she felt inside. She had finally come up with a plan of escape. If she had any hope of carrying it out, she needed Silas to stay calm.

"I'm hungry," she said.

"Ah, getting your appetite back. That's good." He untied the rope from around her wrists, handed her the canteen, and went about opening a can.

Abby used her fingers to scoop beans into her mouth, listening as he spouted off his plans for their future.

"We can do a lot with this money, ya know. I'm gonna find us a nice parcel of land. Build us a home. Keep you pregnant." His mouth twisted into a crooked, manic grin. "It might be just what we need. Hell, Abby, can you imagine? We might end up having four or five boys."

She glanced over at him and forced herself to smile.

He reached down and patted her leg. "Hey, don't you

worry. Your hair will grow back. I know I shouldn't have done that, but you know better than to make me mad."

Abby scooped out the last of the beans and eyed the spot where she needed the can to land. If she had any hope of reaching it, it needed to be exact. As carefully as she could, she tossed it, doing her best not to throw too hard. When it landed where she hoped it would, she kept a poker face, careful not to let her emotions show. Inside, she gave a tremendous shout of joy.

Silas had one thing, and one thing only, on his mind. Considering what he knew Abby's reaction would be, he felt it best to tie her hands. He reached for the rope behind her.

"Please don't." She held up her wrists to show where the rope had rubbed her skin raw. "They hurt so bad."

"You'll be fine. Tell you what. I'm gonna tie your hands, but I'll take off the shackles for a bit."

His offer surprised her, and immediately she was suspicious. She eyed him warily. "Thank you."

After Silas had secured her hands, he went over to his saddlebag and began rummaging through it. He pulled out a tiny key and knelt down in front of her. Slowly, he unlocked the shackles. He took one of her bare feet in his hands and began rubbing it. "Doesn't this feel good?"

"It does," she said, biting back the urge to vomit.

No sooner had Abby gotten the words out than he reached out lightning-quick and latched onto her other heel. He pulled her toward him until she was lying flat on her back. She glanced over and saw that his left foot was right next to the can she had so carefully placed. With a sinking heart, she knew if she resisted him in any way, there was a good chance the can would get moved out of her reach. Abby didn't know if she might get another opportunity. She was running out of options. That can was her only hope—the only chance she had to get away.

Silas shucked off his boots. He unbuckled his holster and laid it far off to the side, well beyond her reach. He unbuttoned his trousers, slid them down, and then kicked them off. Kneeling between her legs, he gripped his limp manhood and gave it a brief tug. Hiking up her dress, he ran a hand up her thigh while stimulating himself.

Abby briefly considered giving in to him. It would be like all the other times, she reasoned. She also toyed heavily with the notion of kicking him in the center of the face and trying to crush his nose into his skull. She decided that trying to fight him would be an effort made in vain. With her hands tied, he could easily overpower her, and it wasn't worth the risk to lose the can.

Then it dawned on her there was a way she could fend him off. Quite easily actually, and she wouldn't have to lift a finger to do it. She forced herself to laugh out loud.

His hand came to a sudden stop. "What's so fuckin' funny?"

She leaned up on her elbows as best she could, so that she could look him square in the eyes. "I just realized, there's no way that wife of yours had any children by you. They must've been some other man's. That thing of yours is about as useless—"

Silas slapped her with the back of his hand and her head snapped to one side. Abby turned back to face him, grinning with bright red teeth. She spat blood at him, which was coming from a split in her top lip. She chortled gleefully. "I couldn't even go fishing with that itty bitty worm of yours! Hell, I've picked up night crawlers bigger than you."

He reached for his knife, grabbed her face in his hand, and squeezed until her eyes watered. Still, she blustered with laughter. Blood rolled from her lip and ran down her chin.

Silas placed the blade next to her mouth. "I should cut out your fuckin' tongue." He laced a handful of her remaining hair through his fingers and jerked her head back. With a fury he could barely contain, he pressed the knife against her cheek. It dimpled the flesh just below her left eye. He pushed the blade into the soft skin, sliced downward, and made a three-inch gash. When he was finished, he threw the knife off to the side, where the blade stuck in the ground. He looked down at her, eyes seething with rage as he untied her hands.

Instinctively, Abby's hand flew to her face. When it came away, her palm was covered with blood. "Oh my God! What've you done?"

He laughed, stood up, and slipped on his pants. "Now you're really an ugly bitch." He tossed her his handkerchief and then turned his back on her.

Abby snatched it up and pressed it against her cheek, wincing. Blood continued to spill from the wound despite the pressure she applied. Already the cloth was saturated beneath her fingertips. She flashed her eyes at him.

Silas placed the shackles back on her feet. "Lookin' at you makes me sick," he said, his lips drawing back in a snarl. He tossed her feet aside roughly and then left the tent in a huff.

Abby couldn't help the frightened tears that sprang to her eyes as she continued to apply pressure to the wound. She had always known Silas was twisted, but this was much worse than she had ever imagined. His words came back to her. For once, she thought this time, maybe he was right. She probably was sickening to look at.

A few minutes passed before Silas returned. He pushed through the flap of the tent and knelt down beside her. "Damn you woman," he said, shaking his head. He placed his hand over the one at her face in an attempt to help staunch the flow. "Why do you always make me do it?"

CHAPTER TWENTY-FOUR

Throughout the night, sharp pains from the laceration throbbed with each tormented heartbeat. What little sleep Abby got was brief and laced with nightmares. The few sporadic moments of rest were only because Silas had taken pity on her. By binding her hands in front of her, rather than to the stump, he had allowed her the ability to keep pressure on the wound.

Her children were never far from her thoughts. Abby replayed the events in her mind, choosing to deny what she already knew in her heart was true. She knew Gwen was like Jesse, strong and capable. It would take more than a bump to the back of her head to stop Gwen. She'd move heaven and earth to save her brother. This was what Abby chose to believe —had to believe. Without faith that her son was alive, she couldn't find the strength to breathe.

In the darkness, Abby could see the bean can vividly in her mind. She stared toward it with razor intensity, concentrating on her plan until she had it perfected. The long, miserable hours passed slowly and the more she contemplated, the more she became convinced that the can was her only means of escape.

By the time the first modest rays of sunlight shone on the walls of her canvas cell, Abby was resolute. She was going home today—even if it meant dying in the process.

Abby glanced over at Silas, who was sleeping soundly. She studied his face and wondered how she had ever been attracted to such a vile man. She thought back to when they had first met. He had been tall and handsome, and she was a naive sixteen-year-old who was easily taken in by how kind, gentle, and patient he was. Her lip curled in anger as she remembered the monster he had become on their wedding night.

A sharp pain spasmed in her cheek and pulled her from her thoughts. "Silas," she said, her voice powerless. "Silas, wake up."

"What now?" he asked, barely turning his head in her direction.

"I need to go see a doctor."

He pushed the blanket off and leaned up on an elbow. "Let me see." When she lowered her hand, he looked closely at his handiwork. "Hell, it ain't even bleeding."

"Please, I need to see a doctor. You really hurt me this time."

"Nah." He rolled back over, taking the covers with him. "You'll be fine. Just keep it covered."

Abby gingerly placed the handkerchief back on the wound. "If you've ever cared about me and want us to start over like you say, then you'll take me. I'm in so much pain."

Silas groaned and sat up. He flung the blanket off and

lazily scratched at his groin. "We can't leave yet." He hocked up a mouthful of phlegm. "I'll get the money tonight. Then we'll go." He rubbed her leg. "I promise."

Although only a faint line of concern appeared between Abby's brows, her heart faltered. Come hell or high water, there was no way she was letting him go back into her house. Fresh determination flowed through her veins, but she kept her expression blank.

"If you need to go," Silas said, loosening the rope from around her wrists, "best do it now."

Abby realized her mistake the moment she pushed through the flap in the tent. Expecting to feel the warmth of the sun, she was struck instead by a bolt of pain when a blast of cold air came into contact with the laceration. She hurried to cover the wound as she shuffled over to the designated spot and then quickly squatted.

As soon as they were back inside, Silas told her to lean back against the stump.

"Don't tie my hands to that," she said, her eyes pleading. "I'm begging you. I won't be able to keep my face covered and the air makes it hurt worse."

It seemed that the pity she had cashed in on during the night had all been spent. With lips compressed into a thin line, he shook his head. "Don't worry. I'm gonna fix ya up." He pulled a savagely wrinkled shirt, redolent with body odor, from his saddlebag. After folding it, he wrapped it diagonally around her head to keep the handkerchief in place. He checked to ensure that her nose and mouth were uncovered, and then tied the sleeves of his shirt into a knot at the back of her head. "It won't have to be like this much longer." He reached for the rope and fed it through the hole in the wood. "I'll be back soon."

"You're leaving now?" Abby couldn't keep her voice from shaking. "I thought you were waiting 'til it got dark."

Silas rolled his eyes. "Woman, I know what I'm doin'. I'm goin' back tonight while they're asleep. I just wanna see what's goin' on at the house." He retied her hands at the base of the stump and double-checked the knots. "I'll be back in a few hours."

"Can you at least take these off?" Abby gestured toward the metal restraints. "I can't go anywhere, and my ankles are so sore. Please?"

Silas considered it briefly. "Best not. Be still and they won't hurt so bad." He cinched his holster, then leaned over and kissed the top of her head. "Tonight, we'll get out of this hell-hole." He slipped on his coat and left the tent, taking his bridle and saddle with him.

Abby waited for several minutes and then waited for several more just to be sure. Once she was confident he had ridden away, she sprang into action. Scooting down until she was flat on her back, she stretched out to her full length. Her toes were still just out of reach. She pushed her limbs until it felt as though her wrists and shoulders were going to slip out of their sockets. When she felt the lid slip between the tips of her toes, she couldn't help but let out a tiny squeal. Slowly, she pulled the can closer until she could clutch it more securely between her shackled feet. Moving into a seated position, she wriggled her body in unnatural ways, like a contortionist in a freak show. Finally, she had the can close enough that she was able to grip it with her right hand. She closed her fist on the metal and exhaled in relief.

With one hand, she wiggled the lid back and forth until she heard a small metallic ting. This time, she didn't pause to celebrate. It was possible Silas could return at any minute. Craning her neck at an awkward angle, she managed to bite down on the sharp lid. Holding it firmly between her teeth, she strained her head down as far as was physically possible while moving her hand back and forth. She watched with great satisfaction as her makeshift knife frayed the edge of the rope.

Abby was vigilant and anxious, struggling to cut while keeping her ears attuned to any cracking branches or shuffling leaves. It seemed to take much longer than it should have for her to manage to slice through the binding. When the rope finally snapped, she shook her hand loose and quickly worked at releasing the other. Once both hands were free, she got to her feet and shuffled over to his saddlebags, the clanking chains as loud to her as the ringing of a church bell.

Abby plunged her hand inside the leather bags and frantically patted around for the key. She turned the bags upside down when she couldn't find it and rifled through the contents on the ground. The key wasn't there. All her careful planning had been for nothing.

Barely containing an agonized wail, Abby clutched at the remaining tendrils of her hair in frustration. She collapsed to the ground, her mind racing through any remaining options. Glancing down at the abrasions covering her ankles, she knew there was no way she could get to the house by nightfall in the heavy restraints. Even if she hid in the woods to ensure her safety, her family was still in danger. Somehow, she needed to find a way back to them before dark to warn them.

Abby remembered the axe leaning up against the tree. She

hurried toward it, the metal around her ankles ripping at the skin, creating fresh wounds. Sitting on the ground next to the tree, she placed the links of the shackles on a large rock and lifted the axe. With single-minded determination, she brought the blade down on the chain as hard as she could.

When Jesse woke, her first impulse was to look over at her kids. She needed reassurance that they were still there and safe. So much had happened in such a short amount of time that she was having trouble discerning what was real. It all seemed like one never-ending nightmare.

Gwen was asleep in Abby's usual place, clutching at the pillow like a beloved toy. Willow was curled in the middle between them. Jesse had spent most of the night consoling them, doing her best to reassure them that their mother was okay. She mentioned Abby's strength and determination, and then reminded them of how much Abby loved them. She worked so hard convincing them that Abby was safe and would return home soon she found herself believing it, too.

Jesse had held onto Willow as she cried herself to sleep. Gwen kept her eyes closed, but it had taken a while for her to finally drift off. Jesse woke up every time one of them cried out and stayed awake with them until they fell back to sleep. With Jim's passing and Abby still missing, she wasn't sure how much more any of them could take.

Sluggishly, she rolled out from under the covers and sat on the edge of the bed. She felt as though she had just gotten them to sleep and now she had to wake them. The thought made her miserable. "Hey, you two," she said gently, reaching around to shake Willow. "C'mon. It's time to get up. We need to start getting ready."

Willow stood in the bed and wrapped Jesse in a bear hug from behind. "Ma's going to miss it, isn't she?" She rested her head on Jesse's shoulder.

"I think so." Jesse tenderly squeezed her daughter's hand. "So it's up to us. Let's be strong for her today." She turned to look at both of them and noticed Gwen's chin was trembling. With her own tears threatening to fall, she did her best to remain strong for her girls. "Hey," she said, reaching out to take hold of Gwen's hand. "I know this isn't going to be easy, but we'll get through this. If it becomes too much for either of you, it's all right with me if you want to hide out in your room. I'll understand."

Gwen locked eyes with her and nodded somberly. "Same goes for you, Pippa."

"Alright, let's start getting ready." She hugged them both and watched as they left her room.

Jesse pulled a suit from the wardrobe and laid it out on the bed. She washed up and combed her hair, paying careful attention to detail. It seemed like a mundane and tedious task, but she wanted to represent Jim with dignity and pride.

She had just tucked a crisp white shirt into black trousers when there was a knock on her door. Thumbing up the right side of her suspenders with one hand, she reached for the knob with the other.

"People are st-starting to get here," Toby said, entering the room. "You should probably be down there to greet them." He handed Jesse a black crepe band. "Hannah told me to g-give this to you."

Jesse turned it over in her hand. "What am I supposed to do with a garter belt?"

"Here. Hold out your arm." Toby wrapped the band around the sleeve on her bicep and tied the strings. "It's supposed to show p-people you're in mourning."

"Pfft. I'm sure people can tell I'm mourning by lookin' at me." Although she knew it was the stress taking its toll, she still felt as though she had aged fifty years in the last few days. It was difficult to keep the terseness from her voice.

"Well," Toby said patiently. "This is wh-what people do."

"When I die, just put me in the ground and cover me with dirt." She walked over to her tallboy dresser, pulled open the top drawer, and reached for her cufflinks.

"Me, too. But you know you're doing right by Abby." He looked thoughtful for a moment. "After Aponi died, this is wh-what Abby wanted me to do for her, so I know this is what she would want for Jim."

Jesse sighed and plopped down in the small chair in front of Abby's vanity. She glanced over the many perfume bottles that were neatly arranged on the top. Many of them had been gifts from her. She picked up the one closest to her. It was more than half-empty and one of Abby's favorites. She pulled out the stopper and brought it to her nose. The familiar fragrance was enough to bring tears to her eyes, so she quickly sat it back down.

"You know I wish more than anything Abby was here," Jesse said, glancing at her brother in the mirror. "But there's also a part of me that's glad she's not." She studied her reflection. Her skin was pale and her eyes had a hollow, haunted look. Suddenly, her throat felt constricted and she fought to hold back her emotions. "Being here is killing me." She fastened her cufflinks and stood. "I can't imagine how she'd handle any of this."

"I'm here for you." He picked her suit jacket up off the bed and handed it to her. He waited by the door until she had finished dressing. "Anything you need, just ask."

Jesse nodded. She slid her arms into the sleeves and adjusted the silk lapels in the mirror. "I'm going to see if the girls are ready. I'll be down in a minute."

Toby nodded and opened the door. "Don't be too long."

"I won't." After he had gone, she glanced at the ceiling. "Please give me strength." She released a heavy sigh and headed down the hallway, her boots feeling as though they were made of cement. "Hey," she said, tapping her knuckles lightly on their bedroom door. "You two ready?"

Celia opened the door and stepped out into the hall. Jesse's heart clenched when she saw the girls standing there. Gwen and Willow were dressed alike, in similar versions of a simple gray dress. They stood quietly with their heads bowed beneath matching black bonnets.

Jesse immediately went to them and wrapped her arms around them, drawing them close. "Remember," she said, holding them tightly. "If this gets to be too much for either of you, you can come up here." She stepped back to look at them. "Any time you need me today, you come find me right away." She cupped their faces in her hands. "I mean it. No matter what's happening, I'm here for you." She extended her hands to them. "We'll get through this together."

Willow and Gwen each took one of Jesse's hands and together, the three of them made their way down the hall, holding on tightly to one another. When they got to the top of the stairs, they paused. A long line of people spilled out from the parlor and across the foyer. It extended all the way outside for as far as they could see from their position.

When they reached the bottom step of the staircase, Jesse gave each girls' hand one final squeeze and then reached out to shake Mr. Plunkett's. "Thank you for coming…"

For the next hour, Jesse stood stiffly next to Gwen and Willow beside Jim's coffin. They numbly thanked the mourners who shuffled past offering condolences. The line of people seemed to be endless.

At last, Reverend Tucker nodded to her, signaling it was time to begin the service. He raised his hand, gathering everyone's attention, and softly announced to the crowd that it was time to make their way outside.

Once the room had been cleared, the reverend stepped out into the hall. He respectfully closed the parlor doors behind him so that the family could have some privacy.

Jesse reached into her pocket and pulled out Jim's watch. She rubbed the initials with her thumb and then slid it into his coat pocket. "'To everything, there is a season, and a time to every purpose under the heaven.'"

Ecclesiastes, Gwen thought and then asked, "Can I put something in, too?"

"Of course," Jesse said. "Anything you want."

"Me too?" Willow asked.

"You too, sweetheart."

Gwen left the room, followed closely by Willow.

Jesse placed her hand on top of her son's and noticed his bangs were hanging in his face. She recalled how the cowlick used to annoy him and he'd get so frustrated. She lovingly brushed them aside and felt a sudden pain in her chest when she realized it was the last time his hair would ever do that.

She leaned down and kissed his forehead, her chin quivering uncontrollably.

Toby placed his palm on her back but didn't say anything.

"I don't know how I'm supposed to go on without you," Jesse managed to say, her voice thick with emotion. The tears that had pooled in her lashes finally spilled over, but she didn't acknowledge them. "You were always the best part of me. I was a better person because of you." She took hold of Jim's hand. "We were so blessed to have you in our lives." It was impossible to hold back the sob that escaped her. "I hope you always knew how much I loved you. I always will."

When her daughters returned, Jesse moved to the side to give them space.

Gwen stepped up to the coffin, holding her brother's favorite book, *The Adventures of Tom Sawyer*, in her hand.

Willow was right behind, holding a crude, stick figure drawing she had done many months ago. In it, the entire family was depicted standing in front of their house.

"Here, Pippa," Willow said, handing it to her. "We can all be in there with him now so he won't be alone."

Jesse could feel the dam inside her starting to crumble. She was powerless to stop the tears and the wave of emotion that threatened to crash down. Jesse took the book from Gwen with a shaking hand and slipped Willow's drawing under the cover. There was a bookmark midway through the pages, threatening to slip out. She secured it so that Jim wouldn't lose his spot and then placed it underneath his hands. Finally, she made herself step away so that she could regain some of her composure.

Toby stepped next to the coffin. He tried to say something, but when he opened his mouth to speak, no words would come. With a trembling hand, he lightly patted Jim's shoulder.

Willow peered into the coffin. "Goodbye," she said. "I love you."

Jamie moved next to Willow. "I love you, Jim."

Gwen clutched her hands in front of her, fighting to hold back her anguish, and stepped up to her brother. "You're my first memory. Remember when we were little, and I wanted to play with your top?" She shook her head. "I wanted it so badly, but I couldn't get to it. You saw how frustrated I was and reached for it." A tear rolled down her cheek. "At first, I thought you were going to put it up higher because you didn't like me playing with your things. I'll never forget the way you smiled when you gave it to me." Streams of tears poured down her cheeks. "You were more than my twin," she said, her voice cracking, "you were my best friend. I love you so much." She gripped the edge of the casket. "How am I supposed to live without you?"

Jesse moved forward and enveloped Gwen in her arms. When she finally felt her shaking slow, she nodded to Toby to indicate they were ready.

Toby opened the parlor doors and motioned for Emery to come inside. A heavy silence filled the room as the undertaker attached the coffin lid. When it was secured, Jesse, Toby, Armand, and Emery each took hold of one of the brass handles and lifted it off of the stand. Armand and Emery were the first ones through the front door, ensuring Jim's body left the home feet first.

Jesse didn't believe in the superstition, but she obliged for the sake of others. There were those that believed the deceased had to be carried from the home feet first in order to prevent a spirit from looking back and gesturing for anyone to follow them over to the other side.

The guests parted, clearing a path for the coffin as it was carried across the backyard. As soon as it passed, they closed in ranks behind it. The procession made its way to a spot underneath the large oak tree. As gently as possible, the coffin was placed onto three planks of wood, which were laid out over the freshly dug grave.

Reverend Tucker clutched a bible in his hand. "'But they that wait upon the Lord shall renew their strength; they shall mount up with wings as eagles; they shall run and not be weary…'"

Jesse took hold of the girls' hands and let the reverend's words fade into the background. She stared at the fine lines ingrained in the wood of the coffin, memorizing the pattern. Her mind wandered into worry about Abby. The lingering question of not knowing where or how she was made her want to scream out loud. The fact that Abby was missing her son's funeral was absolute torture. She didn't know how much more of not knowing she could handle.

She felt Gwen squeeze her hand gently, pulling her away from her tumultuous thoughts. Quietly she mouthed the words, joining in with the others as they recited the Lord's Prayer and then Psalm 23.

After a nod from the reverend, Emery looped a rope around the coffin. Carefully, he pulled on the end hanging from a pulley, which was fastened around a sturdy tree branch. After his son pulled out the boards, he cautiously lowered the coffin into the ground.

Several people paused to toss freshly cut flowers down into the grave. After a brief moment of silence, the guests made their way over to a group of tables, which had been set up behind the house. There was a large offering of food available for the bereaved. They respectfully left behind only those in the immediate family.

The reverend cupped Jesse's palms in his own before he left. "'May his angels keep watch over you wherever you go.' Psalm 91:11."

Later in the day, Jesse stood looking out across the backyard. It was loud, filled with the babble of many discussions. She couldn't understand how anyone could talk about weather, crops, or recipes as if it were merely an ordinary day. It wasn't an ordinary day. Her only son was lying in the ground only a few yards away.

Jesse had never been more grateful than when people finally started coming over to her to say their goodbyes. By late afternoon, only the Baptistes and the Shumakers remained.

Jesse approached Emery and Hannah. "Thank you for everything."

Hannah smiled warmly. "I'm sure Abby would've been pleased."

"She absolutely would have been," Celia said. "It was a lovely service."

Jesse didn't say one way or the other. She just wanted it to be over and for everyone to leave. "Here, let me help you clean up," she said, picking up a casserole dish from the table.

"No," Emery said, taking it from her. "We'll clean up everything. That's what you're paying us for."

Jesse glanced around and then noticed that Gwen and Willow were gone. "Have any of you seen my girls?"

"I haven't," Celia said, continuing to gather the silverware.

Toby said, "I saw Jamie go inside with them a little while ago."

Jesse nodded and turned to face the Baptistes and Shumakers. "Thank you, again, for everything you've done for us. Toby and I should go and check on them." She went inside to be with what remained of her family.

CHAPTER TWENTY-FIVE

Silas had been keeping a watchful eye on the McGinnis household from the edge of the tree line all afternoon. His eyes darted around, taking in all of the commotion and understanding the purpose of the gathering. He waited until the last wagon had rolled away before he jumped down from the tree he was perched in. Quickly, he mounted his horse and rode back to the campsite. Come nightfall, he was breaking into that house and getting his money, regardless of the risk involved.

Reining his horse next to the tent, Silas dismounted near the tether rope. He uncinched the saddle and placed it on the ground. Humming, he pulled the bit from the horse's mouth and leaned over to place it next to the saddle.

Abby lunged out from behind one of the trees where the tether was fastened and struck him on the head with the blunt end of the axe. The horse spooked and reared up, barely missing him when the hooves came down in a blind panic. The mare fled as though running for its life.

Abby let the axe fall from her hands and stood staring at

the unconscious body of her ex-husband. As hard as she had tried, her attempts at cutting through the chain had been futile. Undaunted, and in order to silence the restraints, she had woven long blades of grass through the links to keep them from clanking together. Now, the only thing she needed was the key, and Silas was the only one who knew where it was. It was the sole reason why she hadn't lopped his head clean off of his shoulders already.

Abby pulled his pistol from the holster, tossed it behind her, and then hurried to snatch up the rope he had used to bind her with. She had barely finished tying his wrists together when his eyelids fluttered. She positioned herself in front of him and slapped him across the cheek as hard as she could.

"Wake up, you son of a bitch!" She grabbed a greasy lank of his hair and yanked his head back so that she could see his eyes. "Where's the damned key?" When he didn't respond, she hit him again. This time, she used her fist, connecting with the hinge of his jaw and putting all of her strength behind it.

Silas's eyes unrolled from the back of his head. He groaned and tugged against his restraints. He lifted his hands to rub at the growing goose egg on the back of his head.

Abby took a few steps backward, picked up his gun, and aimed it at him. "Where's the key?"

"It's…it's under that rock," he said, pointing to one a few feet away from where she was standing. "There. The one with the crack."

Keeping the gun trained on him, she shuffled toward the rock he'd indicated. No sooner had she turned the stone over, than from the corner of her eye, she saw him reach inside his coat pocket.

"Lookin' for this?" He held up the key. "Hmm?"

Abby tried to reach him in time, but she wasn't fast enough. She watched him pop it into his mouth. "Spit it out!" She leveled the gun on him. "I *will* shoot you."

Although Silas initially struggled to swallow, the smile he gave her when it went down was one of pure satisfaction. "Guess you won't be gettin' it anytime soon. Don't you fret. You may get it tomorrow—if you're lucky."

Abby cocked the colt revolver.

"Go ahead." Silas pointed to the bridge of his nose. "Right here."

She put her finger on the trigger, closed her eyes, and squeezed.

Click.

Abby looked down at the gun.

Silas had known there was a chance something like that could happen. He didn't want his own weapon to be used against him, so, each time he neared the campsite, he removed the six cartridges from the gun.

"They're in my pocket," he said, leaning to one side. "Come and get 'em."

Something inside of Abby finally snapped. She didn't stop to think. She reacted. Tossing the pistol aside, she picked up the axe and hefted it over her head.

"You crazy bitch! Don't you fuckin' da—"

His threat ended in a shriek as she plunged the blade deep into his thigh. He leaned forward, fighting for control of the wooden handle.

Nostrils flaring, her blue eyes glacial, Abby kept hold of the wood and wriggled it feverishly, trying to dislodge it from the bone.

Silas screamed.

A slow, sadistic smile spread across her face when she finally managed to pull it free. Splinters of bone came out with it, along with bits of his clothing. A large pool of blood quickly formed beneath his leg from where it poured out of the wound.

"You fuckin' bitch!" Silas moaned and squeezed his leg. "You wait 'til I get—"

Abby sank the blade into his kneecap, the sound of shattering bone loud in the still of the forest. The axe nearly severed his leg. She freed it easily and prepared to strike again.

He saw her wielding the axe and managed to get his hands up in front of him. Unable to stop the blow, there was an audible snap when the axe split through his humerus.

Abby smiled as she swiped at the droplets of blood spattering her face. It smeared like war paint.

He stared at her incredulously. "I'm gonna fuckin' kill you!"

She rested the axe casually on her shoulder and shrugged. "No, Silas," she said, staring him in the eyes. "I'm going to kill you."

"Wait," he said, his expression suddenly pleading. "You don't have to do this. I'll let you go."

Abby scoffed, rolled her eyes, and brought the axe down with every ounce of strength she could muster. It struck him dead center on the top of his head and sank all the way to the cheek of the blade. His skull split like two halves of a walnut.

Abby collapsed to her knees. Through bleary eyes, she watched Silas warily until he stopped convulsing. When he was still, she released a breath that felt as though it had been trapped for years.

For a while, all she could do was sit there. Her teeth chattered and her hands shook uncontrollably. It felt as though she would never be warm again. She tucked her hands into her armpits, rocking herself.

You know what you have to do. In her mind, Jesse's voice was as clear as if she were standing right beside her.

Finally willing herself to move, Abby reached under Silas and pulled out the knife. She laid it on the grass beside her and rolled him onto his back. With numb fingers, she unfastened the buttons on his coat and shirt until the pale-skinned underbelly was exposed.

Picking up the knife, Abby closed her eyes. She heard Jesse's voice again. *You can do this. I've shown you how.*

The way Abby saw it, Silas was no longer human—he was an animal. It was the same way as she had prepared other animals when hunting with Jesse. She pushed the blade into the hollow above his groin and slid the knife up to his sternum. In her mind, she convinced herself that she was simply field dressing a deer.

Her work was quick and effective. It didn't take long until she had him splayed wide open. She identified the stomach and then reached in and pulled it out without any hesitation. Another quick slice and the key was in her hand. It was slippery against her fingers and she struggled to keep hold of it as she inserted it into the lock.

It was late when Jesse lowered the lights and wearily climbed the stairs. She was still wearing her black pants and white shirt, but the suspenders flapped loosely at her sides. Opening her bedroom door, she discovered Gwen, Willow, and Jamie, already dressed in their nightgowns, lying in bed waiting for her. She forced a smile.

Gwen had claimed Abby's pillow again and was curled up against it. Jamie had tucked herself in next to Willow, who was holding up a book. "We thought maybe you could read to us before bed."

Time with the girls was exactly what Jesse needed. She knew if she went to bed right then, she would be up again within minutes. Sleep had eluded her for days. She couldn't justify curling up in a warm, safe bed when Abby was still out there possibly cold and hurt.

Jesse kicked off her boots, set her cufflinks on the dresser, and rolled up her sleeves. She reached for her spectacles on the bedside table and got into bed. With her back resting against the headboard, Willow and Jamie scooted over until they were curled up on either side of her. Gwen stretched out across the foot and stared up at the ceiling, her palms tucked comfortably underneath her head.

Jesse read aloud until, one by one, the girls fell asleep. When the last one drifted off, she placed the book on the table. Carefully, she maneuvered herself over Willow so as not to wake her. Before leaving, she stoked the fire to keep them warm, grabbed her boots, and then tiptoed from the room.

She paused at the bottom of the stairs, unsure of what to do or where to go. For a moment, she considered walking over to Toby's house so she could have someone to talk to. Not wanting to burden her brother, she stopped in the foyer long enough to shrug into her coat and step back into her boots and then slipped out onto the porch.

It was eerily quiet outside, the creak of the rocker the only sound she could hear. Her mind was restless, roaming over the events of the last several days. No matter how far her thoughts wandered, they always came back to Abby. The questions of who took her, where she was, and if she was ever coming home tortured her. The other burning question, was she even still alive, was one Jesse refused to consider.

It wasn't more than an hour later when she heard a noise that made her bring the chair to a stop. Still wide awake and quite alert, she strained to listen. The sound seemed to have ceased. Shivering, Jesse realized she had been sitting out in the cold for far too long. She stood, stretched her aching limbs, and turned toward the door. Before she could take a single step, the strange noise came again.

Jesse froze. Squinting, she peered out into the darkness. Nothing moved. Whatever it was had gone silent again. She insisted on chalking it up to her tired mind. As she opened the door, though, the noise came a third time. She pivoted in the direction of the sound. Whatever it was, it was close, somewhere in the vicinity between her house and Toby's. There was no doubt in her mind anymore. Something was definitely out there.

Jesse closed the door and quietly walked down the porch steps watching for any signs of movement. As she started out across the lawn, she could barely make out the huddled figure in front of her. In the dim light of the crescent moon, at first, it seemed to be some sort of injured animal, perhaps a dog. As she drew closer, however, she realized it was a person. Though she was startled, her first thought was that it had to be Abby. There were no thoughts of danger, only a hopeful heart soaring with relief as she ran.

Jesse knew it was a woman by the dress she was wearing. Even in the dark, she soon discovered there was nothing familiar about her. The stranger's face was caked with blood and dirt, her dark, matted hair shorter than Jesse's.

She could tell by the injury to the woman's face and the heavily tattered dress that she had been in some sort of accident. "Ma'am, are you alright?"

The woman was shaking wildly and didn't speak. The only sound she made was an awful, high-pitched keening that could have come from any wounded animal.

Jesse took off her coat, knelt, and draped it around the woman's shoulders. Whatever she had been through must have been horrific. "Ma'am, you're safe now."

Without warning, the woman balled her hands into fists and pounded them on Jesse's chest. "Why didn't you come for me?"

Jesse recognized the voice instantly and reached out to grab hold of Abby's hands. Before she could respond, she felt Abby's body go limp. She slid an arm under her knees, gathered her in her arms, and cradled her tightly against her chest. As fast as she could go, she raced over to Toby's house, kicking at the door. "Toby! Open the door!" She glanced down at Abby. "You're going to be fine. You're safe now."

The moment Toby opened the door, Jesse pushed her way inside. He held up a lantern while she gently lowered Abby onto his sofa. Despite the dim glow in the room, Jesse was still able to see the large gash on her cheek. Silas's dried blood covered nearly every inch of her ripped and ragged clothing. Her face and hands were caked in it. Underneath the filth, Jesse could see the raw skin around her wrists and ankles, which appeared infected. Her long, blonde hair had been carelessly hacked off and looked as if someone had dyed it a macabre, rusty brown.

"Who's that?" Toby asked, taking a step closer.

"It's Abby!" Jesse said, nearly screaming.

"Oh, my God! What do you need me to do?"

"She needs a doctor. It's faster if we take her. Go hook up the carriage, and hurry!"

Toby turned, snatched his coat, and raced out the door.

Though it was painful to look at the damage done to her, Jesse kept her eyes trained on Abby's face. "We're going to get you help." She took hold of Abby's hand and laced her fingers through hers. "You're going to be okay."

"The twins? My babies..." She grabbed Jesse's shirtsleeve. "Our babies—are they okay?"

"Gwen's fine." Jesse dropped her gaze.

"Jim?"

The only thing Jesse could manage was a small shake of her head. She placed her hand on Abby's forehead. "Where all are you hurt? Who did this to you?"

Abby's eyes turned icy cold. "I killed him."

"Who? Who did you kill?"

Abby turned her head away and yanked her hand free from Jesse. "If you'd've been home, our son would still be alive." She pulled her knees up to her chest and began her frenzied whining again.

Jesse had sustained many injuries over the years, but none of them hurt as badly or cut as deeply as Abby's words did. She had never felt more worthless in her entire life. Unsure of what to do or say, she sat there helplessly as she waited for her brother to return.

Once the carriage was parked out front, Toby ran inside and picked Abby up in his arms. "Why don't you go get the girls?" he said to Jesse. "That man could c-come back here."

"He won't be coming back," Jesse said numbly. "She killed him." She grabbed her coat from the sofa and draped it over her arm.

"Jim?" Abby gasped and looked up at Toby. "Jim? Is he alright?" Her voice was heavy with worry.

"No," Toby said, shaking his head. "Jim's gone." He repositioned her in his arms. "We may have lost him," he said softly, "but we're not g-going to lose you." He turned toward the door and carried her outside.

Abby let out a painful moan and burrowed her head against his chest.

Jesse couldn't understand why Abby asked about Jim again. For the moment, though, she simply brushed it aside and followed them to the carriage. She hefted herself up and tossed the coat onto the seat. Holding her arms out in front of her, she took Abby from Toby and gently lowered her onto the leather bench seat. Once she had Abby's head secured safely in her lap, she covered her up with the coat.

"Gwen!" Abby sucked in a deep breath and looked at Jesse. "Is she alright? Willow?"

"Yes. They're fine."

"Jim?" Abby asked, clutching Jesse's arm. "Where is he?" She lifted her head slightly and glanced around. "Where is he?"

Jesse blinked in confusion. Though the illumination provided from the lanterns mounted on the sides of the carriage was dim, she could still see Abby clearly. However, Jesse struggled to recognize the woman who was lying in her lap.

Abby looked like a vagrant in her dirty, torn dress. Her hair was a short, rust-colored mess. The side of her face had a large laceration. None of these things bothered Jesse more than realizing that something in Abby's mind seemed to have been damaged. She wasn't sure there was a fix for that, and that terrified her.

As Toby raced the horses through the night toward Doc Montgomery's house, Jesse lightly caressed Abby's forehead and traced her brows with her thumb. "Shh, now," she said, holding her tightly. "It's all over now. You're gonna be fine."

CHAPTER TWENTY-SIX

The black Landau carriage flew down the dirt road leading to Neva. Pitted with numerous ruts and holes, Abby whimpered louder each time one of the wheels struck an obstacle. Her skin was clammy, her breathing shallow, and her pulse galloped as fast as the horses. Still shivering uncontrollably, the only sound coming from her was a terrible, feeble moan. If she had been a wounded animal, someone would have already put her out of her misery.

The noise was so unnerving and constant that Jesse felt helpless to comfort her. All she could do was hold on to her tighter and try to keep her body from jostling as they sped along.

"You're going to be fine," Jesse whispered, cradling her head gently in her lap. She lovingly picked detritus from what remained of her beautiful, golden hair, tucked her coat around her, and tried her best to keep Abby warm. "Don't you worry. Doc's going to mend you right up."

It didn't take long, perhaps only minutes, but to Jesse it felt like hours before Toby steered up in front of Doc Montgomery's home. Both horses and carriage skidded from the force of the abrupt stop. The draft horses' breath clouded in the chilly air as Toby leapt from the seat and ran to the door. He pounded his fist against the wood, rattling the threshold and vibrating the glass of a nearby window.

Jesse placed her cupped hand on the top of Abby's head. The hair felt like a hard and matted clump against her palm. "We're here. Help is coming."

"Owww." Abby turned her head slightly and continued to moan. "Aughhh."

It was late, but Doctor Montgomery was used to emergency calls coming in at all hours. He flung open the door, his nightshirt hanging over the top of his pants. His white hair was tousled from sleep. "Toby! What is it?"

As soon as Toby had finished giving a hurried explanation as to why they were there, the doctor grabbed his black bag and a lantern and hustled down the walk in his bare feet.

Climbing up into the carriage, the doctor handed the lantern to Jesse. "Hold that for me, right there," he said. "Let me see what we got here." If Toby hadn't already told him who it was he was looking at, he wouldn't have recognized the badly bruised and beaten woman. "She's definitely going to need stitches," he said, inspecting Abby's cheek.

"Let's get her inside," Jesse said, removing the coat from Abby, "so you can treat her."

"No," he said, shaking his head. "She needs better care than I can give her." He shot Jesse a glance. "You need to get her to a hospital." Turning, he ducked through the door. "I'll be right back," he said over his shoulder.

Doc Montgomery returned moments later with a blanket. "She's in a bad way. Best to keep her as warm as possible," he said, laying the cover over Abby. He took Jesse's coat and draped it over the blanket.

He opened his bag and reached inside to retrieve a brown bottle. Using his teeth, he pulled the cork and poured liquid onto a folded square of white cloth. "Here," he said, after replacing the cork. He gently applied the dressing over the wound. "Keep this on the laceration." He wiped his hands on his nightshirt. "I wish there was more I could do to help."

"Thank you," Jesse said, cautiously holding the bandage in place.

"You're welcome." He stepped back down and closed the door behind him.

Toby was worried about the girls being home by themselves. Although Jesse had no trouble believing that Abby had killed the man who took her, he wasn't so sure. Abby wasn't acting like someone who had their wits about them.

"Psst," Toby said, leaning over the side of the carriage. "The girls are alone. Can you g-g-go out to the house and stay with 'em until we get b-back?"

"Of course. Now you should go. And hurry."

Toby acknowledged the doctor's words with a crisp nod, pausing only long enough for him to step back onto his flagstone walk before flicking the reins. Within seconds, he had the horses charging in the direction of San Francisco.

The next forty-five minutes were some of the longest, most excruciating ones of Jesse's life. She sat holding Abby's head on her lap, counting every breath and hoping it wouldn't be her last. She had never felt more useless, with no way to help the person she loved most in the world. The noise of the road and Abby's unsettling refrain weren't enough to drown out the words still thundering in her mind. Abby blamed her for everything. Jesse knew she was right. If she'd been home, maybe their son would still be alive.

She looked down at Abby's face through her blurry, green eyes. "I'm so sorry," she said softly. "Can you ever forgive me?"

As dawn slowly broke over the horizon, shades of orange and pink peeked through the trees as the carriage flashed by. Jesse remained focused on Abby until Toby brought the horses to a sudden halt. Jesse jolted on the seat. She cast a glance out the window and saw a two-story, wood-clad building. The hospital wasn't much bigger than their house in Neva. "We're here," she said, placing Abby's hand on the bandage. "You hold onto this until we get you inside." She lifted the coat and pulled back the blanket.

Abby's hand slipped and the dressing slid down from her cheek. It had been traumatic enough for Jesse to see the weeping sores and bruises on Abby's wrists and ankles—seeing the dirty, gaping wound carved into her face in the daylight made her visibly cringe. She couldn't imagine how much pain Abby was in.

When Toby opened the door, Jesse transferred Abby into her brother's outstretched arms. On trembling legs, weak from stress and exhaustion, she grabbed the bandage and hopped from the carriage. She ran up the walk ahead of them, stumbling with effort. Underneath the carriage porch, she took the stairs two at a time. Once she reached the top, she turned the knob, pushed open the door, and stepped to one side to make room for Toby and Abby.

They were in a large, open room, which smelled of disinfectant and chemicals. Two of the walls had five beds lining them. Patients who were resting comfortably occupied three of the beds. The room was completely quiet.

A woman seated at the far end jumped to her feet when they came in. The white smock she wore over her blue dress rustled as she rushed toward one of the empty beds. "Bring her over here!"

Toby crossed the room swiftly in several long-legged strides and gently lowered Abby onto the bed.

Jesse looked at the nurse with pleading eyes. "Can you help her?" she asked, shifting her weight from one foot to the other. "She's hurt real bad."

"Doctor Sarver is in the other room," she said, pivoting on her heels. "I'll be right back."

Jesse bent down and placed the medicated cloth back on the wound. "The doctor's coming," she said, her voice cracking. "You're going to be okay."

Moments later, the nurse returned, followed by a short, rather portly gentleman. Though she was relieved to see the doctor, she was rather annoyed by his casual entrance. Jesse moved out of the way and watched as the doctor lifted the fabric.

His forehead puckered. "Hmm," he said, turning Abby's head. "Uh-huh." He replaced the bandage and then motioned for them to follow him.

The doctor was still lacking the sense of urgency Jesse had been hoping for.

"It's a good thing you brought her in when you did. You can leave now. I'll see to it she gets taken care of." He turned to go.

"Wait!" She grasped his arm. "I'm not going anywhere!"

He turned to face her and peered over the top of his spectacles. "Why? Do you know this woman?"

"Of course," Jesse said indignantly. "She's my wife."

"Oh," the doctor said, coloring slightly. "I'm sorry. I mistook her for a woman of…limited means. We receive quite a few here. Usually they're dropped off." He reached out his hand. "I'm Doctor Sarver."

She gripped his hand. "Jesse McGinnis."

Doctor Sarver kept hold of her hand as he processed her name. "I've heard of you," he said thoughtfully. He flashed a grin. "Ah, I remember. I think you did some work for my in-laws a few years back. Mr. and Mrs. Benjamin Johnson."

Jesse recalled that particular job quite well. "Yes, I did." She couldn't understand why he thought the time was appropriate to be discussing work when Abby needed his full attention. She massaged the crescent shaped scar on her forehead impatiently. "Can you please hurry? She's hurt."

The doctor was fully aware of the kind of money his in-laws had. He also knew they had paid a small fortune for the custom woodworking, which had been done in their home. A switch flipped in his mind and he now looked at Jesse and Abby as part of his social class. This granted them a new level of respect.

"What happened to her?"

The muscles in her face tightened. "A man broke into our home and took her. I don't know how Abby did it, but somehow she managed to get away from him."

"Well, he sure did a number on her, didn't he?" Doctor Sarver glanced over at Abby. "It's obvious the laceration is festering. It's going to need quite a few stitches, too." He sighed, shaking his head. "Unfortunately, the wound isn't fresh. I'm going to have to remove some of the dead tissue before I can do anything." He lowered his voice. "Do you know if she was violated?"

Jesse suddenly felt lightheaded, as if all of the blood in her body had surged to her feet. That thought hadn't even crossed her mind. "I-I don't know." She felt tingly all over. "She hasn't said much. When she does talk, she seems confused."

"That's understandable," the doctor said. "It's obvious she's been through something traumatic."

"She's going to be okay, isn't she?"

"Oh, I believe so," he said, pushing up his spectacles. "I need to get her sedated so I can clean and stitch up the injury. She'll need to stay here for a couple of days."

"That's fine. Do whatever you need to, Doctor."

The doctor glanced from Abby to Jesse. "There's nothing else you can do for her right now," he said quietly. He put a comforting hand on her shoulder. "Listen, I know you're worried. But she's probably going to be out of it for the rest of the morning. Why don't you check on her later this afternoon?"

"I'm not going anywhere!"

The three other patients glanced in her direction.

For the first time, she didn't care that she was the center of attention. "You'll have to drag me out of here."

"With all due respect, sir," he said, gently steering her toward the door. "The longer you stand here and argue with me, the longer it keeps me from giving your wife the treatment she needs." He stopped and faced her. "I'll see she gets the best care possible. You have my word." He took a step closer. "I'll also make sure she's moved into one of the private rooms."

"C'mon, Jes," Toby said, taking hold of her arm. "We'll come b-back later. Let him do wh-what he needs to." When

Jesse still showed no sign of leaving, he went on, "'Sides, we need to get home to the girls."

Jesse looked over and briefly locked eyes with Abby. For a moment, she wasn't sure if Abby was even capable of seeing her. When Abby rolled her head away a second later, Jesse had to bite back a sudden swell of emotion. She really did blame her for Jim's death. As she reached for the door, Jesse couldn't help but wonder if she would ever see love shining in Abby's brilliant, blue eyes again.

"Wait," Jesse said to Toby. "I'll be right back." She turned around, crossed the room, and took hold of Abby's hand. "Listen. Doctor Sarver is going to take good care of you…" She paused, waiting—hoping—Abby would at least look in her direction. When she didn't, Jesse continued, her voice strained. "I need to run home and check on the girls. I'll be back as soon as I can." She held Abby's hand against her cheek. "I love you, you know." She kissed her palm, placed it under the blanket, and forced herself to walk out the door.

As they made their way down the brick walk to the carriage, Toby asked, "Did she s-s-say anything to you about what happened?"

"Only that she killed the man. Not much else. She wasn't making much sense. But…" Jesse's voice faltered. When she could speak again, she said, "She blames me for Jim's death." She hurried ahead of him, fetched her coat from inside the carriage, and climbed onto the driver's seat. Though she was heartbroken, her face was an exclamation of rage. She knew how much she hated herself. She could only imagine that Abby had to feel the same way.

Toby took a seat beside her. "She actually said that?"

"Yes." Jesse held his gaze as she slipped her coat on. "It was the only thing she was clear about." She clutched the reins so tightly her knuckles were white.

"I'm sure she didn't mean it," he said gently. "I know Abby. There's no way she w-would blame you. She's just been through a lot. She isn't th-thinkin' right."

Jesse shook her head. "She's not wrong, ya know," she said, steering the horses onto the road. "She didn't say anything that I haven't already thought of myself."

"Remember when Aponi died? I th-thought the same thing. Had my-myself convinced her death was my fault." He chuffed out a breath and glanced over at her to make sure she was listening. "You remember wh-what you said to me?"

She nodded, but said nothing.

"You told me it wasn't my fault. Were ya lying?"

"No." She understood what he was doing. "Of course not."

"Well, none of this is your fault, either." When she didn't respond, he continued. "I know everything seems hopeless r-right now, but if anybody can get past this, it's you and Abby."

"I'm not so sure." She swallowed hard, trying to dislodge the quiver in her voice. "I don't think she'll ever forgive me— hell, she can't even look at me."

"She will, Jes," he said confidently. "Give her some time."

Willow was in her bedroom, watching out the window with a vigilant eye, when she finally spotted the carriage coming up their lane. She raced down the hall and bounded down the stairs, shouting as loudly as she could. "They're back! They're back!"

By the time the carriage pulled up, Doc Montgomery and

all three girls were standing on the lawn out in front of the house.

Before Jesse had reined the horses to a stop, Gwen was sprinting alongside them, frantically craning her neck to look inside the window. "Is she in there?"

Jesse set the brake and jumped down. "No, she had to stay at the hospital. But she's going to be fine." She extended her hand to the doctor. "Thanks for looking after them."

"No trouble at all. Don't mean to be rude, but I've got to go. I'm late making my house calls."

Jesse nodded. "Thanks again."

"You're welcome. And I'm glad she's going to be okay."

After Doc had boarded his buggy, Jesse turned to the girls. "Have any of you had breakfast yet?"

"No," Gwen said. "We've been too worried."

"Toby and I have something to do. I'm going to need you to go on inside and fix you girls something to eat. Then, I want you to go upstairs and pack up some clothes. When your uncle and I get back, you and I are going to go stay in the city for a couple of days."

"Can I go?" Willow asked.

"Not this time, sweetheart." Jesse kissed the top of her head. "I need you to stay here with your uncle."

While the girls busied themselves in the kitchen, Jesse and Toby strapped on their guns and met up in the barn. After saddling their horses, Jesse walked over to the back corner and grabbed a shovel.

They cantered the horses across the pasture beside the house, following Abby's footprints that led toward the woods. When they neared the edge of the tree line, Jesse spotted a small piece of fabric which had been snagged in a patch of briars. Knowing it had to have come from Abby's dress, she plucked it off and picked up the trail from there. Most of the time she was able to see the footprints by leaning over in the saddle. Other times she had to dismount, forced to crouch low to the ground in search of the tracks.

It took her nearly an hour to trace the prints to where Abby had been held captive. When she saw the eviscerated body of a man with an axe lying near his cracked skull, Jesse had to look away.

She didn't turn away from disgust or out of pity for the man. Whatever fate had dealt him, he had most certainly deserved it. After all, he was the one responsible for her son's death. She was bothered by the fact that Abby—her sweet and innocent Abby—had been pushed to a point where she had been forced to do something so heinous.

When Jesse slid down from her mount, her legs buckled beneath her. She jammed the tip of the spade into the dirt and leaned on it for support.

"You can leave, if you want," Toby said, tossing his leg over the saddle and jumping down. His stance was steady and firm. "I can take care of th-this."

A fresh ribbon of guilt floated over her—one more merciless and unforgiving than the ones before. "That's not it. My God, Toby, she was right here the whole time, and I didn't even try to look for her."

"I don't th-think any of us thought they would still be in the area. I didn't. Hell, Garland and McCreary d-d-didn't even think to search our woods."

Jesse had never felt more disgusted with herself. She had always taken pride in her tracking ability. Yet, at a time when it mattered most, she had failed miserably. Everybody had told her to wait at home, and like a fool, she had listened. It crushed her to know that Abby would have to wear the proof of her negligence for the rest of her life.

"So," he said, interrupting her thoughts. "Wh-what are we going to do with him?"

"We're gonna bury the piece of shit," she said, holding up the shovel. "That's what we're going to do."

"Don't you th-think the sheriff n-n-needs to see this?"

"I don't know," she said, tossing the shovel on the ground. "And I don't care. If he wants to see him, he can come dig him up."

She walked over and pushed through the flap in the tent. Toby fell in behind her, holding open the flap to allow for more light in the shelter. The stump in the center, where strands of Abby's long hair lay scattered all around, immediately stole their focus.

"What do you suppose he used th-that for?" Toby asked.

The images Jesse had tried hard to suppress for decades came rushing back at her. Even though she had only been ten at the time, what happened to her sister in the barn all those years ago was still just as vivid in her mind as the day it had happened. The thought of Abby being tied up and assaulted was so similar to what had happened to Jamie that it brought hot bile shooting up into her throat.

"I'm not sure I can handle knowing." She clamped her hand over her mouth and backed out of the tent. Walking over to the body, she had an overwhelming desire to smash in his ugly face. Even though he was dead, she felt an urge to try and make his corpse feel the pain she was going through. Before she could lift her boot, something in the corner of her eye caught her attention. Lying on the ground was a knife. Next to it was man's shirt with the sleeves tied together. Although dried blood made the knife appear old and rusted, she recognized it immediately.

Toby came over and stood beside her. "You th-think that's what he used to c-cut her face?"

"Don't know." Jesse shrugged and glanced at the handle, noticing the small, perfectly preserved fingerprints. "But it looks like she used it to gut the son of a bitch."

"Any clue who he was?"

"No idea," she said, squatting next to the body. "Maybe he's got something on him that'll tell us." She was grateful for the cooler temperatures keeping the stench at bay. Still, she had to shoo away several flies as she patted around at the man's pockets. It was all she could do to not retch as she fumbled through them.

"What is it?" Toby asked when he heard her gasp.

Jesse held up Abby's ring. With everything that had been going on, she hadn't noticed it was missing from her finger. She placed it in her pocket and continued to search.

"There's nothing else," she said, swiping her hands on her pants. She stood and gestured toward the tent. "Could you start tearing that down?" She stabbed the blade of the shovel into the ground.

Jesse dug with a fury until her arms shook and her muscles burned and then handed the shovel to Toby. While he was digging, she spread the canvas out on the ground next to the body. After that, she picked up the axe, walked over to the stump and chopped it off as close to the ground as possible. Lastly, she rolled the body onto the canvas and tossed the axe on top of him. She reached down and picked up her knife. For a split second, she considered keeping it. After all, it had been a cherished gift from Abby. Though she hated to part with it, she knew neither one of them would ever be able to look at it again. She tossed it next to the axe and then rolled everything, including the body, up in the canvas.

"This should be deep enough," Toby said from inside the hole. He threw the shovel onto the surface and climbed out.

Together, they lifted the bundle and tossed it into the hole as casually as they would a piece of trash. They pitched in everything else of his as well, including his tack, the shackles, and all the provisions. Once they had ensured everything had been placed in with him, they filled the hole with dirt.

When they had finished, Jesse nodded at Toby. They walked away without so much as a backward glance—the only indication that anyone had been there was the oval-shaped patch of freshly turned soil.

CHAPTER TWENTY-SEVEN

J esse let the reins dangle loosely in her hand and kept the horses at a measured pace. She wanted to use the time on the return trip to the hospital to explain to Gwen what had happened to Abby. She sat there solemnly, staring out over the horses' heads as she contemplated on which parts and how much of the story she should reveal. There were not many times in her life that she remembered having this much difficultly gathering the right combination of words. She cast a sideward glance at Gwen. It made her sick being the one to have to tell her such horrifying things. She knew it would destroy some of her daughter's innocence, and she cursed herself for having to do it.

The day was cold, but Jesse could feel lines of sweat running down her spine. She sighed deeply and then, as calmly as possible, told Gwen what had transpired out in the woods. She altered some of the details, including the manner in which the man had died. Choosing something more benign, she told Gwen he had died of a gunshot wound, which she thought would be easier for her to accept than the gruesome truth.

In an effort to prepare her for the visual shock of seeing her mother, she went on to explain about the large cut on Abby's face, and also how most of her hair had been cut off.

When Jesse finished speaking, the steady clip-clops of the horse hooves on the road were the only sounds in their vicinity. They rode without talking for several miles. Gwen's silence was worrisome. Jesse's body was tense, a rippling storm of emotions causing her anxiety to mount. As they closed in on another quiet mile, she couldn't help but think that telling Gwen had done more harm than it had good.

All at once, there was a loud clatter as the carriage rumbled over a hole in the road. Jesse leaned over for a better look. The black exterior, normally polished and shiny, was covered in a thick layer of dust from the previous night's ride. With a frown, she wondered how she could have ever cared about something so trivial.

Jesse's nerves were frayed by the time they reached the city limits. As concerned as she was for Gwen, her thoughts kept drifting back to Abby. It was hard to admit, but she was scared to see her. Not because of the injury. Nothing anyone could do to her would ever make her seem less beautiful. It was the fact that Abby blamed her for Jim's death, and that was a hard pill to swallow.

She thought of the broken tree up at the cabin. Her frown deepened as well as the lines around her eyes. She wondered if they would end up like the sapling—broken and in pieces.

Gwen squeezed her eyes shut against the afternoon sun and hugged herself. Though she tried to picture her mother with short hair and an angry slash carved into her cheek, the image was impossible to form. It made her feel sick to even try. Instead, she focused on the rhythm of the carriage bumping along the road and tried to hold it together.

Jesse glanced over at her and thought about how much she looked like Abby. She had seemed so grown up the night of the dance. It was hard for her to believe that it had been less than a week ago. It seemed inconceivable that in the span of six short days, their lives had been turned completely upside down. She reached over and placed a hand on Gwen's arm. "Hey. You okay?"

Gwen flinched. "I'm fine." She used the cuff of her coat to wipe at her eyes.

Jesse pulled out her handkerchief and handed it to her.

Gwen's tears blinded her. "I know this sounds kind of awful," she said, using the hanky to wipe her cheeks, "but I'm scared to see her."

Jesse chose her words carefully. "I think it might be hard for you to see her at first, but for your ma's sake, we have to try to act normally. She needs us now more than ever."

When they entered the hospital, the first thing Jesse noticed was that Abby was no longer in the room. She hurried over to a nurse who was tending a nearby patient. Pointing to the empty bed, Jesse asked, "Excuse me. Do you know where the woman who was in that bed is?"

The nurse pulled the patient's sheet up to his chest. "I'll be right back," she said to him. She pivoted toward Jesse and Gwen. "Come with me and I'll take you to her." She led them down the hall to one of the private rooms.

They paused outside the doorway.

From where they stood, Jesse could see that Abby had been bathed and put into a clean gown. Her hair had been washed and was back to its normal honey shade of blonde. One side of her face was completely covered with a bandage.

Abby turned her head to look at them.

"Oh, Ma," Gwen said. A sob broke in her chest. She ran to the bed and knelt down beside it, reaching out a tentative hand to her mother.

Abby slipped her arm out from beneath the covers, unwilling to let the pain keep her from draping an arm around her daughter. "I'm so glad you're here," she said, holding Gwen as tightly as she could manage. "Don't cry, sweetheart. I'm okay." She gave Jesse a swift look and then pinched her eyelids shut.

Jesse quietly stood watching them from a safe distance. Part of her wanted nothing more than to run over and fall into Abby's embrace. Another part of her, one that feared rejection, stood frozen in the doorway. She didn't know if she could handle heartbreak on top of everything else. She bit her bottom lip to keep it from trembling.

The nurse angled her head toward Jesse. "Doctor Sarver asked to see you as soon as you got back. Can you come with me, please?"

Jesse cast a wistful glance at Gwen and Abby. Resigned, she nodded and turned to follow the nurse down a long, dark-paneled hallway.

"Ah yes," Doctor Sarver said amiably, looking up when she entered his office. "Have a seat." He sprinkled tobacco onto a small square of paper.

Jesse sat down in the chair on the other side of the desk.

"I cleaned her laceration and stitched it up the best I could." He ran his tongue along the edge of the paper. "I also gave her a complete examination. There were a few superficial wounds. Other than that, I found nothing significant." He gave her a kind smile.

"So, she wasn't…" Her mind briefly revisited the horrors she had tortured herself with since seeing the stump. "You know?"

"I don't believe so. But, I'm very concerned about her. Not so much physically as I am mentally. Her face will probably heal long before her mind does." He placed the cigarette in the corner of his mouth.

Jesse looked beyond his smile. "Did she tell you anything about what happened?"

"Yes…well, as much as she can recall." He struck a match and touched it to the end of his cigarette. "The last thing she remembers," he said, shaking out the matchstick and dropping it into a ceramic ashtray, "was being tied to a stump. She doesn't even know how she got here." He took a long drag, studying Jesse through the smoke for a moment. "I'd like to keep her here for observation for a couple of days. I want to keep an eye on the wound in case it starts to fester." He blew a thick stream of smoke and then flicked away the ash. "I also want to make sure the stitches hold," he said thoughtfully.

"You were able to close the wound then?"

"I did the best I could with what I had to work with. I had to remove a lot more of the flesh than I would have liked. There was an abundance of necrotic tissue." He leaned forward and rested his elbows on the desk. "Unfortunately, she's going to have quite the scar. Your wife hasn't seen it yet, but I imagine she'll take it pretty hard when she does. You know how women are about their appearances."

Jesse slouched in the chair. "Do you think she'll ever be okay up here?" She tapped her temple. "She keeps asking about our son. My brother and I already told her he didn't survive, but she keeps asking if he's okay."

"Whatever she went through caused her brain to shut down, so to speak." He took another long hit from his cigarette and then exhaled a plume of smoke toward the coffered ceiling. "It's her body's way of coping with the extreme duress she was under." He flicked off his ash. "She's fully aware of your son's passing. She mentioned it when she woke from the anesthesia." He stared pointedly at her. "I believe she's suffering from melancholia. With your full support, she can overcome it sooner rather than later. Only time will tell."

She raised her eyes to look at him. "You know she blames me for our son's death. She won't even look at me. How am I supposed to help her?"

He crushed out the butt of his cigarette. "There are places for women who struggle with this sort of thing. Doctors who specialize in wounds of the mind. I can recommend a few, if you want. Let's see how she does in the next day or two before we think about going down that road."

"Okay." Jesse inhaled a deep breath and blew it out slowly.

"Oh, and whatever you decide," he said, getting to his feet, "she's still going to need to have the stitches taken out in a couple of weeks." He glanced at the clock hanging on the wall. "She's actually due now for another dose of morphine." He moved toward the door and held it open for her. "After I administer it, you should know she'll probably sleep for the rest of the day. Why don't you come back in the morning?"

Jesse nodded reluctantly. "My daughter and I are going to be staying at the hotel just down the street. Could you please let me know if there are any changes to her condition?"

"Of course." The doctor extended his hand warmly. "You can rest easy tonight. She's in good hands here."

Jesse gave him an uncharacteristically limp handshake.

When they entered the room, Gwen was sitting on the bed beside her mother, running her hand over Abby's hair. "It doesn't look bad at all," she said in a quavering voice.

Abby looked skeptical but didn't argue. She looked up as Jesse came into the room. Immediately, she turned her head away.

Although she'd been expecting this reaction to her presence, the snub hit Jesse like a sucker punch and knocked the breath out of her lungs. She came to a shuddering stop. Like a coward, she backed toward the door. "We need to leave so the doctor can give your ma some medicine," Jesse said to Gwen. She stuffed her hands into her pockets and looked down at her boots. "Abby, we'll be back in the morning to check on you." When there was no response, she turned crisply and waited for Gwen out in the hallway. The thought of those words hanging there in space without acknowledgment or response was eating away at her already.

Jesse was grateful it was only a short distance to the hotel. She wanted to be as close as possible in case Abby's condition worsened. She parked the carriage and saw to it that the horses were taken care of for the night. Her legs felt heavy and slow as she headed inside to the front desk. After speaking to the clerk, she paid for a suite with two bedrooms and then headed upstairs with Gwen.

In the back of her mind, she knew it probably seemed a bit haughty to get a suite, but it honestly couldn't be avoided. Quite simply, she didn't feel comfortable sharing a room with her daughter knowing they each needed some privacy. There was also no way she was willing to let Gwen stay in a room by herself. A suite was the only option that suited their individual needs perfectly.

She tipped the bellboy handsomely after he had placed their bags inside the room and waited for him to leave before she turned to Gwen. "I'm starving. Wanna go downstairs and get something to eat?"

Gwen nodded. "I'm hungry, too."

When they entered the dining room, Jesse noticed the tinsel hanging from the sconces and the colorful bells resting on all of the tabletops. That's when she remembered it was Christmas Eve. Most people were at home with their families, enjoying their holiday traditions.

Since only a few of the other tables were occupied, they were able to choose a table near a window.

"I don't like that Ma has to spend Christmas in the hospital," Gwen said.

Jesse pulled out a chair for her daughter. "Me either. We'll go spend the day with her tomorrow. Hopefully, she'll get to go home the day after." She took a seat across from Gwen.

A waitress approached the table and poured water into their glasses. "You folks know what you'll be having this evening?"

Jesse picked up the menu and glanced over it hurriedly. The idea of enjoying a meal made her feel a fresh sense of guilt, so she just blurted out the first thing that caught her eye. "I'll have the lobster bisque."

The waitress jotted it down and turned toward Gwen.

"Chicken and dumplings, please." No sooner had the waitress taken their menus and stepped away than Gwen let out a worried groan. "Ma is going to need something to wear home."

Jesse pulled out her pocket watch and checked the time. "Everything is probably closed by now. I can't imagine any place will be open tomorrow, but don't worry. We'll pick her something up before she gets released." Jesse looked out the window and noticed the store across the street, where a woman was just flipping the open sign to closed. "I'll be right back," she said, scooting back her chair.

Gwen watched out the window as Jesse ran across the street and knocked on the door of the shop.

Tenting her hands over her eyes, Jesse peered through the plate glass window. She knew the woman had to still be inside. She knocked on the door again, and then a third time, until at last, it swung open.

A heavyset woman with tight curls stood staring at her. "We're closed," she said through pursed lips.

"I know. I'm so sorry. But can I come in? It won't take long, I swear."

"Come back the day after tomorrow," she said, pushing the door closed.

Jesse wedged her foot between the door and the jamb. "Ma'am, please. My wife is in the hospital. I just wanted to get her something to cheer her up. It's Christmas," she pleaded. "I promise, I'll be quick."

The woman fought with her conscience for a moment and quickly relented. She sighed. "Oh, all right." She opened the door. "But be quick about it."

Jesse knew exactly what she wanted to get and found it almost immediately. She placed the item on the counter and thanked the woman again for her kindness.

She crossed the street, entered the restaurant, and reclaimed her seat.

"What did you get?" Gwen asked curiously.

Jesse laid a copy of *Little Women* on the table. "I thought maybe we could read it to your ma tomorrow."

Gwen knew it was her mother's favorite book and her eyes lit up. "Oh, she'll love that," she said, tears shimmering in her lashes.

Jesse noticed the tears forming in Gwen's eyes. "What's wrong?"

Gwen sniffed. Her parents had always been so close. The distance between them seemed to be growing as wide as an ocean. "You and Ma aren't speaking. Are you going to separate?"

Jesse reached over and placed her hand on top of Gwen's. "I honestly don't know." She squeezed her daughter's hand. "Your ma is very upset with me right now."

"You still love her, don't you?"

"Of course I do. Just because we aren't getting along right now doesn't mean we don't love each other." She leaned on the table and tried to find the right words. "Losing Jim broke something in me. I hardly know how to fix myself, let alone what's broken between your mother and me. But I promise you," she said with a reassuring smile, "I'm not going anywhere."

Gwen gave her a faint but grateful smile. Tears sparkled on her lashes like tiny diamonds. "Pippa, you can fix anything. I know you'll find a way to fix this, too. I hope someday, I have a marriage just like you and Ma."

"You will," Jesse said with a wink. "And what about Jonathan?" she asked. She leaned back to make room for the waitress to set down their dishes. "Thank you," she said to the woman.

Gwen waited for the waitress to leave before she answered. "I care about him. But, it's not like what you two have." She fiddled with her fork but didn't touch her food.

"How so?" Jesse asked, spreading her napkin on her thigh.

"I guess I love him like he was part of our family. I think of him more as a good friend than I do anything else. Is that wrong?"

Jesse shook her head. "You can't force love, sweetheart. It's either there or it isn't. When I first saw your ma…" The frown she had been wearing for days vanished for a moment. "I forgot how to breathe. I didn't have a clue what it felt like to be in love. I only knew I loved how I felt when I was around her." She picked up her soupspoon and skimmed some lobster bisque off of the top. She held it over the bowl and continued. "You'll know when you find it. There'll be no doubt in your mind. When you find someone, you won't be able to imagine life without waking up next to them every morning." She took a sip of soup and swallowed. "If you don't have those feelings for Jonathan, then maybe he isn't the one for you. Life's short. I don't ever want you to settle."

"You won't be upset if I'm not with him?"

"Not even a smidge." Jesse looked surprised. "Why would I be? All I want is for you to be happy."

As they continued to eat, Jesse thought about a conversation she'd had with Abby. Before leaving for the Davenport job, they had made the decision to tell the kids the truth about her. There was no way she could tell Gwen now. After losing her brother and almost losing her mother, Jesse knew that finding out the truth could easily become the thing that pushed her daughter past her breaking point. She decided she would never come right out and tell Gwen. If she should ever stumble upon the truth, however, or start asking questions, then she would come clean.

They had just finished eating when Gwen spoke up. "I'm not the least bit tired. Are you?"

In truth, Jesse was exhausted. She looked across the table at her daughter's expectant face. "What do you want to do?" she asked, pulling out her watch. "It's still pretty early."

"How 'bout we go for a ride?"

Jesse stuffed her watch back into her vest pocket. "Where would you like to go?"

"Why don't you show me where we used to live. The house on Taylor Street."

Jesse stood and offered her daughter her elbow.

Soon, they found themselves riding through the winding streets of San Francisco. They took their time, taking in all of the buildings, which had been decorated for the holiday. Jesse pointed out places of interest along the way, especially those with special meaning to her.

Eventually, Jesse pulled back the reins and brought the carriage to a stop. "There it is," she said. "317 Taylor Street." In the late, evening sunlight, it was easy for her to see not much had changed. Someone had added flower boxes to the windows on the front of the house and there was a fresh coat of paint on the barn. Other than that, it was exactly as she remembered it. She pointed at one of the second floor windows. "That was yours and Jim's…room," she said, her voice faltering." She felt a fresh wave of grief wash over her at the mention of her son's name.

"I still can't believe he's gone," Gwen said quietly. She looked over at Jesse and caught her inconspicuously wiping away a tear. Trying to distract Jesse's thoughts, she continued. "Isn't the house where you built your first staircase around here somewhere? Would you show me?"

Jesse nodded and sniffled. "The Bowman estate. Yes, it is." She took one last look at their old home and shook the reins.

Within minutes, they pulled up in front of Sam and Helga's mansion.

"This is it."

"This place is huge," Gwen said, her hushed voice tinged with awe. "They must be very wealthy."

"Did you know your ma used to work for him?"

Gwen shook her head. "Where?"

"Sam used to own several saloons," Jesse said. "I met your ma in one of them. A place called The Foxtail…" Movement diverted her attention and she turned to look up the Bowman driveway. "Well, I'll be," she said. As soon as the carriage that was coming through the gate had pulled onto the street, she hailed the driver. "How've you been?"

The driver steered his carriage alongside hers and brought it to a stop. He studied her face for a moment and then broke into a wide, easy smile. "I's good, and you?" He propped his elbows on his knees and let the reins dangle loosely from his large hands. "Sho' been a mighty long time."

"It sure has. I'm doing well, all things considered." She leaned back. "Cuffy, you remember my daughter, Gwen."

"How do you do, mister?" Gwen asked.

Cuffy offered her a smile and tipped his hat. "This sho' cain't be one of them baby twins."

"It is," Jesse said. "Fifteen years old, now. Can you believe it?"

"No suh." He shook his head.

"How are the Bowmans?"

"They be fine," he said. "I's on my way to fetch 'em from the depot now, so I needs to git goin'." He gripped the reins and gave Jesse a wide smile. "It sho' was good seein' y'all."

"You too—say, how's Ulayla? She inside?"

"She be good. She be livin' in one of them row houses now."

Jesse knew exactly where he meant. It was one of the poorest sections of the city. The homes were nothing more than shanties. "You mean she doesn't work here anymore?"

"No suh. Mr. Bowman done gone replaced her. She been gone...oh, I's say three years now."

Jesse felt a twinge of guilt. She had been so caught up in her own life, she hadn't once thought of checking in on Ulayla.

"I's gotsta git." Cuffy tipped his hat again. "Y'all take care."

"Hey!" Jesse called out to him, stopping him just as he started to pull away. "Which house does she live in?"

"Hers be the only yeller one. Gots a black shutter missin' on the front."

"Thanks. You take care, too—oh, and Merry Christmas," Jesse said.

"Yes, Merry Christmas," Gwen said.

Cuffy nodded. "Merry Christmas." He smiled and snapped the reins.

Gwen waited until the horse's hooves had faded before she said, "He sure talks funny. Is he slow?"

Jesse laughed. "On the contrary," she said, getting her own horses moving. "He's one of the smartest men I know. The man can fix just about anything. He talks like that because English isn't his first language. He was brought to this country against his will on one of those horrible slave ships. Had to teach himself to speak our language." She nudged Gwen with her shoulder. "It'd be the same thing as you trying to teach yourself to speak…Swedish. Imagine talking to a Swede. They'd probably think you sound funny, too." She looked over at Gwen. "He's a lot smarter than me, because I can only speak English."

"Oh," Gwen said, processing the information. "So who's Ulady?"

Jesse laughed again. "Her name's Ulayla, and she's a wonderful woman. Actually, I'm quite fond of her. What do you say we go try and find her house? I'd love for you to meet her."

"Sure, Pippa."

Only a remnant of daylight remained by the time Jesse steered the carriage through an area packed thick with shanties. She felt Gwen slide closer to her.

Gwen couldn't help but notice the looks they were getting as they traveled slowly down the rut-covered road. "I'm not sure we should have come here," she whispered.

"Don't be scared," Jesse said. "I trust the people around here more than the ones living up on Nob Hill." She looked down the row of houses. "That has to be it!"

"Are you going in there?"

Jesse noticed the house appeared dark inside. "She's probably sleepin', and I'd hate to wake her up. Besides, it's getting late. We'll come by another time." She flicked the reins and headed back toward the hotel.

CHAPTER TWENTY-EIGHT

CHRISTMAS, 1880

Jesse woke to the sounds of laughter and singing. She pushed back the heavy quilt, rolled out of bed, and walked over to the window. Parting the drapes, she peered down at the street below. Several couples hurried past, their arms piled with wrapped presents. It was nearly impossible for her to imagine only a few days had gone by since she had mentioned hiring a photographer to take a photograph of the family for Abby's gift. It was not the Christmas morning she had envisioned. Her family was broken and scattered, with miles between them and one of them lost forever.

She got dressed and pushed open the curtains. The sunlight that came pouring into the room did nothing to penetrate the darkness and gloom that had become her world. She collapsed in one of the side chairs and pressed her fists against her temples, struggling for control of her emotions.

"Pippa, are you up?" Gwen asked, tapping lightly on the door.

"I'm up, sweetheart. Come in."

Gwen pushed open the door and noticed Jesse's swollen,

bloodshot eyes. She crossed the floor in a hurry. "What's wrong, Pippa? Did you get news about Ma?"

"No," Jesse said calmly. "As far as I know, she's fine." She rolled up her shirtsleeves and then ran her hands through her hair. "I just didn't sleep very well. How 'bout you?"

"Not really. I couldn't quit thinking."

"Me, either." Jesse rose to her feet and wrapped her arms around her. "Merry Christmas, Gwen."

"Merry Christmas, Pippa," she said, squeezing back. "It sure doesn't feel like it."

"I know." Jesse let go and stepped back. "You hungry?"

"I don't want anything. My stomach's upset. How 'bout we go see how Ma is feeling this morning?"

"Okay."

Downstairs, Jesse had their carriage brought around to the front of the building. She tipped the hostler a coin, helped Gwen to climb up, and then took a seat next to her. The overwhelming anxiety about seeing Abby, and whether or not she would even be responsive to her, made the already short ride to the hospital seem even shorter.

Jesse pulled back on the reins and brought the carriage to a halt. She saw a nurse dumping water from a bucket next to the street and hailed her attention. "Excuse me," Jesse called out to her.

The woman turned in their direction.

"How is Mrs. McGinnis this morning?"

"She's doing about as well as can be expected." The nurse smacked the bottom of the bucket to get the last of the suds out of the pail. "Still refusing to eat. She's awake if you want to go inside and visit. Maybe you can get her to eat something. Poor thing has to be starving."

Gwen moved to get down and noticed Jesse wasn't making the effort. "Aren't you coming?"

Jesse briefly considered it. Suddenly, she wasn't prepared to face the rejection she knew was waiting for her inside the building. "Uh…I have something I need to do." She handed Gwen the copy of *Little Women*. "You go on in? I'll be back after bit."

"Okay, but don't be too long. I'm sure Ma wants to see you."

Jesse had her doubts about that but gave her a reassuring smile just the same. "I won't. Promise." She watched as Gwen followed the nurse inside. Once she was out of sight, she flicked the reins and headed back to the hotel.

Jesse parked the carriage out in front and went inside to speak to the receptionist. She waited for the woman to return from the kitchen.

"We only have sweet potato left," she said, opening the lid on the box.

"It's perfect. I'll take it."

The receptionist closed the lid and handed it to her. "I'll just add it to your bill."

"Thank you." Jesse nodded to her. "Merry Christmas."

"Merry Christmas to you, sir."

After carefully placing the box on the floor of the carriage, Jesse drove down the street, her mind wandering as she unconsciously maneuvered the horses through the city. Without warning, she was overwhelmed by an unbearable wave of grief. It crashed over her, leaving her breathless. She hurried to rein the horses to the side of the road and jumped down quickly. With hardly a glance around, she climbed into the back of the carriage and pulled the curtains closed. Jim was gone and

Abby couldn't bring herself to look at her. Each thought, every memory, was one more strike to her already battered heart. Her body shook as she gave in to the anguish.

Jesse wept until she had no more tears to shed. Sniffling loudly, she pulled her handkerchief from her pocket and blew her nose. Outside, she could hear the sounds of children's voices. She lifted the edge of the curtain and stole a glance out the window. Several yards away, on the same side of the street, stood a tall, wrought iron fence. Playing just on the other side of it were several children.

Jesse hadn't realized she had parked next to the orphanage. Apparently her brain was foggier than she thought, because she couldn't recall how she had gotten there. She took a couple of minutes to pull herself together, opened the carriage door, and got out.

"Hey, mister!" a boy shouted.

Jesse turned around. Three boys were peering at her through the fence. She guessed their ages to be between ten and twelve. Their faces were smudged with dirt and their clothes were ratty.

"Got any candy in there?" the tallest of them asked, pointing to the carriage.

Jesse latched the door and walked over to the fence. "Sorry, I don't." She studied them through the iron bars for a moment. "Hey, can I ask you boys somethin'?"

"Whadda you want to know, mister?" asked one with blond hair.

"You boys like it here?"

A smaller, redheaded boy cast a glance over his shoulder. When he saw that there were no adults within earshot, he turned back to face her. "Heck no. We hate this place."

Jesse leaned in. "Why's that?"

The blond boy took a step forward and motioned for her to come closer. "The beds are hard and have bugs. The food tastes nasty and is always cold. The grownups are mean." He spat on the ground in disgust. "Hell, Dickie here," he said, elbowing the redheaded boy beside him, "got his ass whooped last week and couldn't sit down for three days. Ain't that right, Dickie?"

Dickie nodded, his auburn curls bouncing. "Sure did. Still got the proof. Wanna see?" He reached for the button on his pants.

Jesse held up a hand. "No, I believe you," she said, quickly. "What did you do wrong?"

"I woke up starvin'," Dickie said. "Snuck down to the kitchen lookin' for food. Mrs. Hartleroad caught me taking a biscuit. Got four lashes with the switch. One for being out of my bed and three for stealin'."

The tall boy snickered. "He didn't even get to eat the damn thing." He turned to Dickie. "You shoulda took off runnin' and crammed it in your mouth, since you were busted anyway."

"Who's Mrs. Hartleroad?" Jesse asked.

"Satan," the blond boy said. "We even wrote a song about her. Wanna hear it?"

Dickie grabbed his friend's arm. "You crazy? He'll run and tattle on us. I ain't getting the switch again."

The blond wrapped his hand around the iron rods and placed his face between the bars. "You won't tell on us, will ya?"

Jesse stepped closer. She knew she shouldn't encourage the boys to misbehave, but couldn't help it. "I won't tell. Swear."

The blond boy began. "Mrs. Hartleroad, she's a toad, horsey teeth, smelly feet." The other two joined in, and the three continued in a discordant harmony: "Saggy skin, mean as sin. Without a twitch, she'll fetch a switch. Strike your behind, several times. So, if you wanna sit, while you eat your grits, best stay clear when Hartleroad's near."

Jesse grinned. "That's pretty clever. Kinda catchy."

All three boys were clutching the bars of the fence now. Whatever trepidation they may have had about the stranger was gone.

"So, what do you boys do for fun around here?" she asked. "Do they take you fishing or hunting?"

The three of them looked at her in disbelief.

Dickie said, "We never leave here."

Jesse was stunned. She couldn't imagine being their age and not getting to do those sorts of things. "What do you do for fun?"

"You're lookin' at it," the tall boy said, gesturing widely at the yard. "They let us come outside."

She looked over the boys' heads to see a large woman marching in their direction.

The woman snaked her way through the group of playing children. She cupped her hands around her mouth. "You boys get away from there this instant!" she hissed.

Jesse watched as the hefty woman approached. She glanced at the boys and lowered her voice. "Is that Mrs. Hartleroad?"

Dickie didn't have to turn and look. He knew the voice well. "No. That's just cranky old Mrs. Coons."

The boys pivoted and sprinted away, their feet kicking up dust as they flew past the woman. She barged straight toward Jesse, her face contorted in displeasure. The scowl she wore made Jesse want to run away, too. The hateful glare froze her in place.

"We don't allow strangers to visit with the children," Mrs. Coons said with a sneer. Her tone was prim and firm. She placed a fat hand on her plump hip. "If you need information, then you need to make an appointment to see Mrs. Hartleroad."

Jesse said nothing.

Mrs. Coons gave a dismissive wave of her ample hand.

Jesse turned on her heel and ambled back to her carriage, feeling like a child that had been reprimanded.

As she drove away, she chanced a peek over her shoulder. The boys were pointing and laughing at her for getting scolded. She couldn't help but chuckle from the encounter and was willing to bet money there was a song about Mrs. Coons, too.

After a few minutes, she brought the carriage to a stop in front of a small, weathered home. The pale, yellow paint was faded and chipped. It was missing a black shutter, just like Cuffy had mentioned. The neighboring houses, she noticed, were all in similar disrepair. She stepped down and reached into the back of the carriage to retrieve the pie. Following the weedy, stone path that led to the house, she nodded kindly to the neighbors who were sitting on stoops and porches as she approached the door and knocked.

Jesse smiled widely when the warped front door creaked open. "Hello, Miss Ulayla." Holding the pie in one hand, she used her other to quickly take off her hat and hold it against her chest.

Ulayla clapped her hand over her mouth, and her eyes

widened. "Well, I'll be. Jesse McGinnis, as I live and breathe. Come in. Come in."

Jesse stepped inside and waited for Ulayla to close the door. "Merry Christmas," she said, offering the pie. "I hope you like sweet potato."

"Why thank you, Jesse," Ulayla said, pleasantly surprised. "And Merry Christmas to you, too." She took the pie box and brought it up to her nose. "Oh, my. It smells wonderful. Sweet potato be one of my favorites. How 'bout we go into the kitchen and I'll cut us a piece?"

Jesse couldn't help but notice the state of the home as she followed her into the next room. Though meticulously scrubbed clean, the floorboards were old and warped, creaking with almost every step. A spiderweb of cracks covered one plastered wall in the tiny living room. Most of the ceiling was covered with large, brownish stains. Jesse presumed they were the source of the musty odor. The smell reminded her of the rainy season at the cabin.

"Have a seat," Ulayla said, gesturing toward the rickety table. "I was just readin' yesterday's paper."

Jesse grinned as she hung her hat on the back of a chair and settled herself onto the seat. "You learned to read? That's wonderful!"

Ulayla set the pie on the counter. "Abby never told you?" she asked, reaching for a knife.

"Told me what?"

Ulayla pushed the knife into the soft pie. "When you used to work next door at the Bowmans, Abby gave me lessons." She placed a wedge on a plate. "After you moved over to Taylor Street, when you went to work, she'd have Aponi watch your youngins. Your wife would walk all the ways over to the house just so's she could keep teachin' me." She placed a second slice on a saucer, grabbed two forks, and took a seat opposite her. "She's got a good heart, your Abby does. How she be anyways? Oh, and those babies?" Ulayla grinned thinking about them. "I bet they all but grown by now."

Jesse was stunned by this new information but not at all surprised by Abby's selfless act. She ran her hand over the back of her neck. "Things aren't good at all." She pushed her plate aside and rested her hands on the wobbly table. "Something awful happened. Last week, while I was working here in the city, someone broke into our home." She took a deep and wavering breath. "Jim was shot and killed."

Ulayla released an audible gasp, and her fork tumbled from her hand. "Oh, sweet baby Jesus," she said, placing her hand over her heart. "I'm so sorry." She reached over and put her hand on top of Jesse's.

"After the man killed him, he took Abby. He hurt her pretty bad before she managed to get away." She gestured over her shoulder with her thumb. "She's in the hospital."

Ulayla patted Jesse's hand. "She gonna be okay, ain't she?"

"We hope so. She's awfully sad and not making much sense. She won't eat." Jesse shook her head. "Things aren't good between us right now. I'm not sure things will ever be good again." She sighed heavily. "She blames me for Jim's death. She's right, ya know. If I'd been home, maybe he'd still be alive."

"Why, Jesse McGinnis! You can't think like that. The Lord works in mysterious ways. He must've had a reason to call your boy home."

"People keep telling me they're sorry for my loss." Jesse crossed her arms over her chest. "But they don't know how it feels. Unless you've lost a child, you can't understand how hard it is to go on. Everywhere you look, life continues as though nothing happened. Birds sing. Rain falls. Yet I can barely breathe." She stared down at her plate. "The pain is so crushing, sometimes, I wish I'd just die."

Ulayla leaned back in the chair. "I growed up in South Carolina. My mammy and pappy was slaves. Means I was born one, too."

"I didn't know that," Jesse said, looking up to meet her gaze.

"I don't talk about it no mo'. Too much pain in them memories. We wasn't nothin' but livestock. Got sold off when I was just twelve years old." She bared her teeth at the memory. "They waited until my pappy was working the field, then they ripped me from my mammy's arms. Oh, did I put up a fight. Got nothin' for my efforts but a good beatin'."

Jesse didn't know what to say.

"They took me away from the only home I knew. Chained me in a wagon. Lawd only knew where they was takin' me. Thought life couldn't get no worse." Ulayla rose to her feet and put a coffee pot on the old cook stove. "I was wrong," she said quietly. She pulled two cups from the cupboard and set them on the table. "After about two and a half hours, we got to a plantation owned by Master Berkholder." She sat back down. "I was took there to be a house slave to his missus." Ulayla discovered a stain on her cup and studied it intently. "She was a nice enough woman, but from the moment I saw that husband of hers, my skin crawled like I was covered with a thousand ants. He was thirty-six years older than the missus." Her lip curled in disgust. "It wasn't long before I found out he had a likin' for young, Negro girls."

Jesse felt a shiver. Her heart ached for Ulayla.

Ulayla scooted back from the table and got up to get the coffee pot. She poured the hot liquid into the mugs. "He cornered me in the barn one day. I tried to fight him off," she said, placing the coffee pot off to one side of the stove to keep it warm. "He beat me 'til he 'bout killed me. I actually begged God to take me that night." She sat back down, blew on the coffee, and took a drink. "Sorry, but I don't have no cream or suga'."

Jesse took a tentative sip. It was strong and bitter. "Doesn't need any. It's good."

"A couple days later, he called me to his bedroom. The missus was out that day so I knew what he wanted." She ran the tip of her finger over a scratch on the table. "When he put his mouth on me, I didn't fight none. My eyes was still swollen from the last time."

"What about his wife? She didn't ask what happened to you?"

"He told her I was clumsy and stupid," she said with a snort. "Told her I done fell down the stairs. Looking back, I think she had to know what her husband was up to." Her voice hardened. "He called me into that room of his more times than I can count." She set her cup down and continued speaking, her gaze an unfocused stare. "One day I realized somethin' was wrong. I was so scared."

Jesse leaned closer, but Ulayla avoided eye contact.

Ulayla ran her finger over the lip of the cup. "The summer of my thirteenth birthday, I gave birth to my first boy." She smiled, her expression one of deep, unadulterated pride. "He was the most beautiful baby I ever saw. Big hazel eyes." She met Jesse's gaze. "Now, I knows what you be thinkin'. How could I love a child fathered by someone so wicked? It wasn't my boy's fault. He innocent."

Jesse smiled at her. "What's his name?"

"Kitch," Ulayla said, her smile broadening. "Good, strong name."

Jesse nodded in agreement.

"Not long after he was born, I took a liking to one of the new field hands, name of June. I think he took pity on me 'cause I was alone with a youngin and all. He was a good man. So we jumped the broom. Even though I was married, Master still had me goin' to his bedroom. By the time I was sixteen I had two more babies, Krimby and Kennard. You could tell by lookin' they be June's."

Jesse simply nodded.

Ulayla busied herself with her cup. "One day, June told me he gonna run. Said he gonna be free. He wanted us be free with him. I convinced him runnin' was no good. We knows what they did to runners."

"I don't know what makes some men so evil. I'm so sorry you had to go through all of that."

Ulayla didn't respond right away.

"I never put up no fuss, cause Master Berkholder always be threatenin' to sell my babies. My youngest, Kennard, just turned five when he bought a new housemaid. It was a blessin' for me cause he quit messing with me as much. I had seven wonderful years with my childrens. One day I went to Charleston with the missus. When we got back, my babies was gone—taken to be sold."

Silence hung in the room.

"June run off that night, searchin' for 'em. He didn't get two miles 'fore the hounds found him. They beat that man nearly to death. Master Berkholder up and sold him the next day." Her eyes filled with tears. "Said he took a loss sellin' him all bruised up, but he figured he'd make an example case anyone else got the notion to run."

Jesse felt as if her heart had fallen into her boots. "Did you ever see them again?"

Ulayla shook her head. "No." She was quiet for a moment and then pulled on the sleeve of her dress, revealing her shoulder and a portion of her back. "That man left me more scars on the inside than he did on the out." She covered herself back up.

Seeing the road map of scars left Jesse speechless.

Ulayla saw the change in Jesse's expression. "Now, I didn't tell you all that so's you could pity me. I told you so's you would understand I know what you goin' through. Some days, all we can do is put one foot in front of the other. Tries to just get through the day." She slid the plate in front of her and picked up her fork. "If that was my June layin' up in that hospital bed, I'd be goin' there and doing whatever it took to win him back. I know Abby. And I'm tellin' you, she don't truly blame you."

"I heard her say it."

"She didn't mean it," Ulayla said confidently. "It was the grief talkin'." She finally took a bite of the pie. She chewed thoughtfully. "It's good. Coulda used a hint of nutmeg."

Jesse picked up her fork and pushed it into the pie. "So why'd you quit working for Sam?"

"He thought I was too slow. Said I wasn't keepin' up with the work. But that's not true. I may be old, but I ain't useless."

Jesse swallowed. "You're right. Needs nutmeg. So, where are you working?"

"I'm a housemaid for the Lipton's."

Jesse took another bite of pie. "Do you like working for them?"

"Puts food on the table and pays the rent. That's all that matters."

Jesse glanced around the dilapidated kitchen. Though Ulayla kept it clean and tidy, the home was falling down around her. She smiled as a thought crossed her mind. "Hmm. That's too bad, because I've been lookin' for someone to help out at my place. It's hard to find someone out where I live. You wouldn't happen to know anyone looking for work?"

"Can't says I do. But I be sure to keep an ear open."

That wasn't the answer Jesse wanted and her smile faded slightly. "Would you ever consider coming to work for me? You'd like Neva. You can live in Abby and I's old cabin. It's very nice. I sure could use your help with Abby. She adores you, you know. Having you around would help lift her spirits. Please say you will."

Ulayla pushed her plate back. She leveled her gaze on Jesse. "I know what you is."

Jesse's body stiffened. "Wh-what do you mean?" She began to feel her face get warm and red.

"Back when you were livin' at Mr. Bowman's, I knew somethin' was different about you. Never met such a kind white man. Couldn't figure you out at first. Then one day, it hit me on the head like a coon fallin' out of an apple tree. You ain't no man." Her face remained impassive. "You a woman."

Jesse's face drained of color. She had always suspected this day would come, but what had always been a mystery to her was who it would be and how they would react. She looked down at her hands and saw that they were shaking. No one, not even Detective McCreary, had been able to see what was right under their noses. Quickly, she clutched her hands together. "I'm sure I don't know what you're talking about." Her foot tapped so nervously against the worn, wood planks it sounded like there was a woodpecker in the room.

Ulayla placed her hand over Jesse's, but the shaking didn't stop. "I know you have reasons for doing what you do," she said kindly. "If I'm gonna come work for you, then I don't want you to have to pretend around me."

"Pretend?"

"I won't tell no one. I swear it. But no secrets. Not from me." Ulayla smiled warmly.

"The relationship I have with Abby isn't pretend. I love her. And I may not be the father of my children, but they believe I am. It's important they continue to believe that."

"I understand."

Jesse forked her fingers through her hair. "You're really comfortable with this?"

"You is who you is."

"Does that mean you'll take the job?"

"If you still want me to."

Jesse's entire body relaxed. She was reeling, but she also felt a great relief cresting over her. "I do."

For the rest of the morning, they sat at the table and made plans for Ulayla to come to work for her. It was agreed that in one week, Jesse would return with a wagon to help her load up her few possessions and make the move to Neva.

CHAPTER TWENTY-NINE

J esse found herself at the mountain cabin. Beside her was Jim, whole and unblemished, sitting on one of the old stump chairs.

"I'm okay, Pippa. Don't cry."

Jesse studied him carefully. She reached out a tentative hand and brushed his bangs out of his eyes. "I'm so sorry." Her breathing quickened. "It should've been me."

Jim looked at her with an expression of pure love. "Don't ever say that."

She twisted her hands in her lap and was unable to conceal the sob in her voice. "You don't know how much I've missed you."

"I've missed you, too." He leaned over and took hold of her hands. "Listen. We don't have much time. There's something you have to do."

"Anything." Tears rolled down her cheeks.

"You have to help those kids at the orphanage."

She cocked her head. "I'm not sure what you want me to do, son."

Jim smiled at her. "Pippa, your whole life has been leading up to this. Don't you see?"

She didn't.

He squeezed her hands. "If my grandparents hadn't died, then you never would've found Frieda. Without her, you never would've learned how to work with wood the way you do."

Jesse shook her head. "Jim, I don't understand. What I do has nothing to do with orphans."

Jim started to fade. "It's time for me to go."

Jesse held on to him with all her strength. "Don't go. Please."

"I have to." He embraced her tightly. "You know what you have to do."

"Jim—please."

"I love you, Pippa."

Jesse woke to find her pillow soaked with tears. She rolled onto her back, her heartbreak as fresh as the dawn that was slowly filling the room with natural light. Although it was only a dream, she hesitated opening her eyes. No amount of time with her son, even if it was imagined, would ever be enough.

Ever since speaking with the three boys at the orphanage, Jesse hadn't been able to get them out of her thoughts. Even with the loss of Jim and anxiety about Abby, they weighed heavily on her mind.

She tossed back the covers and slid to the edge of the bed. Sitting up, she allowed herself a moment to collect her thoughts. Always one who set straight to work, she paused and considered the laundry list of work for clients she had waiting for her at home. She begrudgingly admitted she no longer had the desire, or even the ability, to be creative anymore.

She fell back into bed and rolled over onto her side.

Closing her eyes, she folded her arm under her pillow and tried to call back the dream. It had been so real she could still feel him in her arms. She just wanted a little more time with him. She replayed their conversation, struggling to make sense of it. Try as she might, she still didn't have a clue about what he wanted her to do.

Her thoughts shifted to Abby. Her well-being was the priority right now. She got up and started to get ready, hoping Abby was well enough to be released from the hospital.

Jesse rehashed the events from the day before in her mind as she and Gwen sat and ate breakfast in the hotel dining room. The entire time she had been in Abby's room, not once had Abby spoken to her. She had barely spoken to Gwen and even more rarely looked in Jesse's direction. When they discovered that Abby hadn't eaten anything since being admitted, Jesse had grown increasingly alarmed.

When Gwen finished, she placed her napkin on the table. "I imagine the boutiques are open by now," she said. "Can we go pick out a dress for Ma?"

"Sure." Jesse pushed her nearly untouched plate of food away. "I'll settle the bill and have them pull up the carriage." She scooted back in her chair and stood up.

"Maybe she'll be better today," Gwen said. Her voice was tinged with hope. "Maybe they got her to eat this morning."

"I sure hope so."

After purchasing Abby the appropriate mourning attire, Jesse steered the carriage up in front of the hospital. She opened the carriage door and retrieved the garments she and Gwen had picked out.

As soon as Jesse stepped inside, she noticed Doctor Sarver nearby, examining a patient. They waited until he had finished and then walked over to him.

"Were you able to convince her to eat something?" Jesse asked.

"No, I'm afraid not." He turned to the woman who had just entered the room. "Nurse Glauster, would you take this young lady here," he said, gesturing to Gwen, "and help her get Mrs. McGinnis ready. I need to talk with her father."

Jesse and Gwen showed visible relief. If the doctor felt Abby was well enough to be released, it had to be a good sign.

Handing the garment over to Gwen, Jesse followed the doctor down the hall to his office.

Doctor Sarver sat down at his desk. "I spoke to Dr. Moody over at the asylum yesterday afternoon," he said. "He's willing to treat your wife. He's expecting her this morning to give her a complete evaluation."

Jesse took a seat across from him. "I think it would be better if I took her home."

The doctor rolled a cigarette. "Your wife needs professional help," he said patiently. "If you care about her mental health, then the asylum is the best place for her. Dr. Moody specializes in treating psychological disorders." He lit the end of the cigarette and took a long drag. "With the state she's in, it would be a disservice to take her home." He passed Jesse a piece of paper. "Here's the address. Go there. Talk to him. You'll see that his treatment is the best hope your wife has."

"I'll think about it," Jesse said amiably. "You have the bill ready?"

"Oh, don't worry about that. We'll send it to you in a few days."

Jesse stood and reached for his hand across the desk. "Thank you."

"You're welcome," he said, shaking her hand briefly. "And please, go see Dr. Moody. There's no harm speaking to him."

Although Jesse was adamant about taking Abby home, she didn't want to waste time arguing about it. Instead, she simply nodded. "Okay. I will." She followed him toward the door and then stopped. "Wait," she said. "Has Abby seen the injury yet?"

"Yes."

Jesse grimaced.

"She wanted to have a look, so I removed the bandage this morning. Honestly, either it didn't bother her as much as I thought it would, or she's very good at putting on a brave face…" He paused and put a consoling hand on her shoulder. "I should warn you, I decided it was best not to dress the wound. I put some salve on it. I think leaving it exposed will help it heal quicker."

As Jesse was guided down the hall to Abby's room, she had to remind herself not to react. Stepping into the room, she saw that Abby was already seated on the edge of the bed, dressed from head to toe in black. Her face was hidden beneath a black veil.

Jesse thanked the staff for everything they had done, and then she and Gwen helped Abby to her feet and carefully led her out of the hospital to the waiting carriage.

"Let's get you home, Ma," Gwen said.

Abby continued to stay silent. The lack of food had made her weak and she found it difficult to walk. She concentrated on moving one foot at a time. Though she had always been slender, the weight she had lost over the last week made her look emaciated and frail.

Jesse changed her mind about taking Abby home when she saw her struggle with the simple task of walking. "Actually," she said, helping Gwen to assist Abby into the carriage, "we have to make a stop first."

Once Abby and Gwen were seated inside, Jesse directed the horses toward the address written on the slip of paper.

Not even half an hour later, Jesse pulled in front of a huge, two-story brick building. Just looking at the cold, dreary stone gave her a bad feeling. She felt guilty that she had kept this place a secret from Abby.

A woman in a dark dress came down the walk and approached the carriage. She wore a pristine white smock and a hat. "Are you Mr. McGinnis?"

"Yes, ma'am," Jesse said, stepping down. "We have an appointment with Dr. Moody."

"He's been expecting you. Let's get your wife inside."

Jesse opened the carriage door. She and Gwen helped Abby maneuver the step, and then she put an arm around her.

They followed the nurse inside and were escorted to an office.

The man standing stiffly behind a desk came over to greet them. "I'm Doctor Moody," he said, offering his hand. "This must be Mrs. McGinnis."

Jesse shook his hand.

"Why don't you go ahead and put her in the chair," he said. "The nurse will show you where you can wait while I evaluate her."

After Abby was seated, Jesse and Gwen were led down the

hall to a small waiting room. They took seats across from a well-dressed woman who appeared to be quite agitated. She glanced repeatedly toward the hall, her leg bouncing nervously.

After a few minutes, Jesse could not contain her curiosity. She asked the woman, "Are you visiting someone?"

"My sister," the woman replied anxiously. "I've been trying for a week to see her, but they keep giving me the run around."

Jesse looked at her sympathetically. "Is she suffering from melancholia?"

"Hell no!" the woman spat. "There ain't a damn thing wrong with her. The only reason she's here is because of that son of a bitch she married."

Jesse arched an eyebrow. "I'm sorry. I didn't mean to pry."

"My sister found out he was having relations with another woman," she went on to explain. "He had her committed so he could divorce her and marry that harlot of his."

Jesse stared at her, slack-mouthed.

"Poor Patricia hasn't seen her children in over a week. He gets to rip my sister away from her kids as though she never existed. Now they belong to him." She glared at Jesse. "I'm sure you know all about that."

Jesse wasn't sure how to respond. Before she could even try, the nurse returned to the waiting room.

"The doctor would like to speak with you, alone," she said to Jesse. She looked at Gwen. "You can wait here."

"I'll be right back," Jesse said.

She was escorted to a chair in a room adjacent to the one Abby was in.

Doctor Moody came in and closed the door. "I'm going to

need some history about your wife. Tell me, just how long has she been in this state?"

Jesse explained the situation to the best of her ability, mindful to omit that Abby had killed someone.

"I believe your wife is suffering from acute mania," he said. "I'll need to do further testing of course, but I think I can help her."

"Have you treated other patients with that?" Jesse asked. "Were you able to cure them?"

"Yes, I have. Some heal, some don't. It really depends on the severity of their case."

"I don't know anything about this place, and I don't feel comfortable leaving my wife here. I think it's best if I take her home."

"Your wife needs professional care," the doctor insisted. "Don't you want what's best for her?"

"I do." She scratched the back of her neck. She was getting the feeling that she was losing control of the situation. "What exactly is wrong with the women who are here?"

"I treat a variety of psychological conditions. Disobedience, chronic fatigue, anxiety, melancholia, and more." He tapped his fingertips together thoughtfully. "Some of these women just have no place else to go. You know, it's not uncommon at all for a man to have his wife committed so he can lay claim to all her assets."

"No. I didn't know that." Jesse felt her pulse quicken. She wasn't sure if what she was feeling was anger or fear.

"I actually had one man bring his sister here after their parents passed away so that he would get all the inheritance," the doctor continued, seemingly eager to inform. "Some women develop physical scars, like your wife. It's not unheard of for a man to find his wife unattractive afterward and no longer want to be with her."

The very idea made Jesse go numb.

"Some wives," he said, making a steeple of his fingers, "simply don't know their place in society. Their strong opinions have landed them here." He shrugged. "You see, we treat all kinds of disabled women."

Her eyes narrowed into crinkled slits and she folded her arms. "Do they ever get to go home?"

"Sometimes, with the proper medication and treatment." He studied Jesse's face for a moment. "Let me give you some advice, one man to another. No one is going to hold it against you if you don't find your wife attractive anymore. Most men would struggle with arousal if their wives were as disfigured as yours. Especially on the face."

Jesse thumbs clenched inside her fists.

"Listen," he said pointedly. "I saw you pull up. I can tell you're a man of means. You have my guarantee. You'll have no issues getting a speedy divorce. In a couple of days, you'll be free to carry on with that pretty little filly I saw you come in with."

"That filly is my daughter!" Jesse exploded out of the chair. "And I'll have you know that I'm madly in love with my wife! I have no intentions of getting divorced."

Doctor Moody jumped to his feet. "My apologies. I misread the situation."

"Yes, you did," Jesse said through clenched teeth. She turned toward the door. "I'm taking my wife and leaving."

"You can do that," the doctor said doggedly, "but you won't be helping her. If you care about her at all, then you'll leave her under my care."

Jesse stopped. She was torn between wanting what was best for Abby and getting her as far away from the place as possible. "If I were to leave her in your care," she said, "then I must insist on a tour."

"We don't do that. Our patients are entitled to privacy."

"Then there's no way I'm leaving her here."

The doctor stood his ground a moment longer. "Hold on. Give me a minute."

He left the room. After giving the nurse some instructions, he returned a few moments later. "I'll have the nurse show you around while I do a couple more tests on your wife. When you're finished, perhaps then we can discuss options."

The nurse escorted Jesse back to get Gwen.

They were briefly shown some of the nicest locations in the facility. Several times, as they passed by a closed door, Jesse inquired about what was on the other side. When her questions were deflected, she had a sinking feeling that things were being intentionally avoided. The bad feeling only grew as the tour continued. She was being shown propaganda.

Gwen said quietly to Jesse, "Maybe we can bring her some books to read while she's here."

The nurse overheard. "No," she said firmly. "Reading is strictly prohibited."

Jesse couldn't believe what she had heard. "What? Why's that?"

"Because," the nurse said, "it can be harmful to their delicate conditions."

Gwen's brow furrowed. "What do they do with their free time?"

"The ones that are mentally sound are assigned appropriate work detail. They often help out in the kitchen, preparing meals or cleaning up. Others work in the laundry room. Some sew and mend clothing. You know, idle hands are the devil's work so we try to keep them busy."

A woman's shouts echoed down the corridor. "Excuse me," the nurse said. "I need to go check on her. Wait here."

Once she was out of their sight, Jesse turned to Gwen. "When she comes back, tell her I had to use the privy. Keep her here if you can."

"All right, Pippa," Gwen said. "But hurry. I don't like this place."

Jesse raced off down another corridor. She was slowed by the sounds of whimpers and moans. Though she wanted to see inside for herself, every door she tried was locked. Finally, she came to one that she was able to open. Glancing up and down the hall, she quietly turned the knob and peered inside.

She gasped. Inside the room, which was approximately eight by six feet if she had to guess, there was a naked woman chained to the bed. The highly sedated eyes looked pleadingly at her. Though she didn't speak, Jesse got the sense the woman was screaming inside.

"You are not allowed to be here!"

Jesse whirled around to see the nurse rushing toward her.

"What's wrong with her?" Jesse demanded. "Why isn't she wearing any clothes? And why the hell is she in chains?"

The nurse hurried to close the door. "She's mad," she explained. "Soils her clothes as soon as we put them on her, so we quit dressing her." She pulled a key from her pocket and turned it in the lock. "Now, come along."

Jesse followed her back to where Gwen was waiting.

As the nurse led them back to the waiting room, Gwen

whispered to Jesse, "I'm sorry. She insisted on looking for you."

Jesse whispered back, "It's alright." She gave her a wink.

When they passed by the doctor's office, Jesse reached for the doorknob. "I need to speak to my wife." She went in without waiting for permission.

Abby was sitting in a chair, her hands resting in her lap. She was fidgeting with a handkerchief.

"Mr. McGinnis," the doctor said, looking up. "I'm not finished with my evaluation yet. Could you kindly wait out in the—"

"Can I have the room? I'd like a moment with my wife—alone." She glanced over at Gwen. "Wait for me in the hall."

Jesse waited for everyone to leave and then closed the door. She pulled a chair over next to Abby and sat down. Leaning forward, she put her hands on Abby's knees. "Look at me."

Abby didn't look at her.

Jesse continued anyway. "Fine. Don't. But dammit, you're going to listen."

Abby stopped fiddling with the handkerchief.

"Don't you think I know this is all my fault? I know I should've been home." Her voice broke. "You have no idea how much I wish it would've been me."

Abby finally turned her head to look at Jesse. She peered at her from behind the protective lace of her veil.

"I'd give my life to bring him back if I could," Jesse said, choking on a sob. "Don't you know that?"

"It's not your fault," Abby finally said, faintly. "It's mine."

"No it's not. You have no blame in any of this."

Abby reached under the veil and wiped her eyes with the handkerchief. "Oh, Jes," she said, her voice flavored with despair. "Yes, it is." She exhaled a long, pitiful breath. "It was Silas. He came back for me. Jim…" She started crying; sobbing so hard she could no longer speak.

"I don't understand." Jesse leaned back in the chair and slammed her eyes shut. The grisly image of his splayed body came back to her. She looked at Abby. "I thought he died years ago."

"I did, too. I was wrong. So you see, it is my fault. It's because of me that he was there."

Jesse took hold of Abby's hands. "No, it's not. You had no control over what he did."

"I tried to get him to leave," Abby cried. "I really did. But he wouldn't go. Oh, God, Jes, you have to believe me. And then Jim came in…it happened so fast. All I did was sit there and do nothing. You were right to bring me here. I deserve it."

Jesse sat in stoned silence. "Listen," she said finally, edging closer to her. "I only brought you here because I want what's best for you. I want you to get better."

"Can you ever forgive me?" Abby's voice was meek.

Jesse wanted to hold her close until she felt Abby's strength return. "There's nothing to forgive." She slowly lifted the veil.

Abby quickly covered her cheek and turned her head away. "Don't. I look like a monster." She tried to pull the veil back in place.

"No." Jesse pulled her hand away. "We're going to settle this right now." She stared at the jagged stitches, fighting against the scream she felt building inside her. It wasn't the wound causing her to feel that way. It was the outrage over what Silas had done. She pictured the macabre scene in her mind again, only this time she was the one wielding the axe.

Abby misunderstood her silence. "I understand if you're not attracted to me anymore."

The sound of Abby's sweet voice shook the vengeful thoughts from Jesse's mind. She looked deeply into her eyes. Gently, she ran her thumb along Abby's lower lip. "You're just as beautiful as the day I first laid eyes on you."

"Just stop. I know that's not true."

"Do you really think I'm that shallow? That I'd be less attracted to you because of a scratch on your face? I love you no matter what. I always will." Jesse got down on one knee and turned Abby's hands so they were facing palm up. She kissed one and then the other, tracing the line that ran from her wrist to her ring finger. "I know we still have a lot of healing to do," she said, staring up at her. "But I think we need each other now more than ever."

Jesse reached into her vest pocket and pulled out the wedding ring. She slipped it onto Abby's finger.

Abby gasped at the sight of her wedding band. She leaned forward and wrapped her arms around Jesse. Her face was stained with tears. "Are you sure you still want me?"

"Wanting you is the only thing I am sure of." She pried Abby's arms loose and pulled back. "Gwen, Willow, Toby, and Jamie. We all want you home. We love you, Abs. Don't you know that?" Her eyes searched Abby's face.

At last, a smile lifted the right side of Abby's mouth. "Take me home."

The doctor had assumed Jesse was telling Abby goodbye. He was surprised when the door opened and both of them stepped out.

"I'm taking my wife home, where she belongs," Jesse announced, holding onto Abby.

Gwen rushed over and wrapped her arms around her mother's waist.

"You're making a mistake," Doctor Moody said with a hiss.

"Who are you to tell me what's best for my wife? She doesn't need medication or to be confined in a tiny room. What she really needs to help her heal is the love of her family, not some doctor looking to subjugate her."

Doctor Moody's hand reached out and coiled around Jesse's arm. "You're making a huge mistake." His voice was laced with venom. "I have medicine that can treat her mental illness."

Jesse glanced down at the hand wrapped firmly around her bicep. "The only mistake I see," she said coldly, "is the one you made by grabbing me. I suggest you remove your hand. Now."

The doctor let his hand fall to his side.

As soon as he let go of her, Gwen and Jesse positioned themselves on either side of Abby and escorted her out of the building.

Walking down the gravel path toward the carriage, Jesse chanced a glimpse over her shoulder. Several women were staring out at them, their faces pressed against the windows. She could only imagine the hell they were living in.

"You really let him have it, Pippa," Gwen said, her voice tinged with pride. "I thought you were going to hit him." She shook her head. "This is not a good place to be."

"I couldn't agree more," Jesse said, opening the carriage door. "Come on. Let's go home."

CHAPTER THIRTY

When Abby returned home from the hospital, the entire family believed life would revert to some semblance of normalcy.

They were wrong.

Jesse found it impossible to get back into any sort of routine. She didn't eat. Sleep eluded her. She had always believed she knew what pain was. Many times in her life the loss of one of her loved ones would hit her like a hammer blow to the heart, even years after they were gone. None of that compared to losing Jim. Without her son, nothing would ever be normal again. Her days slowed to a tortuous crawl. She fought her way through each one of them, gritting her teeth against the constant, excruciating void that was crushing down on her.

Abby struggled as well. She slept for as many hours of the day as she possibly could. Her new reality was one she could only face in small, calculated bursts. When she was awake, thoughts tormented her. Hot, guilty tears streamed down her face as she considered a future filled with missed birthdays and family holidays—constant reminders of their incalculable loss. There would never be a wedding to attend with the lovely young lady who stole her son's heart. No grandchildren with Jim's dark, soulful eyes begging her to let them help bake cookies. It wasn't right she should outlive her son. She couldn't stop thinking—believing—the horrible truth she repeated like a mantra: *If it weren't for me, Jim would still be alive.*

Jesse and Abby were so caught up in their own personal turmoil they had no energy to console one another. There wasn't any cure for what was wrong with them—no Native remedy that could take away their pain, no glue that could put back together the shattered pieces of their hearts.

Every second of every hour that Jesse and Abby spent inside the home was a constant reminder of Jim's absence. There wasn't a place they could go to escape their sorrow. It followed them from room to room, lingering in corners and behind doorways. No matter where they turned, it was there, looming and omnipresent. They knew it was something they would have to carry with them for the rest of their lives. Neither one of them knew how to handle their grief. Instead of coming together, sharing the weight of the oppressive yoke, they moved apart, shouldering the load separate and alone.

If not for Ulayla, the entire household would have collapsed. Most days it was a challenge to get Abby to eat much of anything. Jesse rarely set foot inside the kitchen she had once viewed as the hub of her home. Ulayla seldom pressed them about eating. About the only things she could do were keep a hot meal on the table for Gwen and Willow and a soundless prayer on her lips.

Even Toby was at a loss about what to do. Though he did what he could to help, in the end, all he could really do was watch as things went from bad to worse. His sister rarely left the house anymore. When she did, it was only to go into town for more cases of whiskey. He knew most of her time was spent with her hand fisted around a bottle. He also knew she would have to drink more each day in order to find any sort of comfort.

Whenever he tried to broach the subject with her, she became irate and aggressive. Slowly, she was evolving into someone he didn't recognize. Despite all that, he stepped up and worked alongside Ulayla, doing whatever he could for Gwen and Willow's sake. It was easy to convince them to stay at his house most days. Distracting them with things such as hunting, fishing, tending the garden, or even playing Old Maid, he, Jamie, and Ulayla did their best to give the girls a sense of stability.

In spite of Toby and Ulayla's best efforts, Gwen lived in a constant state of fear. She watched silently as the distance between her parents grew further apart each day. They barely spoke to anyone, let alone each other. Gwen's biggest concern was that they would drift so far apart they would never find their way back to one another.

For two months following Jim's death, Jesse suffered from insomnia. She had tried everything to get sleep, but nothing worked. An entire bottle of whiskey did nothing to slow her racing thoughts, and drinking had simply become a way for her to black out. She spent most nights in her office or the barn, alone and inebriated.

It was another sleepless night. Jesse slid the bottle away and pushed back from the desk. It was rare for her to consider sleeping with Abby. Utterly exhausted and not knowing what else to do, she stumbled down the hall, trudged up the stairs, and crawled into bed. She had just closed her eyes when there was a soft knock on the bedroom door.

Jesse threw back the covers and flung open the door. "What!"

"I need you to get d-dressed and come out to the b-barn."

She heaved a sigh. "Why?"

"Just g-get dressed."

Jesse could see Toby's expression in the moonlight streaming in through the window at the end of the hall. She nodded. "Give me a minute." She pushed the door closed, turned up the wick, and reached for her clothes.

"What's the matter?" Abby asked, squinting.

"I don't know," Jesse grumbled. "He wants me to go to the barn."

"Is something wrong?"

"I said I don't know!" She rammed her bare foot into her pants.

Abby quietly got out of bed and dressed.

Wordlessly, they hurried down the stairs and then followed Toby quickly across the yard.

They could hear loud banging noises before they even reached the barn.

Jesse rushed inside and peered over the wooden gate of the stall. Buck was on his side on the ground, thrashing violently. His stomach was obviously distended.

"What's wrong with him?" Jesse lifted the latch.

"Wait," Toby said, grabbing hold of her arm. "You can't go in there. He's in pain, and he might hurt you." He pointed over to the corner. "He got sick."

Jesse didn't know as much about horses as Toby, but she

did know that they didn't vomit. When they did, it meant something was horribly wrong.

He let go of her arm. "He's ruptured inside."

Jesse raked her fingers through her hair. "Is there anything we can do for him?"

Toby shook his head. "He probably won't make it 'til dawn."

Jesse grabbed hold of the gate. She watched helplessly, her chin quivering, as Buck continued his violent rolling. He had been her faithful companion for so many years. The thought of not having him around devastated her. It was soul crushing that she couldn't be in there with him, holding his head and stroking his velvety muzzle.

Abby put her arm around Jesse and then looked at Toby. "How long will he be like this?"

"Hard to say. Could be an hour. Could be several."

Abby ran her hand down Jesse's back. "I'm so sorry, Jes."

For a moment, Buck's thrashing stopped and he looked up at Jesse, his normally soft, brown eyes white with fear. In all the time she had spent with him, she had never seen anything remotely like this, and it chilled her to her core. Her eyes pooled with tears. When the kicking resumed, her tears flowed unhindered down her ashen cheeks.

"I know you don't want to think about it," Toby said, placing a hand on her shoulder. "But we should probably put him out of his misery."

Jesse's head snapped around to look at him. "You mean, shoot him?" She had been expecting these words from Toby, but somehow, they still caught her by surprise.

He nodded. "It's the humane thing to do."

"You don't want him to suffer," Abby said.

"I can't do that." A fresh torrent of grief washed down her face.

"I can do it," Toby said quietly.

"I think you should let him," Abby said.

Jesse couldn't see. She nearly choked on the sob that was threatening to explode out of her. She barely had the strength to nod her consent.

"I'll go get my rifle." He turned on his heels and left the barn.

There was nothing more Jesse wanted in that moment than to go in and sit by Buck's side until the end. Since the day she had gotten him, he had stayed by hers. He'd met every challenge they had ever faced together. Now, at a time when he needed her the most, she could do nothing for him. Her inability to help him made her feel like an even bigger failure.

She leaned over and placed her hands on her knees. "I ca-ca-can't breathe," she said through gut-wrenching sobs that shook her entire body. "He's my best friend. I can't do this."

Abby continued to rub her back until Toby returned carrying his rifle.

He looked at them. "You two should go."

Abby took Jesse's hand and pulled her out of the barn. They had just reached the porch steps when a shot rang out. Both of them jumped.

Jesse fell to her knees and lost what control of her limbs she still possessed before the sound of the gunshot.

Toby came from the barn and he and Abby struggled to get Jesse to her feet, but it was no use. He and Abby locked eyes for a moment and both nodded slightly. Toby swooped Jesse up in his arms and carried her up to the bedroom with

Abby right behind them. Abby pulled back the blanket and Toby gently lowered his sister onto the bed.

Jesse used the last bit of strength she could muster to roll over onto her stomach and bury her face in the pillow, unable to think of anything other than the fact that her best friend had been there minutes before, and now he was gone forever.

The next morning, Abby woke to find herself alone in the bed again. She slipped on her robe and quickly went downstairs. She discovered Jesse asleep in the office, her head resting on the desk. An empty cognac bottle was on its side next to her. Abby walked over and placed her hand on Jesse's back. "Jes," she whispered. "Why don't you go on upstairs and get some sleep?"

Jesse lifted her head and stared around groggily. She looked up at Abby with swollen, bloodshot eyes. Her gaze went immediately to Abby's cheek. The scar was a constant reminder of her failure. She turned her head away without responding. Standing on wobbly legs, she stumbled her way up the stairs and down the hall into the bedroom.

Abby plopped down onto the settee in the office and placed her hand against the scar. She couldn't stand to look at her own reflection. She couldn't blame Jesse for feeling the same way.

She fully understood Jesse's attitude toward her. If not for her, Silas never would have come into their lives. It was her attitude toward the girls that she didn't understand. Jesse rarely spoke to them anymore. When she did, her words were short and gruff. Abby had watched her own father turn into a mean drunk. She worried Jesse was doing the same thing. She buried her face in her hands and cried.

Jesse spent the entire day passed out in bed. When she woke up it was dark out. Abby was sleeping soundly beside her. Jesse slid out from the side of the bed, pulled on her clothes, and tiptoed out of the room.

She headed down the hall to Jim's room, where Gwen now slept, and peeked her head through the barely-open door. Gwen was sleeping peacefully. She pulled the door most of the way shut and headed down the hall to Willow's room. She went over to the bed, pulled the blanket up around her daughter's shoulders, leaned down to kiss her on the forehead, and then slipped quietly from the room.

She went downstairs to her office and sank into the chair behind her desk. The only light in the room was coming in through the window at her back. After what had happened in that room, she wondered if people would think she was crazy for spending so much time there. She found she didn't care. It was where she felt closest to Jim.

Her wet cheeks glistened in the moonlight as she pulled open the bottom drawer and reached inside. The bottle of whiskey she expected to find wasn't there. She leaned down and searched further back. Nothing. She smacked her hand on the desk. She jumped up and opened the cupboards. The bottles she normally kept inside were gone. It didn't matter. She headed out the door. She was fairly certain Abby didn't know about the stockpile she had hidden in the barn.

It hadn't been that long ago when Jesse's sleeping body pressed next to hers was the norm. When Abby woke the following morning to find herself alone once again, she realized they had a new normal now. Losing Buck had been the final straw. The hairline fracture that had been forming had finally cracked completely. Jesse was broken. Abby released a long, weighted breath.

For the first time since Jim died, Abby knew it was time for her to snap out of the state she had been in. She'd have to forget about her own despair and do something drastic if she wanted to save her marriage and help Jesse. She dressed quickly and then went to find Ulayla. Together, they hurried over to Toby's house.

"I'm scared," Abby said frankly.

"It's only gotten worse," Ulayla said.

"Jes has lost so much." Abby sipped at her strong, dark coffee. It paired well with their conversation.

"W-we all have," Toby said.

The others nodded in agreement.

The three of them sat silently for a moment, thinking of the loved ones they had lost. No strangers to pain, they understood completely how Jesse was feeling. While they had somehow been able to find ways to navigate their grief, Jesse had not. She was about to crash upon the rocks. The three of them thought long and hard. Two cups of coffee later, they came up with a plan that would go into effect that day. They were determined to help the person who had always been there to save everyone else.

"Leaving is going to be the hardest thing I've ever done," Abby said. Her voice was hollow. "But I have to. I'm not strong enough to bury her, too."

"I think this'll work," Ulayla said.

"If the th-threat of losing you guys don't s-sober her up," Toby added, "nothing will."

Abby returned home and went straight to her bedroom.

Hastily, she tossed her carpet bag on the bed. After she had packed, she went down the hall and told the girls to do the same.

Gwen and Willow could tell by the look on their mother's face there was no sense in arguing. It was a battle they knew they wouldn't win.

While the girls packed, Abby sat down at the kitchen table and wrote a note. When she was finished, she walked into Jesse's office to place it on the desk. As she had expected, Jesse was passed out on the settee. Her face looked almost peaceful and Abby stared lovingly at her. After a moment, she placed the note on Jesse's chest, swept her hair off her forehead, and bent down to kiss the crescent-shaped scar.

In the time it took the girls to finish packing, Toby had hitched up the carriage and pulled it around to the front of the house. After meeting with Abby and Ulayla, he had made the decision that it would probably be best for Jamie to go into the city with them. He didn't want her around for what he knew were going to be some rough days ahead.

By the time Jesse woke up and found the folded piece of paper on her chest, the rest of her family was well on their way to the city.

Jes,

I can't stay here any longer and watch you slowly kill yourself. The children don't need to see it, either. We'll pray for you every day. Hopefully someday you'll find some peace.

Take care of yourself,

Abs

CHAPTER THIRTY-ONE

J esse crushed Abby's note in her fist and threw it across the room. The spark of sadness that shot through her was followed immediately by a rush of unbridled anger. She swung her legs off the side of the settee and propelled herself into a seated position. From the kitchen, she could hear the sounds of pots and lids clanging together. She jumped to her feet and headed for the door, prepared to confront Abby. She discovered Ulayla instead, standing in front of the stove, stirring a large pot of beet and sweet onion soup. "Where's Abby?" She spat the words at her back.

"Toby done took her and your youngins to San Francisco." She sipped soup from a large wooden spoon and then added a pinch of salt.

"When are they coming back?"

Ulayla whirled around. "Far's I know they ain't."

Jesse rubbed her temples. A massive headache was starting to form. She took a step toward the table and stumbled on the cuff of her pants. She hitched them up and gathered them in at the waist where they were too big from all the weight she'd lost. "Wow…she's something, isn't she?" she said through gritted teeth. She plopped down in the chair. "And that's some brother I have."

"It's what Abby wanted. Don't be mad at him." She picked up the ladle and filled a bowl. "Don't you be mad at her. She just had her limit." She set the bowl down in front of her. "Here. Have some."

Jesse felt sick. She wasn't sure if it was because of everything she'd had to drink or if it was because Abby had left and taken the children with her, but she felt that if she were to eat any of the soup Ulayla had just given her, it would have come right back up. She pushed the bowl away. "No, I'm going to go lay down. Wake me up when he gets back."

Several hours later, a bleary-eyed Jesse woke to find Toby standing next to her bed. She blinked groggily several times, trying to focus on the world around her. "What are you doing in here?" She rubbed at her eyes. "And why the hell would you take my family away from me?"

"No more drinkin', Jes." Toby leveled his gaze at her. He didn't blink or stutter, and the look on his face was one that she had never seen before. "I don't have much family left. I'm not about to lose you, too." His eyes filled with concern. "I will not let you ruin your life. I won't."

Jesse fought her way out from under the covers and stumbled to her feet. The only thing she wanted was a drink. "I'm not ruining my life." She marched toward the door. "I'm not the one who left—she did." Her eyes narrowed. "I bet I can guess where she went. Right back to Sam, didn't she?" she said, shouldering her way past him.

Toby moved to stand in her way. "Don't you dare talk

about Abby th-that way. And you're crazy if you think that. Just so you know, she's st-staying at a hotel."

"Then why'd she leave?"

"'Cause you're a damn f-f-fool, that's why." His stance was rigid, his gaze unfaltering and implacable. "And you're not g-going anywhere."

"Oh yeah, who's gonna to stop me?" She took a step back and eyed him up and down. "You think you're big enough to do it?"

"That's r-r-right." He placed his hands on both of her shoulders.

She flung them off. "You need to get out of my way."

"I can't d-do that."

"I mean it, Toby. Move! Now!"

His jaw clenched and he broadened his stance. "No. I'm not—"

She swung her fist, cutting him off.

He moved quickly, catching the blow in his hand as easily as if he were catching a fly ball. The force of her second jab landed on his bicep before he shoved her away.

She lunged at him. Her feet, already unstable, became tangled in the baggy hem of her pants. She lost her footing and spilled onto the floor.

Toby's arms were exceedingly muscled. The veins stood out like cords of rope. He easily mopped her up and tossed her over his shoulder.

She pummeled his back and kicked her legs, but she was overmatched.

He hurled her onto the bed.

Jesse fell hard, but the soft mattress easily absorbed the shock.

As soon as she landed she sprang up on the bed, nostrils flaring. She swung at him and missed. She drew back and swung again. Her fist found nothing but air, and the momentum of her attempt sent her sprawling. When she landed, the upper half of her body was on the floor and the lower half was knotted in the heavy quilt on the bed. She glared up at him, panting. "Let me go."

Toby picked her off the floor, untied her from the bedclothes, and threw her back on the bed.

Jesse's green eyes were ablaze. She shot at him with any incriminating thing she could think of. Accused him of being dishonest, untrustworthy, and disloyal.

She tried everything she could to get out of that room. No matter what she did, she was no match for her brother's brute strength. Exhausted, she lay back on her elbows, determination flashing in her eyes. "If you know what's good for you, you'll let me out of this room!"

He stood straighter. "Sorry. Can't do th-that."

The battle between the siblings continued for hours. For every move Jesse made, Toby had one to counter it that would leave her upended on the mattress.

The day discreetly passed into the next, and Jesse finally gave up fighting with her brother and began what would become her true battle.

Her demands to be let out of the room turned into pitiful cries as time wore on. "Just one drink," or "One couldn't hurt," she'd plead to him repeatedly. She writhed on the mattress in a silhouette of her own cold sweat. The pain in her head was so violent that she felt like someone had taken an axe to her skull. The thought made her think of Silas. That thought led to Abby. She didn't know if she should cry or scream. Instead, she leaned over the side of the bed and vomited into the pot Toby held for her.

"You better hope I never get out of this bed," she told him through chattering teeth.

Toby looked down, his brown eyes full of sympathy. "I'm s-sorry it had to come to this, but it's f-for your own g-g-good. You'll th-thank me later."

Jesse growled deep in her throat. She wanted to lash out at him, but she had no strength to move. "It's f-for your own g-g-good. You'll th-thank me later," she said, mocking him.

"Feel b-better?"

"Sure do, you stuttering fool."

Her words struck him harder than any blow she could have landed. He knew it wasn't his sister speaking. Still, the sting of her words wouldn't leave anytime soon. He imagined it would hurt long after they had left that room.

"I'm n-not the one who's a fool. I'd never be stupid enough to p-p-push my family away."

"No one told her to leave." Jesse bared her teeth. "It was her choice."

"Jes, I know you're not th-that dumb. She left b-because she loves you. You don't see how lucky you are."

She scowled at him.

"Well, I do. I'm n-n-not going to let you piss it away." He offered her a glass of water.

She pushed his hand away. "You're killing me." Her eyes were red-rimmed. She couldn't remember ever feeling so sick. The fight was gone from her body, replaced by constant shivering. She was as white as flour. "I need a drink so bad. You don't understand." Froth had formed at the corners of her mouth.

Toby continued to stay by her side, holding the pot when she needed it, and bathing her head with a cool rag as her body purged itself. Tremors rocked her so hard it looked as if she were having a seizure. Placing a chair in front of the door, he dozed when she did, which wasn't very often.

After three long days, Jesse announced she was ready to try and eat something. Ulayla's chicken and noodles came back up almost immediately. She begged her brother for one small drink of whiskey on the pretense of helping to keep the food down.

Toby shook his head and stood firm in his resolve, determined to see the mission through to the end.

An entire week had nearly passed when Jesse woke. She noticed straight away that Toby wasn't seated in the chair blocking the door. Pushing off the covers, she sat upright on the edge of the bed. Already thin, the ordeal had taken a toll on her. She glanced down at her body and ran her hands over her ribs and then her hipbones, which were sticking out noticeably. It was hard for her to tell how much weight she had lost, but she knew it was a lot. She cupped her face in her hands. It took her a moment for her to realize her head wasn't pounding. With a sigh of relief, she let herself feel hopeful that the worst was over.

She slowly stood and got dressed. She was acutely aware of how loose her clothes had become. Thumbing up her suspenders, her stomach rumbled when she made her way to the kitchen. Ulayla was frying bacon in a cast-iron skillet. Toby was seated at the table drinking a cup of coffee. She crossed the room.

Toby and Ulayla were happy to see her up and about, however, they kept their expressions guarded.

"Good morning," Toby said.

"Morning." She sat down across from him.

Ulayla poured a cup of coffee and brought it over to the table. "How ya feeling?"

She gave a half shrug. "Okay, I guess."

Ulayla went back over to the stove. "I made your favorite." She came back to the table and placed a heaping plate of French toast and bacon in front of her.

Jesse picked up her fork and began to eat.

Toby took a sip of his coffee and shared an optimistic look with Ulayla.

Jesse chewed one bite, swallowed, and then set her fork beside her plate. "I'm sorry, Toby. I know I said some pretty awful things to you."

Toby set his cup down. He sized her up and was thoughtful for a moment. "I kn-know you didn't mean it."

"I didn't." A line appeared between her brows, and she drew her lower lip between her teeth. "But I know I hurt you, and I'm sorry."

"It's alright. I forgive you."

She looked over at Ulayla. "I owe you an apology, too. I'm sorry I've been so difficult to be around. I know it wasn't what you signed on for."

"We good, Jesse." She smiled warmly at her.

Jesse sighed and released a long breath. She picked up her fork and started eating again. The food was delicious, and she enjoyed it, but she pushed her plate away after a few bites. She didn't want to upset her stomach again. Picking up her cup, she snatched a piece of bacon and headed to her office.

Jesse thumbed through the letters on her desk, hoping to find one addressed from Abby. There were several from potential new clients. One she found was from Edith. But there was nothing from Abby. She picked up the one from Edith and slid the letter opener along the edge of the envelope. Inside were two sheets of paper. There was nothing out of the ordinary. Edith filled her in on their lives, and the lives of everyone they knew in Ely. One paragraph toward the end of the letter caught her attention, though. Burton had shown interest in attending law school. Edith went on to mention she wasn't sure they would be able to afford to send him.

Jesse dropped the papers on the desk and swiveled in her chair. Outside the window, the leaves on the trees swayed slightly in the light breeze. There wasn't a cloud in the sky, but the world outside looked gloomy to her. She thought back to a conversation she'd had with Jim about going to Harvard, which had taken place in that very room. A single tear rolled down her cheek, and she swiped it away with an impatient hand. She had felt lost in a world where her son no longer existed, but now she felt even more lost without Abby and the girls.

The silence in the room suddenly felt oppressive. She pushed back from the desk and headed straight to the barn. Careful to avoid Buck's stall, and the painful memories corralled there, she grabbed a currycomb off a shelf and went down the row of stalls until she reached Phantom's. She toyed with the notion to throw a saddle on him and ride pell-mell to San Francisco to win Abby back. However, she knew she'd never make it; she barely had the stamina to walk across the yard.

When she finished with Phantom, she walked over to a corner of the barn and tossed back a heavy, canvas tarp. Most jobs she worked on in her shop. Smaller, more personal projects, she enjoyed working on in the barn, alongside the horses like she used to up at the cabin. Her chisel was in the same spot where she'd left it months ago. She snatched it up, hoping to forget everything for a while. After a few chips and scrapes, it was obvious it was pointless. Her creativity and passion seemed to have died right along with her son.

She replaced the tarp and then checked all the places where she used to hide whiskey. All her bolt-holes were empty except for one. She reached behind a pile of stacked lumber and pulled out a bottle. Her shaking hand clutched it like a buoy.

A barn swallow landed nearby and watched her with accusing eyes.

She pulled the cork from the bottle and brought it to her lips. Her eyes closed, and she pictured Abby and the girls. Before she had time to think about what she was doing, she turned the bottle upside down. She focused on the smells of woodchips and leather, liniment and oil, rather than the golden liquid pouring on the ground at her feet. When the bottle was empty, she let it slip from her fingers and fell back into a pile of hay.

Right away, the dream she'd had about Jim inched its way to the front of her mind. She still hadn't been able to come up with an idea as to what he wanted her to do. One consideration she had was that she was supposed to make a charitable donation. After some careful thought, she concluded the money she had in the bank wasn't nearly enough to make much of a difference. It would take more—much more.

Her thoughts shifted to the gold hidden beneath the floorboards under her bed. For years, she had been steadfast not to use it. She was proud of the fact that she'd been able to keep the collection of nuggets together. There were seventeen hunks total, all still accounted for. It crossed her mind how foolish it was to hang on to it when so much good could come from it. She couldn't help but wonder what Frieda would think. Surely her old mentor would be proud if the gold were used to help change the lives of children.

Still, it gnawed at her. Even if she sold the gold, there was no guarantee the children would benefit from it. It was entirely possible they would still be forced to live within the confines of bars, with women who would punish them simply for being hungry.

Jesse knew in her heart if she truly wanted to change their lives for the better, then her best option was to sell the gold and use the money to build her own orphanage. It was the only way she could ensure the children would actually benefit.

She had no clue where to begin with such an endeavor. She was already in way over her head just thinking about it. There was something Jim had said, though, about her whole life leading up to this.

Suddenly, she understood what Jim was implying.

The solution was now as clear to her as the crisp mountain air. Through the craft Frieda taught her, she had been introduced to many people. Over the years she had built strong connections with bankers, business owners, tradesmen, and laborers. Jim was right: her life's work had placed her directly in the path of people with massive amounts of knowledge and power. With architects, attorneys, and politicians at her fingertips, she had an entire army of people who could help her. All she had to do was ask.

She closed her eyes and could already visualize what she wanted it to be. The building's façade looked like a home, both comfortable and inviting, and certainly not made of cold, depressing stone like a prison. The structure had plenty of windows for as much light as possible. Best of all, any child would be welcome, regardless of ethnicity or gender.

A genuine smile replaced her frown of despair when she thought of Abby. She could picture her clearly standing at the head of a classroom. Row after row of desks would be filled with boys and girls of all ages, eager to learn. She envisioned herself out in the woods with a small group of children, teaching them how to hunt, fish, and how to live off the land. Then her smile widened when she considered that eventually it might become the life's work for her daughters and niece. It was possible that Gwen, Willow, and Jamie would have a passion to teach.

Then her smile vanished in an instant knowing she had ruined what was most precious to her. Her first priority was figuring out how to win Abby back. That thought weighed her down, pulling her off to sleep.

Nearly an hour had gone by when Gwen and Willow came running into the barn.

"Pippa!" Gwen called out.

Jesse jumped to her feet and held out her arms. "I've missed you so much," she said, clinging onto her daughters. She didn't try to hide the tears that came. They were the first happy ones she'd had in a very long time.

"We've missed you too, Pippa," Gwen said, her own tears welling.

Jesse bent down and kissed Willow on top of the head.

Willow reached up and poked one of Jesse's cheekbones. "You need to eat, Pippa."

Jesse smiled and cried at the same time. "So, are you home for good?"

"I thought so," Gwen said. "But Ma just said we need to pack some more things." She studied Jesse's face. "What did you say to her? She ran out of here crying."

"I didn't say anything to her," Jesse said, her brow creased in confusion. "I don't know why she'd be upset."

"Why don't you come to the house and talk to her." Gwen pulled on her arm.

Jesse allowed the girls to lead her inside. She stopped when she saw Abby standing in the parlor. "Please stay." She curved her arm around Abby, but she pulled away.

"I was going to until I saw you in the barn. With the bottle…" Her voice was steely. She slowly shook her head and took another step backward.

It dawned on Jesse what Abby thought she had seen. She looked over at the girls and motioned with her head. "Go wait in the kitchen, will ya? I need a word with your mother." When they had left the room, Jesse pulled the doors closed.

Abby sat on the edge of the sofa and folded her hands in her lap. "I will not stay here and watch you drink yourself to death. I can't. I won't have the girls watch it either."

"You're wrong, Abs. I haven't been drinking."

Abby stared at her incredulously. "Don't lie to me. I saw the empty bottle."

"You did see an empty bottle." Jesse knelt down in front of her. "But not because I drank it. I poured it out." She looked Abby in the eyes. "Losing Jim destroyed something in me. Drinking was the only thing that numbed some of the pain."

"You think I don't hurt?" She stared hard at Jesse, trying to figure out a way to get through to her. "He was my son, too.

Don't you think I'd like to pick up a bottle? Forget about my pain for a while? I can't. I have two daughters who are counting on me."

Jesse was quiet for several moments. "I can't promise you that I'll never have another drink. But I swear to you, I'll do my best not to. I just don't want to lose you." She choked on her next words. "Please give me another chance."

Abby's response was softer than air. "Does that mean you still love me?"

Jesse sat back on her heels, absolutely dumbfounded at the question whose answer was so blindingly obvious to her. "Why would you ask that?" She searched her face. "I've never stopped loving you."

"Because you barely look at me anymore." Abby lowered her head and her hand went reflexively to her scar.

Jesse moved closer and she pulled her hand away. "Abs, it's not what you're thinking." She took a deep breath. "It's just…" She lightly trailed her thumb over the scar. "It's my fault you have that."

Abby placed her hand on top of Jesse's. "It's not your fault. Don't ever think that."

"If I'd gone to look for you, maybe I would've found you before he had a chance to do that." Her voice finally broke. "I'm so sorry. Is there any way you can ever forgive me?" She hung her head.

"Jes." Abby tipped Jesse's chin and stared deep into her emerald eyes. "There's nothing to forgive." She brought Jesse's hand to her lips and kissed her palm.

The feeling that rushed through Jesse's body was electric.

The heaviness that had washed over the room was beginning to lift.

"I want to talk to you about something," Jesse said, sitting on the sofa next to her. "I had a dream when you were in the hospital. About Jim. He wanted me to do something. I couldn't make sense of it at first, but, I think, I'm supposed to sell off Frieda's gold and use the money to build an orphanage."

Abby didn't respond right away. By far the oddest idea Jesse had ever come up with, it took her a moment to process. When she looked over at Jesse, she could see a bit of the old sparkle in her eyes. Maybe it wasn't such a crazy idea after all. She knew it would take something huge to take Jesse's mind off her grief. The orphanage seemed like exactly the sort of thing that could do it.

"I think it's a great idea," she said, brushing a strand of hair from Jesse's face. "But, Jes, we don't know the first thing about something like that. Where would we even begin?"

"Don't you see?" Jesse's excitement mounted. "The work I've done over the years has introduced me to people who can help us."

"Where would we build it?"

Jesse took both of Abby's hands in her own. Her eyes were lit up like Christmas morning. "We can buy some land and build one here in Neva. Before we get ahead of ourselves," she said, standing and pulling Abby up along with her, "I think we should see an attorney and find out the legalities of such an endeavor. If it's something we want to continue, then we'll take it one step at a time." She studied Abby's face. "So? What do you think?"

"Okay," Abby said after a moment. "After we hear what the attorney says, we'll go from there."

Jesse wasted no time gathering Abby in her arms and

pulling her close. "Oh, and there's something else." She lowered her voice. "Tomorrow, how about we go into San Francisco. I want to hire Obie McCreary to find Ulayla's family. Can you imagine the look on her face if we could manage to pull that off?"

Abby rested her head against Jesse's chest. "I think that's a wonderful idea."

"I got a letter from Edith. She mentioned that Burton wants to go to law school. I don't think they can afford to send him. I was thinkin', if it's alright with you, maybe we could use the money we had set aside for Jim's schooling to pay for Burton's?"

Abby leaned back, gazing up into her eyes. "You know they'd never accept money from us."

"I've already got that part figured out. I'll find out what college he wants to attend and contact them directly. I'm sure there's a way we can pay for it without them knowing."

Abby caught a glimmer of light shimmering in Jesse's eyes again. It gave her hope. Somehow, some way, they just might make it after all.

CHAPTER THIRTY-TWO

CHRISTMAS EVE, 1914

G wen Woodley looked up from the face of her sleeping granddaughter, Frances, and peered out through the etched-glass window of the idling train. A horde of people crowded the Holling's Gulch platform. Her eyes scanned the large group searching for her family, who had gotten off briefly to stretch their legs. Finally, she spotted her husband, Perry, among the other travelers. Walking beside him was her twenty-four-year-old daughter, Arlie, and Arlie's husband, Thorn. Thorn was carrying her five-year-old grandson, Winfield. When they moved past her field of vision, Gwen glanced down at her beautiful granddaughter again and smiled.

"Ma and Pippa are going to be so happy to see you," she whispered. She brushed her fingertips against the girl's smooth, unlined cheek. "We're almost there."

The last time Gwen had been in Neva was seven years ago when she had come home for her uncle's funeral. Toby's passing had come as a shock to everyone. Having spent his life working around horses, he was accustomed to most of the injuries that came with being a farrier. Getting his foot stepped on was an ordinary occurrence. The last time it had happened, the skin on the side of his foot was torn, despite the fact he was wearing heavy, leather boots. Like many of the other times he'd been hurt over the years, he barely gave the injury a thought. It wasn't until the wound started putting off a foul odor that he became alarmed. By the time he decided to have it checked out, the infection was already coursing through his bloodstream. There was nothing the doctor could do. For someone like Toby, who had always been strong and healthy, to die from such an insignificant wound seemed unimaginable.

It was still hard, even after all those years, for Gwen to believe he was actually gone. She thought of her parents—both of them were in their seventies now, and she released a guilty sigh thinking of all the years she'd let slip by. She knew it was time with them she would never be able to get back.

Her gaze fixed on one of the brass light fixtures mounted on the Cuban, mahogany wall in the private Pullman car. Being so close to home, her mind naturally went to her brother and thinking of him always brought on the same reaction. She squeezed her eyes shut, but it did nothing to prevent them from welling up as an image flashed through her mind. In it, Jim looked up at her, his eyes pleading for help, right before the life was extinguished from them forever. Gwen placed a gloved hand on her heart. The pain, even thirty-four years later, was novel and incapacitating. Her eyes burned and her vision blurred from the recollection. If she lingered on the memory much longer, the tears would flow down her cheeks.

Everything she had accomplished in her life had been overshadowed by her brother's death. College, her marriage to

Perry—even the birth of her child had been perceived through the prism of Jim's passing. Throughout every single milestone, the specter of Jim followed her. In the back of her mind, there was always one single thought. *Jim will never get to experience any of it.*

As excited as Gwen was to be going home, she was more than a little apprehensive. She knew everywhere she'd look memories would be conjured of the times she had spent with her brother. With a twinge of guilt, she knew memories of Jim would naturally lead to thoughts of Jonathan.

Gwen was a happily married woman. There was nothing about her spouse she didn't appreciate. Still, over the years, and especially during times when the longing for her family seemed almost too much to bear, she found herself thinking about Jonathan and what life might have been like if she had married her brother's best friend instead of Perry.

She knew she could have chosen a simpler life with Jonathan. He had taken over running the vineyard for her parents after she'd gone away to college. Life with him would have been predictable. It would have been as easy as moving her things into the cabin Ulayla had once lived in and bearing his children, living a life of relative comfort and happiness.

A smile crept across her face at the thought of Ulayla. The four years the retired cook had lived on their property were precious to Gwen. It was the time in her life when her parents were heavily involved with overseeing the construction and running of the orphanage. They had seemed too preoccupied to be involved in her life as much, and Ulayla had become a second mother—not only to her, but also to Willow.

Jesse had hired Obie McCreary to track down Ulayla's family, and the seasoned detective had been able to locate one son, Kennard. He had been thrilled to find out his mother was still living. He told the detective he had given up hope of ever seeing her again. Unfortunately, even he had no idea where his father and brothers were. As far as anyone knew, they had perished.

Gwen thought back to the last time she had seen Ulayla. It had been at the train station in Neva. Ulayla was leaving for Philadelphia to move in with her son. They had stood in the middle of the busy platform, their arms wrapped tightly around one another. Both of them had been crying. People hurrying along the platform had cast sidelong glances at them and given them a wide berth. As happy as Gwen was for Ulayla, it was one of the hardest goodbyes she had ever had to make. She laced her fingers through Willow's and watched as the train pulled out of the station. With her other hand, she began to wave. As the train gathered speed, she kept her eyes trained on Ulayla's face, which was framed in the window of the compartment she was seated in. Gwen stood in place until the train rounded the first bend. By then, Ulayla's face was no bigger than a postage stamp. It was the last time either one of them ever saw her. For ten years, they corresponded with one another. The last letter Gwen had received was from Kennard, who had written to inform her that his mother had passed peacefully in her sleep. As she had no photographs, the image of Ulayla in her mind had all but faded.

Gwen's thoughts shifted to Willow. Although her little sister had the opportunity to go to college, she chose a different path.

Gwen would never forget her shock after reading her mother's letter. It had been the first warm day in spring after an especially brutal and biting Boston winter. Rather than sitting inside, she had taken advantage of the beautiful weather and sat out on the stoop while she flipped through the mail. When she came to a letter addressed in her mother's handwriting, she tore into it, excited for news from home.

Her eyes skimmed the first page. Halfway through the second page she paused and looked out across the street. A young couple was strolling nearby, their arms linked together. A little further away, a mother was pushing a stroller. None of it registered with her. She glanced down at the paper in her hands. She couldn't believe what she had just read. Jonathan and Willow were getting married. She was so surprised to see this news she dropped the letter and gave herself a few seconds to regroup before she leaned over and picked it up.

It was nearly impossible for her to imagine her parents allowing the marriage to happen. Willow was only sixteen, after all. As she continued to read, her amazement turned to understanding. Willow was carrying Jonathan's child. What shocked her even more than the wedding announcement was that her father hadn't killed Jonathan for getting Willow in that condition, but instead, hosted a lavish wedding at the house. Willow gave birth to their first son, Sullivan, seven months after they were married. One year after that, they welcomed a second son, Grant.

Gwen couldn't bring herself to go home for their wedding. For some reason, the thought of seeing Jonathan marry her sister bothered her. She excused herself from the event, blaming her absence on a full load of schoolwork. Although she'd avoided attending the wedding, she hadn't escaped hearing about it.

Gwen had met Perry Woodley while she attended Vassar. It was in the spring of 1888, shortly after she had turned twenty-three. She had gone home with her roommate on a break from school rather than making the cross-country trip back to Neva.

Perry was her roommate's brother and was enrolled at John Hopkins for medical school. Busy with school and work, it was unusual for Perry to go home. Serendipitously, he happened to be there at the same time as Gwen. Though courting was difficult because of the distance, they somehow made it work. Perry took great pleasure in surprising Gwen in different ways whenever they were together, and for perhaps his biggest surprise of all, he proposed a mere eight months after their initial meeting. It took Gwen less than a second to say yes, and two days later, they were standing in front of a Justice of the Peace. It was hard for her to not be a bit jealous of Willow's ceremony, but she reminded herself that it wasn't the ceremony itself that made a marriage great—it was the relationship they would build immediately after it. Her only regret was the pain she caused her parents by not having them at her wedding.

Gwen gave birth to their only child, Arlie, two years after they were married. Although she took after Perry's side of the family with ebony hair and soft, brown eyes, there were times when she would look at her daughter and see a strong resemblance to Jim. She couldn't help but smile.

While Arlie didn't get to spend as much time with her grandparents as Willow's children did, she didn't miss out on the precious relationship entirely. Every year, Jesse and Abby made the three-and-a-half-day train trip from San Francisco to Boston. They would stay in the city, visiting with the family and sightseeing. After a few days, they'd board the train taking Arlie with them to spend the summer in Neva. Once the hot months of June and July passed, they would make the trip again to take her home.

As Gwen's parents aged and Arlie became more involved with other pursuits, the summer visits decreased and then eventually ceased altogether. Jesse and Abby hadn't made the trip since Toby died.

Whenever she thought of her parents, Gwen felt guilty. She knew she had disappointed them. Initially, she'd had every intention of returning home after college and running the children's home. Fate, it seemed, had something different in store for her. Halfway through her first term, Gwen discovered the joy of books and writing. Jim had been with her throughout her studies, giving her an extra push every time she was seemingly too drained to study another hour or revise her paper one last time, and now she felt that somewhere, he must have been shaking his head in disbelief at her career choices.

It was during her second year, when she was home for Thanksgiving holiday, that she decided to tell her parents about her plans. They had been sitting out on the front lawn in a swing her father had built. Beneath the canopy of a large oak, she explained to them how she wanted to become an editor rather than the headmistress at the children's home. Although they smiled encouragingly and told her the only thing they wanted was for her to be happy, they couldn't quite conceal their disappointment. Like the ground around them, their voices were shaded. After that, Gwen's visits became less frequent.

As much as Gwen felt she had disappointed them, she felt they had let her down as well. Taking on the children's home had been an enormous endeavor, and it was one her parents knew nothing about. As they tried to put it all together, she and Willow became afterthoughts. By the time they mastered the running of the orphanage, Gwen was married and raising her daughter in Boston. It was ironic to her that as their own child, for the last few years she'd lived at home, she had been put on the back burner while her parents figured out how to raise other people's children.

In the end, Jamie was the one who came home from college to be one of the teachers. Eventually, she took over the responsibility of running the home alongside her husband, Judge, who was an accountant. Jamie oversaw day-to-day operations of the place while Judge took care of the finances. In 1897, they were blessed with a son of their own, Thad.

"You okay?" Arlie asked, taking a seat next to her mother. "You looked like you were a million miles away."

Gwen turned to face her daughter. "Where's everyone else?" She passed Frances to Arlie.

"Dad and Thorn took Winfield to get some peanuts." She positioned the drowsy baby comfortably in her lap. "You getting excited?"

Gwen nodded. "Yes. It's been a long time."

"Grandma is going to be so surprised." She looked back at her mother. "You don't think Grandpa told her, do you?"

"No. It's probably been killing him having to keep it to himself, though. Your grandpa loves pulling off surprises." She looked up, noticing people were starting to board the train again, and saw her family walking toward them. "I think we're about to leave."

〜

Jesse steered her blue, 1913, Pathfinder automobile along the street next to the train station. Slowly, she pulled into the gravel lot behind the depot and found a spot to park. Jamie's son, Thad, pulled his car up alongside hers. She reached for her cane on the seat beside her. She waited for Thad to get out of his vehicle before stepping carefully out of hers and limping over next to him.

Together, they made their way over to two waiting wagons. Both had been driven to the station by Willow's sons. Twenty-four and twenty-three respectively, Sullivan and Grant were strong, reliable young men. They made their living by either working at the vineyard alongside their mother or by doing maintenance work at the children's home.

Grant looked down from the wagon seat at Jesse. "Grandma is going to flip when she sees them."

Jesse nodded. "Yeah, she is. Once you boys get these loaded, hurry home will ya? We got a lot to get done today."

"Sure thing, Gramps," Sullivan said.

"Alright." Jesse reached down and rubbed her knee. The cool air made it throb more than usual. "I'm going to wait for them at the platform." She turned and joined in the mingle of people headed in the same direction. She checked her watch. There was still plenty of time before the train was scheduled to arrive. She snapped it shut and then walked over to the news-stand to find something to pass the time.

With a newspaper tucked under her arm, she made her way over to a nearby bench. Taking a seat, she kicked out her leg and relaxed back against the wooden slats. The bench was not comfortable in the slightest, but it was highly preferable to being on her feet and dealing with the pain in her knee. The old injury she'd sustained when she fell down the mountain crevasse seemed to hurt worse now than it did at the time of the accident. Resting her cane beside her, she pulled her glasses from her inside pocket and flipped open the paper.

It wasn't long before the platform was thrumming with excitement and energy. The noise of family and friends anxiously waiting for their loved ones to arrive buzzed all around her. Her reading was interrupted often, making it impossible for her to become fully immersed in the newspaper. Sometimes the person was one she knew well—someone who had grown up in the orphanage. Other times, it was someone whose life had been altered by one of her selfless deeds. Whatever their reasons for stopping to talk, their words to her were always the same. They all spoke with great respect and appreciation. No matter who it was, she greeted each of them with a warm, sincere smile.

The opportunity for constructing the orphanage couldn't have come at a better time for the townspeople of Neva. Phylloxera had been rampant at the time. The microscopic louse ate its way through one vineyard after another, and the citizens of Neva were powerless to stop it. Its effect on the community had been devastating. The landowners struggled to pay back their debts. It didn't take long for the entire town to feel the dire consequences.

For the first time since the town's inauguration, the blades at the sawmill stood idle. Miss Dottie's ovens went cold. Even Elmyra Tallent was forced to let go of her hired help. The entire community suffered, and soon, the town fell into a severe economic depression.

Once Jesse sold two of the gold nuggets in San Francisco and purchased a hundred acres just outside of Neva, things began to turn around. Before construction began, Jesse called for a town meeting. A steady income was offered to any local who wanted a job helping with construction of the orphanage. Her neighbors, many of them on the verge of losing everything they'd spent their lives building, rushed to shake her hand after the meeting, their eyes full of gratitude.

Soon, the blades at the sawmill were running nonstop, and the smell of sawdust was returned to the air where it had been missing for far too long. It was all they could do to keep up with the demand of milled lumber required on a project the size of the one Jesse had taken on. With the entire town back to work, people had the money to purchase goods again. The bell above the door at the Tallents' Mercantile jingled all day long. Elmyra was even able to re-hire her help. Miss Dottie had never been busier. Jesse hired her to provide daily meals for everyone working on the home. It was incredible that one project had managed to save the entire town.

Jesse glanced at her watch again and realized the train was set to arrive any minute. She removed her glasses and placed them in her breast pocket, folded her paper, and struggled to her feet. The pain in her knee was radiating, but knowing she was about to reunite with family, she didn't acknowledge it as she leaned heavily on her cane and took a few steps toward the people congregating in anticipation of the train pulling up.

"Excuse me," Jesse said to an employee of the station who happened to be passing by. "Do you know if the train is running on time?"

"Mr. McGinnis, sir. It is as far as I know." A faint train whistle blew off in the distance. The man nodded at her. "Ah, there it is now."

CHAPTER THIRTY-THREE

Jesse stared down the long expanse of tracks running through the tunnel of trees, watching as the large, black engine approached the station. A white plume of steam billowed from it, leaving a trail through the air as it got closer and closer. There was another loud whistle, followed by the screech of metal as the train applied the brakes.

Moments later, the train was standing in the station. It hissed and belched a final, tall cloud of steam from its stack. A porter placed a stool at the bottom of the steps for exiting passengers.

Jesse was nearly engulfed by the mass of people bursting onto the platform when the doors of the train opened. She planted her cane and searched among the faces.

Arlie repositioned Frances and then accepted the porter's hand as she stepped from the train. It had been two years since she had visited her grandparents, and she was more than excited to see them. The last time she had visited them, Thorn had been tied up with work and unable to accompany her. So, she had made the cross-country trip with little Winfield and one of her girlfriends.

Jesse caught a glimpse of her granddaughter and forgot all about the pain in her leg. Her mouth stretched into a crooked grin. Attacking the crowd the same way she would a thick piece of hickory, she chipped her way through until she was standing in front of Arlie.

"I sure have missed you," Jesse said with a squeeze, being careful of the baby in her granddaughter's arms.

"I've missed you too, Grandpa."

Jesse stepped back to get her first look at her great-granddaughter. "She's beautiful, sweetheart." She lightly rubbed the baby's cheek. "I can't believe how big she is already."

In her periphery, she spied her great-grandson clinging to the back of Arlie's dress. "Where's Winfield? Did you leave him at home?" She made a show of looking around but not down. "I can't believe he didn't come for Christmas. What will Santa do with his presents?"

"Probably give them to someone not so ornery," Arlie replied.

"I'm right here, Grandpa Pippa," came Winfield's little voice.

Jesse feigned ignorance of his words and pretended not to hear him. "That's really too bad. I told Santa to bring all of his presents to our house this year. What a shame." She felt a tug on her pant leg but didn't look down.

"Grandpa Pippa, I'm down here." He tugged harder. "See. Here I am!"

"Oh!" Jesse finally acknowledged him, pretending to be startled. She looked down at him. "There you are!" she said, grinning widely. "Let me get a good look at you. You've gotten so big since the last time I saw you that I didn't even recognize you. Is that..." She gasped, leaned over, and gave him the most serious expression she could manage. "...a mustache?"

Winfield placed one hand on each of her cheeks. "I don't have a mustache!" he said with a giggle. "You need your glasses, Grandpa Pippa."

"Oh, my mistake." Jesse stood upright and looked at Arlie. "How was the trip?"

"Let's just say, I'm glad to be here. Traveling with little ones is a challenge. I thought Thorn was going to pull his hair out a time or two."

"Where is your husband?"

"Winfield spilled his peanuts, and Thorn was cleaning up the mess."

Jesse looked around her, beaming with excitement. "Your ma's with you, isn't she?"

"Yes." Arlie smiled. "She's just slow, ya know she'll be turning fifty next year."

Dr. Perry Woodley stepped down and then turned to offer his hand to Gwen. They made their way over to Jesse and Arlie.

Without hesitation, Jesse stepped up to her daughter and wrapped her arms around her. "I've missed you so much it hurts."

"Hi, Pippa." Gwen said. She put little effort into the hug. "I've missed you, too. You look well."

Jesse could feel a palpable awkwardness between her and Gwen. She ignored it, grateful just to have her home, and relinquished her hold long before she wanted to.

Gwen pulled away, the old familiar tension building inside her. It had been that way for years. She felt she barely knew her parents anymore. She would always love them, but the close bond they once had, for her at least, was quite broken.

Jesse did her best to dismiss Gwen's lackluster greeting. The smile she offered couldn't quite hide her doleful expression. "Now, don't be telling lies," Jesse said. Her tears shimmered in the morning light. She reached out and lightly gripped Perry's hand. "Good to see you, Doctor. You look well."

"Good to see you, too."

She released her clasp on his soft, almost delicate hand and extended it to the handsome young man who came over and stood beside Arlie. "You must be Thorn. Glad to finally meet you. Happy you could make it this time."

"Nice to meet you, sir," Thorn said, firmly shaking her hand. "I've heard a lot about you."

Jesse had always been able to tell a lot from a simple handshake. The callouses she felt on the bricklayer's hands told her that her granddaughter's husband was someone well-versed in a hard day's work. This was an admirable characteristic in Jesse's eyes, and she clapped Thorn on the shoulder in approval.

While Jesse continued to speak with the family, Gwen turned her attention to her two nephews. Willow's sons, though they were brothers, looked nothing alike.

"How've you been, Grant?" Gwen asked.

"Real good. Just found out last week, we're expecting number three."

Grant was short and slender. When he smiled, his eyes crinkled in the corners the same way Willow's did. His curly, black beard seemed to take on its own life when he continued.

"Beth's sure hoping for a girl this time."

"That's wonderful. I'm so excited for both of you." Gwen looked over at Sullivan and grinned. "How about you? Anybody special in your life?"

Sullivan was taller and more muscular than Grant. His sculpted jawline glistened in the sunlight. His aunt's question came as no surprise to him. It was the same one everyone always asked. Although his handsome good looks and masculinity had caught the eye of many beautiful women, he had no interest in courting them. He definitely wasn't about to marry one of them for the sake of appearances. What he wished, more than anything, was that he could tell everybody the truth. He did have someone special. It just wasn't a woman. Sullivan kept his attraction to men a closely guarded secret. He knew it would bring shame to his family or even, in the wrong company, get him killed.

"Not yet. Grandma is going to go crazy when she sees all of you," he said, quickly changing the subject.

"She still doesn't know?" Gwen asked.

"No," Grant answered. "We all snuck away before she woke up this morning. Beth and the kids are over at Ma's house waiting for everyone."

Gwen turned her attention to Jamie's son, Thad. The last time she'd laid eyes on him was at Toby's funeral. It was hard to believe the little ten-year-old boy she remembered was all but grown up. She placed her gloved hand on his arm. "You look just like your grandfather."

The seventeen-year-old smiled. "That's what they tell me," Thad said. "It's good to see you again."

Jesse smiled as she listened to their exchange. Gwen was right. There was a strong resemblance between Thad and Toby. She loved that. It was part of her brother she still had with her.

"Alright," she finally said. "I have to go check on a shipment. Shouldn't take long. Then we can get this show on the road."

Thad stayed behind to help Gwen's family get their luggage to the waiting vehicles while Jesse, Sullivan, and Grant went to one of the boxcars at the rear of the train. One of the railyard workers slid open the heavy side door and Jesse peered over the edge. It was filled with crates of donated items for the children's home. She nodded in approval, overwhelmed by the contributions.

Over the years, countless people had been blessed by Jesse's generosity. Many of them wanted to repay her kindness. Unwilling to accept money, she requested they make a donation to the children's home instead. In the weeks leading up to the holiday, train cars brought numerous crates into the station destined for the orphanage.

Most of the cargo she looked at that morning was from Sarah Winslow. As one of the most successful fashion designers in the country, Sarah used her connections to help provide the children at the home with more than enough clothing for the entire year.

Jesse left Sullivan and Grant behind to oversee the unloading of the shipment and met up with the rest of the family out in the parking lot. Gwen and Perry climbed into the car with her while Arlie's family rode with Thad.

Arlie's husband, Thorn, sat peering out the passenger side of the car, taking in the town of Neva for the first time. As the car slowly made its way along the main street, he was surprised to see the names on several of the businesses: the McGinnis Sawmill, McGinnis Dry Goods and Cloth, and McGinnis Feed Store. He turned with amazement to face his wife in the backseat. "Does your grandfather own all those?"

"No," Arlie said. "Some of the owners in town wanted to show their appreciation for everything Grandpa did for them."

Thad shifted gears and then glanced over at Thorn. "Uncle Jesse is a big deal 'round here," he said. "If it weren't for him, this whole town would have vanished off the map. He's kind of a legend in these parts."

In the car in front of them, Gwen leaned over from the back seat. "How'd you manage to keep us a secret?" she asked Jesse.

"It wasn't easy." Jesse chuckled. "She's going to be so happy to have all of you home for Christmas. Willow's making sure she won't see us when we pull in. Jamie and Judge will be over as soon as they can get away."

"How's Willow doing?" Gwen asked.

Jesse paused. "Oh, she's doing okay."

"He's been gone for…what? Eight years now." It was quiet for a moment. "Is she seeing anyone special?"

"No," Jesse said. "I don't think she will, either. Running the vineyard keeps her pretty busy. Plus, she helps look after the grandbabies."

Silence filled the car. Although Jesse and Gwen's minds wandered, they took the same route.

Gwen still found it hard to believe Jonathan was gone. No one could have predicted that when he set out one morning for San Francisco to pick up some supplies for the home remodel he was doing he would never come back.

Halfway through loading the goods he'd gone after, the added weight of a heavy, claw foot tub caused the axle on the wagon to break. He was forced to spend the night in the city until the repair could be made, which they had promised him would be completed by the following morning.

Gwen remembered reading about the massive earthquake in the newspaper. The paper had called it an act of God, and it was estimated to have taken three thousand lives. No one had seen one of that magnitude in those parts in recent history. She had nearly fainted when word came from her parents that Jonathan was one of the casualties. Nearly a decade later, his funeral was as clear in her mind as if it had just taken place. It seemed so recent to her that sometimes she swore she could still smell the flowers from the mourners.

Jesse recalled when she and Toby went to search for Jonathan right after the quake. She would never forget her first glimpse of the city on fire. They travelled block after block in complete shock. The scale of the destruction was unimaginable, and there was almost nothing familiar left. It was so unrecognizable that even a person who had been born and raised there would have lost their bearings and been unable to orient themselves. It was difficult to maneuver around the crumpled buildings and pop up fires. Travel was difficult, as they had to share the road with horse-drawn fire engines, which were also trying to make their way through the rubble-strewn streets.

Their search for Jonathan was delayed when they joined in the recovery efforts. By dawn of the second day, she learned most of her own creations had been destroyed. The Davenport Mansion, which held some of her finest work, was in ruins. The biggest shock came when she found out Sam and Helga Bowmans' estate had been nearly leveled and that their bodies had been pulled from the rubble.

On day three, she and Toby barely had the strength to join the mix of refugees, aid workers, and soldiers moving through the streets. They had all but given up on finding Jonathan until they entered a makeshift morgue tent. His remains were located among several others inside. Though his face was recognizable, his body had been crushed from the waist down.

Jesse and Toby transported his body to Emery Shumaker. Having been like a son to her, she wanted to make sure that his remains were taken care of. The only thing that brought Jesse comfort was the fact she was at least able to take Jonathan home. Per Willow's wishes, he was given a proper burial and laid to rest behind their home.

Gwen gazed out the passenger side of the car. On the edge of town, standing next to the road, stood a large sign impossible for her to miss. It bore the name: The James McGinnis Home. There was a large, well-manicured lawn, cut in a precise, interwoven pattern. Children of all ages, genders, and ethnicity were playing gleefully outside. Seesaws, swings, and slides were placed beneath the canopy of several large shade trees. A group of kids were skipping rope in one area. Staff members sat a picnic table, keeping watchful eyes on a group of younger children who were digging in sandboxes. Gwen's eyes drifted to the sprawling building set back from the road. It had doubled in size since the last time she'd seen it.

"It looks so different," Gwen said.

Jesse snapped out of her recollection, slowed the vehicle, leaned over in the seat, and pointed. "Over there is the new bell tower we just put on the chapel. Those are the staff quarters. Right there is the new dining hall." She pointed to the white house near the back of the property where Jamie, Judge, and Thad lived. "We just finished the wrap-around porch a few weeks ago. Turned out pretty nice." She leaned back and clutched the steering wheel.

Gwen's eyes shifted from Jamie's home to the children playing. "How many are there now?"

"We're up to a hundred and twenty-three." Jesse shook her head. "It's heartbreaking when you think about it. A hundred and twenty-three kids that had nothing."

"Are you going to play Santa in the morning?"

"Oh, no," Jesse said. "I gave that up a few years ago. Sullivan does it now."

The car picked up speed again.

Gwen knew how hard that time of year was for her parents. It was hard for her, too. It was impossible not to associate Christmas with Jim's passing. In the years following his death, her parents could no longer bring themselves to celebrate the holiday. They still gave out presents, but they quit decorating the house or putting up a tree. It wasn't until the grandkids came along that they finally put aside their anguish and started participating in the holiday again. However, it was always done at the last minute on Christmas Eve because her parents couldn't handle seeing the constant reminders.

Jesse turned onto Willow's driveway. "Need to let Beth and the kids know we're back."

Thad drove in behind them.

Gwen sat silently, taking in the beautiful, two-story home where Willow lived. Once belonging to the Baptiste family, it no longer looked like the place she remembered from her childhood. Every time Gwen returned here, everything became more and more unrecognizable.

Jesse had bought the homestead, not long after Willow and Jonathan were married, when Armand learned of a two-hundred-acre spread not too far away he wanted to buy.

Because it was a failing vineyard, he was able to get it at a good price. Still, the only way he could afford it was to sell Jesse his old home and let her buy him out of their partnership. With clippings from their existing vineyard, Armand was able to turn the vineyard around relatively quickly. Within a few years, he finally achieved his dream of producing his own wine. The supply of his delicious port could not keep up with the demand, and it was not long before Armand did not have to worry about affording the things he wanted.

Soon after Jesse purchased it, she turned around and gave the Baptiste home to Willow and Jonathan as a wedding gift. Over the years, Jesse helped Jonathan make several changes to the place. They transformed it into one of the finest homes in Neva.

"How are the Baptistes?" Gwen asked.

"Armand and Celia are doing well," Jesse said. "Armande and her husband are still in San Francisco. From what I hear, Dr. Claire's practice out in Oregon is doing well."

"Is she married yet?"

"No." Jesse stopped the vehicle. "Armand says she's too busy to take on a man."

Beth came out of the house, followed by her two sons. She waved to the idling car parked behind Jesse and then stepped up to the vehicle. "Good to see you," she said to Gwen and Perry as she opened the rear door.

Gwen scooted over to make room on the back seat. "Good to see you, too. I hear I'm going to be a great aunt again."

"Yeah. Talk about a surprise."

Beth's son, Will, scooted next to Gwen and scrunched up his face. "I don't want a sister."

Will's younger brother, Tim, crawled over the seat and sat

between Jesse and Perry. "Are we going to get a tree now?"

Jesse tousled his hair. "Soon. We have to give your great-grandma her present first."

"What did you get her?" Will asked from the back seat.

Knowing the boys might let it accidently slip, no one mentioned the homecoming plans to them.

"The best present ever," Jesse said. "Family." She glanced at both boys. "When we get inside the house, I need you to be extra quiet. Can you do that for me?"

"I can," Will said.

"Me too, Grandpa Pippa," Tim said.

Jesse waited until everyone was settled and then pulled out of the drive and headed up the long lane to her house. Thad followed right behind them.

As they neared her old home, Gwen studied the two log houses that sat on the property. Grant, Beth, and their two boys resided in Toby's old home since Jamie preferred to live next to the orphanage. Sullivan lived in the one Ulayla had used. Gwen shifted her focus to Willow when she saw her coming down the porch steps.

"Where is she?" Jesse asked as soon as she stepped out of the car.

"Upstairs, sleeping," Willow said. She waited for Gwen to get out of the vehicle and then wrapped her arms around her. "It's great to see you. Welcome home."

"It's great to see you, too. You haven't aged a day."

"I don't know about that." Willow's smile said she appreciated the compliment. "Ma is going to be thrilled to see all of you."

"Come on," Jesse said to the group. "Go hide in the parlor. I'll go get her up." She looked down at Winfield, Will, and

Tim. "Remember," she said, placing a finger near her lips, "be very quiet."

The boys nodded and quietly followed the adults into the house.

Jesse climbed the stairs and found Abby asleep on their bed, a letter clutched in her hand. She sat down next to Abby and placed a hand on her forehead. She lightly ran her palm over her soft, white hair. "Good morning."

Abby opened her eyes. It took her a moment to fully get her bearings. "Good morning," she said, yawning. "Did you get the shipment already?"

"Yes. The boys are takin' care of it." She motioned with her head at the letter. "What's that?"

Abby sat up. "You're not going to believe it. It's a letter from Edith."

"Edith?"

"Yes. It's the one she swore she mailed but we never got. Burton forwarded it. It must have gotten lost." She handed it to Jesse.

It had been over twenty years since her last letter from Edith. Her old friend used to write all the time. The pages were mostly filled with praises about Burton. She told her about his school days, on up into law school, and then finally about his move back home to Ely. She was especially proud that he had set up office in her old home. Edith and Felix never did discover Jesse and Abby had paid for his entire schooling.

Jesse's mind flashed back to the day she'd gotten a letter from Burton. The news that his parents had died in a stage-coach accident had hit her with the force of a locomotive. The only good thing to come from the tragic accident was that they had gone together. Jesse hoped that when she and Abby perished, they would be lucky enough to go at the same time. Neither one of them could imagine a life without the other.

Jesse pulled her glasses from her pocket and began to read.

When she was finished, Abby said, "You know, if you had gotten this letter back then, you would have gone right before the attack." She looked pointedly at Jesse. "You probably would've been killed. God only knows what would've happened to Willow. It's actually a blessing it never came."

"Let's not think about such bad things," Jesse said. "Not today."

"Would you get my journal for me, please?"

Abby was eager to put pen to paper and write about the letter from Edith. Ever since Jim's death, she adopted writing as a coping mechanism. She had started at the very beginning, telling about her life growing up in Missouri. She wrote about meeting Jesse and divulging both of their secrets—how Jesse was actually a woman and how Sam Bowman was the twin's father. She kept nothing back. Nine journals later and she was up-to-date. Knowing they contained things of utmost secrecy, she kept them hidden in the compartment under their bed.

Also hidden beneath the floorboards was the one remaining nugget of Frieda's gold. Jesse had kept it purpose-fully. One day, she reasoned, long after she and Abby were gone, someone would have to repair their old home. She wanted to reward whoever that person was. Hopefully, they would come to love the house as much as she did.

"Could you maybe do your writing later?" Jesse asked. "I need you to get dressed because I need your help downstairs." She patted Abby on the leg and kissed her cheek. "I'll go put on the coffee. Meet ya in the parlor."

CHAPTER THIRTY-FOUR

A bby went to her tallboy dresser and pulled out a pair of pants and a blouse. After dressing, she sat at her vanity and stared into the mirror. She pulled her long hair up in a bun and then reached for one of the jars and dabbed some makeup on her cheeks. When she was finished, she turned her head one way and then the other, inspecting her work. Never completely satisfied, she got up from the seat and headed down the hall.

Abby hobbled down the stairs. Already heavily distracted by Edith's letter, it never occurred to her to wonder why the house was so quiet. She nearly fell over when she stopped in the doorway to the parlor and saw her family seated all around the room.

"Surprise!"

Abby brought her hand to her throat. "I-I can't believe this!" she stammered, eyes twinkling.

Gwen hurried across the room and fell into her mother's arms.

Abby held onto her tightly. After a moment, she forced

herself to take a step back. "Let me see you." She was practically bouncing on her toes. "It's been too long."

"Yes it has." Gwen cupped her mother's cheeks. "You're still so beautiful."

Abby's attention was diverted when she felt Winfield tug on her pant leg. "Hello there," she said, looking down. "You're getting so big."

"Gamma Abby, Mommy said we get to go pick out a tree," Winfield said. "Can we go now?"

Arlie stepped forward. "In a bit, honey. Hi, Grandma."

Arlie gave Abby a warm hug and then stepped aside to introduce her husband. "Grandma, this is Thorn."

"Nice to meet you, ma'am." Thorn extended his hand nervously.

Abby pushed his hand aside and pulled him in for a hug. "It's nice to finally meet you. Thank you for coming."

Arlie could tell by the look on Thorn's face he wasn't prepared for the kind of warm welcome her grandmother gave him. She smiled as she watched her husband awkwardly pat Abby's back.

Abby looked at everyone in turn. "I can't believe you're all here. I had no idea." She spun to face Jesse. "I don't know how you managed to pull this off, but thank you." She kissed her on the cheek and gave her arm a loving squeeze.

Sunlight streaming in through the window reflected off of something creating starbursts of light around the room. Jesse glanced out and saw Jamie and Judge's automobile coming up the drive. She flashed a grin knowing their vehicle was loaded with all sorts of food she'd arranged ahead of time for the Christmas Eve feast. "Alright," she said, eagerly. "Everybody put your bags upstairs and get changed. This room needs a tree."

After everyone had changed out of their travelling attire, they met up again in the kitchen. Abby fussed over making sure they all got something to eat while they waited on Sullivan and Grant to return from unloading the wagons.

The kitchen soon filled with conversation and laughter as the great-grandkids screamed and chased one other through the house. Abby was overjoyed with all the commotion and found herself standing there taking it all in with a wide smile on her face.

The chaos made it easy for Jesse and Gwen to slip away to the barn. As soon as Jesse slid open the door, Gwen went right over to Gypsy's old stall. Inside was a horse the same color as the snow that used to blanket the cabin up on Mount Perish.

"What's his name?" Gwen asked.

"Cotton."

"Hey there, Cotton." Gwen ran her hand down his neck. "He's beautiful, Pippa."

"Let's turn them out," Jesse said, opening Phantom's old stall. She took hold of a lead on a midnight-colored mare named Pepper.

When they got to the paddock, Gwen opened the gate and both horses took off in a slow trot.

Jesse leaned over and petted Toopy on the head. "Who's a good boy?" she said to the dog. She took the stick out of his mouth and gave it a toss. Then she looked over at Gwen. "I can't tell you how happy I am you're here. It means a lot to your mother and me."

"It's good to be home. I miss it here."

"Ya know, this will all be yours one day. Think you'll ever move back?"

"No." There was no hesitation in her answer. Even though she loved her old home, there were too many painful memories there and she had no desire to move back. "Perry would never leave his practice."

"There's sick people in California," Jesse reminded her. "He could always work here you know." She turned back toward the barn. "I need to toss the horses a couple of flakes."

"I'll do it."

When they stepped back into the barn, Gwen noticed something in the far corner covered by a large tarp. "What's under there?" She started walking toward the canvas, glancing at Jesse over her shoulder. "Are you carving again?"

Jesse quickly reached out to take her arm. "Naw. It's just a bunch of old lumber."

Gwen took Jesse at her word and turned toward the hay bales.

Jesse's shoulders relaxed. Even though what was under the tarp was some of her finest work, she didn't want her daughter to see it. In fact, besides Abby, she didn't want anyone else to see it. It was a project she had been working on for the past few years. She whittled away at it whenever she got the chance.

Made out of oak, though identical in shape, everything else about the coffins was completely different. On Abby's, she had carved a scene depicting flowers, birds, and butterflies. On her own, she had done a mountain landscape, complete with wildlife and a lake. They had to be perfect. After all, they were where she and Abby would spend eternity.

Jesse glanced over her shoulder to see Sullivan and Grant pulling up in the empty wagons. She was surprised her grandsons had already unloaded everything into the outbuildings at the orphanage. She pulled out her watch and checked the time. The day was flying by. Time spent with her family was never long enough, and she knew their visit home would be over in the blink of an eye.

While most of the family stayed behind to prepare the Christmas Eve feast, Jesse corralled Gwen and Arlie's families, along with Sullivan, Will, and Tim, out of the house to go on the hunt. It was chilly, but the children were oblivious to the cold, laughing as they piled into the back of the wagon. Their faces were lit with excitement.

Winfield looked up at Abby as she gingerly took her seat. "Gamma Abby," he said. "Can I sit beside you?"

Abby inched closer to him and wrapped a blanket around both of their shoulders. "Bless your little heart," she said, beaming. "Of course you can."

Winfield snuggled closer and smiled up at her. "This is gonna be fun," he said when the wagon started to move. His eyes flashed with curiosity.

Abby remembered that expression all too well from when the twins were young. It was often followed by one of calculated mischief. She could already tell Arlie was going to have her hands full. "Oh yes," Abby agreed. "Tree hunting is always fun."

"I've never been before," Winfield said, his expression thoughtful. "Daddy has one delivered to our house. How do we know which tree to pick?"

"Oh, it's easy," Abby told him. She smiled and leaned in confidentially. "Would you like to learn the secret?"

Winfield's eyes were huge. "I like secrets," he whispered.

Seeing her mother happily engage in the old family tradition was good to witness, but in the back of Gwen's mind, she was concerned. She couldn't remember the last time her mother had even come close to stepping foot in their woods. Her fear was that tree hunting would trigger the horrible memories she kept closely guarded since she'd been attacked.

It didn't take long for Gwen to realize they weren't traveling toward their woods. Instead of heading toward the back of the property, her nephew was steering the wagon down the lane. A few minutes later, they were moving across the pasture owned by one of the neighbors, Norm Gallo. Obviously, some kind of arrangement had been made ahead of time giving them permission to harvest a tree from his property.

After the wagon came to a stop and everyone had gotten out, Jesse reached into the back and picked up her handsaw. She walked over and stood next to Abby. Winfield, Tim, and Will huddled close by, unable to keep still and eager to start the pursuit of the perfect tree.

Winfield tugged on one of Abby's gloved hands. "Gamma Abby, let's go find it together!"

"I bet I find it this year," Tim said, stomping his feet in anticipation.

Will took off running.

"I'll go with you," Arlie said to Abby. "You'll need some help with these rascals."

The family disappeared into the woods.

Hearing the shrieks of joy from the boys brought back precious memories of the twins and Jesse quickly swiped at her eyes so Abby wouldn't see her tears. She didn't want to drag her down on such a happy day.

Since Will and Tim had picked trees in the past, and had already picked out one for their home that year, Jesse and Abby had decided to let Winfield have the honor. Several times, Abby rejected perfectly good selections made by Will and Tim as she waited for Winfield to choose one.

"Gamma Abby, how 'bout this one?" Winfield squealed. "See!"

Abby cringed inwardly when she saw the pitiful tree he was pointing at. Between its crooked trunk and dying needles, it would have made for a most underwhelming Christmas tree. "It's pretty nice," she said, smiling brightly. "But I think there's a better one. Keep looking."

Tim shouted. "Did you see this one, Grandma Abby?"

"Not green enough," she called back with a wink.

Abby caught Gwen watching her. She smiled at her daughter and then went off after the giggling children who were chasing one another through the foliage.

Winfield tugged on her coat sleeve. "Gamma Abby, how 'bout this one!"

Abby stepped toward a modest fir. "This one might be perfect," she said with a smile that reached her eyes. "What do you think?"

Winfield looked the tree up and down. "It's my favorite so far."

"It's beautiful," Arlie said. "Good job."

"Let's get it," Tim added.

Abby looked down at Winfield. "Ask your grandma what she thinks."

Winfield turned to face Gwen. "Gamma, can we get this

one?"

Gwen came over and stood next to the tree. She made a show checking the branches and the trunk just like her mother used to do when she was a child. Glancing over her shoulder, she saw all three boys' faces staring at her hopefully. "Yes," she said finally. "I think it might be the most perfect tree I've ever seen."

Although it was nowhere near as big as some of the other trees they had in the past, Jesse knew from experience not to dawdle. She also wanted Arlie's husband to feel like part of the family. "Trust me," she said, handing the saw to Thorn. "You better hurry or we will be out here all day."

Thorn knelt beside the tree and feigned difficulty sawing it, causing Winfield to giggle and offer his strength and teamwork.

Once the tree was loaded into the back of a wagon (again, Winfield's assistance was "needed" to hoist it up), everybody else piled inside to head back to the house.

Winfield climbed up beside Abby. "Gamma, this was fun."

"It was the best time," Abby agreed. Her eyes had their own merry twinkle.

As they rode back to the house, Abby began to sing softly. "*Silent night, holy night, all is calm, all is bright…*"

As the melody grew, the volume of her voice grew louder and the entire family soon joined her, creating a fragmented harmony that was delightful to everyone.

By late afternoon, the kitchen was once again bustling with energy and intoxicating smells that were dizzying to the senses.

The children stayed in the parlor with the men while the women were busy creating their signature dishes. Jesse wandered between the rooms, often just to stay in the center of everything, but also to make sure Abby was having a good time.

A bottle of Armand's best port had been opened, and Abby's cheeks soon glowed with warmth. Jesse cackled along with the rest of them about some inside joke she would probably never understand. She flavored Abby's face with a brief smooch and then disappeared back into the parlor with the men.

Jesse studied the room. Grant, Thorn, and Judge were discussing baseball, loudly arguing over the proper mechanics of throwing a curveball, a pitch none of them were actually capable of throwing. Adjacent to the lively sports talk, Perry was telling a story that held the children captivated. Even little Frances stared at her grandfather as he spoke.

Sullivan and Thad were focused on their chess game. They were lying prone in front of the fire, studying the carved, wooden pieces maybe a bit too carefully. Sullivan was plotting to have Thad in checkmate in three moves if he didn't move his knight. After a lengthy pause, Thad finally took a pawn with his bishop; unaware of the trap Sullivan had set.

The tree stood proudly in the corner, waiting to be trimmed after supper. The boxes of baubles and ornaments were brought down from the attic and placed next to the tree. Though some were painful to remember, having the children around helped remind Jesse of how precious moments like these were. She much preferred to be in a loud, crowded room with family to being alone with just Abby and her thoughts.

That evening, everyone gathered in the dining room and

crammed close around the table. Except for the empty plates in front of each of them, there wasn't a spot available that didn't have a platter of food. There were three types of bread, including Willow's famous cornbread muffins, Jamie's sourdough bread, and Gwen's buttered biscuits. Three different animals were served up for the main course of their homecoming feast. A goose, stuffed heavily with cornbread dressing, was leaking brown gravy onto the serving tray. There was a ham from one of the pigs they had raised and cured in their own smoke house. A huge roast sat in the center of the table, so tender that the moment a fork touched it, the meat flaked away. A large chocolate cake, which Abby had baked, sat on the sideboard. Large carafes of sweet tea dotted the table. Cups waited to be filled.

"Let us join hands," Jesse said from the head of the table. She bowed her head. "We thank you, Lord, for this bountiful feast you have provided for us. We thank you for this glorious day and for this blessing of family. Thank you for the abundance we have always received and for the skills and strength to get through it all, no matter how you challenged us, Lord." She squeezed Abby's hand on her right, Gwen's on her left. "We are so grateful for the adventure of life you have gifted us and for the memories and people that will never be forgotten. In Our Father's name we pray, amen."

"Amen."

Conversations and laughter filled the room as sounds of silverware scraped against the fine china. The food was delicious, and everyone ate until they couldn't hold another bite.

Once the meal ended, everyone pitched in to wash and put away the dishes. When the work was finished, everyone returned to the parlor except Jesse and Abby. They lingered in the kitchen working on a batch of hot chocolate.

Abby and Jesse locked eyes.

"This has been one of the best days of my life," Abby said. "I mean it. You reminded me of everything that's important."

"I love you, Abs." Jesse gathered her gently in her arms and held her for an extra beat. "All I've ever wanted is for you to have the best day. Every day, no matter what. Ya know?" She kissed her forehead.

"Yeah," Abby said, kissing the corner of Jesse's mouth, "I know."

Together, they carried trays of hot cocoa into the parlor and passed them out.

Winfield had been starting to get drowsy, but the appearance of a warm, chocolaty drink gave him new energy that was unmatched by the tired adults.

Abby took a seat on the sofa near the box of ornaments. As she pulled each one from the box, she explained its significance to the little children. She would hand one to each of them and laugh as they raced to place it on the tree. Every few minutes she would have to remind them that the entire tree needed to be covered, as they were neglecting the back section that lined up with the wall.

"Grandpa Pippa," Tim said. "Will you read us the story?" His eyes were glassy from a full day of excitement.

"Please," Will chimed in.

She glanced at the others and then smiled. "Of course. Let me go get it." Jesse left the room and returned a moment later with a worn book in her hand. She sat down on the sofa. "This is my favorite," she said, holding up the book so they could see the cover of *Twas the Night Before Christmas*.

When she finished reading it aloud, she closed the book and turned her attention to Gwen. "Hey, can you come with me?"

Moments later, Gwen was seated at the piano in the den. Her skill had gotten considerably better over the years, and her collection of songs had grown significantly. It wasn't long before the entire family was in the room, listening as her fingers curled out one melody after another across the delicate keys. For the next forty minutes, they sang Christmas carols together until kids started to yawn and Frances began to get fussy.

"That's the signal," Arlie said. "Bedtime."

"Aw, do we have to?" Winfield asked.

"You do if you want Santa to come," Jesse said.

"Santa!" gasped Winfield. He scrambled to get up. "Can I sleep at Tim and Will's house?"

Arlie looked to Beth and Grant for confirmation that it was okay with them.

Grant tousled Winfield's hair. "It's fine with us."

With all the kids over at Grant and Beth's home, the remaining adults gathered back in the parlor. They worked quickly, setting out presents and filling all of the stockings. They managed to drink two more bottles of wine while they finished the work. Finally, the last to leave the room, Jesse and Abby disappeared into their bedroom.

"Thank you for the perfect day," Abby said, rolling over into Jesse's arms. "I love you."

"I love you, too," Jesse said. "So much."

They turned down the lights, hoping to get at least a couple hours of sleep before they had to get up and leave in the morning.

CHAPTER THIRTY-FIVE

CHRISTMAS DAY, 1914

G wen woke to a tapping sound. Barely audible at first, it did little to rouse her from the edge of sleep. When it became louder, she opened her eyes and sat up. She didn't give her eyes time to adjust to the darkness as she crawled out of bed. Easily picking her way across the floor of her old bedroom, she opened the door and peered out.

"Merry Christmas," Willow said softly.

"Merry Christmas. Are the grandkids up already?"

"Not yet. You two get dressed and come downstairs."

Gwen arched an eyebrow. "Is something wrong?"

"No, of course not. I just want you to go see something."

"Okay," Gwen said with a nod. "Let me wake Perry and we'll be down."

Several minutes later, Gwen and Perry entered the kitchen. They were surprised to see that Arlie and Thorn were already seated at the table with Willow. Arlie was holding a sleeping Frances in her arms.

"What's going on?" Gwen asked. She felt no less

concerned than she had moments before. She looked from Willow to Arlie with confusion.

Arlie rose to her feet and transferred Frances into Willow's arms. "Aunt Willow is going to watch the baby," she said. "Grant is waiting outside."

"Waiting for what?" Perry asked.

"He's taking us over to the children's home," Arlie answered. "Grandma and Grandpa are there."

"Already?" Gwen asked. Her parents hadn't changed after all, she thought with some contempt. She knew she shouldn't be surprised. Even though she hadn't been home in years, it was obvious to her that the orphanage still came first. In fact, over the years, she had come to believe that the orphanage had become their most precious baby.

"They went over hours ago," Willow said, rocking the baby slowly in her arms.

Arlie and Thorn gathered with Gwen and Perry in the foyer to put on their coats. When they stepped out onto the porch, light from the gas fixtures gave them a clear view of Grant in the driver's seat of a waiting carriage.

"Sorry," Grant said. "Grandpa and Sullivan took the cars this morning."

The family filed into the carriage without any follow up questions.

Ten minutes later, Grant steered the horses around to the back of the orphanage. They hadn't even stepped down from the carriage before smelling the wonderful aromas coming from inside the building.

Grant held the door open and everyone filed in through the back door, trailing behind him down a long hallway into a large room. Above the door was an oversized, elaborately carved wooden plaque proclaiming it The Frieda McGinnis Dining Hall. The overwhelming scent of yeasty cinnamon buns and hickory-smoked bacon being prepared in the adjacent room saturated the air.

Gwen stepped inside and scanned the large, open room. In the center was a massive Christmas tree, standing easily twelve feet tall. Presents spilled out onto the floor well beyond the span of the ornately decorated boughs. On the wall opposite her was a large stone fireplace with a crackling fire on its grate. There were thirty well-used tables, each one with six chairs pushed in around it. The ceiling was peaked and covered with planks of oak that had been brushed with a light coat of varnish. Several large rafters spanned the width of the room. The pale green walls were covered with framed photographs and artwork. The photographs were of the children who had lived or currently lived at the home, and the children's artwork was displayed just as proudly as the portraits.

Sullivan came through a door on the opposite side of the room dressed up from head to toe in his Santa attire. Every detail of his ensemble was perfect, right down to the polished buckles on his belt and boots. He put his index finger over his lips and motioned for them to follow him.

Gwen walked into the kitchen and found her parents working right alongside Jamie, Judge, Thad, and a few other cooks.

Jesse flipped the flapjack on the griddle and placed it onto a large sheet tray. She glanced up and was surprised to see her family standing near the doorway. Handing the spatula to the cook closest to her, she wiped her hands on a towel and approached Abby. "Look who's here."

Abby turned and smiled wide at her family. Quickly, she

pulled a pan of cinnamon buns from the oven and sat it next to the stove. She took off her oven mitts and skillfully spread a thick layer of icing over the tops of the buns before untying her apron and hurrying over to the group. She extended her arms to them. "I didn't expect to see all of you here. What a wonderful surprise."

"Is there anything that we can do?" Arlie asked.

"No, we're just about done. Hey, you want to have some fun?" Jesse asked, waving for Jamie, Judge, and Thad to come over and join them.

"Sure, Grandpa!" Arlie said with a smile.

"Why don't you help us wake up the children this morning," Jesse said with a twinkle in her eye. She looked at Thorn and Perry. "You two go with Judge and Thad." She turned her attention back to Arlie and Gwen. "You two go with Jamie."

"Aren't you coming?" Gwen asked.

"No. Not this year," Jesse said. "You do it."

When they left the kitchen, Jesse and Abby went into the dining hall and joined Sullivan. He had taken his place in an oversized chair next to the tree. Jesse and Abby took seats at a long rectangle table, near the fireplace at the front of the room, and waited.

It wasn't long before the silence in the room was broken. A cacophony of merriment filled the space as children rushed in and took their seats. Their clothing was disheveled from dressing in haste; their hair was still messy from sleep. By the time the rest of the immediate family had taken their places at the table with Jesse and Abby, the children could barely contain themselves. They were bursting with excitement for a chance to go up and see Santa.

Jesse stood up and the room went quiet. She looked out

over the room, chuckling inwardly at the puffy, tired eyes filled with wonder staring back at her. "Merry Christmas, everyone!"

The entire room responded as one. "Merry Christmas, Mr. McGinnis!"

Jesse smiled. "Okay, let's get moving so Santa can be on his way." She held up a stocking. Normally, Abby was the one who conducted the first part of the tradition. This year, however, Abby insisted that Gwen should take over the role.

Gwen was dumfounded when Jesse held the stocking in front of her.

"Well, go on," Jesse said, with a wide grin. "Pick one."

Gwen reached inside and pulled out a slip of paper. The cracking fire was the only sound as everyone in the room seemed to be holding their breath while waiting for her to unfold it. She showed the number to Jesse.

"You say it," Jesse said.

Gwen looked out over the room and noticed everyone was watching her. Her gaze locked on a small girl with blonde curls and cornflower blue eyes, who was clinging to a threadbare doll. It dawned on Gwen how fortunate she was. She had never known a single hardship in her entire life. If not for her wonderful parents, she could have easily wound up just like that young girl. It was the first time she realized how blessed her life had been.

Jesse nudged her. "They're waiting, sweetheart."

"Number fourteen!" Gwen finally called out.

The children seated at table fourteen leapt from their chairs. All of the other children expressed their disappointment with loud exhalations. Six children formed a line and made their way to the front of the room where Sullivan waited. He looked on the floor around him for the pile of presents designated for that particular table. One at a time, he handed each child a package and then watched as they raced back to place their gifts on the table in front of them.

The process continued until every child in the room had a gift. Several times during the procedure, Sullivan had to yell out the warning: "No peeking!" Finally, the floor underneath the tree was bare. He looked out over the room and said in a booming, husky voice, "Merry Christmas!"

Those were the magic words they had all been waiting to hear. The room erupted in rapture, the sounds of ripping paper and shrieks of glee echoing from the rafters. Jesse and Abby had learned, through personal experience with their children and those at the orphanage, that clothes didn't elicit much of a response. They chose instead to mostly give toys, doing their best to personally select a gift that they knew each child would like. Still, it wasn't unheard of for some of them to exchange their gifts. There were never any complaints, however, and each child expressed gratitude for their present.

After Santa had waved goodbye and left the room, the immediate family left to help bring the feast in from the kitchen. An assortment of tempting food covered the tables that ran the length of one wall. There were flapjacks and cinnamon buns, chocolate and vanilla cakes, bacon, and sliced ham. More than enough was available for everyone to get their fill. Jesse waited until every child had a plate and then rounded up her family. It was time to go home and have their family Christmas.

As soon as they stepped through the door, Winfield, Will, and Tim came rushing out of the parlor. "Hurry!" they exclaimed. "Santa came!"

"They've been so excited," Willow said, following behind them. She waited until Arlie took her coat off and then handed Frances to her.

Jesse noticed Gwen move stealthily up the stairs. "Why don't you all go into the parlor? I'll be back in a minute."

Jesse tapped on Gwen's bedroom door. "Hey. You okay?"

Gwen pulled a hanky from the sleeve of her blouse and wiped at her face. She exhaled a long breath and turned the knob.

Though Gwen tried to make her expression blank, the emotion was impossible to erase and Jesse could see something was bothering her.

"Why are you crying?" Jesse asked, her brows knitted with concern. "What's wrong?"

"I'm sorry." Gwen dabbed at her eyes with the handkerchief. "I'm not trying to spoil today. Things just got to me."

Jesse ran a loving hand down Gwen's arm.

Gwen sniffled. "I've been angry for years. Mad at Jim. Mad at you. Mad at Ma. There were so many times I could have come home. I chose to stay away. Time I could have spent with you—gone, forever." Her chin quivered. "I'm so sorry."

Jesse closed the door. "Sweetheart, you have nothing to apologize for. It's okay."

"No, it's not!" Gwen took in a ragged breath. "I lost so much more than Jim that day. I've always felt like I lost you, and Ma, too." She felt the familiar twinge and covered her heart. It ached dreadfully. "I've been carrying this resentment around for all of these years."

Jesse walked over to the bed. "Come here," she said, patting the space beside her. "Have a seat."

Gwen made her way over to the bed and took a seat next to her.

"I was a mess after Jim died. Remember?"

Gwen remembered but didn't say anything.

"I had to have something to focus on, or I would have lost my mind." Jesse picked at a hangnail. "I had no idea what I was getting myself into. Your ma and me, we were in way over our heads." She took a deep breath of exasperation, fussing with her fingernail a moment longer. "There was so much for us to learn. Permits. Licenses. And dealing with the state of California was an absolute nightmare." She turned to Gwen, focusing her attention. "Listen. I know that there wasn't much time left over for you. I spent so much time taking care of other people's children that I failed to take care of my own. I know you needed me more than I was ever available." She shook her head. "I'm the one who's sorry."

"Until this morning," Gwen began hesitantly, after a moment of thought, "I never thought about the lives you and Ma have touched. Those children needed you more than I did —so much more." She choked on a sob. "You know, I never thought I'd hear myself say something like this, but something good did come from losing Jim. If we hadn't gone through that, you never would have started that wonderful place."

"I've thought of that, too," Jesse said. "But I feel it came at too high a price. You and I were never as close after we started building it." She sighed regretfully. "That's on me. I really thought we'd have more time together after you finished college. I thought you'd move back here and run the place with me." She paused. "But it didn't work out that way."

"It's hard being back here. Despite the great memories, there are too many painful ones."

"Mm." Jesse couldn't argue. "But you know, I've always wanted you to come home. I've missed you so much. Not a day goes by that I don't think of you and wonder about how you're doing."

"I think of you and Ma all the time," Gwen said. She covered her face with her hands. "I feel like I've wasted so much time. I should have just come back after graduation. I'm so sorry I disappointed you."

"You've never disappointed me." Jesse put her arm around her daughter. "Not once. You have always followed your heart and for that, I couldn't be more proud."

The hug they shared lifted a bit of the sadness. The moment was healing for both of them. When they let go, some of the tension was released as well. They smiled at each other through their tears.

"How about," Jesse said, "from now on, we both try to do a better job keeping in touch. I promise to write more."

Gwen wiped the trail of emotion from her cheeks. "And I promise to visit every chance I get."

"You two alright in there?" Abby asked, knocking lightly.

"We're fine," Jesse said. "Come on in."

Abby stepped into the room and closed the door behind her.

"Come sit for a minute," Jesse said.

"Okay," Abby said. "But fair warning, the kids can't take much more waiting." She sat down on the edge of the bed.

Gwen said, "I'm glad you're both here. I've been wanting to talk to you about something."

Her parents angled their bodies toward her.

"I know that you want this house to stay in the family and that you're planning on leaving it to me one day. But, my life is in Boston. My home is there. And since Willow would rather stay in her home, I was wondering how you'd feel about leaving it to Arlie."

Jesse cocked an eyebrow. "She would like to live here?"

"Arlie has always loved this place," Gwen said. "She has nothing but good memories here. Last night, she asked what I thought about her moving out here to help take care of both of you."

"Are you implying that we're getting old?" Jesse asked with a crooked grin.

"No, of course not," Gwen said, smiling. "But I know she could be a big help to you two."

"What about Thorn?" Abby asked. "How does he feel about all of this?"

"He's always told Arlie he would never move to California. But, being here has changed his mind. He really likes it." She nodded in approval. "He's a good man and he works hard. I'm sure folks around here could use a good mason, too. Now, they'd have to take care of some things back home," she continued. "But it is possible that they could make the move out here as soon as this summer."

"What about you?" Abby asked. "Are you okay with this? I know how hard it is to be away from your kids and grandkids."

"It will be difficult," Gwen agreed. "It will just give me another reason to come visit."

Jesse patted Gwen's leg and nodded, smiling. "We'd love to have them here."

"I don't mean to interrupt," Willow said from the other side of the closed door. "But Mr. Greer is here."

"Ahh!" Jesse pulled out her pocket watch. "How'd it get to be so late?" She rose to her feet. "Come on."

"What's going on?" Gwen asked, slightly startled.

"I picked out my own Christmas present this year," Jesse said, grinning as she hurried to the door. "Mr. Greer is here to take some photographs of all of us together."

Gwen stood up quickly, touching her hair. "Well, give us a few minutes to get ready, at least."

"No!" Jesse pivoted in the doorway. "That's not necessary. I don't want one with everyone in formal dress. I just want one of us, the way we always are."

Jesse coaxed her injured leg to speed up and hurried down the stairs as quickly as she could. Somehow, she managed to collect her family together in record time. She was even able to convince Winfield, Will, and Tim to wait just a bit longer to open their presents. With matching pouts, all three boys followed the adults out onto the front porch.

She made her way down the steps and across the lawn to where the photographer was adjusting his field camera, which was set up on a tripod.

Jesse was one of Mr. Greer's best paying customers and had hired him several times over the years. She had made it clear to him how important the photo he was about to take was to her. Her entire family was rarely together and it needed to be perfect.

"Sorry," she said, extending her hand in greeting. "Time got away from me this morning."

"It's no problem," Mr. Greer said, looking up at the sky. "I was hoping it would've cleared up by now, though. I didn't want to have to use the flash lamp." He shrugged and then fussed over several intricate pieces, ensuring everything was set properly. "Better safe than sorry. Why don't you go take your places? I'll finish up here."

Judge and Thad moved the weathered rocking chairs from their usual spots to a place near the top of the steps. Jesse and Abby sat down and then the entire family surrounded them. Gwen and her family were on the right; Willow and her family were on the left. Arlie and Jamie's family took seats on the stairs.

"Ah, that's perfect," Mr. Greer said, satisfied. "Don't anybody move." With one hand holding up the flash lamp tray, he ducked his head underneath a dark cloth and ignited the powder.

Whoomph!

CHAPTER THIRTY-SIX

Abby woke early and was unsurprised to discover the other side of the bed empty. As usual, Jesse had still managed to beat her out of bed, despite the fact she was up much earlier than normal on that particular morning. She tossed back the blankets, crossed the room to her wardrobe, and pulled a dress from one of the hangers. She slipped it on and then went over to her vanity, tucking a few stray hairs behind her ears before using a bit of makeup to hide the dark splotches under her eyes. Satisfied, she went over and pushed open the drapes and then headed out the door.

The smell of coffee led her to the kitchen, and she came down the hall wearing a smile as she thought about her family arriving soon. After nearly six months of planning and preparation, Arlie and Thorn were finally coming to live with them and were leaving on the train in Boston that morning. Gwen and Perry were traveling with them on the cross-country trip to help with the move. Abby's smile deepened and the lines around the corners of her eyes sharpened knowing they'd be in Neva in a few days.

As soon as Abby came into the room she saw Jesse lying on the floor, and she dropped down beside her. Like the light in Jesse's green eyes, Abby's smile quickly vanished. "Jes?" She gently pulled Jesse's head onto her lap and stroked her hair. "Jes?" When there was no response, her body shook and tears burst from her eyes. "Jesse," she whispered, quietly, over and over again.

Abby and Jesse had been through many discussions about what needed to be done when the inevitable happened. Abby was acutely aware of what Jesse's final wishes were. No friends and only certain family were to be notified. There was to be no wake or funeral. No embalming. No undertaker would see what she'd been hiding for more than half a century. She wanted to be in the ground long before anyone even knew she was gone. She had also made it clear not to bury her in a fancy suit. Whatever she was wearing when she departed would be good enough to spend eternity in.

Abby stayed that way until mid-morning and then wiped her eyes on the cuff of her dress. She brushed her warm lips over Jesse's one final time. As easily as she could, she gently placed Jesse's head on the floor and then walked across the yard on legs that had gone long numb to tell her grandsons the awful news.

The family followed Jesse's wishes exactly as Abby instructed. Abby and Willow stayed inside with Jesse's body while Grant and Sullivan dug a grave next to Jim's. Beth kept watch over the great-grandkids at her and Grant's house—Jesse had been crystal clear she didn't want her great grandkids' final image of her to be one that would haunt them.

Once Grant and Sullivan had the hole prepped, they went to the back corner of the barn. Grant pulled back the heavy, canvas tarp and the brothers grabbed an end of her casket—one that was intricately carved with a lush, woodland scene.

They placed the casket next to the gravesite and then went inside to retrieve Jesse's body. With great respect and care, they carried her out, placed her in the handcrafted box, and secured the lid. Abby and Willow watched as the two men carefully lowered it six feet into the ground. Tears fell from everyone's eyes, rolling down their cheeks until they were wiped away by a shaky hand and a cloth.

~

One week had passed since Arlie and her family had moved in. Even though everyone had been devastated by Jesse's death, they held no resentment for not being able to attend her funeral. Jesse had always made it clear she did not want any fuss when she passed away.

After staying up late with Gwen, who was leaving early the following morning to return home to Boston, Abby turned in for the night as the clock struck eleven. As was now her custom, she crawled into bed thinking of Jesse. She readjusted her pillow and fought with the covers as things weighed even more heavily on her mind that night. Whenever she got into bed now, her thoughts were like a whirlwind. Images and concepts swirled through her head, relegating her much-needed sleep just beyond her grasp as her hand stretched out to the cold and vacant spot that, until just recently, had been occupied by warmth and love.

When the grandfather clock downstairs chimed twice, Abby felt hard wood pressing against her cheek. Slowly, her eyelids fluttered open, and her fingers traced the familiar

pattern of the wood grain on the kitchen table of her childhood home. When she shifted her gaze, she saw a slender
woman standing at a counter arranging flowers in a vase.

"Hello, sweetheart," the woman's sweet voice said, turning
around to face her.

Abby didn't blink. She was afraid if she did, the woman
would disappear. "Is it really you?"

"It's really me." She dropped the remaining flowers onto
the counter and hurried over to the table. "I've missed you so
much."

Abby stood quickly and held out her arms to her mother.
"I-I've missed you, too."

Abby's mother stepped back and held her at arm's length.
"Let me see you. You're absolutely beautiful."

Abby knew her mother was just saying what all mothers
said. After all, she was pushing seventy-six. Her beauty had
faded years ago. She glanced down at the flawless skin on her
hands. She looked past her mother, shocked to see her own
reflection in the little, grilled window.

"It's not there," her mother said in a musical voice.

Abby reached up and felt her left cheek. The three-inch
scar was gone. "How…how is that possible?"

"Hello, Baby Girl."

The husky voice sent a shiver through Abby's entire body.
Only one person had ever called her that. She was scared to
turn around. She flinched reflexively when she felt a hand land
on her shoulder.

Her father gently turned her around so she was facing
him. "I'm sorry I failed you. I wasn't strong enough. Can you
ever forgive me?"

Abby finally understood what it meant to lose a child and

spouse and now knew why he wasn't able to cope with the unbearable grief. "It's okay. There's nothing to forgive. I love you, Papa," she said, reaching out.

His body trembled as he took her into his arms.

Out of the corner of her eye, Abby caught sight of someone else entering the room. She stepped back from her father to look at the young woman who she never had the chance to meet. No one needed to tell her who it was. Although they were nine years apart in age, it was almost like looking in a mirror and seeing a younger version of herself.

"Hi, Sis!" the young woman said. "I've wanted to meet you for so long."

"I can't believe this. How is this happening?" Abby asked. "I must be dreaming."

"No, Baby Girl. You're not dreaming. We're all here."

Abby looked around the room. Although she was happy to be reunited with her family, she was upset that not everyone was there.

Abby's mother smiled warmly at her. "They're waiting for you."

Abby took a quick, audible breath. "Where?" she said, hurrying over to the window. "Where are they?"

Her mother came over and stood next to her. "Just close your eyes."

Abby turned to look at them. "I don't want to. I can't lose you again."

"Oh, sweetheart," her mother said with twinkly eyes. "We'll always be here. You can come back anytime you want. Now, close your eyes."

Abby squeezed her eyelids together. When she opened them, she was standing in the shade of a huge oak tree. Tilting her head back, she stared up through the bright, green leaves. She took a deep breath. It was crisp and earthy. Without a doubt, she knew the tree was the one she and Jesse had planted more than half a century ago.

Abby stepped back slightly and again peered up at the tree with wonderment. The sky above her was clear blue and an eagle glided through the air high overhead. She lowered her gaze and her heart soared like the bird when she saw Jim and Jesse sitting on the old stump chairs on the porch of the cabin atop Mount Perish. Her fifteen-year-old son looked exactly the same as he did the last time she had seen him. Jesse, however, had changed drastically. She looked as youthful as she did on the day they first met at The Rowdy Rabbit.

Jesse and Jim ran down the porch steps and enveloped her in their arms. Tears rocked Abby's body so hard it caused the bed frame to creak.

"Hi, Ma."

"Jim," Abby managed to say. "You have no idea how much I've missed you." She looked at them in turn. "Jes, it's been so hard without you."

Jesse cupped her face in her hands, letting her lips linger on Abby's for an extra beat, just as she always had when they had been apart for an extended period of time.

Abby waited until Jesse pulled away and then opened her eyes. That was when she noticed Aponi and Toby standing on the porch along with two teenagers. She didn't know how she knew the children, but she did. In an instant it came to her— these were the two fetuses stolen from the miscarriages Aponi had suffered. She paid it no mind that they weren't infants or grown adults by now, they were forever young. Surrounding the cabin next to Toby's family were the members of the Ponak tribe.

"Come on," Jesse said, gazing into her brilliant, blue eyes. "There's so much to see."

Abby hurried up the steps only to be embraced by Toby and Aponi as soon as she reached the top. The reunion was short-lived because Jesse was tugging on her arm. She allowed herself to be pulled away and followed Jesse through the door of the cabin.

The large group of people seated around the room was familiar to anyone who had listened to Jesse's stories over the years. Most of them she recognized. She spotted Jesse's entire family right away. One woman, who was quickly approaching, confused her, though.

The attractive woman wrapped her in a hug. "I've heard so much about you. Welcome home, Abigail."

"Abby, this is Frieda," Jesse said with a wide grin.

The woman standing in front of her was nothing like the image she had conjured up in her mind all those years. In her mind, Frieda was old. This woman was young. Not to mention, she was a pretty brunette who hadn't a line on her face.

Frieda turned and motioned behind her. "Abigail, this is my husband, Nathaniel, and my son, Patrick."

Quickly, she was pulled into another warm embrace. "I couldn't be more proud to have you as my daughter-in-law," Sarah Pratt said.

In all her days, Abby had never felt more warmth coming from one room. A thought occurred to her then, and she glanced over at Jesse. "How are we all going to fit in here?" she asked.

Everyone in the room gave a lighthearted chuckle.

Jesse put her hands over Abby's eyes. "Close them. And no peeking 'til I say open."

"What's going on?"

"You'll see." Not a moment later, Jesse said, "Okay. You can open 'em now." She lowered her hands.

Abby and Jesse were standing on the shoreline next to the mountain lake. It was the exact spot where Jesse had taught her how to skip rocks—the same place where they had made love in the water.

"I don't understand. How'd we get here?"

Jesse smiled. "It's easy. You just close your eyes and think of the place where you want to be." She kissed her cheek. "I don't know how it works, but when you open your eyes, you're exactly where you want to be."

"You mean if I want to see my parents, all I have to do is close my eyes and wish to be with them?"

"Yep. You can see anyone you want who has passed on before you."

Abby looked out over the shimmering lake. "It's just as lovely as I remember."

Jesse put her arms on Abby's shoulders and turned her so that she was facing away from the water. "Well? What do you think?"

Standing several yards from the shoreline was the most beautiful home Abby had ever seen. The roof had several gables and wide, overhanging eaves. The front porch had tapered columns, and the front door was one Abby knew Jesse had carved herself. Nothing had been overlooked. It was perfect—right down to the hanging flowerpots that lined the long covered porch.

"Everyone lives wherever they choose. Surely you didn't think you, me, and Jim would have to live in that damp, old cabin again, did you?"

"You mean this is for us?"

Jesse nodded.

Abby laced her fingers through Jesse's. "If I'm dreaming, I don't ever want to wake up."

Seeing the ones she loved and holding Jesse in her arms again, it all felt so very real. Her heart swelled with emotion. The tears streamed down Abby's face as she wept in her sleep. She reached out across the mattress to Jesse's side and could feel the warm, familiar memory snuggling up close to her one last time.

Abby released a blissful sigh. It truly was the perfect dream. One she never wanted to wake up from—and one that she never would.

A NOTE FROM THE AUTHOR

Dear Reader,

Thank you for choosing to read *The Devil that Broke Us*. I truly hope you enjoyed reading *The Devil's Trilogy* as much as I enjoyed writing it. I'd like to ask for a minute of your time to please consider leaving a review for the books on Amazon, Goodreads, or your favorite book website. Even if it's only a few words, it would make all the difference to me and I'd appreciate it very much. Thank you again for your continued interest in the incredible life story of Jessica Pratt.

S.C. Wilson